Written in the Oceans

JEANNIE CHOE

Written in the Oceans

Copyright © 2022 by Jeannie Choe

This is a work of fiction. Names, character, place, incident, brands, and/or media are the product of the author's imagination and/or are fictitiously used. Any resemblance to actual persons, living or dead, or locales is entirely coincidental.

Cover design and formatting by Books and Moods
Editing by Katie Wolf

NOTE TO THE READER

This book contains themes and subject matter that some may find triggering. For more information, please visit jeanniechoeauthor.com for a list of content warnings prior to reading.

Furthermore, triggers are not listed in this book to avoid spoilers in consideration for those that would like such information to be left out.

To anyone that has ever felt like they aren't enough.
You are so irrevocably and remarkably enough.

PROLOGUE
Ellie

TEN YEARS AGO...

"Eleanor, do you know why we're here today?"

"It's just Ellie," I correct him.

"Okay, Ellie," he concedes. "Let's start from the beginning. What happened two nights ago?"

The doctor, whose name I've already forgotten, looks at me, disinterested and impatient. His shirt, a color of blue I've once heard described as cerulean, peeks through the front lapels of his white coat, right where his name badge is neatly secured. His ankle rests on his opposite knee, with a flimsy plastic clipboard balanced on his thigh. My gaze stays fixed on his finger lightly tapping the armrest as he waits for my answer. The dim light situated just above his head spotlights the center of the room as if we're on a stage, my life meant to be on display for entertainment.

What happened two nights ago?

The events of that night hang in the stiff air between us, floating and waiting for me to transform them into solid words so he can write them down in my file, making them permanent.

My thumbs run over the worn leather as my eyes flutter, trying to push away my most recent memory.

Seventeen, eighteen, nineteen. Nineteen pills. Maybe if I coat my mouth first and wet it so the pills don't stick to my throat, I can swallow them in one go.

Tap, tap, tap.

My foot sits impatiently below the sink, waiting for the fragile glass to fill with tap water.

Yeah, the water should help. Maybe if I just take fifteen of them. It should still do the trick, and I can swallow them all at once. What difference does it make? It doesn't matter; none of it matters. I won't be around to reexamine my actions anyways.

My hand lifts to my mouth, my lips scooping the pills before the gush of tepid water washes them down.

Okay, I did it. Hard part over. Now I just wait. Wait and wait and wait.

I feel dizzy, like I might pass out. My trembling hands move to grip the sink, my palms slipping against the cold, hard surface instead.

I jump, startled by the sudden noise, like someone bashed in a window with a baseball bat. Was that glass? Why is the floor wet?

I wince, the sharp pain puncturing the bottom of my foot. And then there's blood. At least, I think it's blood. Everything's so blurry.

"Ellie?" The voice calling my name sounds distant. And familiar.

It's the last thing I hear before everything goes black, the empty bottle hitting the floor as I go with it, and we land on the soft, fuzzy rug in unison.

"Ellie!"

"Ellie?"

I squeeze my eyes shut, gripping the cushion of the chair, the harsh leather making a creaking noise against my hand. I lower my head so that gravity can bring my hair in front of me, creating a makeshift drape for me to hide behind. Like a beaded curtain, still able to be seen through but managing to hide the fine details.

"Okay." The doctor sighs. "How about we meet again tomorrow? It's up to you when you're ready to talk. In the meantime, the nurses can reach me at all hours." He raises his hand and signals towards the nurse waiting quietly by the door. I stand, and she moves her hand to my back to guide me to my room.

We walk in silence. The sounds of our footsteps echo off the sterile walls of the hospital hallways underneath the dull fluorescent lights, the quietness between us spreading the length of the hall. It fills every wall and corner, making our every move sound loud and menacing.

"Dinner will be served in a couple of minutes. Make sure you're in the dining area on time, please." She turns away after I nod to inform her I will follow instructions this time. Unlike last night, when I stayed in my room with my eyes squeezed shut, trying to erase everything. Trying to pretend that none of this even happened.

My gauze-covered feet peek through the flat, cold slippers that were issued to me when I arrived at the hospital in nothing but sweatpants and a dress shirt, no shoes. I curl my toes as my feet flexure against the weeping cuts still bleeding intermittently. All the while, my fingers cling to the shirt, wrapping it inward to grasp the soft material, the plastic buttons digging into my palms, leaving small crescent indents in my skin.

I squeeze my eyes shut, never wanting to open them again. Every time I do, I think to myself, *This is it.*

But it doesn't work out that way. Otherwise, I wouldn't be here.

CHAPTER 1
Rhylan

The smudge on my slacks is from the chocolate donut that I just inhaled while I've been waiting for the last hour. I realize that now, seeing the crumbs of my indulgence littered around my feet. But man, these studio catered sweets are hard to pass up on. It isn't coming off with a simple wipe of my thumb. Even after a couple more swipes, it's still there, spreading and dissolving into the cotton fibers. Luckily, I'm wearing black, so it won't be too noticeable. At least, I hope. Shana stands over me, her hands moving rapidly through a stapled stack of papers and her eyes scanning over the words.

"They aren't supposed to ask you any personal questions, Rhy," she says, her eyes still focused on the paper in her hand. "But those assholes never listen, so if they do, deflect. Make a joke instead. Deflect as much as you can."

I nod.

We're in the fancy greenroom at *The Late Night Show with Jack Stuber,* minutes before I am to take the stage and meet Jack Stuber for the first time. My elbows dig into the soft spot above my knees, my body enveloped in the leather loveseat pushed against the wall. I would sit on the more comfortable cushioned stool in front of the mirror adorned with large globe-like lights, but having to stare at myself in the mirror feels vain, even a little narcissistic.

Jack Stuber made a name for himself as the number one late-night talk show host, beating James Corden in the unofficial race, which meant an interview with him to promote my new movie, *Unrestrained*, was already written in the books before post-production even began.

Shana, my highly paid publicist, is here to make sure that I look good and to keep up the image of Rhylan Matthews: A-list celebrity, Hollywood's hottest *it* star, the silver screen's golden boy.

But she's here for another reason: to make sure I actually showed up. Exactly three days ago, when the European leg of our press junket had ended, I called her, asking if I could skip this very interview. The extensive tour that lasted two weeks left me physically spent and emotionally exhausted. As soon as my plane landed on the tarmac and I stepped on American soil, I didn't want to think about anything else. I didn't want to worry about promoting this damn movie and sit down for more of these draining, menial interviews. I was so fucking exhausted, and I just needed an out. Something, anything.

When Shana answered the phone, she had assumed I was just checking in. But when my tone turned grim and my request was one that wasn't feasible, she had difficulty understanding why. "You're asking me if you, the star of your own movie, can miss an interview with Jack Stuber?"

"Um, yeah," I answered. When I heard it repeated back

to me, I realized how ridiculous it sounded. I shook my head, regretting even calling her.

"No, Rhylan. You have to go," she finally said, stern and mother-like. "Is there something going on? Are you ill?"

I whispered a quick "never mind" and hung up the phone before she could say anything else. Before she could further remind me of the laundry list of commitments I had signed up for in the months to come. Red carpets, movie premieres, charity events, public appearances.

The thing was that even if she had asked for specifics, sat me down and dug deeper as to why I would want to skip such a pivotal point in my promotional responsibilities, I wouldn't have had an answer. I couldn't explain the inward exhaustion that had taken over me, resulting in a physical burnout.

Deep down, I knew I needed to be here. I didn't need the tabloids speculating on why I missed such an important interview when all of my other co-stars would be present. I knew this, and Shana knew this. It's why she's here now, working hard to keep my head in the game and settle my nerves.

But I'm suffocating. I can't breathe, and all I want to do is scream. Literally scream as if to purge all of the dark, disgusting thoughts in my head. To let it all out instead of pretending I'm fine. Because the last thing I am is fine. I'm not *fine* about anything. The fame, the attention, the scrutiny. I want to tell everyone that all of that shit isn't okay, to back off and leave me alone. But I can't. I can't because I've been conditioned not to. To always put on a smile and wave. Smile and *fucking* wave. So that's what I've been doing.

"The good thing is, you have the movie to talk about, and Charles and Bella will be with you." Shana finally peeks up at me and sees me groan at the sound of Bella's name. My head rolls back against the plush cushion just as the back of my thighs rub against the leather, creating friction and mimicking the unpleasant sound of someone unapologetically passing gas.

"But that might not actually be a good thing," she says more to herself than me as the realization sets in.

I sigh. "It is what it is."

Along with my co-star Charles Bradley and me, Bella Raven had been cast as the female lead in *Unrestrained*. She played my love interest that eventually turned on me, leading up to some angsty scenes between two scorned lovers. While I had played a role, Bella was fixated on the chemistry that she claimed we had off-screen as well as on-screen. I tried to convince her that our acting was the work of two talented actors playing their roles, but she took that as a challenge and continued to pursue said chemistry.

I should have been flattered. Bella wasn't cast in the movie just for her acting skills. Her looks played a huge part in it. Her sex appeal was what forced the producers to add in some extra bikini shots, even though they weren't really necessary for the plot. Because sex sells, and why the hell not. But beneath all that, she's shallow and stereotypically superficial.

The paps had a field day when they snuck in some behind-the-scenes shots on the streets of Paris with an overly handsy Bella clinging to my side. When those photos leaked, I got a call from Shana asking me what the deal was. But this was the life of a celebrity, always answering to false rumors, made up through the magic of a thousand words splayed out on an image.

"You know, that girl is as sexy as they come, but she cannot take a hint for the life of her." Shana hands me an individually packaged wet wipe taken from her crocodile Birkin as she eyes the chocolate stain on my thigh. I guess it's a bit more noticeable than I thought.

"Whatever," I answer, taking the wipe from her and cleaning off the stain completely like it was never there in the first place. I repeat my words. "It is what it is. And like you said, if all else fails, I'll talk about the movie. That's the whole point of tonight anyways, right?"

"Right, the movie," she concurs, refocusing her attention to why we're here in the first place. "Bring up the scenes, especially the intense ones that involved all the stunts and whatnot. And talk about the logistics of filming them. That'll take up the time."

She brings up her wrist to her face, checking the time on her diamond-encrusted Rolex. The light reflects off of the pricey timepiece onto her preoccupied face before she lowers the papers still in her hand.

"You're going on any minute now," she says, her pep talk voice in full effect. She lowers herself to face me. "You've got this. Don't be nervous, and have fun."

I nod again, the knot lodged in my throat acting as a roadblock as I try to speak through my nerves.

"They're going to kick me out, but call me once it's over. I don't care if it's late. Call me and let me know how it goes."

I clear my throat. "Okay, Shana. I will."

We're interrupted by a sharp knock on the door and the handle clicking open. Both of our heads turn at the same time.

"We're ready for you, Mr. Matthews."

I look back at Shana one last time. "Break a leg, kid," she says.

A man with a headset attached to his ear and dressed in all black walks me down a row of maze-like hallways, walking briskly around sharp corners as if he's being timed. We finally land in front of a dark curtain, the lights from the other side peeking through the small slits at the bottom hem. "We're going to have you wait here until we give you the signal."

I nod, holding back the flex in my jaw by giving a purse-lipped smile instead, before he nods back and hurriedly steps away.

A low whisper makes me jump. "Nervous?"

I whip my head around only to face Charles wearing a relaxed expression in contrast to my unsettled one. His smirk, curved up in one corner, is surrounded by a day's worth of stubble, making me think that maybe I hadn't needed to worry so much about my appearance if Charles didn't even find it necessary to shave.

I finally smile, the first time since I walked through the studio's doors. "Always."

Charles Bradley, A-list movie star, close friends with equally famous Rhylan Matthews.

That's what all the tabloids labeled us as. We met ages ago through auditions and numerous unsuccessful callbacks. We found that we kept running into each other, going to the same casting calls and auditioning for the same roles. We discovered a common ground, a foundation to build a friendship on. He was the one that showed me the ropes in this big new city that I found fiercely intimidating.

Charles gives my back a firm pat, making my shoulders hunch forward. I'm about to punch him back in equal strength, as his vivacity has somehow become infectious enough to bring out that side of me, when Bella rushes in. She comes to a stop a few steps away from us, her glam squad fawning over her as they finish the final touches to her makeup. We haven't spoken a word since we arrived separately, making this the first time I'm seeing her since we left the airport in London.

While Charles and I settled on a casual and simple suit attire with no tie, Bella looks perfectly camera ready. Her silver sequined dress, cut just below her knees, clings to her, flattering her slender body and sparkling in every direction. And her hair is pulled back in a tight bun, not a single strand sticking out in the wrong place. Her team made sure of that.

Just as Bella shoos away her team, loud instrumental music plays from the other side of the curtain. The drums snare as they signal our entrance. The same man that led me to this very spot gestures for us as the curtain slowly slides open. And the crowd goes wild.

Once the curtains fully open, the lights blind us. Bella walks in front, already in the arms of Jack Stuber as Charles and I follow close behind.

We take turns shaking hands, the applause overpowering our verbal exchange, and when it's my turn, I take Jack's extended hand in both of mine. Jack Stuber is every bit as charming as he is handsome. He tilts his head slightly when he smiles and nods his greeting, a congenial act of endearment that I don't expect. My nerves have shaken awake the butterflies in my stomach in anticipation for tonight, but Jack's hospitality somehow settles them.

We're ushered into our seats on the blue velvet couch perfectly wide enough for three people, as if they measured it for us before our arrival. We situate ourselves in an orderly row, with me nestled between Bella and Charles.

"Charles Bradley, Rhylan Matthews, and Bella Raven are here to promote their newest action-packed film *Unrestrained*. And I have to say, I don't think we've ever had such a star-studded cast on our couch before."

We hear a *whoop* come from the audience, followed by a faint "I love you, Bella" from deep within the sea of people.

Jack turns towards the crowd. "Calm down, guys. I don't think she's taking any marriage proposals tonight." The polite laughter dies as Jack turns to Bella. "Bella, you're sort of a new face to the action genre. What was it like working with two of Hollywood's hottest men?"

Another *whoop* from the crowd.

Bella laughs, her eyes batting at Jack as she crosses her legs in his direction. "It was so exhilarating! Both of them are so talented, and there was so much physical work involved. They were very supportive, teaching me the ropes and not treating me like a complete loser when I got scared. Especially Rhylan."

She turns to me, placing a hand on my forearm and batting her eyes up at me.

"And there was some onscreen chemistry between you and Rhylan. I hear that you two have somewhat of a steamy scene?"

"Oh, yes. It was very heated. But, you know, it hardly feels like work when you have such a willing participant. And Rhylan was *very* willing."

She slyly places her hand in mine, and the crowd once again hollers, whooping from every direction and growing out of control.

I finally interject. "Bella is an extremely talented actor that I felt I had amazing chemistry with on camera." Bella looks at me, her smile waning as she listens to me speak. "She's become an amazing colleague that I've come to respect and love."

Jack nods and leans his head to the side to address Charles. "And Charles Bradley, I hear you're in the movie as well?" Jack says, friendly banter laced into his words. "What was it like working with Bella and Rhylan?"

"It was amazing. Bella is a fast learner, and she might say she needed a lot of support from us, but she caught on very quickly."

Thankfully, Charles takes control of the interview from there while I sit and watch, mindlessly nodding along to keep myself present. In the midst of Charles explaining the logistics involved when he and I had to jump out of a helicopter mid-air, I finally break free of Bella's firm grip on my arm. I bring my hands together, intertwining my fingers and placing them on my lap, away from Bella's reach.

As I'm listening to Charles, I realize that the accounts of our time filming feel so different being told from his point of view. Because that isn't how I remember it at all. While Charles enjoyed the thrill that came along with being attached to stunt wire and surrounded by fake explosives, I have different memories of our three-month-long shoot.

All I remember is feeling tired and angry and so debilitatingly weary. All because I didn't want to keep going. Even with the pressures of my work, I wanted to stay in bed and hide underneath the covers. There, surrounded by the rustling Egyptian cotton and the hazy darkness, I felt like I had disappeared. I hated myself, not fully understanding why underneath the weight of the goose down comforter, it felt tolerable. Why I felt that I even needed to create a sanctum at all. But it seemed the only sliver of solace that I could get was when I sectioned myself off from the rest of the world, completely destitute and isolated.

I rub my hands down the fabric of my pants, my eyes landing on where the chocolate stain was when I was sitting backstage, now gone as if it were never there. Luckily, the interview is over before any more questions are directed to me. Instead, the slot is filled with questions about Bella's workout regimen that kept her bikini-ready and a small clip of Charles and me tussling in an intense fight scene.

Once I'm back in the greenroom, alone and empty, I sit for a moment. The pent-up nerves that had filled my chest release when I inhale and exhale. But the heaviness sits at the pit of my stomach.

This shit is so fucking lonely.

There, I said it. Even if I say it to myself, not even out loud, I've acknowledged it. It doesn't make sense how, just minutes ago, I was surrounded by adoring fans waving and cheering at me, and now, I feel like someone sucker punched me in the gut. But this is the life that I've created for myself. Full of people but no one to truly share it with. Never alone but always lonely.

"Rhy?" I look up and see Charles peeking through the doorway. "You about ready to leave?"

I stand. "Yeah, I was just making sure I didn't forget anything."

"Let's walk out together. I'm sure the crowd outside is going to be just as wild as the one in here."

I hesitate.

"Bella already left. Something about an after-party."

I visibly sigh, not meaning to express my relief, but I can't help it. It feels like the first piece of good news I've heard all night.

"Yeah, let's head out," I finally say.

When the metal doors to the back entrance swing open, the crowd lining the streets clamors wildly. On one side, they're screaming our names, calling out adoringly with words of love and admiration. And on the other side, there are the paparazzi. As we step closer towards our waiting cars, I hear the taunting, the ridicule to incriminate both myself and Charles. To get the reaction they want.

Questions prodding into our personal lives. Asking Charles about his kids, where his wife is tonight, why she isn't by his side, insinuating another scandal to add to his already growing list of false rumors. The last one, a low blow to his marriage, was an allegation that he'd been cheating on Amelia with the nanny.

And the questions to me are just as direct, just as personal, trying to poke at a giant that they want to be woken.

"Where's Bella?"

"Did you two have a fight? Is that why she left without you?"

And then the demands.

"Come on, Rhy! Give us a smile!"

I don't engage. I know better. Actually, Shana knows better, and she instilled that mentality in me years ago. Her mantra has always been: "Don't give them what they want."

I duck my head, my eyes glued to the passenger door of my waiting car. I don't turn and wave farewell to Charles. Instead, I keep my eyes on the prize, my exit out of here.

Once in the quietness of the car, the muffled sounds of the paps flowing in from the other side and the dark tinted windows providing me some sort of refuge, I sink in and sigh deeply. I allow the gentle thrum of the engine to take me home while the quiet driver behind the wheel provides me the comfort and privacy I know I need after this chaotic night.

"Ellie, I just think that you need to start looking into other options. You can't work at the bookstore all your life." My mom's voice is turning whiney. Her tone, meant to be encouraging, is now pushing me away, making me want to avoid the topic altogether. "I mean, you're graduating from UCLA for crying out loud. Albeit a literary major, but I'm sure you'd be able to find *something*." She pokes at the white, creamy pasta on her plate with her fork, almost half gone, as is the sweet wine that she served us all.

With my head ducked low, I nod, bobbing along to my mom's words as if I were listening to music. Like a monotonous and repetitive tone that I've learned to let play out.

My cousin Walter is sitting at the far end of the dinner table, engrossed in the screen of his phone, AirPods lodged into his ears, making it difficult for me to signal an SOS in his direction.

"She's right," my aunt Janice chimes in. "That goes for the both of you." Her voice raises a decibel as her statement is directed towards Walter, implying he quit his job at the music store where he teaches guitar lessons.

Walter lifts his head, pulling his gaze away from his phone screen while removing an earpiece out of his ear. "Huh?"

Aunt Janice rolls her eyes. "I was saying that you and Ellie can't work at those minimum wage jobs for the rest of your lives. You need to think more in the long run. Think about what you want to do after you two graduate."

"Like Hector?" he says through a sarcastic undertone and a shake of his head. Our being the same age means that we met many of our milestones together. When we said our first words, when we got our driver's license, and now, graduating college. Something that our moms have been looking forward to for the past twenty-two years: planning a dual graduation party in the coming months.

"Exactly!" Aunt Janice beams. Her eyes turn bright as she talks about her more successful son, the one that she denies but obviously favors between the two.

Walter lifts his wine glass. "Sorry, Mama. We can't have it all. A house in the 'burbs, a high six-figure job—"

She gasps and turns to my mom. "I almost forgot! Hector sent me a video of Hailey the other day. She's walking!" She reaches into her purse and extracts her phone. She swipes through it as she squints and brings it further away from her line of vision for focus.

"A picture-perfect family, a 401(k) and health benefits…" Walter continues, ignoring Aunt Janice's sudden shift of her attention. When he doesn't stop, Aunt Janice covers his mouth with her hand, turning up the volume on her phone and handing it to my mom as Walter's voice becomes muffled behind his mom's hand.

My mom takes the phone and smiles warmly. "Oh, she is so sweet!" she says affectionately.

Aunt Janice finally removes her hand off Walter's face and peers at the screen to watch along, even though I'm sure she's seen it a dozen times. I can hear the happy squeals that only young children can make and the words of encouragement from Hector's familiar voice. She brings a napkin to the corner of her eye, sniffling as her eyes mist over. My eyes meet Walter's as he rolls his eyes at me. I stifle a smirk as both my mom and Aunt Janice look at us, their eyes narrowed and lips drawn together in a firm line of disapproval.

"You know, missing my only grandbaby just means that I actually have a heart and I'm not *dead* inside," Aunt Janice says.

I'm not meant to see it, not meant to notice the small movement of my mom's hand lightly tapping Aunt Janice's forearm, but I do. And when it happens, Aunt Janice realizing her poor word choices, everyone stills. The awkwardness settles around us, replacing the warm scent of alfredo and garlic bread.

The words had left her lips before she even had a chance to think about them.

But there it is. Dead. Death. Dying.

Taboo words in this house. It's the fluffy pink elephant in the room taking up space and filling every corner, barging into our lives in the most unwelcome way possible.

Up until ten years ago, we said those words callously and tossed them around like you would the words *orange* or *butter.* But that was before. Before death was such a common presence in our house.

I pretend not to notice. Instead, I swirl pieces of thick pasta around my fork, cooked al dente and wrapped in the creamy sauce my mom makes from scratch. I eye the glass of wine sitting in the two o'clock position of my plate that's almost empty and waiting to be finished. I drop my fork to pinch the stem, rolling it between my fingers before tilting it back and emptying the contents.

"Anyone want more wine?" I say clearly, void of any emotion.

Walter raises his hand. "I'll take some."

My feet slowly trudge to the kitchen, reaching for a new bottle to uncork. The tension follows me, breaking the silence as I hear my mom and Aunt Janice shuffle in their chairs.

"I'm so sorry," I hear Aunt Janice whisper sharply.

I don't hear anything from my mom, but I know she's shaking her head, dismissing her sister's apology in a way that it wasn't necessary in the first place. It was an accident, just like so many things in this house. My dad's death. My attempt to end my life.

But the simple matter of the fact was, accident or not, death happened. It surrounded our lives and became a stale, lingering presence that we tried our best to ignore.

And when the sudden presence of death entered our lives as intrusively as possible, we managed through it as we mourned. We were warned about the stages of grief, all five of them when my dad died. Denial hit the moment we got the call from the hospital.

"Hello?" I hear my mom answer a call from the kitchen. The TV

is blaring so loud that my mom whispers at me to lower it while her hand covers the mouthpiece. She stands over the steam rising above the stove, her hand still on a ladle sticking out the top of a large pot. And then I hear her go silent, listening carefully to the voice on the other end.

"Oh my God."

My attention piques. I turn from the couch to look at her just as her phone drops to the floor with a clatter.

"Ellie, we have to go."

She doesn't say anything to me. Just whizzes through traffic, desperately urging people to move out of her way. I don't even know where we're going. Not until we pull up in front of a building with large red lit up words that read EMERGENCY do I realize where we are.

Still no answers from my mom, but I follow willingly, moving quietly as my gaze focuses on the urgent steps of our feet.

"I'm looking for my husband. His name is Dan Salerno." Her voice is breathless, hitching when she says our last name, the one commonality that the three of us share.

And then everything just happens. Neither I nor my mom have control over it. We move wherever we're ushered to. Bodies and hands lead us through hallways, from the receptionist to the nurse, until we're at a doorway. And we finally see him.

It's then I hear it. The shrill, guttural sound erupting from my mom's small, fragile frame. I don't wince. I don't even move. My feet are planted into the linoleum floor. I register the mangled face that used to belong to my dad, now wrapped in white gauze with stains of red seeping through it. My eyes trail the wires that come running out of his body like a maze, connecting to beeping machines next to *his bedside.*

"Mrs. Salerno…"

I don't hear anything else. Just bits and pieces of a conversation.

"Deadly impact."

"Brain dead."

"Organ donation."

And every memory after that moment blurs. It drifts off into a space that I can't fully retrieve it from and only fragments of it stay embedded in my brain. Like how I sat in a cold plastic chair for hours, the bones of my butt digging into the hard plastic while my mom and I waited. As we sat and waited, the stages of grief continued to course through us without permission, inherently passing by as we processed the biggest loss of our lives.

We returned home, his belongings in a small bag, a shell of our former happy family. We left with our hearts in that hospital on a cold bed, buried with no chance of returning into the hollow hole in our chests.

Sometime after my dad's death, years after it happened and when everyone assumed we had picked up the pieces of our lives, my grandma visited us. She mentioned the words *ebb and flow*. She used the phrase to describe her grief over the loss of her only child. While she didn't always remain in a constant state of mourning, it was always there. It came and went as it pleased, never fully allowing her to move on. That was exactly how I learned to manage my grief, through the ebb and flow of my own heartache. It would come during the moments I would least expect it, hitting me hard and placing me into a deep depression that I couldn't explain. It would sit there while I stared off into nothing, often that nothing being a television screen, for hours, days, watching the flickering light in the stale darkness of my room. I wouldn't think about anything during that time. My mind would be blank. Not because I wanted it to be but because it would already be full from the soul-crushingly heavy weight of my grief, making no room for anything else. And then those days would pass as if they never happened. I would come out relatively the same and go on with my life. The ebb and flow would continue in waves, sometimes small enough that it didn't become debilitating and sometimes so hard that even the shrill screams that expelled from my lungs weren't enough to dull the pain. But that's the thing with heartache that comes and goes. While it may leave for a short period of time, it always comes back. And all I can do is welcome it like an old friend.

So in the meantime, while I wait for the next wave of grief to show up at my door unannounced and unwelcome, I go day to day. I try to make it to the next morning and keep my head held as high as I can, evading the rush of water trying to drown me. Sometimes I feel like I'm waiting to be rescued, but maybe it's my way of believing that I don't have to live like this forever. That there'll be some sort of consolation at the end. But that sounds more like senseless optimism at this point, foolish and imprudent.

I leave the still intact wine bottle on the kitchen counter, the desire to drown my sorrows in a second glass sitting alongside it, and walk to my room. My hands trace over my shelf of books lining the wall next to my door. The collection of leather and clothbound books has grown in number throughout the years, all scattered alongside paperbacks with tattered spines and dog-eared pages. I slump into my mattress, my body feeling heavier than it actually is.

When Aunt Janice leaves, both she and Walter calling out their farewells from the living room, I'm sitting in the dark. My knees hug against my chest and the TV screen flashes silently, creating a strobe-like effect in my small room. When my mom knocks softly on my door, I don't answer. I listen to her whisper "goodnight" through the cracked opening and her footsteps fading away. Sometime in the night, I drift off. My mind is finally numb enough to turn everything off, muted enough for me to fall into a dreamless sleep.

It's the numbness I crave. Because when you're numb, you don't feel. And when you don't feel, there's no pain. No joy, no excitement, no sadness. Just a paralysis that feels like a dream.

Beep. Beep. Beep

God, has my alarm always been this annoying? My outreached hand hits the decade-old digital clock flashing neon green numbers.

07:47.

Crap! I overslept. I know I hit the snooze button a few times, but I must have lost track of how many. My upper body springs to life, the covers flying off me, and my bare feet hit the rough carpet. The blood drains from my head, leaving me disoriented and dizzy.

My closet door slides open with a loud crack, and my hand

slices through the vertical lines of hanging clothes, sliding them left to right as the clicking of hangers makes my urgency louder. Angus, our elderly black lab, pokes his head through the small opening at my door as he announces his arrival and extends his morning greeting, most likely hearing the commotion coming from my room. I'm in the world's biggest hurry but can't resist the temptation to scratch his ears. When I do, his tail thumps heavily on the thick carpet. At fourteen, his once shiny black coat is gradually being replaced by coarse patches of white fur, and his down-turned eyes look heavier with each passing day.

"Excuse me," I croak through my morning voice as I sidestep past him, glancing quickly at my wall clock.

08:03.

I have exactly seven minutes before I need to be out the door and hurdle into rush hour traffic. I take those seven minutes to splash water on my face, brush my teeth, and run a brush through my thick, wavy hair. Breakfast is out of the question at this point.

"Ellie! Are you up?" I hear my mom call from the kitchen.

One last stop in my room to shove my laptop into my backpack, and I walk into the kitchen.

"Oh, there you are," my mom says, setting down a coffee mug before stuffing papers and her laptop into a brown leather briefcase, readying for her day as an HR manager at Hoffman & Abermann Law Group. The coffee smell is inviting, calling to me to forgo the first thirty minutes of my lecture so I can enjoy a cup. The crisp blouse my mom paired with gray dress pants looks so executive and professional in contrast to my lightweight hoodie and worn jeans. So much so that if seen in public together, most would assume that we were strangers.

"Shouldn't you be on the road already?"

"I overslept," I mumble, still not fully awake yet.

"Oh, that's not fun. There're some granola bars in the pantry. So you have something in your stomach."

"Okay. Thanks, Mom," I say, thinking to myself how I hate the texture of granola bars and how sweet they are.

That's the last thing I call out before I rush out the door, hopping into my maroon-colored Converse with the irresistible scent of coffee wafting behind me.

As soon as my foot hits the cement pavement of our driveway, my hand moves up, hovering above my forehead to shield my eyes. It's spring. The normally chilly winds from the lingering winter are past us now, and the air is becoming warmer, more comfortable, reminding us that summer is just around the corner.

Southern California has always been inordinately bright and fiercely blinding. And I've never learned how to fully embrace it. After twenty-two seasons in Los Angeles, I would assume that my senses would have adapted to the persistent sunshine but instead, I simply exist in it.

I hurl my backpack into my beat-up Honda Civic, and my body follows, settling into the driver's seat and buckling in. The engine ticks before finally coming to life as it vibrates under my feet.

Most people assume LA residents live off sunglasses and iced lattes, but I require neither to start my morning. My preference for my car's sun visor alongside hot black coffee in an insulated travel mug pulls me away from the norm, the absence of the latter making this commute longer than necessary.

"It's called a blinker, asshole. Learn how to use it!" I mutter to myself.

I'm twenty minutes into my commute, and I've muttered the words *idiot* and *dumbass* under my breath about five times. I pull into a parking spot once I arrive on campus with just enough time to speed walk into my class. I sigh a breath of relief once I enter the building, and my stomach growls, reminding me that I skipped breakfast. This isn't a good start to my day or my week.

CHAPTER 3
Rhylan

've always wondered why people keep plants. I mean, yeah, they look nice, and they're supposed to resemble some sort of responsibility towards a living object, but I've never understood the appeal. The one I'm looking at right now sits in a large mauve pot on the floor that comes off as snobby. This whole room screams pretentious. From the minimalist décor to the color-coordinated books on the shelves, nothing about it says: *Your deepest, most intrusive thoughts are welcome here.* At least, that's the thought I have every week when I walk into this office for my regularly scheduled sessions with Dr. Rosalin Greene.

"Rhylan, this is a safe place. We aren't here to pick apart every single emotion you have. We're here to try to understand where these emotions come from," says Dr. Greene, interrupting my judgmental thoughts on her interior design choices.

She, too, has a pretentious aura to her presence. Her olive-green pantsuit fits a little too loosely to be considered attractive, and she continues to look at me over her gold-rimmed glasses that hang at the tip of her nose.

I nod my head. "I understand."

"So we were talking about your work. What made you want to pursue acting?"

"Well, at first, it was all I thought about. When I told my parents I was coming to LA to fully pursue acting, they had one condition: I was to go to college while I did it."

Her pen moves furiously against the clipboard. It's distracting, but I continue.

"When I got accepted to UCLA, it felt like fate. And when the semester started, I enjoyed it. Acting classes, meeting people that had the same interests, and then finally auditioning for actual acting roles. It was exhilarating."

"And now? How do you feel about acting?"

"Now?" I sigh deeply. My hands move to my face, covering my eyes in an attempt to rub the tension out of them. "I'm exhausted."

"And why do you think you feel that way?"

"I don't know. I mean, you're the professional. Aren't you supposed to know?"

She chuckles politely. "I'm here to help you better understand your emotions. I can't tell you why you feel a certain way or why you think you have an opinion about something. Those are emotions and thoughts for you to decide."

I sigh again. "I don't really know. I used to be so eager. Levi, my agent, would have to tell me to calm down and take a few deep breaths so that I could collectively decide my next steps. I wanted it all. I was a greedy nineteen-year-old kid."

She nods, again writing furiously on her clipboard. "And do you feel like that motivation isn't there anymore?"

"I mean, I'm literally at the height of my career, and I should be even more motivated and confident than ever." I lower my head, unable to understand how I got here. So low, so beneath anything I ever expected. "I guess… I don't really know."

"Okay," she answers. "It's okay not to know. Can you tell me something that you do know?"

My hands rub against my thighs. Back and forth, back and forth, as I mull over her question. "I know I'm getting frustrated, and it's making me angry. And that's not who I am."

"What do you mean by angry?"

"I feel like I have no control over my actions, and it scares me. For example, I was on set a couple months ago, and a production assistant brought me an iced coffee like she did for the rest of the crew. I had asked for a hot coffee, black. I could have taken the iced coffee, it wasn't a big deal, but I made it a big deal. I threw it against my trailer, right in front of her, and stormed off." I'm starting to ramble, these moments of anger that I regret so badly now rolling off my tongue. The words are laced with guilt and embarrassment for my behavior. "And just last week, I was attending a wardrobe fitting, and I lost it because I had to try on the same shirt for the third time. It's all part of the job. I knew it, no one needed to explain it to me, but I'm becoming a ticking time bomb. And I can't even place why."

"It can be difficult to understand emotions that you didn't expect, especially when it's the complete opposite of what you thought you would feel," she explains. "But you have to understand, it's completely normal."

"But I'm taking out my frustration on people that don't

deserve it. People that work hard and are just doing their damn job," I retort. "This isn't who I am, and I hate the person I'm becoming."

"Okay, let's change pace a little bit, try a little exercise." She faces me, sitting upright. "I want you to think of one word that encompasses your emotions as of late. Just one word."

I mull over her request. And then it pops into my head. It makes sense, apt for the feeling of sinking with no end. "Drowning."

"Why drowning?"

"Because I feel like I'm suffocating."

"And now I want you to think of the opposite of that feeling. Not necessarily the opposite of the word drowning. I want you to think deeper. The opposite of that thought that makes you feel like you're drowning."

I don't hesitate. "Freedom."

"That's a good one," she encourages, her hand scraping across the paper on her lap. "What does freedom mean to you?"

"Being able to do what I want," I say, breathing out, the thought of it liberating from deep within. "And to not have to worry about what people will think of me or my image."

She suddenly glances at the numberless clock on her wall, the hands slowly gliding around its circumference. She brings the backside of her wrist up to her face, confirming the time and signaling the end of our session. "That's it for today. We'll pick up here at our next session. Same time?"

"Sure," I answer as I stand up.

"That was a good session. We opened a lot of closed doors today." She sounds like she's trying to convince herself more than me.

I remain silent as I shake her hand and turn my heels towards the door. Every time I leave her office, I leave a little lighter but a little bit more confused. I guess it's not bad, but I can't figure out if it's good. For now, all I can do is keep coming and hope that one day I can understand it.

Right now, with everything that I had put out for Dr. Greene and having to draw it all back in just as quickly, I'm irritated. Frustration is pent up in my chest, and I want to punch something, anything. I want to hole up in a corner for a week. I want to sit in silence and do nothing. I want to do all of these things, knowing that none of it would ever fulfill the void in my life. It would all leave me just as empty as I feel right now.

My intention after leaving Dr. Greene's office was to hit up Charles for lunch. They were loose plans we had mulled over earlier in the week, but I don't feel like forcing a smile and socializing while stuffing my face with overpriced gnocchi and bitter wine, so I keep driving. The gentle roar of my 1980 Camaro Z28 purring under my feet gives way to a direction I don't really have control over. I just need to clear my head.

I continue to stare at the asphalt in front of me, the Los Angeles heat causing the road to sizzle as I speed past it. I knew when I moved here from Nevada, I would be trading in the high desert for the cool beachy air that comes with the Southern California coast. At the time, it sounded so glamorous and exotic. Now, it feels mundane, completely lackluster, and repetitive.

Dr. Greene's office is situated right in the center of

Westwood. Office buildings and restaurants line the streets, and people flood the sidewalks on every sunny day that Southern California has to offer, which is almost every day now that spring is in full gear.

The streets that I drive through are familiar, the trees and buildings ingrained in my head in the form of memories. Memories that came from a busy college life in acting technique lectures and improv classes. Flags are randomly pitted into the streets that wave UCLA in bright yellow and blue.

My car sits idle in front of an intersection when my eyes catch something equally familiar as the university seals that are strategically placed everywhere as the campus draws nearer. A coffeehouse. It has no quirky, unique name, just the word *COFFEEHOUSE* all in bold capital letters adorned with coffee beans sprinkled at the edges of the sign.

When you look back nostalgically at a time when you were happy, you generally think of your childhood. Time spent with your friends climbing monkey bars and riding bikes late into the summer nights. My days spent at this exact coffeehouse felt much like that. Gathering with classmates and drinking coffee while studying the allure of method acting and script memorization. Having something to look forward to, knowing that making it big, chasing that high of having a box office hit was the only thing that I looked forward to. No weight of a thousand shades of grief sitting square on my shoulders. Only anticipation and hope.

I miss that feeling. The expectation that every day could bring something unexpected and exhilarating instead of dread.

As a last-minute decision, I pull into the coffee shop. It's not busy, but the in and out of customer traffic is still there. Students engulfed in their studies and the chitter-chatter between friends keeps the atmosphere light and natural. I haven't decided if I can pull off going in unnoticed as I park my car in a spot at the far end of the parking lot. The folded baseball cap sitting in my glove compartment feels loaded, like it's warning me that I'm a fool if I think I can go out and about in public without being recognized. I stifle that thought, ignoring it completely by adding a pair of Ray-Bans before I open the car door. I slowly exit my car and look around before walking towards the entrance. The tall trees sprinkling their loose leaves to the ground shelter me from the sun, allowing me to move discreetly through the parking lot. A hop onto the sidewalk, and I'm faced with the curved metal handle attached to the heavy glass door.

The long counter with a chalkboard menu board behind it is situated right at the entrance. There's barely enough room for me to take a step past the closed doors once I'm inside. With my hat lowered, I approach a girl with short, straight hair that's too dark and eye makeup that's too heavy.

I clear my throat. "Can I get a table for one, please?" I ask.

She looks at me, confused, her face drawn together in what I can only describe as disgust. She blows a bubble with her gum, the translucent pink ball growing bigger and bigger before it pops with a loud smack.

"It's self-serve, buddy," she says. She looks as bored as she is annoyed. "Just order what you want here and sit wherever."

"I uh… guess I'll just have a black coffee then."

She raises her brows, eyes widening with judgment as

she turns behind her, moving between a glass coffee pot and papered cups. Her movements are minimal, everything she needs being within arm's reach. She turns back around to face me and slips a sleeve around the cardboard cup, then places it on the counter between us.

"$3.57," she says, her face emotionless. The entire transaction, me pulling my card out of my wallet and sticking in the card reader, her doing everything to avoid rolling her eyes at my stiffness, feels so awkward. Like I'm inconveniencing her, and I need to apologize.

I take my coffee and walk away from the counter. The rest of the shop faces an outdoor area. The small, intimate patio is set over a cobblestone pavement, and above it hangs large round string lights tied to the massive trees that create a shelter for this little sanctuary. The iron-wrought tables and chairs fit the setting perfectly, creating an inviting atmosphere. It's fairly empty, aside from a couple of other patrons enjoying their mid-day break.

As I place my coffee on the uneven tabletop, my phone vibrates in my pocket. I pull it out and see Levi's name on the screen.

Shit. That's the second time today. I've been blatantly avoiding him all week. While I was in London, he'd been calling and emailing me, trying to decide what my next project would be. In all honesty, I don't know. I don't know what I want to do or what I should do. What I *do* know is that I don't need to jump into anything that I can't commit to. I need a minute to sit on things and decide carefully before I sign up for something that I can't get out of.

My thumb hovers over the answer icon, still deciding if I want to talk to him. To face the music that I know Levi is going to rain down on me. In the middle of my delayed decision, the phone stops ringing, making my decision for me.

My eyes start to wander, my hands fidgeting with my sunglasses that now rest on the iron table before moving against the fabric of my jeans in an attempt to relax, trying to keep my hands busy.

Everything seems to be happening around me. The steam rising above my coffee, birds chirping in the trees, the hearty laughter of a group of students gathered around each other, engaged in their own riveting storytelling.

A woman sitting in the far corner of the patio.

When you recognize something familiar, you're drawn to it. It calls to you, sometimes in excitement for something that feels reassuringly nostalgic and sometimes with dread, knowing that what you see isn't good. It's discomforting. Like when you see a storm coming with the same dark clouds you've seen before, reminding you of the destruction it's sure to leave behind. Those are the eyes that I see staring off into nothing, exhausted and dispirited to the point of absolute heartbreak. And they feel familiar.

She's a student, I assume. She has her books lying out in front of her, the pages blowing in the wind, but she maintains no effort to keep them in place on the table. Instead, she keeps her hands tucked into the kangaroo pockets of her sweater as the tips of her dark hair lift around her face every time a soft breeze blows by. The bottom curve of her chin twitches as her jaw sets, and she gnaws on her upper lip, exposing the white tips of her teeth. Her eyes look lost. Like all of the energy that fuels her has been drained and emptied. And every time her eyes flutter and her gaze shifts to something else, it looks as if she was convincing herself to hold it together. To bind everything that held her in place tighter instead of loosening those bindings and letting it all fall apart.

Up until now, I've never seen what I feel reflected in another person. I always assume that I'm going through this all alone, that no one can ever understand the battle my mind plays out in my head each day. And I can never tell anyone I feel this way. They would just respond with disapproval and misunderstanding.

How could you complain when you have such a blessed life?

What do you have to be so sad about? You're so successful.

Just focus on your success. You won't be sad anymore.

So instead, I wallow in my depression alone, surrounded by the whispers of criticism and judgment.

But this woman…

I watch as her eyes continue to search over her surroundings. As if she's looking for a distraction from her own thoughts. She buries her face in her hands, her breathing evening out before she pulls at her face and wraps her hands around her neck as her fingers meet at her nape.

When she looks back up, her eyes meet mine. The middle edges of her brows turn up, right where a single vertical crease forms, pleading. Begging me to… I don't even know. Help her? Drag her out of this incessant pull of water trying to keep her under? The corners of her mouth pull downwards in a deep frown as her chest rises and falls. Her breathing picks up pace as her eyes never leave mine. The air continues to shift around her, breezing through her hair as it cuts across her face in light sweeps.

I know it sounds absurd, but as our eyes remain locked in what feels like a conflict of push and pull, I feel her pain transfer on to me. Like I'm taking on whatever hurt was piercing through her heart, leaving it spent and beyond repair. I feel the moment I see right through her guise and recognize the hurt in every single facet of her heart. It's as if I can physically see her heart breaking in front of my eyes and for some reason, I want it to stop. I want to fix it because whatever hurt she's feeling, I'm feeling it too.

Everything in me is telling me to look away, fearing that she might recognize me, but I can't. I can't tear my eyes away from hers. They look at me as if she's willing me to help her, to pull her out from the dark waters that she's drowning in. I want to tell her that I want to help, but how? How can one person who's already drowning help another from drowning too?

CHAPTER 4
Ellie

t always happens gradually, the ache, the heaviness. It always starts in my heart, right at the center of my chest. It starts there because that's where it's the most painful. And then it spreads. It slowly and painfully spreads to my shoulders and settles into my limbs. At that point, it feels physical. It's no longer an emotion but an ache that becomes tangible, making it impossible to move, to subsist. So I sink, I drown. I let the harsh water rush over me, smiling at the thought that I no longer have to fight because I've surrendered.

It's the fresh wave of the ebb and flow that I've become so familiar with rushing towards me. No warning, just the knowledge that once this too passes, I'll have to welcome it once again. That old foe that keeps showing up, unannounced and always unwelcome.

It clouds my vision, blurring and clearing as everything in front of me focuses and goes out of focus. All I hear is the happy conversations of the people around me, now a muffled sound that thuds against my eardrums. The iron table in front of me feels cold, my hand catching on the small holes so that I can grasp something real, something concrete. Even my books that were causing me nothing more than a passing moment of frustration a minute ago distort right in front of me.

That's when I see him.

He watches as I take down every safeguard I surround myself with because I'm so tired. So tired and weary, and I want… My head instinctively shakes. The disbelief of actually knowing what I want, knowing what will take me away from this feeling of being submerged by the pull of dark, angry waters is almost euphoric.

But I can't look away, not when I feel like he's the only thing keeping me grounded. It's as if I can somehow send him a beacon, a call for help. So I can hope. Maybe hang on to some sort of surety that I don't have to live like this forever.

I have to leave, get the hell out of there. I blink away the blurriness and try to focus as I gather my things. My feet and hands move faster than my brain, every neuron signaling my muscles to move faster, quicker. My books find themselves roughly shoved into my backpack before I beeline towards the exit, tossing my half-empty coffee cup in a nearby trash can. I feel embarrassed, indignant even. After trying so hard to be complacent and never letting anyone have reason to be concerned for my well-being, I let a moment of weakness expose me.

Call it curiosity, call it self-sabotaging, but I instinctively stop on my way out. I turn to take one more look at the man, and he's still staring at me with an impassive look stretched over his face. The lip of his hat is pulled low, hovering over his eyes that reflect like a kaleidoscope of varying blues. Cobalt, aquamarine, cornflower, all blending together seamlessly. His hand is shielding the bottom portion of his face with his elbow propped against the arm of the chair, fingers fanning over his mouth and jaw. Only the upper curve of his nose is visible over his index finger.

I look away, disheartened yet thoroughly bemused, and continue to walk out, unsure of how to comprehend this out of place exchange between two complete strangers.

When I'm met with a gaggle of people crowding towards the coffee shop, I feel broken free of whatever stupor seemed to tether me to the coffee shop behind me. I look down at my phone to check the time. After trudging through classes all morning and not being able to get my coffee until close to lunch time, I still have another half hour until my next class. I take my time walking towards the lecture hall where my statistics class is located, leaning against the cold wall once I arrive, just as my phone vibrates in my hand.

It's Claire.

We've been friends since our freshman year at UCLA when we sat next to each other in a crowded auditorium. We were both fresh-faced eighteen-year-olds, ready to face the world of adulthood only to find out how ill-prepared we were. Her bright smile and confident spirit drew me to her right away. She has always been a welcoming presence since. We've been looking forward to graduating together at the end of the semester. A culmination of the last four years and our hard work finally paying off in one ceremonial day.

Claire: Hey. When are you done with class?

Me: I just got to class. I should be done by about 3. What's up?

Claire: Nothing. I just wanted to see if you wanted to hang out after.

Me: Yeah, that sounds good. I think I could use a little pick me up today.

Claire: Happy hour?

A smiley-face emoji follows.

Me: I guess. Only cause it's you.

Claire: Better be only for me! Ok, text me when you get out of class then.

I respond with a thumbs-up emoji before sliding my phone to my back pocket. I smile at our exchange. While heavy alcoholic consumption has never been my preference, I know a small chat with Claire will temporarily lift my spirits.

My toes wiggle into the linoleum floor, and my eyes fixate on a small hole that's starting to appear at the edges of my canvas shoes. I lift my head up as my professor breathlessly jogs to the door to our classroom and unlocks it with an armful of papers and a stained paper coffee mug.

"Sorry, guys. Just running a bit behind today," he explains over his shoulder as he enters the room and flicks on the lights.

I slowly find my unofficially assigned seat towards the back of the auditorium and get settled. The familiar faces of students start to trickle in, and we all silently take our seats. This is my last class of the day and usually takes me into the afternoon, leaving me drained and tired by the end of it.

"Have you looked at the study guide?" a breathless voice whispers to me. Austin, the one classmate I managed to make friends with, sits in the empty seat next to mine and looks at me with worried eyes.

"Yeah, I tried for a bit, but nothing's really sticking."

"Okay, I thought it was just me. And I don't even understand half the stuff he talks about."

Austin is a senior, just like me. We bonded over our hatred for this class and everything that involved statistics. Still, it's been nice to have an ally while working through distribution models and endless hypothesis testing.

"I think he's going to go over some of the questions today," I say in an attempt to provide some reassurance. "If not, they have some tutoring sessions available at the learning annex."

"I think I might have to attend one of those. You want to go with me? Next week? Maybe we can both get some help."

"Uh, yeah. I'm sure I can use it."

We set up our laptops as our professor turns on his and begins his lesson for the day. I sit quietly with the screen brightly lit in front of me, clicking away at the keyboard and struggling to follow along. My attention wavers in and out, catching only glimpses of whatever our professor is writing furiously on the whiteboard. He's so animated, eagerly answering every question and passionately describing the material in minute detail.

I continue to see Austin to my right peering at the screen of my laptop to see if my notes look any better than his. Mine are sparse, barely getting the important markers that are highlighted on the projector. I continue to sit through my class while occasionally glancing at the clock hanging at the front of the auditorium, willing it to move faster.

When I look again at the large dials moving at a snail's pace, it's 1:46 p.m. More than an hour left. I resist the urge to bury my face into my hands and try to focus on the notes. I guess I actually will be needing that tutoring session.

CHAPTER 5
Ellie

My drive to work the next morning is gloomy. The fog lingering along the empty roads is shrouding my vision as I drive slowly but make it in time for my early shift. After happy hour with Claire followed by a restless night of going back and forth from TV to overdue homework, I pulled myself out of bed this morning with a large amount of will on my end.

When I enter the store, the copper bell hanging from the door handle jingles, announcing my arrival. I'm greeted by the drifting scent of stale books and fresh coffee. The latter, which I assume, is coming from the Styrofoam Dunkin' Donuts cup sitting next to Mrs. Le on the glass counter.

"Good morning, Mrs. Le." I wave towards my boss, a middle-aged Vietnamese woman whose love for literature convinced her to open a small local bookstore some twenty years ago. I've always loved this place. The Cottage Bookstore, aptly named after the street it's located on, sits in a busy strip mall that's frequented by locals and popular amongst angsty teens looking to get away from their parents. As a teenager myself, I used to beg my mom to drop me off and leave me there for hours on end. Any excuse to get out of the house. I would usually settle into a small corner after having collected a stack of novels ranging from romance to psychological thrillers. Now, my weekends are spent working here, stocking books rather than buying them.

"Good morning, Ellie." She smiles sweetly at me. "There's a new shipment in the back. Do you think you could stock those before you take over the register?"

I nod. "Sure."

I walk myself to the back storage room and open one of the boxes stacked against the nearest wall. The first book sitting snugly, nestled right on top in the packed box, is *The Perks of Being a Wallflower* by Stephen Chbosky, one of my favorites. I frequently have to stop myself from reading books I find in the store, reminding myself that I am an employee and no longer just a customer.

"Umph!" Unable to actually lift it, I drag the box out towards the sales floor and begin sifting through to organize it alphabetically. A calming quiet fills the store while I sink into a comfortable routine, shelving book after book with the smooth classical music playing off of Mrs. Le's small speaker system situated behind the counter.

Claire and I had enjoyed our happy hour session last night. We talked about our lengthy and anticipatory plans for graduation. The realization that it would happen in just a short couple of months was barely settling in, and it brought on a new slate of dread. For me.

"This semester has seriously kicked my ass. I can't wait for it to be over," she said, a relaxed smile spreading across her face from the second margarita she was sipping on.

"Me too. I'll be glad when all this is finally over," I responded. I didn't mention my run-in with an overly observant stranger or my near emotional breakdown. I just nodded along and listened to Claire's chatter over the faint Spanish music that played above us.

Claire pulled her curly hair into a makeshift ponytail before letting it fall down. Her silky golden ringlets bounced as she rested her elbows on the table. "I just hope this internship pays off. My boss told me yesterday that they're going to announce really soon who they're hiring full time once the internship ends."

"So if you're hired, you would be working for Paramount?"

"*If,*" she emphasized.

I waved a hand at her, brushing off her modesty. I knew Claire. She was as fierce as she was ambitious. Her acceptance into an internship for Paramount, one of the most prominent production companies in the world, showed evidence of that. "I know you don't like to toot your own horn, but toot away! Especially when your boss is saying… What were your words? That you're the type-A firecracker the office needs?"

"He *did* say that." Claire giggled, blushing behind her hand. "Have you thought about what you want to do once you graduate?"

I sighed. "My mom and my aunt were just talking about that last night."

"Oh, that must have been fun," she said sarcastically.

"Yeah," I agreed, an acknowledging scoff coming out of me

at the same time.

"What did they say?"

"Just that I shouldn't work at the bookstore after college, maybe look into more promising ventures. Like an actual career."

She shrugged. "I mean, it doesn't hurt to start looking now."

"Yeah, I guess. I might look into it soon." I sighed, my agreement unconvincing.

The truth is that I don't have the eagerness that Claire has. I knew I wanted to study English in some way or form when I started college, but I don't have an ambitious bone in my body. To be completely honest, I don't have the faith in myself to be successful. Fear mixed with uncertainty is the perfect combination to keep ambition at my fingertips, never coursing through me to propel my future the way it should.

We had ended our night with me dropping Claire off at her apartment, our stomachs full of salty tortilla chips and watered-down margaritas for Claire and multiple refills of Coke for me, and I drove back home. I enjoy Claire's company, but often it leaves me feeling that I'm lacking in some way. I don't understand why my approach to our future is so different. I know our lives aren't the same, with Claire having been brought up in the posh parts of Beverly Hills surrounded by country clubs, charity galas, and a long line of extended family and social acquaintances, while the latter half of my childhood was spent alongside my mom fulfilling her duties as a single parent. Yet her optimism radiates from her while I suppress mine. I realize how uncomfortable I am with simply being happy, so much so that I actually intentionally work to remain somber.

With my mind wavering in and out with thoughts of my future, I finish stocking the books. I walk my way over to the register and settle behind the counter, ready to spend my day ringing up local students while helping them locate their books. I often wonder if they, too, have doubts about their future like I do or if they have everything figured out, waiting for their next move so they can live out their dreams.

"Hey, what happened last week? Weren't we meeting for lunch?" Charles's voice fades behind my fridge door, the upper half of his body disappearing with it.

"I uh… I went to school," I answer hesitantly.

His face reappears, along with a confused expression. "School? What are you talking about?"

"There's this coffeehouse right off campus near UCLA. I just went in for a bit."

"Ah, I see. Mingling with the common folk."

I roll my eyes at him. "I just needed to clear my head."

He hands me a beer and sits in the seat across from me. He groans as he settles in and leans back, running his hand through his chestnut-colored wavy hair before draping his arm along the backside of the couch.

Our premiere, and the last event that will close the chapter for our *Unrestrained* promotional responsibilities, is tonight. Which means another red carpet event and even more interviews that both of us will have to sit through. I'm not necessarily looking forward to it. Actually, if I'm being completely honest,

I would skip it. I would avoid it altogether and stay home if I *could*. And I think that's part of the reason that Charles is here instead of at home keeping Amelia company as she spends the better part of the afternoon getting ready.

"How was your session? With Dr. Greene, is it?" he asks. Charles is one of the few people that know I regularly attend therapy. In fact, he's one of the only people that has seen me in my darkest moments.

"It was… whatever." I wave off his question.

We're interrupted by the thunderous boom of my front door opening, followed by the clamoring that can only be Chuck and Jackson.

Chuck, given name Charles, was given his nickname so that we, amongst our friends, could differentiate between the two Charleses. He's a big trust fund baby that comes from very old money in Manhattan. He moved to LA against his parents' wishes to be free from the social demands of his very high-profile family name. He thrives off going against the grain and proving to his parents that his lifestyle is thriving despite their lack of moral support. Jackson was born and raised in LA, just like Charles. The two have been friends since grade school, and Jackson currently works as Charles's assistant. He's modest, as he lives an unassuming lifestyle in West Hollywood, but he's patient. He's always putting up with the chaos that comes with our hectic lifestyle, even though it's not necessarily his style.

The four of us have formed a sort of posse, a comradery that can only develop through trust, loyalty, and a lot of partying. The former two being a scarcity in our way of life.

"Where the fuck have you guys been?" Chuck screeches,

his voice echoing against the hard interior of my home. "Jacky here has got no game whatsoever. I need my boys to be my wingman. This guy's a good-for-nothing pussy."

"Those girls didn't want anything to do with us. Why even try when they were so clearly repulsed by us?"

"They were repulsed by *you*. The blonde one thought I was cute. She even gave me her Snapchat," Chuck says proudly.

"Snapchat? What are you, twelve?"

Charles and I both chuckle. The bickering that continues between the two is ever so present, just like every other time the four of us are together. If it's not about women… Well, actually, it's always about women. For as long as I've known these guys, they argue about how to get women, who gets more women. Hell, they even argue about the women they don't get.

"So what's on the agenda tonight?" Chuck asks, rubbing his hands together, insinuating another night of debauchery.

"We have the premiere," I answer, pointing between myself and Charles.

"Oh shit, I forgot about that," Chuck answers.

Right on cue, my doorbell rings. The four of us look at each other, our conversation halting as we silently assign a person to answer the door.

Jackson sighs, volunteering. "I guess I'll get it."

As soon as the door opens, Levi pushes past it and storms into the foyer.

"Dammit, Rhy, I've been calling you all fucking week!" he blurts out. I stand as Levi stalks towards me. I tower over him, not in an attempt to intimidate him, but because our height differences give me no choice. While Levi's stature may be subpar, he makes up for it with his spunk. His arrogance and assertiveness are what have made him one of the most sought-after talent agents in the industry, and he makes no apologies for it. With his iPhone permanently glued to his hand, he's always about business. No room for formalities, just straight to the point.

I've been ignoring his calls since I landed back in LA. Knowing he wouldn't want to waste any time deciding my next project, even sending a gofer to deliver a cardboard banker's box full of scripts, I didn't want to face him. Now it's been over a week, and he's driven all the way from his office in Central LA to confront me. I have no choice but to face him.

"Sorry, Levi. I've just been busy," I explain. But he sees right through my lie.

He rolls his eyes and deadpans, "Come on, Rhylan. Look, I know you've been going through some shit. And I'm here for you, I really am. But we've got this premiere tonight, and I need you to be on your A game."

"I know, I know," I answer with my hands up, palms facing him in surrender.

"Then why the fuck have you been avoiding me? What's going on?" he demands.

"Relax, man," Chuck calls from his seated position on my couch. "Sit down, have a drink with us."

Levi doesn't answer Chuck. He just looks at me, annoyed and at the tail end of his patience.

Chuck stands and walks right up to Levi, leaning a hand on his shoulder. "You seem tense. Are you under a lot of pressure?" Chuck croons.

Levi looks at Chuck, his mouth opening and closing before looking back at me. "Why is he talking to me?"

Chuck smiles obnoxiously at Levi, completely unfazed. He's used to Levi's cold shoulder and limited patience. In fact, he takes pleasure in pushing Levi's buttons and gets a kick out of making him peeve.

"Um, why don't we talk in my office," I suggest, suppressing the urge to smirk as Chuck clings closer to Levi.

I walk the narrow hallway towards my office to lead the way, passing by the wall that showcases multiple movie posters framed in glass and gold embossed borders with my face blown up into oversized proportions. Levi shakes Chuck off his shoulders and follows. Once we're in private, I close the door behind me.

"Look, I just needed some time. That's all," I explain. Defeated, I collapse onto one of the matching armchairs facing my large desk with a sigh. My hand moves to my face to rub my temples with my thumb and middle finger in an attempt to release the built-up tension.

"Rhy, did you want me to go with you tonight? We can make an appearance and leave," he suggests. He sits down on the opposite armchair and faces me, his elbows resting on his knees. His anger has subsided, and genuine concern is written all over his face.

"No, I'm fine. I just needed a couple of days to clear my head. I'll be there. You have nothing to worry about."

He continues to look at me, unconvinced.

"I'm sorry, Levi. I've just been distracted. That's all."

"Rhy, I don't mean to overstep, but are you still seeing that therapist I recommended?"

"I am," I answer. My brows are drawn together, recalling the conversation I had with Dr. Greene last week. And the specific encounter near the UCLA campus that I haven't told a soul about.

"Okay. And is the therapy helping?"

I look up at him, remaining silent while bobbing my head up and down, indicating an extremely unreassuring affirmative answer.

"I'm fine, Levi. I'm going tonight, and you have nothing to worry about. I even have Carrie dropping off my suit right now," I add, trying to sound convincing and hoping it would add to my already thinning argument. I realize I've said that I'm fine twice in a five-minute span. Not very convincing at all.

"Well, you should have had that here already, but I guess I'll take what I can get," he says, loosening up.

Levi is starting to slacken for now, but his trust in me is starting to wane thin, and I don't necessarily blame him. Avoiding his calls and emails isn't helping, and I know forcing him to show up at my door just so he can talk to me is his last straw.

"You have nothing to worry about. I'll be there on time." I start to walk towards the door to walk him out when Carrie, my assistant, bumps into me with a garment bag in one hand while balancing what looks like a dozen shopping bags in the other. I rush to help her, my hands fumbling as I walk back to my desk.

"Okay. Just call me when you're back home tonight. Let me know how it goes," Levi answers with a hint of hesitation.

"I will. Now go, enjoy your night with your family," I say as I wave him off.

His phone rings just then, ending our meeting and naturally ushering him out the door. He waves his hand with his back facing me, already talking a mile a minute to whomever is on the other line.

Carrie is in the middle of my office, moving efficiently, just as she does with her job on a day-to-day basis. As another integral member of the Rhylan Matthews team, she manages the ins and outs of my days. Without her, Shana, or Levi, I would probably be standing on a street corner with a cardboard sign that says Will Act for Food.

My hand goes to the silver hanger peeking off the top of a black garment bag. "This is the Tom Ford I asked Shana for?"

"Yep. She also got you some Louboutins," she answers, pointing to the tan shoe box sitting on the floor next to three other shoe boxes. Options, as Shana always stresses. *It's good to have options.*

"Great. Hey, thanks for getting these at the last minute. I know I should have asked you to grab them sooner. Sorry," I apologize.

"Don't worry about it," she answers as she waves off my concern of having to inconvenience her. "By the way, Shana told me something. She asked me not to mention it to you."

My brows draw together, confused as to what Shana could have told her but doesn't want me to know.

"Bella Raven is going to be there," she answers my unspoken question.

"Well, yeah. She's *in* the movie," I explain.

"Yeah, but I guess her publicist called after your interview with Jack Stuber and… She's basically stating you guys are dating. And have been since the movie wrapped."

I groan and shake my head. "It's fine," I answer with a surrendering slap to my thighs. "I can't avoid her. I guess I'll just have to deal with her."

"Okay," Carrie responds, her face apologetic for being the bearer of bad news.

"The car's going to be here at five. I'm just going to shower and get ready," I say, changing the subject and keeping my eye on the time. "You can go. I'm good here."

Carrie looks down at her watch and nods, confirming that my itinerary is accurate. "You sure? I can wait until the driver gets here. Just in case you need anything," she offers.

"No, I'm fine. Really. I'll see you on Monday."

"Okay." She nods in my direction. "Call me if you need anything." I follow her out of my office towards the living room as she waves at the guys before letting herself out.

"I better get going," Charles says as I turn to face him. He stands as he points a thumb towards the door. "Amelia had her whole glam squad at home. I'm hoping they'll be finished by the time I get back."

"Yeah, I got to hop in the shower and get ready too," I explain.

"I guess we'll head out too then," Jackson says. "Good luck, guys."

Chuck and Jackson follow Charles towards the door, taking their cue to exit and give me time to get ready.

Once the door closes behind them, I head towards my

massive master bedroom, suit in hand. Stripped out of my jeans and white undershirt, I step into the steaming hot shower equipped with a waterfall shower head. The heat trickles down my body while the stall fills with heavy steam. I linger for a moment too long as I mentally prepare myself for tonight.

I've always accepted the responsibilities that come with my job. As much as I want to focus my attention on the *acting* part of my career, I'm still a public figure. A role model to some, and I have to present myself as such. But all I want to do right now is disappear. Or whatever it is that I need to do so that I can feel like myself again. My mind keeps wandering to my phone, ready to call Levi to tell him I've changed my mind, to go back on my word and weak assurances that I'm fine.

I'm just hoping that I have enough of me leftover to get through the night. I guess the silver lining is that I don't need to be alone with my own thoughts. A welcoming distraction, because I don't know what I would do if left to my own devices.

CHAPTER 7
Ellie

The sniffles I hear are coming from Claire, a wrung-out tissue held up close to her eyes in an attempt to not ruin her perfectly done makeup. She's holding up a large, fluffy makeup brush, held midair as her attention has shifted onto the small television screen on my desk.

She had barged into my room after her last class, an overnight bag filled to the brim with makeup, hair care products, and three different types of curling irons varying in barrel sizes, ready to primp herself up for her first movie premiere attendance. And, undoubtedly, not her last.

"This is my favorite part," she whispers, her tiny voice breaking as her chin trembles.

"Brent!"

"Katherine!"

"Brent! I didn't mean it! Any of it!"

"I know. I knew the whole time."

"I love you, Brent."

"I love you, my Kit Kat."

I wait for the tears to spill from my own eyes or at least

some form of emotion that mirrors the empathetic tears coming from Claire as we watch the scene between two reunited lovers unfold, but nothing comes. So instead, I huff out a laugh in Claire's direction, finding her reaction to a movie that she's seen a dozen times endearing.

The End.

Written in perfect cursive with a flourish, the words sit dead center on the screen, with Brent and Katherine, played by Rhylan Matthews and Sarah Hyland, driving off into the sunset. The dramatic music turns into a melancholic tune as the names of the cast and crew scroll upwards.

"I would let that man do whatever he wanted to me," Claire says wistfully, methodically dabbing the moisture from the corners of her eyes. "If he wanted to throw me over his shoulder and carry me into a dark dungeon to do unmentionable things to me, I would go willingly."

"I'm sure Wes would love that," I counter sarcastically.

She rolls her eyes and waves her hand at me, making a *tsk* sound with her tongue, telling me her boyfriend's protests wouldn't matter. "He would have to just deal with it. But can you blame me?" Her hand extends towards the screen, presenting me with exhibit A in the long list of reasons why she would leave her boyfriend for Rhylan Matthews.

She's not wrong. Even now, as the credits roll, his dark unruly hair and eyes the color of the waters in the Maldives are all I see. His height is a whole other subject. An entire chapter going into detail about how he sprouted from the ground and took residence on every screen he appeared on. Even through a flat-screen TV, I can tell he's tall. Like, unnaturally tall. The kind of tall that takes up a room no matter how big it is. With shoulders and a chest broad enough to take up what's left of that room. And that smile, the way it curves at the edges and softens his normally sharp, jutted jawline, would make any girl swoon.

Jesus, I'm no better than Claire.

Claire's phone dings, interrupting our ogling and bringing us back to reality. Her brows furrow, glaring at her phone screen. "What?!" she exclaims.

"What?" I ask.

"Wes can't make it tonight!"

"Why?"

"He said he's sick. Fever and everything." She extends her phone towards me, presenting me with a blurred image of her boyfriend riddled with illness in bed, proof that he's actually sick and not standing her up for some other incredulous reason.

"Oh, that sucks," I say, genuinely apologetic that her plans fell through.

Her hands are moving furiously over her phone screen, tapping away a message that I'm sure Wes is glad that he isn't able to hear in person. Her wrath is one that both Wes and I know not to be the object of. She lifts her head up in defeat. "I can't go alone!"

I shrug. I don't have any solution for her. The premiere is in two hours, and she isn't going to find a replacement, or a cure for the common cold, in that short amount of time.

"It was for work anyway. Do you really need a date?"

"It's a red carpet event! I'm not even working tonight. It's just an invitation to the premiere. Rhylan Matthews's premiere!" she says, emphasizing that it was very much Rhylan Matthews's movie premiere she was attending. When her boss proudly presented her with an exclusive invitation, she squealed. He then shushed her and requested she keep it on the DL, as not everyone was extended the same invitation.

I nod, shrugging again, wishing I could offer more help than that.

"Wait," she says with that sinister tone of a plan concocting in her head.

I look at her sideways while nervous for her next words. "What?"

"*You* can go with me!"

"What?" My face deadpans.

"Yeah! You can be my date," she explains.

"Claire, no," I start to protest. "I don't even have anything to wear."

My eyes scan her from head to toe, knowing that if I were to attend said premiere, I would have to fix myself to look something like Claire does right now. She looks beautiful naturally, and now, with a full face of makeup and hair styled in a sexy updo, she looks stunning. Her normally curly blonde hair is straightened to look sleek and clipped neatly to the back of her head. And her slender figure is displayed in a two-piece, skintight dress the color of peacocks, exposing just enough of her midsection for it to be sexy yet tasteful.

"It's okay! You don't even have to dress all fancy. It's not the Oscars."

I'm contemplating my decision, already leaning towards a refusal, when Claire walks over to my closet and starts rummaging through my inventory.

"I'm sure we can find something in here," she calls out, elbow-deep in the accumulation of jeans and T-shirts, with the occasional sundress that I like to indulge in. "This is perfect!"

I turn to see what particular outfit she was able to find in my curated collection of clothing picked to my taste. She presents me with a red knee-length dress with thin straps, sleek and slit to the mid-thigh. My eyes widen, trying to figure out where that came from.

"It's mine," Claire explains as if she were reading my mind. "I completely forgot I had it here. Remember when we snuck out to see that band? I think they were called 100 Monkeys? I changed my mind last minute and wore one of your dresses instead."

"I can't wear that!" I protest.

"Yes, you can! It's sexy and chic. And it's perfect for this premiere," she argues. "Here, just try it on."

"Claire, I don't know," I answer, already going in through one of her ears and out the other. She pulls my arm and stands me up, shoving the dress into me. I have no choice but to give in to her demand.

I pull the oversized T-shirt I was wearing over my head as Claire holds open the dress, making it easier for me to step into it. She zips me up from behind, and we both look into the full-length mirror hanging off my door.

"Holy shit. Girl, that dress looks amazing," she squeaks. "I'm not even kidding."

I turn to the side to examine the full look and confirm the accuracy of her statement. While Claire has the height and svelte shape that's built to model any look, I have the subtle curves that fill this dress. I remember the dress hanging loose on Claire's slender frame. But on me, it's form-fitting, clinging to my hips and exposing my silhouette in a flattering manner.

"Okay, but I can't go out in this! I feel so exposed and *naked*," I protest to Claire. I already don't feel comfortable in my own skin. Standing in front of a mirror with my best friend to prod my newfound appreciation for skintight dresses is one thing, but to be out in front of strangers is another.

"You look too good to waste that dress away in your closet, or mine when I take it back. Come on. And if you have a horrible time, I'll take you out for milkshakes after. You wouldn't want me to go alone?" Claire continues, pleading her case and giving me a downturned pout with perfected puppy eyes. I finally sigh, defeated and running out of excuses.

"Fine. I can't be out too late though. I have work tomorrow morning," I groan, reminding her of my responsibilities at the bookstore on the weekends. I slouch forward from the regret I'm already feeling from my decision.

Claire jumps with joy, clapping her hands and squealing. "You aren't going to regret it! In fact, you're going to be the one taking me out for that milkshake to thank me. And I promise to get you back home before midnight, Cinderella," she states matter-of-factly.

I smile and roll my eyes at her as I slowly start digging in my closet for an appropriate pair of shoes to match my dress.

"I need to do your hair, and then we can work on your makeup," Claire says. "You're lucky I finished mine already."

"Yeah, so lucky," I respond sarcastically.

"Here, sit down. What do you think about curls? Like, soft curls to make you look like an old Hollywood starlet," she says with wistful eyes. She's envisioning the look she has in mind for me, and I know she has high hopes. I don't want to break it to her that while she might be imagining an overall sexy, glamorous look, I would probably only be able to deliver a slightly better version of what's in front of her.

I comply and pull out my swivel chair from my desk to sit, facing the mirror as she digs through her large overnight bag filled with every cosmetic product known to humankind. She begins brushing through my hair and plugs in her curling iron, then sections off chunks of my hair to make it easier to work with. Her expression turns serious as her head bobs up and down behind me.

"Wes talked to me about moving to Australia with him." She says it so casually, I quickly turn to look at her to make sure it isn't some random joke.

I can't believe what she's saying. *Australia?* She would be so far away. "What's in Australia?"

"Wes's job is opening up a headquarters there, and his boss asked him if he would be interested in starting it up." She says all this so nonchalantly, it's almost as if she isn't even serious about it. But I know Claire. She wouldn't be bringing this up if she wasn't even remotely considering it.

"And you want to go? What about Paramount?"

Her shrug is subtle as she tries to remain indifferent. "I'm not even in yet. I don't know what's going to happen after graduation."

I look at her through my full-length mirror, her focus fully on the back of my head. All glee has left her face as she focuses with pensiveness. This has been on her mind for a while, and she wears the worry from it all over her face.

"Are you worried he's going to break up with you if you don't go?"

She sighs at my question, evidently worried that she may lose this man that she has come to love over the last three years. They met when Claire was a freshman and Wes was a senior. He majored in finance and quickly found a job with a large finance company in the heart of Los Angeles. Its headquarters is here, but now it looked as though they planned to expand.

"I guess. I mean, if he wants to go without me, I can't stop him."

She reaches for her curling iron and lightly taps the wand to check the heat. She begins meticulously curling sections of my hair and pinning them to my scalp, working her way from the bottom up. I remain compliant as she continues to work on my hair and I start on my makeup. I keep an eye on her, ready to offer whatever advice I can give. At the very least, I can listen to her, be a welcoming ear to talk through her situation.

I look at her through the mirror. Her expression is serious, and she catches my eyes.

"Claire, whatever he chooses, you guys are going to be okay. I can't imagine him just throwing away a life you two built over the years without thinking twice about it."

"I know," she answers while focusing on wrapping my thick hair through the rod of the curling iron and letting it fall in her hand carefully.

She smiles at me. "Sit still before I mess up your hair.

Otherwise, you're going to end up looking like Bellatrix Lestrange when I'm done."

I burst out into laughter, imagining myself with hair like the crazed aunt of a blonde-haired bully.

CHAPTER 8
Rhylan

Once I'm showered and dried, my hands swipe side to side on the foggy mirror in my en suite bathroom to create small, streaked reflections of myself. The air is still thick and warm from the hot water that I just stepped out of. I don't have any big pre-premiere ritual, no glam squad to primp and pamper me. Instead, I simply towel dry my hair, run some pomade through it, and dress in whatever designer outfit Shana picks out for me. In interviews, I've been asked how I coif my hair so perfectly in the right places. The same insignificant, unoriginal questions that I get asked and laugh through politely. I say it's a secret while I know all I do is create some friction with a terry cloth towel.

My phone lights up and vibrates, the thrumming off the counter echoing loudly against the tiled walls.

"Hello?" I answer, my voice worn and tired.

"Hi, Rhylan." My mom's voice rings through the receiving end. Her reassuring voice makes my chest tighten, homesickness taking over me. "The premiere's tonight?"

I clear my throat before I speak, covering the wavering in

my voice. "Yeah, I'm heading out in a bit."

"Oh, I'm glad I caught you before you left."

"Yeah. Is Dad there?"

"He's here." She laughs. "Just puttering around in the garage, working on that ancient car of his."

I smile, imagining my dad hunched under the hood of his old Corvette. The same Corvette that he taught me how to do an oil change and replace spark plugs in. The same one that persuaded me into finding my own classic car, something to remind me of home.

"I miss you guys." My voice finally gives, cracking at the sentiment of missing my parents and everything that represents my former life.

"We miss you too." Her voice is soft and comforting, everything I need right now. I just don't realize it until I hear her say those four little words letting me know that my absence is noticed and there are still some remnants of the son I used to be.

"I got the video of Brooklyn that you sent me. She's getting big."

"Oh my goodness! Isn't she?" she says in a singsongy tone. Even through the phone, I can picture her face lighting up. "And she has those big, bright eyes that are aware of everything. Robert is such a good dad. He even gets up at night to change diapers!"

"I'm sure Natalie appreciates that," I say fondly in regards to my oldest brother and his family. His wife had delivered a baby girl barely a month ago, and the news of the newest addition to the Matthews brood was all anyone could talk about.

"You need to visit so you can meet her. She needs to know who her Uncle Rhy is."

I sigh. "I will, Mom. When I have some time off, I'll visit."

She does this every time she calls: guilt-tripping me into visiting more often. If it's not to see her and my dad before they get too old for them to remember who I am (her words, not mine), it's to coerce me using my nieces and nephews as leverage. There are five in total between my oldest brother Robert and the middle sibling, Jacob. They remain close to home, raising a family and living a picture-perfect suburban life. Jacob even has a white picket fence that surrounds his front lawn, and he coaches his oldest son's little league while Robert is stepping in to take on Natalie's PTA responsibilities while she recovers from her recent delivery.

Their completely contented and idyllic lives are something that I haven't been able to witness firsthand but can't necessarily bring myself to. Knowing that they're living normal lives only makes me realize how far from reality mine has strayed.

"I should finish getting ready. The car's going to be here soon to take me to the premiere."

"Of course. Have fun tonight and call me later," she calls through the phone.

"I will."

Her call comes like clockwork before every movie premiere to check in and give me words of encouragement, knowing that I need it more than I think I do.

The first call was filled with more excitement and enthusiasm that I was able to reciprocate at the time. I was only twenty-one years old, and there were whispers going through

Hollywood of an Oscar nomination. Those whispers got to my head. My ego blew up, thinking I could do whatever I wanted in this town. My sweaty, glazed-over face appeared on every episode of *E! News*, plastered through still images with whatever girl was linked to my arm, usually bleach blonde with big tits, after a night of binge drinking and late-night partying. I didn't win an Oscar. I didn't even get nominated. My ego cloud burst, and I was left feeling empty.

The calls from my mom always bring me down to earth, reminding me of where I came from. But it isn't a happy wave of nostalgia. It's more of a melancholic one. I had left the comforts of my childhood and stepped into a world that still feels foreign to me, and those moments of doubt are becoming more frequent and even harder to ignore.

I know people always think that actors look cool and collected, confident to a fault. But that's not always the case. A lot of the time, I feel like I don't even know what I'm doing. Like I'm just following along with what I'm supposed to do and whatever is expected of me. But that's what we actors do. We *act*. We act like we know what we're doing, like we're comfortable with the fame and attention. Never giving way to the intimidation of the world and having to embrace it instead.

I'm fastening the minimalist gold cufflinks and shrugging into my jacket when a message dings on my cell phone, alerting me that my driver has arrived. I slip on my shoes, adjusting myself to the roughness inside since I didn't have time to break them in, before my stride leads towards the door and into the brisk night.

"Good evening, Mr. Matthews. We should be at the

theater in about an hour with the traffic," he informs me. I nod back at him and hop into the car as he holds the door open for me.

Uncomfortable with idle hands, I scroll through my phone. Nothing important to look at, just something to keep my hands occupied. My thumb finally stops on an email from Levi. He's been badgering me about a romantic comedy where I would star opposite Reese Witherspoon. The premise of the story is that of an older woman dating a younger man, myself, with a hint of comic relief, making it a typical rom-com. It's a role that I've done one too many times. And yet, I can't wholeheartedly commit.

I weigh out the pros and cons every time Levi brings it up, which is often. I would be comfortable in the role. It's familiar. And I would be working with one of the most talented actresses of our time. But the cons are too hard to ignore. Like my wavering commitment and inability to stay focused. My tenacity was what had kept me going in the past but as of late, I've become hesitant, fluctuating between can't and won't. These personal qualms are what keep my answer the same each time Levi broaches the subject: I'll think about it.

I leave the email read, no answer, and lean back into the plush leather seat. The quiet hum of the engine is the only sound that fills the interior of the car. And for a moment, just a moment, I feel relaxed. All the noise and chaos have stopped, and I feel like I actually disappeared, and no one noticed. Until the lights that manage to peek through the dark tinted windows remind me that evanescence is just a dream and that being Rhylan Matthews is the furthest thing from being insignificant.

The sound of Claire tapping her perfectly manicured nails on her phone screen is distracting. It's harsh even over the drone of the engine and the low hum of music coming from the car stereo. When I look at her with one brow raised, she stops.

"Sorry." Her hands move to the seat belt strapped across her chest as she glides her fingers over the bumpy material.

"Are you nervous?"

"Kind of." She lifts her hand to run her fingers through her hair before she stops, remembering the hours she spent to have it styled perfectly. "My boss said that Paramount's studio head is going to be there. If I'm lucky, like *super* lucky, I might be able to meet him. I guess that's making me a little on edge."

"A little?"

"Okay, a lot." Both our bodies slump to the left as the driver takes a sharp turn, causing Claire to swear under her breath. The sleek town car she called to take us to the premiere isn't proving to be well worth her money, as the erratic driving of our driver is only adding to Claire's already frazzled nerves.

I tug at my own seat belt to ensure that it's secured properly.

"Deep breaths," I say, my hands moving upwards as I take a closed mouth breath of my own, providing a visual for her to mirror. "In and out."

She takes a long breath, her chest heaving before relaxing as she exhales.

"Just remember, you're a professional. You got this."

"I got this." She nods, only half believing her self-affirmation.

"And if you don't, there's alcohol, right?"

She giggles at my attempt to lighten the mood and sighs, just a fragment of her shoulders relaxing. "I still can't believe we get to see Rhylan Matthews tonight. And Bella Raven!"

"Hmm."

"I heard they're dating," she states matter-of-factly. "God, they look so good together."

I *hmm* again, acknowledging her intel on celebrity news while I mull over her gossip. Bella Raven is as sexy as a woman can be. Legs that go on for miles and a seductive smile that makes me question my own heterosexuality. Pair her with Rhylan Matthews, and you can't help but wonder what their kids would look like. I don't fully acknowledge it, but the baby butterflies that have suddenly appeared in my stomach are a small indication that I'm just as excited to see them as she is.

Our car pulls to a gradual slowdown. The crowd of people and flashing lights indicate that we have arrived at our destination, as if the monotone voice on the automated GPS system isn't enough. When our practically matching black stilettos hit the red carpet, I can't help but feel the rush of Hollywood's biggest party of the night rattle through me. Glitz and glamor surround us, and I'm engrossed by it all. I look over at Claire and smile. She feels it too.

"So, I guess you owe me a milkshake?" she says to me, her voice barely able to be heard through the noise. She extracts two lanyards crammed into her clutch, both attached to a laminated miniature version of the movie poster along with a bold VIP across the center. "Here, wear this."

I comply, ducking my head to hang the lanyard around my neck. "I feel so very important."

"You should," she says with a flirty wink. "You're with me."

I nudge my shoulder into hers before we move our right feet further onto the red carpet, our steps moving in synchrony. We move in deliberate and calculated strides as our eyes scan everything in our periphery, taking in every bit of the flair that has been flawlessly placed around us. From the red carpet backdrop to the searchlights swiveling in every direction and everyone dressed so chic and stylish, it's all so glamorous.

Claire suddenly gasps, her hands firmly grabbing hold of my arm to stop me as our steps lead us towards the entrance of the theater. "Oh my God! It's Rhylan Matthews! And Bella Raven." Her eyes twinkle as if in a daze, the sudden presence of Hollywood royalty making her speechless. I trail her eyes, landing on the stars of the night as they wave towards the throng of fans reaching out for them as they hastily sign autographs and pose for pictures.

With their backs turned to us, we're only able to observe and admire them from afar. Our necks are strained, and our feet are balanced on our tiptoes so we can get a better look.

For a moment, we shamelessly stare. We watch as Bella Raven brings her hand up Rhylan Matthews's arm and leans against him. Her hand glides into his, looking innate and comfortable in her movements. He releases her hand and tenderly moves his hand to her back, holding her close while his eyes stay on the crowd. Bella continues to look at him, and he finally turns to smile at her, outlining his profile as she leans her head on his arm. The action is affectionate, something a couple would do but not overly intimate.

Having watched the entire exchange, Claire nudges me. "Oh, they're definitely having sex," she says, quite loudly. I giggle and nudge my elbow into Claire's side when a passerby looks at us, having overheard our conversation.

"Claire! You made it!" Both of our heads turn to the voice coming from an older gentleman dressed in a stark white suit over a silk purple dress shirt. His hair is slicked back, exposing the narrowing point of his widow's peak. While on anyone else, the entire look may have looked clumsy and distasteful, he looks elegant and charming.

"Hugo! We just barely got here." Claire places her hands on his arms, hovering over him by a couple inches, and kisses both his cheeks. So Hollywood of her. "This is Ellie. She's my date for the night."

"No boyfriend?"

"He's indisposed." Her small frown shows her disappointment.

"Well, looks like you have a very stunning plus one by your side tonight." He smiles at me, extending his hand. "Nice to meet you."

The three of us are interrupted when a very relaxed and slightly intoxicated man brushes his arm up against Hugo, his smile infectious. Hugo turns to face the man, their noses inches away from each other.

"You came to say hi to the commoners?" They laugh, clutching onto each other, making it obvious that they're close. "Claire, this is Michael Perry."

Claire's eyes widened. "Yes, of course! It's such an honor to meet you, Mr. Perry. We're so excited to see the movie tonight."

He smiles, waving his hand towards her. "Michael, please."

"Claire's the intern I was telling you about."

"It's nice to finally meet you! This man talks nonstop about you. You've made quite an impression on him."

The way Michael's hand grazes down Hugo's arm, finally settling into his hand, doesn't go unnoticed. And when Hugo cups Michael's face only to pinch it affectionately, it confirms that the two are more than just acquaintances. As the three interact, dipping into topics related to the movie and Claire's work, I sidle to the side lines, trying not to take away from Claire's spotlight. I hadn't realized how important tonight was. Yes, it's an opportunity to see some very famous faces, but it's more than that for Claire. These are opportunities for her to network and build her already growing reputation.

It makes me envious. Not in a way that I wouldn't wish this sort of success on Claire. I'm overjoyed for her. She worked hard to get to where she's at, and this interaction shows it. But seeing her hard work pay off only brings to light how little I've worked for my own future. We're both slated to graduate this spring, yet I feel so ill-prepared while Claire looks ready to take on the world.

Claire looks over at me as the conversation thins now that introductions are over.

Hugo reaches for Claire's hand, fondness twinkling in his eyes. "We'll see you inside."

Claire nods, her smile beaming as she watches Hugo and Michael walk away.

"Is that Michael Perry, the director?" I ask.

"Mm-hmm. He directed *this* movie!"

"Oh, wow. I didn't know. And he's dating your boss?"

She nods with a smug smile that doesn't come off as snobby but full of pride instead.

"Wow, that's impressive." I nod approvingly. "You really know how to meet the right people."

She turns to face me, one shoulder lifted up in modesty as she reaches for my hand. "Come on. Let's go inside."

CHAPTER 10
Rhylan

Blinding lights, ones that temporarily leave bright white spots on the back of my eyelids, are all I see. The shouting surrounds me from every angle, calling my name, trying to get my attention from every direction possible. Photographers, fans, and any other attendees that would be present yelling, "Over here, Rhylan! Can we get one of you two kissing?"

Bella stands by my side, dressed in a floor-length black silk dress slit to her hip and her long blonde hair pulled back in a sleek, low ponytail. She oozes seduction.

As my Louboutin-clad feet move along the red carpet, I choose to ignore the way Bella's hands glide over my suit. They rest in places that I don't feel comfortable with her touching, so I attempt to minimize our contact to the occasional hand-holding or my hand pressing to her bare back. All with a smile on my face.

It doesn't matter how many red carpet events I've attended. Instinct always tells me to run. But I don't, of course. Instead, I become a puppet to any puppeteer taking on the reins. Smile and wave, stand and pose, take a pen and sign, answer questions while hoping they don't ask about my personal life. Everything done in the name of fame.

My steps are calculated alongside Bella, stopping at little markers, making it easier for the puppeteers to control my movements so I can smile for the cameras a little more gracefully. My waves are deliberate, minimal, and working through what little confidence I have left.

When I feel a familiar hand rest on my shoulder, I relax a bit. A friend in a time of need, just when the overwhelming pressure is making me feel like my tie is tightening around my neck like a noose.

"I guess the circus found us," a low voice says in a hushed tone.

When I turn, Charles is already looking at the crowd, smiling and mirroring my waves with his wife, Amelia, by his side.

"And it's a hell of a circus." I turn to Amelia, extending my greeting with a warm hug. "Hi, Amelia."

"Hi, Rhy." She smiles. "I swear, the crowd seems to get bigger and louder each time."

Charles and Amelia met in high school. The two dated all throughout college and finally married right before Charles's career took off. Just before they had the first of their two boys, she quit work as a grade-school teacher to stay at home and out of the public eye. As soon as the media caught wind of Charles's more personal life, they had a lot less privacy along with a much less normal life. Meaning no more day jobs and a lot more of raising a family in secrecy.

We continue our walk down the red carpet, our hands

permanently in the air and our smiles never waning, when a young woman with frizzy red hair approaches us. Her clipboard is clutched to her chest, and a headset drapes around her neck.

"I'm so sorry, but we have an interview with *E! News* before the three of you head into the theater." I don't even know who she is, but we've learned to not question those kinds of details. Just follow along and do as the puppeteer commands.

We all duck our heads in unison, following the woman, and move towards the end of the red carpet where the interview is to be held. Director chairs are set side by side, cocooned by the bustle of lights and cameras and people working hurriedly to get the stage ready. Inherent habits take over as I unbutton my jacket before sitting as still as possible while a small mic gets clipped to my collar. I smile politely at the interviewer as her own mic gets clipped to her blouse. She looks more confident than I do as she glances down at her cue cards, her eyes scanning over the words with assurance.

Bella's glam squad, following her around like little ducklings, touches up her makeup one last time before she sits next to me. I'm sandwiched between Bella and Charles, making me the centerpiece of this interview.

"Charles Bradley, Rhylan Matthews, and Bella Raven, the stars of *Unrestrained*, are joining us live for their star-studded premiere at Grauman's Chinese Theater." The interviewer's statement is directed towards the camera, towards an audience that would most likely include my own mother. "This movie has already gained an unrealistic amount of buzz, and you three are at the center of it. What has the success of this movie meant to you?"

Charles speaks first. "Well, we have a good team, an amazing production crew, along with Michael Perry, our equally amazing director. I think it would just mean a lot that our work was for something. We created a great movie that the fans will love, and we're all really proud of it."

"And Bella, the leading lady of the hour, you look amazing, by the way," the interviewer fusses, her hand politely pointing towards Bella's dress. "What did it feel like to kiss one of Hollywood's hottest men?"

She's referring to me, obviously.

God, do they really have nothing better to ask? It's always the same damn questions.

I lower my head and smile, trying my best to remain polite and collected.

Bella practically purrs, her hand purposefully landing on mine. "Oh, Rhy Guy here was an amazing kisser." She laughs, smiling at me while urging me to share her enthusiasm.

The interviewer laughs, clutching a hand to her chest. "And you have a sweet little nickname for him! Oh my, does that mean there was some off-set chemistry between you two?"

"One could say that," Bella answers.

My hand covers Bella's, my attempt to take control of the interview and to squash any insinuating remarks Bella is trying to make.

"Bella is such a talented actress, and we all worked really hard to make this movie what it is," I explain. "And like Charles said, this team that we had was one of the best we've all worked with. Everyone was very dedicated, and we're just happy that our hard work is paying off."

The interviewer nods and refocuses her attention on Bella. "Bella, what did you do to prepare for tonight? It looks like you have a whole village here to make you look as beautiful as you do. Any beauty tips or secrets to share with your fans?"

Bella rambles mixed words of hair, makeup, and designer labels. My attention wanders, scanning the now exceedingly large crowd and other familiar faces of Hollywood trickling in.

I smirk fondly when I see Michael Perry, our director, standing at the far end of the red carpet. His laughter rings across the scattered crowd, loud enough that I can catch the peak of it. He's talking amongst a small group of people. One of them, a woman with dark hair facing my direction, has twinkling eyes curved above full cheeks that round when she smiles politely. I blatantly stare, wondering why she looks so familiar.

It's when her smile fades and her eyes avert to her surroundings, the inner corners of her brows lifting in a furrow that creases above the bridge of her nose, that I realize why she stands out to me.

It's the woman from the coffeehouse.

What the fuck?

What is she doing here? Was she somehow involved with the movie? Maybe she's an actress? And why is she talking to Michael?

I can barely believe that she's here and that I actually remember her face. She's no longer on the verge of tears, but I still see the same eyes that reminded me of a warm pool of honey, sweet and inviting. They twinkle against the hovering lights, making them shine even brighter. As she listens to

Michael speak, she smiles politely, the edges of her mouth twitching slightly with each movement.

I don't know why, but I hadn't noticed before how... stunning she looked.

"Rhylan?"

"Huh?" My eyes shift from the interviewer to Charles and back to the interviewer. It's obvious a question or some kind of statement is directed toward me, but I haven't been paying attention. The heat from the lights beams down on my face, a thin sheen of sweat starting to form across my forehead and my neck.

Charles laughs. "You have to excuse Rhy here. He's just excited to see his pretty face on that big screen. He can't seem to focus on anything else."

I don't smile. I don't even laugh politely at his joke. Instead, I stand, the mic attached to my jacket pulling me back before I remove it completely and leave it on the chair. I don't even look back to confirm the dumbfounded looks on everyone's faces as the cameras connected to the live feed wait for the interview to continue without me. I can't even bring myself to care.

By the time I've finally walked around the chairs, carefully stepping over the fat cords that run along the hard floor to the lights and cameras, the woman is gone. In a flash, she disappeared, and I feel panicked. *Where the hell did she go?*

I start towards the steps leading into the theater, then change my mind. I look over the sea of people, the laughter and happy commotion of people frustrating me to no end, hoping to find her, but it's hopeless. My head swivels back and forth, frantically searching for this woman. But I don't see her anywhere.

"Rhy!" I turn to see Charles jogging towards me, finally catching up after I left the interview. "What the hell was that?"

"I saw someone."

"What? Who?"

I keep searching, scanning the entire entrance to the theater, but it's impossible to locate one single person in the crowd. A needle in a haystack. I shake my head, my eyes meeting Charles's.

"No one."

CHAPTER 11
Rhylan

This feels like the longest two and a half hours of my life. The seconds actually feel like they're ticking slower than the usual sixty seconds that take up a minute. I repeatedly have to remind myself to keep my eyes forward instead of turning around to scan the dark theater. I can't focus my attention on the movie for the life of me. I'm *in* the damn movie, but if someone asked me what it was about, I'd be better off talking about narwhals.

Charles sits to my left, and every time my body shifts, I can feel his eyes look my way. When I look to my right, Michael's face is practically glowing towards the flickering screen as his dumbfounded smile never leaves his face. He doesn't seem to notice or isn't even bothered by the tapping of my feet or the occasional impatient hum that I let out. My body is intolerably restless, even annoying me. When the credits finally, *finally* roll, I see the light at the end of the tunnel.

The lights flicker on, and the crowd applauds. I'm the first one to stand. My head pops up over the sea of people languidly standing and unhurriedly herding towards the exit. I scan the faces, hoping to see this woman whose name I don't even know and face I barely recognize. Still, I search, my eyes impatiently seeking her out and making second glances any time I see a woman with dark hair and a red dress.

Not wanting to get stuck in the crowd, Charles and I are the last to leave. When the last of the audience has walked out in front of us, we walk out into the night where darkness has fully settled above the hazy Los Angeles lights, and I realize that I *still* haven't found her. A part of me feels like I dreamt her. Like she's an illusion that my mind forged into reality because… I don't even know why.

"Are you going to the after-party?" Charles asks. Amelia is close to his side after having spent most of the night apart so that Charles could tend to his duties.

I don't really want to go, but looking into Charles's concerned face with his firm smile and wrinkled forehead, I give in. "Uh, sure. I guess I'll pop in for a bit." There's also the matter of finding this mystery woman.

"Great. We'll see you there." He pats my shoulder and turns towards the line of cars. His arm snakes around Amelia's waist as he leans down to kiss her, only for her to turn her face to give him her cheek, no doubt not wanting to ruin her makeup. I follow behind, locating the same black Lincoln Navigator I had arrived in parked up against the curb.

"Hey." I hear the familiar voice of Bella, hushed down to a seductive tone, right at my ear.

My hand is halfway towards the handle of the passenger door when I turn to look at Bella, her coy smile peering over her turned-up shoulder. "Hi, Bella," I answer, my tone distant and distracted.

"Can I catch a ride with you to the party?" she asks with narrowed eyes.

"Um, sure, I guess."

"We can be carpool buddies," Bella responds with a hearty laugh.

I open the car door for her as a wave of flashes blinds us, a rush of photographers caging in the two biggest stars of the night. I already know Bella's angle, but I have no choice but to comply. Any disagreement on my end, she's sure to cause a scene.

I watch her scoot herself down the length of the back seat. She makes sure her dress doesn't catch on the leather beneath her as she smooths out the material. Once she's settled, I enter the car and close the door behind me, keeping a fair amount of distance from her. When she realizes that I've situated myself as close to the opposite door as possible, she slinks up to me.

"I don't bite." Bella giggles as she moves closer, her bare arm grazing my suit sleeve. Then her voice turns serious. "I've been thinking about our time in Paris a lot lately. I miss you."

"Bella, we talked about this then. You're a great friend and a talented actor, but I really don't see us going beyond that," I reason.

She responds with annoyance, a huffy expression on her face and her arms crossed. It's definitely not the answer she was hoping for. Noticing a new idea simmering within her, I can see she's carefully contemplating her next move.

She shifts her body towards me, flicking her ponytail over her shoulder, and places her hand across my chest, running her manicured fingers along the thin fabric of my shirt. She looks up at me, her eyes rounding and lashes fluttering, and I stiffen under her touch.

"I think I recognize a challenge when I see one," she whispers into my ear. The scent of muted florals and alcohol invades my nose. I turn my head to avoid her closeness. While any man would succumb to her advances, her cluelessness makes me frustrated, wanting to get away from this situation even more.

Thankfully, Chateau Marmont, the location where the after-party is located, is nearby, and we arrive at our destination quickly. Without any further words, I open the car door, unable to wait for the attendant to open it from the other side, and both Bella and I spill out of the car. Photographers go frantic, eagerly pointing their cameras toward us. I can't focus on what's in front of me, but I rush to gently remove Bella's hand off my neck, where she had quickly and conveniently placed it in an attempt to regain her balance. I slowly exit the car, leaving behind Bella to wave at the cameras with a big, flashy smile.

Flustered, I walk away and make my way into the building. The sounds of the commotion behind me fade into the background with my plans to avoid Bella and maintain my stance on our nonexistent relationship blowing up in my face as I walk past the attendants manning the doors.

The whole night feels so chaotic. The crowd, the noise, the suffocating attention. I want it all to go away. The strain in my neck settles throughout my whole body, the tension twisting tighter and tighter. I shouldn't even be here. Maybe I just need a drink. Or two.

The bar is easy to track down, as it's constructed in the middle of the ballroom, right under the massive chandelier. I order my scotch, requesting the unopened Macallan on the top shelf, and lower my head towards the spotless counter, the reflection of the floating crystals bouncing in front of me.

I'm rethinking my decision to come here instead of heading straight home when Charles sidles up to me, a fresh drink already in his hand and his expression turning serious.

"You okay?" he asks.

I clear my throat into my fist. "Sure."

His hand lands on my shoulder, giving it a supportive squeeze. When I lift my face to look at him, he firmly presses his lips together and nods. He gives me the same look he made when he found me, one month into shooting *Unrestrained* in Paris and hours late for our call time. I had completely missed hair and makeup, unable to leave my hotel room. When I heard the door swing open and his voice calling out my name, I didn't have the strength to hide or make excuses. So instead, I looked up at him, slumped on the floor next to my bed, pleading for help. I wanted to scream or cry or anything that reminded me that I was alive. But I couldn't.

He covered for me, told Michael that I had come down with a bad case of food poisoning, and even claimed he rushed me to the hospital. Instead, we stayed in my room. We silently watched TV, and he listened to my aimless conversation about my family and how exhausted I had become. How I lost my way, and that wayward path had somehow brought me to that exact moment.

I knew then he didn't fully understand what I was going

through, but he didn't have to. His being there, a presence that I didn't know I had needed, was enough.

"So no date tonight?" he asks, changing the unspoken subject we had somehow landed on.

I look at him, an amused look on my face at the absurdity of his question. "Uh, no, not tonight."

"I just thought you might have someone special on your arm."

"Maybe the next one," I answer jokingly. Up until about two years ago, I always had a date by my side. It was never anyone important. Sometimes I would even forget the woman's name by the end of the night. It was all in the name of good fun, and the tabloids sure got a kick out of it, labeling me as Hollywood's playboy. The bachelor that would succeed the likes of Clooney or DiCaprio. Gradually, those dates became fewer. I completely defaulted to attending events solo, not wanting to struggle as I chewed over any sort of meaningless conversation with a woman, every word sounding superficial coming out of their vacant smiles.

"Charles Bradley!" The booming voice interrupts us and even causes a few heads to turn. When we turn, we see Richard March, studio head at Paramount Studios, stalking towards us. His heavy steps vibrate at our feet as they come to a stop, and his hand stoutly outreaches towards us. He smiles wide, a sliver of his gold crown peeking from the curved corner of his smile.

"My congratulations on the movie's success!" He aggressively shakes both of our hands, his enthusiasm unwillingly transferring onto us. His suit, looking just as heavy as his steps, envelops his awkward shape while his slicked-back hair hides just enough of his baldness to still leave a gleam of sweat to show through on his shiny scalp. We both smile politely, nodding our appreciation.

"I'm glad I ran into you," he practically bellows, his deep voice ringing loudly in the packed ballroom. "I have some ideas that I want to bounce off of you. The both of you, actually." He turns to look at me, his smile eager and optimistic.

"The both of us?" I ask.

"We're greenlit for a movie that I think you two would be perfect for," he explains, his voice in a lower tone in an attempt to maintain the confidentiality of our conversation. "It's going to be an all-star cast. I want to set up a meeting, maybe some time next week, to go over the script. What do you guys think?"

"If you want to send the script through to Levi, I can take a look at it," I answer. That's usually how we do things. Levi does his research, and I give my two cents before accepting or declining. I don't do much without Levi. Many of my decisions are based on his approval.

Richard huffs. "I was hoping we could be a little discreet about this. Maybe just involve the necessary parties."

"You know how we do it. The agency usually gives us a go for any movie we sign on for," Charles explains. He works the same way as I do with his own agent. We've both gotten comfortable allowing our agents to do a lot of the leg work when it comes to seeking out movie roles, and, honestly, it's the least messy way to go about it.

"If that's how you gentlemen want to handle it, I'll talk to the producers. But—"

"Dick!" The cheerfully taunting voice comes from Michael Perry, who appears to be even more relaxed and inebriated since leaving the theater. It's obvious that he's basking in the movie's success. His partner, Hugo, whom I've had the pleasure of meeting a number of times while on set, follows close by his side.

Richard's boisterous laugh echoes across the ballroom as he embraces Michael and heavily pats his back. "I hope the box office numbers don't go to your head when they start trickling in."

"Too late," Hugo interjects. "I have to keep reminding him tonight's just the premiere and we still have the box office release before getting shit-faced." He turns towards Charles and me to shake our hands, and he greets us warmly. "It's good to see you guys again."

The four of us stand close to the bar, taking up enough room for people to discreetly surround us, hoping to catch glimpses of our conversation or blatantly stare.

I'm staying relatively quiet, listening to the conversation and sipping my scotch, when I see Hugo wave someone towards him. When I curiously peek in the same direction, I see a young woman excitedly walk towards him smiling bright and eager. Normal activity at a premiere, networking and making informal introductions in the hope of meeting the right people. It's the typical cog of the industry, everything moving a mile a minute and never taking a break, not even to celebrate at a premiere.

This woman approaching Hugo isn't who catches me off guard. It's the woman who's following close behind. The same one in red that I've been looking for all night. The two walk close to each other and come to a stop right in front of me. As if brought to me by the universe, urging me to introduce myself, to awkwardly extend a greeting, to *talk* to her.

"Richard, I'd like you to meet Claire. She's one of our interns out of UCLA."

The woman that Hugo had flagged down extends her hand, assertive and professional. "Mr. March, it's such an honor to meet you." Her nerves give her away with her shaky voice, though Richard doesn't seem to notice as he's focused on her smile that never falters.

"And this is Charles Bradley and Rhylan Matthews," Hugo adds, gesturing towards myself and Charles. Both women glance at us as Charles nods a greeting to both. Me, on the other hand, I can't even attempt to tear my attention away from the woman standing behind Claire almost hiding in the shadows as if wanting to blend in.

"UCLA, that's my alma mater," Richard says proudly, interrupting our introductions.

"Yes, I know. I've followed your career closely, Mr. March. My peers and I very much look up to you."

Richard laughs deeply and proudly, basking in the recognition he's getting for his success. "That's quite a compliment, young lady." His eyes then wander to the woman standing behind Claire, his hand gesturing towards her. "Is she also an intern like you?"

"This is my friend, Ellie," Claire says, her hand gently landing on her friend's arm. "We both attend UCLA, but she's not an intern, no."

Hugo dives deep into how much work Claire has done for Paramount, expressing how her efforts as a fresh face in the office have been noticeable and that he has hopes to hire her full-time once she graduates.

Ellie.

I repeat her name in my head as I watch her face. I study it, noticing the way her eyes nervously shift side to side or how her smile only curves up in small fragments. Her face is full of shyness and reserve.

I only hear snippets of the conversations around me because I'm too busy watching Ellie. I know I'm staring, practically glaring at her, but I can't seem to look away.

She's standing there, looking completely out of place but belonging at the same time. Her subtle charcoal makeup makes her deep honey-colored eyes stand out even more while her dark hair is piled on her head into an organized mess. My eyes linger on her shoulders, the thin straps of her cherry-colored dress digging into the plush skin, right where a thick strand of hair has managed to come loose. Her arms cross her chest as her hands reach to squeeze her elbows, her fingers nervously tracing her own skin. On the outside, she looks like she's part of this absurd Hollywood crowd. But beyond that, she looks hesitant. Almost apologetic that she's taking up space when she's the one that stands out the most.

Ellie finally looks at me quickly enough for our eyes to meet for a second before her eyes fall back on her friend. Her eyes are cautious but curious. Our eyes meet again, not in passing this time but held in what feels like a trance. I can see the moment she realizes that I look familiar, beyond the expected recognition as Rhylan Matthews. As someone that saw a fraction of her exposed soul when she wasn't guarding it as tightly as she normally did. I see it when her eyes widen and her lips part. When her chest heaves as she inhales a sharp intake of breath.

She looks away, her eyes absentmindedly searching for answers, before she reaches for her friend's hand, squeezing it lightly to get her attention. Claire turns to watch her walk away before continuing her conversation with Richard and Hugo.

I, too, watch her walk away, her steps quick and hurried as the heels of her stilettos click against the hard floor. My eyes narrow, following her path. Her steps lead her away from the crowd—somewhere quiet and secluded—as I push past Charles to go after her. I don't know what I'm going to say or why I'm even trying to catch up to her, but I do it for no other reason than my own nagging curiosity.

I finally follow her outside to an outdoor patio area that's empty. The only things present are the potted plants that somehow create a makeshift fence that blocks us off from everyone else. The moonlight skirts down over her, bouncing off her shoulders as she lightly paces against the far railing.

She's facing away from me, and I don't think she's heard me walk through the door. So I take a slice of a moment to watch her. One hand rests on her hip while the other is brought to her face. She traces her cheek before bringing her hand to the back of her bare neck. I wish I could see her face, know what she's thinking. I want to know if she's remembering our last encounter and how it wasn't just two people that incidentally locked eyes. It was more than that.

I clear my throat. "Uh," I say, my voice awkwardly loud in the quiet space. She jumps, turning to face me. "Hi, I'm Rhylan."

The unease on her face fades and she finally smiles, exhaling a light giggle. "I know who you are."

This is the first time I've seen her sincerely smile. And it's absolutely radiant.

Her eyes turn into tiny dancing crescent moons that end at the corners with little wrinkles that fan out like feathery wings. Another set of fine lines runs down the bridge of her nose, where a light smattering of freckles is sprinkled like fairy dust. The fact that she smiles with her eyes, completely genuine and sincere, is so utterly charming. And her giggles sound like a rhapsodic melody, so infectious that I can't help but smile back.

"Your name is Ellie?"

She nods. "I saw you the other day. At that coffeehouse," she says. Not a question but a fact. "I–I didn't recognize you then, but that was you, right?"

I nod. Our faces are serious as our conversation quickly lands on the verity of her statement. Although we both realized it in the ballroom.

"What were you doing there?"

"I, um…"

She shakes her head and clasps her hands in front of her. "I'm sorry. That's really not any of my business."

"It's okay," I answer, smirking through my answer. "I don't… really know why I was there."

"And you kept staring at me. Why?"

She doesn't apologize this time, and her question catches

me off guard. Not because it isn't warranted, but because it's so unpretentious, no overtone or implication. Just honest curiosity that allows her to ask a question that would be kept between us two. But I don't know how to tell her that I did it because looking away from something that struck a chord in my fragile heart wouldn't have been feasible. That if a fire had suddenly emerged between us there at the coffeehouse, I would've just continued to stare straight into her eyes through the flames.

But I try. I attempt to make sense of my answer, hoping she'll understand. "I saw something in you that I recognized."

Confused, she answers, "I don't think I know you."

"No." I shake my head. "I mean, you looked like you were dealing with some things that made you feel… hopeless. And maybe even a little lost. I–I guess it felt familiar to me."

Her brows knit together, her expression growing pensive. But she isn't upset, not even a little bit. Instead, her face slowly begins to soften as if to tell me something. A deep secret, a piece of good news, anything to connect that familiarity to something real. To make it comprehensible instead of just an inkling. She got it. She understood when I said the word *familiar* because she felt it too.

"You… want to get out of here?"

Her brows raise. "I'm sorry?"

"I mean, do you want to go somewhere? Maybe get away from this crowd." I say the last word with a trace of bitterness in my voice.

"Where?"

I smile. "Anywhere."

t was Rhylan Matthews. Rhylan Matthews who watched me fall into a scattered mess waiting to be picked up by anyone other than myself, even though I knew it wasn't possible. It was him that watched me expose a part of myself that I had kept covered under layers of shame, along with everything that told me to move on and make some paltry attempt to be happy. How did I not realize it was him before? Maybe it was because my focus was narrowed in on trying not to completely break apart under his glaring scrutiny, as if he was trying to figure me out while I prevented it from happening. Maybe it was the fact that all I saw when I looked at him was his eyes. How they had somehow pierced through an exterior that I had unwillingly built over the past decade.

I follow close behind with my eyes on his broad back as he walks with confidence and urgency. He pulls open the heavy doors with ease, the same doors that I had to use my entire weight to push open. When we reenter the ballroom, we realize that we have to walk through the heavy crowd to get to the exit on the other side. I look up at him, wondering if he still wants me to leave with him, knowing it may cause a scene. But I don't see an ounce of doubt on his face. Instead, he turns to me with a curved smile and a hint of mischief, which causes me to smile back at him.

He takes my hand, firmly grasping it in his as he walks quickly through the crowd. My steps become urgent as I try to keep up with him, the clicks of my heels the only indication that I'm still behind him. And the fact that my hand is still in his, wrapped in his long fingers tightly gripping mine so we don't separate.

I feel the eyes following our path as we walk through the parting crowd. And when we walk swiftly past Claire, I see her mouth drop open. But Rhylan doesn't stop. His eyes are glaring straight ahead in an effort to ignore everything and everyone. All the murmurs and stares are background noise at this point.

Once outside and on the other side of the stifling crowd, we don't stop. He doesn't let go of my hand either, which I'm all too aware of. We don't stop walking until we're in front of an excessively clean black SUV that he opens the door to, stepping aside for me to get in.

My eyes go from the interior of the car to Rhylan. His face turns grave, and I wonder if he's having doubts. Second thoughts just like I have about him so impulsively asking me to leave with him. As I mull this over, I feel like my feet have been nailed to the ground.

He takes a step towards me, my face meeting his chest. He lowers his head so our eyes meet again.

"You can change your mind," he says, his voice low and

husky. "You can go back inside. I won't stop you."

I don't answer. His face is so close to mine, just inches away. No matter how deep the pensiveness is stretched on his face from his knitted brows and tense jaw, he keeps his eyes on mine.

I shake my head, but it's so slight. All it does is express my uncertainty.

"But…" His voice trails off. "I would like it if you didn't… change your mind."

When he pulls away, his eyes still bore into mine. I don't realize I'm holding my breath until he finally looks away, his gaze settling past me back towards the entrance to the hotel with his hand leaning up against the frame of the car. My breathing finally steadies before I move into the car. I carefully step up to the raised step and slide all the way to the other side.

He follows suit, lightly slamming the door shut before facing me.

"I–I, um," he stammers, releasing a breath before collecting his words. "We won't go far. And I'll take you home whenever you're ready to leave." For some reason, there's a strain in his voice. But he doesn't sound nervous or scared but more virtuous. Like he's more worried about gaining my trust than about escaping the chaos we've just shaken free of.

"Are you going to tell me where we're going?" I ask gently.

He finally smiles, his face softening. "I want to show you LA. At night."

"LA?" I ask, confused. "I've seen LA. Actually, I've seen it every night for the past twenty-two years."

"Not this side of LA." No other explanation follows.

My phone vibrates in my purse in sequential buzzes, indicating multiple messages rattling through, and I know it's Claire. I quickly read the messages that are flashing on my screen, confirming my assumption that Claire is the one who's blowing up my phone.

Claire: Where did you go?

Claire: Are you seriously with Rhylan fucking Matthews?!

Claire: Ellie! Answer me now!!

I punch out a quick message to Claire, telling her I'll call her later and to head on home without me.

The car starts moving right after Rhylan leans forward and whispers to the driver what I assume is an address or directions. Not knowing how to fill the silence as we sit quietly during the drive, we both stare out the window, occasionally stealing glances at each other but avoiding eye contact. From the corner of my eye, I watch his strong, masculine hands as they fidget, clenching and unclenching against the leather of the seat. His hands go to his lap, running against his thighs, causing friction as they rub against the fabric.

After a drive that consists of winding roads and frequent turns, we come to a stop atop a hill overlooking the city. Rhylan steps out from his side of the car as the driver pulls to a stop and waits patiently for me to exit. I follow him out the same door and come face to face with Los Angeles.

I close my eyes and inhale, the cold air filling my lungs like cool spearmint. Refreshing and icy. It's so dark, I can barely see my feet in front of me. So I move slowly, my uncomfortable heels adjusting to the uneven dirt and gravel. And then I see the twinkle of the city in the far distance. The beautiful side of Los Angeles that only comes out at night. It's like a dark lake, still and quiet, reflecting the moonlight along the ripples. A gentle reminder that maybe I wasn't meant to be left drowning in the dark. Maybe I was meant to shine, to radiate through life instead of merely fading away.

"It's beautiful, isn't it?"

My thoughts are interrupted. I turn to look at Rhylan, the breeze carrying my hair in the same direction. Even through the dark, I can see the lights bouncing off his pale eyes looking at me as he marvels at the view in front of him. He clenches his jaw as he lowers his head and looks up at me, peering through the veil of his hair.

He smiles, the corners of his mouth perking up before he speaks. "I come up here a lot when I need to get away from everything. It helps me clear my head when I feel like I'm suffocating. It's hidden from tourists and people in general, so it works in my favor."

I nod and smile in understanding. "It's beautiful. I've lived in Southern California all my life and I've never been here," I say with a wistful tone.

"I did a lot of touristy things when I first moved to LA. I was getting used to the city, and I found a lot of little gems like this along the way," he explains.

"You're not from here?"

"No, I grew up just outside of Reno," he answers.

"Where's that?" I ask.

"It's, uh, just past Lake Tahoe, in Nevada. I moved out here right out of high school."

I nod. "Huh, I always assumed famous people grew up in Hollywood. Like they were bred here or something."

He smirks, cocking his head to the side with his brows raised in amusement. "Bred here?"

"I–I'm sorry. I didn't mean to offend you. I guess… I just never really realized movie stars had a life before they got famous," I stammer. I can feel the redness spreading through my face, traveling to my ears and leaving the tips of them hot with embarrassment.

"It's fine," he says coolly. "I'm not offended. It's just a funny concept that just because I do movies, I would've appeared out of thin air into LA. Like a magician or something."

"Uh, you don't 'just do movies.'"

His right brow flicks up into an arch. "I'm an actor."

I roll my eyes, and my embarrassment fades as his smile rings clear with playful wit. "You know what I mean." With my head tilted to the side, shaking it slightly to brush off his modesty, I smile coyly.

"I do," he affirms teasingly. "But do enlighten me."

I suppress a laugh thinking how I would explain to Rhylan Matthews his celebrity rank. "I mean, I was just watching one of your movies at home, and now you're literally in front of me," I point out. "I think that's pretty surreal."

He laughs, flashing his perfectly straight I-never-skipped-a-night-wearing-my-retainers teeth. "I hope it was half decent," he says, rubbing his chin as he talks.

"Meh, it was fine," I tease.

His open palm reaches up and lightly grazes my lower back in the midst of our banter. And I know he does it as a response to my playful barb, but it feels so tenderly affectionate.

We turn our gazes back to the view, and our smiles fade into a look of satisfied contentment. No exaggerated laughs or forced smiles, just quiet gratification. We stand there in silence, relishing in the clarity the night air provides as I notice him watching me through my peripheral vision. The cool winds continue to sweep between us, lifting the silence and taking any speck of vulnerability with it. It's comforting in a way that feels effortless. I've never felt this way with anyone where I could let my guard down so naturally.

"Can I ask you something?" Rhylan asks, breaking the silence. I turn, and he's standing there with his hands in his pockets, the bottom hem of his jacket curved up like drapes. "What was going on in your head at the coffeehouse?"

I sigh at his question and bring my eyes back to the view of the city, everything blurring until all I see is a fogged cloak of twinkling lights. I don't know how to answer his question. So instead, I think about how it feels to drown, a feeling that I've become so intimately acquainted with.

Whenever I picture myself drowning, it's always in the middle of the ocean. Where it's dark and empty, making me scream for help out of sheer desperation. But nothing comes out. My screams are eerily silent as I sink into a shadowy void. And that outright terrifies me.

"I can't really explain it," I finally say. "I guess… I have moments where I feel overwhelmed. Like I'm suffocating. It feels like I'm being pulled down, and there's nothing to keep me afloat." I take a deep breath. "Kind of like I'm…"

"Like you're drowning."

My eyes flutter back to him, my lips parting ever so slightly to draw in a breath. "How did you know?"

"I feel like that too sometimes. Like I can't breathe, and when I saw you, for some reason, it felt like you knew exactly what that felt like. You… didn't look like you were just having a bad day."

When I say I'm drowning, I mean it. Not in the actual physical sense like I've been thrown into the deep end of a pool and a teen in a uniformed red swimsuit has to save me. I mean I'm sinking because the enervating attempts to ride the waves with freedom and confidence have failed. So I have no choice but to plummet down the deep depths of the ocean, where I surrender. I don't fight anymore. I don't endeavor towards anything. I just accept my fate.

And Rhylan understands this.

I turn and look back at the view, hugging myself as I shiver in the cool spring breeze. I feel a welcoming heat surrounding me, covering my shoulders and draping over my torso. Rhylan has taken off his jacket and envelops me in his warmth and scent. His fingertips brush the sensitive spot at the base of my neck, making it buzz with electricity as a chill runs down my back.

He's now dressed in his white dress shirt tucked neatly into his seamless pants. The shirt blows in the wind and clings to his broad chest, exposing his physique. I smile softly at his kind gesture and whisper a quiet "thank you."

"Thank you for coming up here with me," he says softly as

he steps back. "I'm usually up here alone, and it's nice to share this with someone."

"Thank you for bringing me up here."

He smiles at me. And then it suddenly hits me how tangible this moment feels while feeling illusive at the same time. How I've actually met someone that somehow understands me, just as equally as I understand him.

I look away from Rhylan, my gaze focusing forward while I wrap his suit jacket inwards. Words that I didn't realize were bubbling up inside me start to spill. As if they had reached a boiling point and they tipped over the edges.

"My dad was quite literally my most favorite person in the world." My voice pours out of me like a bundle of silk ribbon against the cool wind, flapping so vividly but somehow placid in contrast to my galloping heart. "His favorite thing to do was to take me out on weekends in his pick-up truck to run errands like browse random pawn shops. He would always slap my hand away every time I tried to change the radio station, saying I needed to expand my taste in music away from the 'shrill pop music' that I played in my room." A light laugh ripples through my lips, the surprise of describing my dad feeling so foreign. "And he used to be obsessed with books. He started my library when I was six. Even though I couldn't read them, he passed down to me books like *Fahrenheit 451* or *Animal Farm*. And when I got a little older, he added classics like *Wuthering Heights* and *Sense and Sensibility*."

"Was?" he asks. Without looking, I can see the curiosity laced into his cautious tone. He treads carefully as he waits for an answer that I'm not sure I want to share.

I lower my face, tucking my chin towards my chest. "He died when I was twelve. And after he died, I started to pretend that if I closed my eyes long enough, then everything around me would disappear and I could go back to how things were before he died." My breath catches, a shake rumbling through me as I say words that I've never said out loud. I've never said anything about my dad and his death to anyone beyond the simple "my dad isn't with us anymore" vagueness.

"I thought that if I kept my eyes closed long enough, I could shut out the world and pretend I didn't exist in it," I continue. I look back at him, the crease between his brows deepening. "It felt easier to pretend that none of this was happening around me, like my dad dying or the grief that I never got over. It felt easier to think that if I didn't exist... just, anything so that I didn't have to carry all of it with me."

He clears his throat. And for a second, I fear that I might have unloaded too much. Regardless of if it felt right, it also felt too raw and naked. Until he speaks. "I've always considered what it would feel like to stop existing. To let all this fade away." He pauses, as if to mull over what it means to disappear, to stand on the other side of chaos and look in instead of standing in the center of it. "It feels... freeing."

"Do you almost feel like if... if you didn't exist... maybe it would be easier?"

I see his throat bob, a deep swallow rolling down the center of his neck as his shoulders square.

"You mean, like if you were no longer here, then everything that was weighing you down in the first place would just disappear?" he elaborates. "And... you're left wondering what was holding you down in the first place?"

I nod and take a deep breath, my eyes slightly closing to

let the possibility of freedom skim over me. "I know we're supposed to fear death, and I do, of course. I'm not going to go base jumping to play with death. But, when I look past the actual dying part, the fear seems to disappear. And I feel *calm*." My insides twist as my voice fills with an eerie sadness knowing that while I don't necessarily want to die, I don't want to live either.

"Death being a comfort," he affirms.

We stay silent. An instant passes where we have a moment to absorb the idea of death being a comfort, a solace. I feel a sense of dread cloak over me. And for some reason, that makes my heart feel even heavier. As if on top of this sinking feeling, a thousand-pound anvil was placed on my heart, telling it, *I know you're already heavy, but here's some additional weight you need to carry.* And that heaviness shifts into a familiar aching pain.

"I guess dying isn't really the scary part. It's living," I finally say, my throat constricting through the words. "It feels easier to die, to pass all of your problems on to your loved ones and leave unfinished business for others to work through. But living…"

"Living…" he says, repeating my last word. "Maybe if there's something worth living for, it would make a difference."

"Maybe," I think out loud.

He keeps his distance while he looks at me, his eyes serious and thoughtful. I notice that this whole time we've been talking and I've been looking out into the city, he hasn't looked at the view once. He's been looking at me, listening to me, hanging on to my words like a compass directing him away from oblivion. And I finally feel *seen*.

CHAPTER 13
Rhylan

B eauty isn't always blissful. It isn't always happy, full of rainbows and butterflies coming from every direction. There's beauty in things that are sad.

It can be a dusky sunset on the horizon of the sea that paints the sky a hazy orange and purple. It can be a string quartet, humming along the doleful sounds of "Clair de Lune." It can even be the light rainfall that takes over the day, keeping away the bright sunshine behind a curtain of dark clouds. Beauty isn't always full of joy. It can be twisted and woven with pain. But it doesn't make it any less significant.

Ellie carries that beauty on her shoulders. The same beauty that emanates through heartbreak. Her pain doesn't make her dull or mundane. It makes her bewitching. It's what pours out of her through that pain that leaves her beauty shining through. And I'm completely enamored by it.

I watch her lean forward against the wooden posted fence that separates the tumbling hillside from the flat graveled dirt we stand on. She closes her eyes as she takes in the air and allows it to heal her, to absorb the pain so that it can feel a little less heavy. I disappear in her moment of healing. So I don't disturb it. Instead, I watch as she cleanses away everything in her heart that causes it to ache.

I slowly sidle up to her, our arms not even touching. I can feel the heat coming from her. She must be able to feel it too, because she opens her eyes and looks at me. There's no smile, no anger, no sadness. Her face is expressionless, enervate and weak. I look back at her, mirroring her expression because I feel the exact same way. I'm spent. So completely exhausted trying to work through my emotions and attempting to come out strong in the end. But I'm so fucking tired of trying to be strong.

We don't say anything. Only silence stretches between us before Ellie shifts her gaze straight ahead again. Then, as if she, too, is acting on impulse, she tilts her head to the side of my shoulder. Her eyes close again. And while I expect her to relax with her head lying heavily on my arm, she doesn't. Instead, her brows furrow, causing the creases between them to deepen. Like her wounds are just beginning to heal, inflaming into a hot, swollen mess to signal the start of the healing process when it's most painful.

I still, my fists clenched, tampering down the urge to circle my arms around her and wrap her towards me. Because every bit of my insecurities is telling me that I'm too broken. That I would never be able to take on any part of her pain and replace it with a warm solace.

So I stand there, minimizing my movements, so she doesn't move either. So that she knows she can stay leaned up against my shoulder as long as she trusts me to do so. While I do that, I let all of my self-doubt and reticence sit in the pit of my stomach where I feel I could bury it deep. And the illusion of me being more than a figurative shoulder to lean on is no longer just an illusion but a reality. I do it even though I know it's temporary, and I hold on to that thought while I inhale the scent of her hair—roses and another floral mixture that I can't place—as the steadiness of her breathing calms my racing heart.

When she shifts her feet, her shoe hooks on the loose gravel, and it causes her to miss her step and lose her balance. Her hand immediately wraps around my forearm for support while her warm skin grazes mine through the thinness of my sleeve, and she suddenly stills. She must realize that her hand has subconsciously moved there, her actions having been played out before thought through, because she slowly moves her hand away. But I hold on to it. I carefully thread my fingers through hers and look down at the tangled knot of our hands. In the dark, I can't tell where her fingers start and mine end. Her hand feels so small in mine, enveloped and caged in a protective armor that my long fingers seem to have created.

This is it. The fallacy that I want so badly to be true but know that it can never be. I want to protect her heart, bubble wrap it and place it in a large wooden box labeled Fragile. And it sounds crazy when I've never had an inclination to protect anyone, to keep them from every harm and hurt that the world had to offer. But it's because we are the same. Every puncture of hurt that poked through her heart, I've felt it. We both know what it's like to feel as if there's no other choice but to yield and sink into a deep void. For the first time in… ever, I don't want to feel like drowning. Death feels terrifying, and living feels hopeful.

We stay up on the hillside for a couple of hours with the occasional words passing between us in the long stretches of silence. We don't need to keep talking. Instead, we stay in the hushed silence of contentment with an air of understanding that I don't want to ever leave.

Just after two o'clock in the morning, when I turn my wrist to check the time, I suggest we head back down the hillside.

"It's getting late. Can I give you a ride back home?"

She looks down at my watch, her eyes adorably squinting to see through the dark. "Wow, I hadn't realized it was this late. Yes, please," she answers softly.

Once we sit back in the car, she meekly gives my driver her address and we drive her home. She sits quietly as she looks out the window with an air of melancholy. Her hair, now an unruly mess from the hillside breeze, makes her look demure. She looked glamorous before in her perfectly done curls but adorable now as her pouty lips twitch with every thought and unspoken word between us.

We pull to a stop in front of her house, a modest home in the Huntington Park area. A beat-up Honda Civic and a dark-colored Lexus sedan sit parked in the driveway leading up to a poorly lit stoop and a rustic Welcome sign hanging on the front door.

A small sigh leaves her lips, followed by a twitch of a smile curving at the corners of her mouth. "Thank you for this. I don't know how to explain, but I really… just, thank you," she says with a sigh.

"I know. Thank you too," I respond in understanding. I can't put it into words either. I just know that what just happened between us was healing. And then, I act on impulse again. I move my hand to hers, covering it with mine, and bring it towards me. She doesn't resist, instead allows it to happen naturally. I turn her hand in mine as I bring the back of it to my lips. My action is so paltry, so discreet that it feels like it happens in an instant. But I can't ignore the emptiness I feel when her hand leaves mine.

We don't say anything else. She turns away from me, smiling softly as she closes the door behind her. Her hips sway side to side as she strains against the height of her heels walking up her driveway. She looks back at me one more time, and I give a small wave. Her eyes are soft with gratitude for the escape I provided us both, even if it was just for the evening. She waves back in return, and I watch as she enters her home.

I tell my driver to head home.

Once inside my big, empty house, I realize how tonight was therapeutic. Instead of walking towards the bar for my usual nightcap to fog my mind, my feet gravitate to my home office. I look at the pile of scripts sitting on my desk that I've been avoiding for weeks and flip through the one on top with the title *Aurielle*. It's the last script sent to me. A love story about a woman named Aurielle dying of cancer. I would be playing the role of the doting husband in this heartbreaking romance. I sit down and read the whole script, start to finish, enlightened by the passionate marriage shared by this couple that would eventually be ripped apart by the death of the wife. Tragic yet beautiful, with a bittersweet ending. It calls to me, catching my attention and drawing me in as I imagine myself a part of a relationship so meaningful. It pulls emotions out of me that I thought didn't exist, causing me to mourn over the death of this fictional woman.

Once I finish, the light outside slowly brightening, I slump into my room and strip down before climbing into bed. For the first time in a long time, I feel that maybe I'm no longer sinking. And instead of gasping for air, maybe I'm floating, looking up at the sky with certainty that I might be okay. I drift off into a deep sleep and, for a change, look forward to what the following day will bring me.

CHAPTER 14
Ellie

The following day at work, my mind is a complete fog. Lack of sleep and the disbelief of the night before makes it incredibly hard to focus. It's almost as if last night was a weird dream where nothing and everything makes sense. The kind of dream that makes you disoriented when you wake up, but as the day progresses, you realize how ridiculous it is of you to actually believe it all happened.

But it *was* real. Every moment of it. It awoke emotions I thought were long gone. Emotions I never knew I could feel again. A smile spreads across my face that comes from my core, where I thought any remnants of elation had been buried long ago. It leaves me delirious and noticeably distracted. At the very least, it keeps me awake.

I continue my workday, stocking shelves with books and ringing customers until I clock out at four p.m. My phone rings right on time with a call from Claire, who knows exactly what time I get off.

"Ellie! What happened last night?!" she screams into my ear.

"Hi, Claire."

"Don't you 'hi, Claire' me! What were you doing with Rhylan Matthews?"

"We just took a drive," I try to explain.

"Why do you say that so nonchalantly? You took a drive with Rhylan Matthews, and you say it like you're telling me you just ordered a blueberry muffin with your caramel macchiato!" she yells into the phone. "What time did you even get home?"

"Um, I think close to three?" I answer sheepishly.

"Three?!" she screeches. "Did you guys, like, make out in the back of his car?" I can practically hear the smile that's spreading across her face as she asks her ridiculous question.

"No!" I yelp. "Claire, it wasn't anything like that." As I say it, I don't even know if it was true. I spent the better part of the morning thinking about what last night had meant to both myself and Rhylan. The only conclusion I have is that we shared a reparative connection. Something that we didn't realize we needed but grasped as soon as it was within reach, no matter how ridiculous it felt to have that connection between two people that barely knew each other.

"Okay. So, are you seeing him again?" she urges.

I furrow my brows, considering her question. There's no indication of a future visit from Rhylan Matthews after last night. I haven't realized how odd that is until Claire poses the question. "No, I didn't even get his number. I think… I think we just needed to get away for a moment, that's all."

"What the hell are you talking about? You spent the whole night with him, and you didn't even get his number? What was the point?!" she shrieks into the phone.

I pull the phone away from my ear to drown out the shrill sounds of Claire's voice, wincing from the sudden change in the tone and volume. My car door clicks, unlocking, before I open the door and slide into the driver's seat. A high-pitched chugging indicates the engine coming to life before I sit there, letting the car run idle while I finish my conversation with Claire.

"I don't know. Seriously, I'm not going to see him again. It really wasn't anything special. He just dropped me off at home at the end of the night," I explain to her. The cynic, the realist in me, keeps rolling its eyes, telling me to stop living in la-la land, to wake up from my ridiculous daydream. But I can't ignore the small, itty-bitty whisper of a voice inside my head that keeps saying, *What if this is something more?*

"Wow, I am just speechless, Ellie."

"I know," I whisper, more to myself than to Claire. "I know he's Rhylan Matthews, and I'm sure he does things like this all the time, but I can't believe I met him and *talked* to him!"

Claire squeals through the phone like a schoolgirl gushing about her crush before we say our goodbyes.

I drive home, all smiles after my conversation with Claire. I think about Rhylan's eyes, the darkness that covers them when he's thinking, reasoning with himself as he fights some internal battle that he's too considerate to share and too scared to say out loud. I think about how his smile always starts from the corners of his mouth, lifting into a little curve and traveling up to the edges of his eyes. My hand still tingles from when he brought it so gently to his lips only to kiss the soft spot where my thumb and index finger intersect. And I can't help but *smile.*

By the time I pull into my driveway, I've squabbled with myself enough to realize how ridiculous it is thinking that there may have been something more between us. I bring myself back down to earth and gather my things, letting go of any future thoughts of myself and Rhylan.

As soon as I walk through the door, I find my mom sitting comfortably on the couch cuddled up to Angus. They both turn their heads in my direction as I quietly walk in.

My mom smiles as Angus eagerly sits up to greet me. "How was work?"

"Good, kind of boring."

She pats my back as I snuggle up to Angus and inhale his scent. His warm fur feels so inviting, I want to fall asleep like this. He responds with a loud thump of his tail and a wet lick to my cheek.

"How about we order a pizza for dinner tonight? I'm kind of too lazy to cook," she suggests, talking to my hunched-over back.

"Hmm," I answer, still nose deep in Angus's neck. I feel my mom shift on the couch, her hands smoothing across the blanket draped across her lap and her legs pushing deeper into the cushions.

"Um, Ellie? I've actually been wanting to talk to you." She lowers the volume on the television. She sits up and lets out a small sigh, preparing herself to tell me whatever it is she's about to say. "I've sort of started seeing someone."

I sit up, the cold hitting my cheek from the absence of Angus's fuzzy warmth. It takes me a moment to understand what she's saying.

She's seeing someone? How? And when did this happen?

"Who?" I ask, not even bothering to hide the confusion on my face. My mom doesn't *date.*

"I work with him. He's a new associate at the office," she explains.

I raise my brows and nod, still silent while trying to take in this bombshell news.

"We've been spending some time together. And, eventually, I'd like you to meet him. Eventually," she repeats at the end. *Eventually.* Meaning inevitably.

"Oh," I say.

"Is it weird?"

"I…" I utter before I remain silent.

"It's okay, Ellie," she finally says, smoothing her hand down my arm. "I'm not rushing into anything. I guess… Things were getting a little serious between us, and I wanted you to know."

"How long has it been?" I ask. "Since you've been seeing him," I add.

"Oh, maybe like… seven, eight months."

"What!" I don't mean to sound so surprised, but I can't help it. She's been keeping this from me for *this* long? It really shouldn't surprise me. Secrets and unspoken topics, along with big pink elephants strategically placed in each room, are how we live our lives. But still…

"Sorry," I say more softly. "I guess I'm just a little surprised, that's all."

The TV remote in her hand rotates, her fingers gently running over the buttons. "It's not just me wanting you to meet him. He wants to meet you too," she says.

"Okay," I finally say, forcing a small smile.

"Okay?"

I nod and she smiles, a relieved shift evident in her sigh.

"I'm going to turn in early," I say softly.

When her brows furrow inwards and a slight frown curves her lips downwards, I smile again, a little wider and brighter.

"It's fine, Mom," I assure. "I'm just tired."

I almost imagine it, my mom whispering my name as I walk away, but I don't turn around to face her. Instead, I continue my path to my room, my steps dragging heavier as I reach my door.

Everything around me seems to be shifting, changing at what feels like lightning speed while I linger, muddling through and evading change. And I suddenly feel exhausted.

I spend the following week trudging through my classes. I can't concentrate. The bomb that my mom had dropped in my lap over the weekend keeps replaying in my head. My mom has a *boyfriend*. And she wants me to meet him. Every time I think about that, my hands gravitate towards my face, gripping my temples as if to massage away the dread that comes over me thinking about meeting this boyfriend.

And on top of that, I'm still high from my rendezvous with Rhylan. I thought it would have dwindled down to a mere afterthought by now, but it hasn't. I'm still thinking about him. It's been almost a full week since I met him, and my fingers still find their way to my hand, caressing the parts where his lips had lightly touched it, reliving the moment he held my hand in his like a constant daydream.

Even as I sit in class today, having spent the entire hour not paying attention to the lecture, it's all I can think about.

"Okay, class. We'll stop here." My attention is brought back to the small classroom as my professor announces the end of our class. "For now, I want you all to work on your critical essay. It will be about a piece of literature that you've been drawn to in a unique way. Make it personal! The guide to the essay is in your announcements. Email me if you have any questions."

Everyone is rushing to gather their laptops and notebooks as they rush toward the door. We funnel towards the exit, and I find Claire leaning against the wall outside my classroom waiting for me.

"Ellie! Come with me to Starbucks. I need some coffee," Claire requests. Both our classes are located right next to each other. At least one day during the week, we like to end our day with a late lunch or a quick coffee run before parting ways. Sometimes, it's the only chance we get to see each other because of our busy, clashing schedules.

"Sure, I could use a pick-me-up. And I think it's your turn to buy." I smile at her.

"Fine," she reluctantly agrees. "But I think *you* owe *me* a Frappuccino after the night you had with Rhylan Matthews."

Her voice is so loud, and there are so many people around us, that I can feel a few heads turn at the mention of Rhylan's name.

"Can you shush?" I whisper. "You're going to start rumors that aren't even true."

"Well, you *were* with him," she protests.

"Yeah, but not like you're suggesting."

"Whatever. You were off gallivanting with Rhylan Matthews, and I was stuck listening to how Michael Perry and Hugo met. Which actually was a really sweet story."

I smile at her, linking my arm through hers.

"But if it were up to me, I would have switched places with you in a heartbeat."

I roll my eyes as we step up to the glass doors of the Starbucks just walking distance from our classes. Once inside, we stand in line as we silently decide what to order. From the far corner, I see Austin leaning up against a wall, waiting for his drink while thoughtfully looking through his phone. When he looks up and sees me, he smiles brightly and waves.

"Who is that?" Claire asks, noticing our exchange.

"Just one of my classmates."

"He's cute," she says, her tone suggestive.

I shrug in answer.

"But no Rhylan Matthews, huh?" she adds.

"You're never going to let that go, are you?"

"Do you know who you're talking to?"

I nudge her before we dissolve into giggles, reminding me why we're friends. It's because of moments like this. How she manages to bring out a smile from me when I need it most. How she gives me these moments of contentment through laughter and friendly banter.

We get to the front of the line and place our orders. I brandish my credit card before she has a chance to take out her wallet.

"I got it," I say to her.

CHAPTER 15
Rhylan

Days go by. Those days turn into weeks as I spend the greater part of that time thinking about Ellie. I keep seeing flash images of her every time I close my eyes. Like how goosebumps scattered her skin when my finger grazed the sensitive spot at the base of her neck. Or how she gently laid her head on my shoulder, and I actually felt her chest tighten with pain. Even the moment that she looked up at me, her bright eyes so lifeless and weak, as I told her that I knew *exactly* how she felt.

I keep thinking about how all I want to do is hold her pain in my hands and let her walk away without it. Just so that she can leave it behind and not have to think about it again. But that can't happen. I can never look into her sad, misty eyes and find out what it would feel like to brush her hair out of her face and tuck it neatly behind her ear. I will never know how the soft skin of her nape would feel under the pads of my fingers as they knead out the knot of ache that only I know is there.

To distract myself, I do what I can to stay busy. I go to the gym with the guys, not having gone since I finished filming

Unrestrained when I had to keep up my physique. I go on long drives, often ending up nowhere and driving home long after nightfall, turning off my engine and sitting in the quiet, empty driveway of my house, unable to actually walk inside where my thoughts feel even louder.

But I'm running out of things to do to stay busy. And my mind doesn't feel any less cluttered.

Today, at the hour when the sun feels the hottest and the brightness has peaked, I walk out of my house and settle into my car. With nowhere to go, I just drive. I drive and drive, hoping the road can provide some sense of clarity. But it doesn't. It never does. All it does is leave me alone with my thoughts, giving me time to rake through them and pick apart every thought that I want to avoid, making me feel emptier than ever.

And then it dawns on me. I need to see Ellie. I need to talk to her, see her face, something. Once I do, I'll be able to sift through my thoughts and gain some clarity.

It sounds crazy in my head, but it somehow makes sense. It feels right to want to see her, to talk to her, even if all she can give me is an open display of her pain, not hidden or secured in any way, visible only for me to see.

So I begin driving in the direction of her house. As my hands move over the gear shift and the steering wheel gliding between my fingers, I fight the nagging voice in my head telling me to turn back around and go home. That night of the premiere was about encasing a single moment where we shed our shielded exteriors. That's what I should leave it at. Isn't that why I didn't ask for her number? Why I hadn't implied or outwardly suggested any type of follow-up meeting, like an actual date? Without the promise of more, I was able to walk away knowing that nothing else was expected. That I didn't need to lay out the false hope of something more. But staying away is turning out to be more difficult than I thought, not without looking back and wondering why the fuck I can't stop thinking about her.

I barely remember where she lives, but the roads start to look vaguely familiar, just vaguely. The twists and turns of the streets bring me to her neighborhood, and I drive in a slow crawl for what seems like forever, carefully examining each house and looking for something familiar to see if this is even the right neighborhood.

Then I come to a stop in front of her house. I know it's her house because she's standing right in front of it. She's just gotten out of her car, carrying her backpack over her shoulder, walking towards the entrance. Her hair is thrown back in a loose ponytail, lightly bouncing and flowing behind her.

Holy shit, it's her.

Now I feel like a fucking stalker.

And no, my car doesn't make a U-turn and go back home where I don't feel like a total creep. Instead, I tap lightly on the brakes, stopping right in front of her driveway.

She's still getting into her house, fumbling with her keys, when the sound of my engine cutting draws her attention. She turns to look at me, her eyes squinting as she searches for any signs of recognition.

I don't really have a choice now.

My body feels like it's dragging, pushing the door open,

stepping my left foot out while my right foot follows. When I fully stand, her eyes go wide.

Every inconsistent and complicated thought that I have balled up in my stomach, making me physically sick, loosens. That knot untangles, and I deeply, *deeply* sigh. I haven't even spoken to her, haven't yet heard her soft, cautious voice, and already, I feel that her being in front of me is the answer to all of my problems.

The disbelief throws me completely off guard, making me shake my head.

But as soon as the silence lingers around us for a minute too long, my nerves return tenfold, making me shy and flustered. I don't know what to do with myself. My hand moves up to my hair, running rakes of rows through it, then stops to scratch my chin before being stuffed into my pocket. My heart races a thousand beats per minute as I try to still the shake in my hands. But instead of clamming up like I normally do, I find the words spilling out of me. Words that are so embarrassingly awkward that I know I'll cringe thinking about them for weeks.

"I swear I'm not stalking you." *Ugh, did I just say that?*

She doesn't smile, her expression unchanging. She doesn't say a single word, making me feel even more flustered.

I laugh, in an unbearably awkward way that sounds more like a cough, before speaking again. "I just came to say hi." I bring my hand up to wave at her.

I *wave* at her.

With her standing no more than a couple of feet away from me, I wave at her, all clumsy and aloof, trying my best to be cool but coming off as creepy and awkward. After I told her I'm not stalking her.

"Anyways, I guess I'll get going." I turn to walk away, mentally banging my fist into the side of my head.

"Rhylan?" I hear her soft voice call after me.

I stop in my tracks, not fully turning to face her.

"What are you doing here?"

I finally turn around as she takes slow, gradual steps towards me before stopping no more than a foot away at the edge of her driveway.

With her face just inches from mine, I'm able to study it. Remember it so that the painful beauty she so cautiously exhibits would be engraved in my mind forever. I notice details that I didn't before. Like the dark rings surrounding her deep sepia eyes that can only be seen in the sunlight. Or the bottom curve of her face that's round enough that it leaves an innocent impression on her silhouette. She pulls her full lips into the grips of her teeth and nibbles on them, just as the flush of her cheeks deepens and spreads.

All the apprehension and anxiety disappear. The butterflies quickly settle, and I can't help but smile.

"I–I, uh…" I sigh, tucking my head down and gripping the back of my neck. When I look back up at her, the confusion on her face has softened. A small smile spreads across her face as she waits for my answer and silently lets me know that whatever the reason I'm standing in front of her house, she'll understand. "I just wanted to see you," I finally confess.

She nods. "I don't know whether to be scared that you showed up out of nowhere or impressed that you remembered where I live."

My rattled nerves calm to an excited quiver. *She's making a joke.* "I had to drive around a bit to finally find your house. Which actually makes me sound more stalkerish, now that I think about it."

She laughs, turning her head to the side to look away. We stay quiet for a moment. I haven't thought this far ahead. I've been so focused on actually finding her that I realize I don't know what to do now that she's in front of me. Until I think of the only thing that feels right.

"You want to go for a drive?"

She tilts her head, her smile fading just slightly.

"Or maybe I can get your number so that I can call ahead next time. If you're busy or something."

She nods. "Okay. Let me just go inside and set down my things."

close the door behind me, my heart racing and practically beating out of my chest. Rhylan Matthews is outside my house, waiting for me so we can go for a drive.

I plop my backpack on the floor next to the couch and look down at what I'm wearing. I see the splotch of coffee on the bottom hem of my oversized sweater, dried and crusted, from this morning when I unsuccessfully tried to balance my books along with my travel mug. And my black leggings are covered in Angus's fur, prickly hairs matted over the spandex material that are more stubborn than Angus's obsession for his monkey squeaky toy. I need to change.

I rush to my room, ripping off my clothes before throwing them in a heap next to the hamper. I only see flashes of my own hands in front of me. I don't even know what I'm doing. All I know is that my fingers finally grasp a dress, floral and navy blue with thin straps and cut mid-thigh, and I pull it over my head, struggling as I try to get it down past my armpits. I brush out my hair and touch up my makeup before reaching for my purse and keys to leave my house, taking a deep, calming breath before stepping off my stoop.

Rhylan is waiting, leaned up against his car with his hands shoved into his pockets, looking so perfectly handsome. He's dressed casually, like any other twenty-something guy that I see at school or on the street. He wears a plain black T-shirt that's pulled taut against his chest and arms, and it blends into his black jeans that are slightly faded and worn. I can't help but let my eyes linger on the tight hem of his sleeve cutting across his tan bicep, leading down to his muscled forearm. His ankles are crossed in front of him, and he peeks up at me through his hair when my sandals take that first step onto the pavement.

His body stands upright as he pushes himself off the car and his eyes scan over me, trailing from my bare legs to the dipped neckline of my dress. "You ready?" he says, taking a step closer to me. I tilt my head up to look at him and lean slightly back when he hovers over me. The upturned curve of his lips that I've acquainted myself with causes me to chew on the inside of my cheek to suppress a smile as he turns to open the door to his vintagy car. I don't know what kind of make or model it is, but it looks like a classic. The kind of car that would be considered collectible and expensive. Once we're both nestled and buckled up in his front seat, he drives.

We drive on with no specific destination. I enjoy the cooled-down air of the late afternoon coming in through the open window with the sun shining high above us as the loose waves of my hair flow wildly behind me. I feel free. Like we could drive off and disappear, and I would have no regrets.

Nothing about sitting in Rhylan's car is unnatural. Not synthetic, as if we were forced into an awkward situation. It's the complete opposite. It's comforting. Like being alone with an old friend, familiar and ordinary. But not ordinary as in boring. This type of ordinary feels like coming home, like being in a place where comfort is the whole point and the only purpose.

"So," he says, speaking over the sounds flowing in from the busy streets. "Can I take you somewhere?"

I peer over at him, tucking in my hair behind my ear as his eyes linger on my hand. "What did you have in mind?"

"I know of a few places. Some that might interest you. Some that may not." He looks back at the road ahead as his playfully ominous words sit between us. I see the corner of his mouth lift, forming a teasing smile.

"Will there be milkshakes?" I ask boldly. I bite my lower lip, anticipating his answer.

The sound of his laugh booms between us, echoing off the storefronts lining the sidewalks filled with people. "You read my mind."

After about another half hour of driving, we pull up to what looks like an outdoor diner equipped with waitresses on roller skates and loud music coming from a jukebox settled under an awning. A large, rotating neon sign reads Marie's at the entrance to the parking lot. He pulls into a spot that lines an outdoor checkout counter and rolls down his window.

"What is this?" I ask. I lower my head and peer through the windshield to look up towards the diner.

"This is one of my hidden gems I discovered a long time ago," he explains with a smile full of excitement as I take in the scenery.

A young waitress wearing a pink poodle skirt and thick cat-eye glasses approaches the car, ready to take our order. She's gliding on white roller skates and is skilled in maneuvering herself on them as she comes to an effortless stop at Rhylan's window.

"We'll take a strawberry and vanilla shake. And a basket of fries," Rhylan says.

"Coming right up!" answers the waitress in a cheerful tone.

He turns to face me. "I come to this place all the time. At first, I embarrassingly enjoyed the recognition when the staff saw me, but now they just treat me like a regular," he explains. "And the milkshakes are to die for."

Excited about the milkshakes, I smile and wait patiently for the waitress to bring them out. Rhylan lifts his butt from the seat as his hand goes to his pocket, extracting his phone and unlocking it before extending it towards me.

"Here. Put in your number. So next time, I won't look like a stalker just showing up at your house," he says with a wink.

I smile and take it, carefully pressing the ten digits that'll connect him to me with a single press of a button. When I'm done, I hand his phone back to him and smile.

"I swear I wasn't stalking you, by the way," he says. He tosses his phone on his dashboard, the clatter ending his sentence.

I can't help the amused laughter that creeps through my lips. "You showed up at my house unannounced. I'm getting some slight stalker vibes from you."

"I wish I could explain to you why I did that. But I don't even know why."

"Try me," I urge.

He sighs. "I don't want to sound obsessive or anything, but I couldn't get you out of my head. Everything we talked about and said to each other... I hadn't felt like that in such a long time. I just... I had to see you."

I don't know what I was expecting, but this isn't it. I'm no one, practically a stranger. So completely forgetful in comparison to those that Rhylan must encounter on a daily basis, and yet here he is, telling me I left an impression on him. Like I had imprinted on his life somehow. And for some reason, it doesn't scare me. I feel hopeful that I could do that for him, hold his hand and tell him it's okay to feel everything that he's feeling. Because maybe he could do the same in return.

"Are you and Bella Raven dating?" I ask abruptly. I don't mean to ask such a personal question, but I blurt it out. Claire and I had come to the conclusion that the two were together, and I wonder why he isn't turning to her.

When, instead of answering, he chuckles and shakes his head, I blush in embarrassment. Maybe I shouldn't have asked him that.

"No, Ellie. We're not," he answers. He says my name the way someone would to scold. To assertively correct the inaccuracy in my question, leaving no room for doubt. He lowers his head towards his lap before turning and looking at me through his thick lashes, his smile gone.

"I'm sorry, I guess that's a little personal," I say, embarrassed.

"Don't look too much into everything you read out there. A lot of the gossip is exaggerated to draw in an audience."

"I've never read anything like that," I say, shrugging to

show indifference. "I saw you two at the premiere. Just the way she touched you and looked at you. Like you belonged to her."

"I don't belong to anyone," he answers seriously. His expression is dark, his intensity alarming as he stares straight ahead. His eyes shift, pensiveness glazing over them as if he's thinking about belonging to someone. As if any possibility of it, to be a half of a whole, isn't something that's attainable for him. It's just an illusion filling his days, fleeting as a mere afterthought.

"I'm sorry. I didn't mean to intrude." I look away, apologizing once again and embarrassed to have spoken so impulsively.

"No need to apologize," he says. He shakes his head, a grim smile appearing on his face. "Things are just complicated, and I wish they weren't."

When I look back at him, there's a hidden softness in his features. His eyes are tilted downwards, and his jaw relaxes into a small smile. We continue to look at each other when we're interrupted by the waitress bringing us our shakes and fries.

"Thanks," Rhylan says to the waitress as he takes our order from her before turning to face me again. "So do you want strawberry or vanilla?"

I reach for the strawberry, one hand gripping the Styrofoam cup while the other takes one of the two straws in Rhylan's hand. The devilish grin that cuts across my face draws a loose laugh from Rhylan just as I take my first sip. I groan in excitement and look at him with surprised eyes. When he said they were to die for, he wasn't kidding.

"I told you," he says with his eyebrows wiggling. I groan again through a second loud slurp, inhaling it bit by bit.

"Try dipping a fry in the milkshake," he suggests. My smile drops to a frown, confusion and disgust spreading through every inch of my face.

Rhylan laughs. "It's good! Trust me," he says. He takes a fry, still steaming from the fresh grease it had been boiling in, and dips the entire length of it into his vanilla shake. He takes the whole fry into his mouth, and my mouth drops open.

"That was gross," I finally say.

"You can't knock it till you try it," he says, reaching for another fry. He dips the fry again, the milkshake pooling from the hot, oily fry, and extends it towards me. "Here."

I tentatively take it from him and eat it. I chew, realizing that it actually isn't that bad, and make a sound of approval.

"See! It's good, right?"

"It's not bad," I say, my mouth still full. "I wouldn't say it's good though."

"But don't dip it in the strawberry one," he adds. "It doesn't taste the same."

"Oh, *that's* where you draw the line," I deadpan, reaching for a packet of ketchup.

We continue eating our fries, covered in vanilla milkshake for Rhylan and dipped in ketchup for me, and we slurp up the last of our milkshakes, conversing in between. People gather in a small open area in front of the entrance, excitedly dancing to fifties rock 'n' roll music and decked out in rockabilly attire. The sun is slowly setting behind us yet still gives a bright enough glow for the dancers to enjoy the ambiance.

"This is so amazing. I can't believe people still dress up like this."

"They do this almost every night. People just come together and relive the fifties," he explains to me.

"It's so nice. And entertaining." I giggle as an Elvis impersonator takes the makeshift dance floor. His awkward steps cause him to lose his balance, but he gracefully moves along to the music as he catches his own feet.

"So, is Ellie short for something? Or is it just Ellie?" he asks. He bobs a fry into his milkshake, concentrating on creating the most accurate fry to milkshake ratio.

I purse my lips through a small smile, a little surprised that he knows that Ellie isn't my full name. "It's short for Eleanor. I was named after my grandma."

"Eleanor. I like that. I think I like that better than Ellie," he says thoughtfully.

"But no one really calls me that," I explain. "At least, I ask people *not* to since it sounds so formal. Except for my mom and my friend Claire. They usually reserve it for when they mean business. Claire especially, when she's trying to convince me to join her for her daily fill of caffeine or margaritas."

He smirks, the corners of his mouth lifting up in a genuine smile.

"How did you know that it was a nickname?"

"I have an aunt we call Ellie. Her real name is Elaine though," he explains.

The music changes from an upbeat tune to something slower paced. I hear the crowd make *aw* and *ooh* sounds in approval of the shift in song.

"You go to UCLA? What are you studying?" he asks me, eyes peering at me from the side and his straw hanging out the corner of his mouth.

"I—um… I'm a literature major." I smile shyly. "Mainly because of my dad."

He smirks, a small gust of a breath rushing through his nose to signify understanding. "That makes sense."

"I didn't realize how much our relationship influenced my future, even after he's been gone for so many years. It's sort of paved a pathway for so many things I didn't even realize. I still read the books he gave me. They're all worn and soft now, but I sort of love that about them."

"Then you have to have a favorite book. One that you could take with you if you were ever to be stranded on an island."

"That's like asking someone to pick their favorite food," I say skeptically.

"Pizza."

"Pizza," I parrot back.

"Yeah."

"If you had to live off one food for the rest of your life, it would be pizza?"

He nods.

I give an exaggerated eye roll and a smirk. When I don't answer his question, he patiently waits.

"Fine. If I *had* to bring one book with me if I somehow planned to be stranded on an island, it would be… *A Walk to Remember.*"

I watch as his lips twitch, a suppressed smile peeking through the corners of his mouth before they downturn instead, nodding along with a fake approval.

"You're going to judge me now on my choice of literature?"

He shakes his head. "No, I just… It's not what I expected."

"It's called a comfort read, for your information. A book that you gravitate to because it brings you comfort, of all things."

He chuckles.

"And you've read it?" I ask, not even bothering to hide the accusatory tone in my voice.

"Me?" He shakes his head vigorously. "No."

"And why that doesn't surprise me." I poke my finger into his shoulder.

"But…" He trails off, peeking at the spot where the tip of my finger pressed into his hard muscle. "So my mom is obsessed with it. She made my brothers and me watch the movie remake, the one with Mandy Moore, at least every full moon since we refuse to read it. She says she settles for that since she can't get her boys to read the best romance story of her time."

I laugh. "She has good taste."

"She even bought the soundtrack and stuffed it in my suitcase when I moved down here to go to college."

I giggle through a wide smile. "I can just picture you dancing along to Mandy Moore's velvety voice while it plays obnoxiously loud over your sound system."

"My best dance moves are saved for my living room and a hairbrush microphone."

I laugh. Not the shy kind but the kind where my head tilts back and my hand instinctively covers my mouth.

"Where did you go to school?" I ask when my laugh dies.

"UCLA."

My eyes boggle. "UCLA? Like the one I'm going to?"

"I'm pretty sure there's just the one." He winks.

My brows furrow through my surprised expression. "Oh, I never realized you went there."

"I didn't graduate though," he explains. "My acting career started picking up the following year, so I quit when I couldn't juggle school and work."

I hum, acknowledging his words. When he doesn't elaborate further, settling for silence instead, my curiosity nags at me. "Do you wonder how your life would have turned out if you stayed and finished?"

He nods. "I do. Especially nowadays when I'm feeling more overwhelmed. All the what-ifs kind of fill my time."

"Those what-ifs can be debilitating. Uncertainty is a scary thing."

"Yeah," he huffs.

"I'm actually graduating in a couple of months, and my biggest what-if is… What if when I'm out in the real world, I'm lost? Right now, everything is sort of decided for me. I go to school, to work, to home. But… without school, I–I don't think I'll know…" My breath catches at the last word, my throat choking on a knotted ball of fear. "What if everything around me passes by while I stay stagnant? And I don't go anywhere."

"Kind of like everyone around you is living their lives, but you're just at a standstill."

I nod.

"Yeah," he whispers, his lips catching between his teeth as his jaw squares. I don't really know what it means, his uncertain yet affirmative response. All I know is that he seems to understand. Not in a grim, brokenhearted way, but in a way that simply says *Everything you feel, I feel it too.*

He looks ahead, eyes serious, and huffs out a sigh before looking back at me.

"I don't usually keep people close to me," he says, biting his lip. "They usually don't understand my life, and everyone involved seems to get hurt. Especially me. People seem to really easily walk away when things get to be too much, and I've learned to not get so involved if I can help it." He swallows, his jaw muscle ticking as his brows furrow deeper. "So I let them… pass through, live whatever life they need to without me. And I've learned to never really be a part of anything. Celebrations, birthdays, weddings. They all sort of happen around me without me being a part of it."

He pauses, lowering his gaze as his eyes scan over the space between us. "I've gotten really good at pushing people away. It feels easier that way."

As he talks, I watch him, trying to remain indifferent. The way he explains his life sounds so isolating. But even as he describes what his life is like, separated from everyone around him, placing them at arm's reach but never close enough to hold dear, it doesn't feel like that with me and him. I don't feel like someone that's going to simply pass through and move on. Even now, sipping milkshakes and being surrounded by smooth blues and jazz, I can't believe that I've seen this much of him already. In this space in his car, in places that he claims are his hidden gems, or even how he prefers his fries dipped in milkshakes. Those are intimate details, ones that I shouldn't know, but for some reason, he's shared with me.

"Sounds kind of lonely," I finally say.

His expression lightens, a sad smile lifting his lips. "It's complicated. Let's just leave it at that."

Watching him, I realize that the Rhylan Matthews sitting next to me isn't the celebrity that I've always known. He isn't the same person I saw confidently and effortlessly walk the red carpet, waving to his fans with a smile that hid any single moment of insecurity. He's bared raw, entirely vulnerable and exposed. He's himself.

He's himself around *me*.

What I told her is true. I don't keep people close by. They're always at an arm's length. It's an easy solution to not get hurt. But it gets excruciatingly lonely. The people that do wander into my life and stay have stuck around because I've made it feasible. It's always been easy to keep them close from a distance because I've never felt this urge, this compulsion to completely be myself.

I haven't let anyone in for a long time. Actually, ever. I've never let someone get close enough for them to *see* me. To allow me to let my guard down and speak freely about how I feel exhausted. How I feel consumed by every morbid, bleak thought that crosses my mind.

When I talk to Ellie, I don't need to explain myself. There's no learning curve or adjustment period that most would need to fully grasp what I feel. No moment where I wonder if she's put off by what I say, as twisted and unhealthy as it sounds. I'm able to talk without any explanation. She just understands. The thought that someone does, so plainly and simply, makes me feel weightless. And a little too good to be true.

She looks at me as I drink what's left of my milkshake. "Do you ever miss home?"

"I do. More so now than I did when I first moved out here."

"Why's that?" she asks.

"I don't know. I think I was just too busy to miss home back then, but now… I kind of have a moment to miss my family."

"I would probably miss home," she says wistfully. "I've never been anywhere else but here, and I can't imagine dropping all that and relocating myself."

"It wasn't easy. And my brothers still give me a hard time about it," I say, a smile teasing my lips thinking about them. "They say I'm missing out on my nieces and nephews growing up."

"I bet you are, being away from home and all." She smiles sweetly, her eyes turning into those little crescent moons.

"Yeah, but they send me pictures."

"Still, that can't beat the real thing. Holding them and spoiling them like every uncle should."

"No, I guess not," I agree. "What about you? Do you have any siblings?"

"Oh, no. I'm an only child." I see her swallow, the knot in her throat rolling down the center of her neck. I can see it travel down her chest where it settles, taking residence and reminding her of the grief that she still feels. "It's just me and my mom."

She looks down at her lap, her fingers linked together and twisting around her cup. She doesn't say anything before looking back at me. "I have Claire," she finally offers. "She's my friend that was at your premiere. She's majoring in film production. That's actually why I was there that night. She got invited by her boss, and she dragged me along with her," she explains. "She's the best friend I've ever had. From the moment we met, we just kind of clicked. No drama, no competition."

"So she's like your person?"

"My person?" She looks at me, confused.

"Yeah, like the person that you turn to for anything. To make you laugh, to hold your hand when you're scared. To hug you when you cry."

"Huh, I guess you're right. I never thought of her that way." She smiles a hint of a smile. "My person," she whispers to herself.

She looks up at me, her small smile still curving her lips. "Do you have a person?"

I chew over her question. "No, I don't. I mean, I have people. And I have friends but not really someone I would call my person."

"Not even your brothers?"

"This sounds kind of weird, but I've never been that close to them. I'm the youngest, and they always seemed to have a close bond with each other. I mean, I love them to death, but…" I trail off. "I've always sort of kept to myself. Even as a kid."

"Little introvert Rhylan," she teases. "Who would've thought?"

I chuckle, finding her taunt endearing. "I have my group of friends though," I continue to explain. "They've been there for me through a lot and kept me company, so I don't feel so lonely.

But I feel like they each have their own person. Like Charles, he has his wife. And my other friends, Chuck and Jackson, they have each other." My hands move to my chin, scratching my jaw as I consider what my close-knit group of friends here in LA means to me. "I think we all keep each other company though. This can be a pretty lonely life, and it's good to have friends that kind of get it."

"Charles? Charles Bradley?"

"Yeah, we've been friends for a while now. Probably close to six, seven years?"

"Oh, I didn't know you two were so close."

"I guess we kind of are. We see each other pretty regularly, and his kids are amazing," I explain. A smile spreads across my lips, thinking about the two boys that always welcome me into their chubby little arms. "They call me Uncle Rhy."

Right then, my phone sitting on my dashboard chirps with a familiar tone.

"I'm sorry. That's probably my assistant." When I look at the message, I see Carrie has texted me, reminding me that my gift to Levi was sent to his house this afternoon ahead of his party. My mind blanks for a minute.

Shit! Levi's party!

It's Levi's birthday. He had extended the invitation over a month ago, explaining that it would be a small dinner party with some of his close friends. His wife had insisted on it, saying he was getting to that age where his birthdays were numbered and he needed to celebrate every one of them, even if it was just a small gathering of people. I would skip it and spend my time here with Ellie instead, but since it would be a small party, it'd be easier for Levi to miss me if I didn't show up. At least with a larger reception, I would be one person in the crowd of people.

"Is everything okay?" Ellie asks.

I don't say anything as I start my car, buckling my seatbelt before looking over my shoulder to back out of the parking space. With my hands on the steering wheel and my feet lightly tapping the pedals to guide us out of the parking lot, I turn to Ellie as she waits for an answer.

"Uh, so I had this thing I had to go to tonight. And I didn't realize it'd gotten this late."

Her brows raise, urging me to continue.

"We're going to have to stop in for a minute."

"We?" Her brows raise even higher.

"It's my agent's birthday, and he's having a party at his house. I need to at least make an appearance, or I'll never hear the end of it."

"And you're taking me with you?" Her voice squeaks with the last word. "Can you just drop me off at home? Or I can take an Uber from here." Her mouth scrunches into a small pout as her fingers twist on her lap.

"There's not enough time, and no, I'm not letting you take an Uber," I scoff but smile at the same time, finding the way her chin scrunches under jutted lower lip adorable.

"Rhylan, I'm not even dressed for a party," she says a little more quietly and defeated.

"What you're wearing is fine. It's just some of his close friends getting together for drinks and dinner, nothing fancy."

I hear her sigh and slump back in her seat.

I tap the brake, my car coming to a stop in the middle of the parking lot before I turn to face her, my hand hooking over the back of her seat.

"I can take you home," I offer.

She lifts her head. "But then… you're going to be late," she says softly.

"I know," I say. "It's fine. I can be a little late."

She chews on her lower lip as her eyes finally meet mine.

"But to be completely honest, I'd rather keep you to myself for a little longer."

Her brows slightly furrow as her lips purse together.

"If you're okay with that," I finish.

She nods, the furrow in her brows remaining as she slowly buckles her seat belt. I turn to face forward as my foot lifts off the brake.

Instinctively, I reach for the hand that she has placed on her lap. When my hand covers hers, it feels tense, wound up in a fist and clasping her other hand, wringing it out in stress. But then she relaxes. Her hand slackens, and her fingers loosen, allowing my large fingers to intertwine with her slender ones. And the pads of her fingers wrap around to rest on the back of my hand. I reached for her in an attempt to comfort her, to reassure her, but it seems that I'm the one being comforted. I haven't realized I need reassurance, but when she holds my hand in hers, I feel calmer. At ease.

Out of sheer intuition, I bring her hand up to my lips and kiss the back of it before bringing it back to her lap. The gesture seems so slight, so fleeting, but the buzz of the exchange can be felt in the air. It's palpable as it brings me nothing but peace.

Contentment that makes me smile, knowing that a feeling like this actually exists.

We drive in silence, finally coming to a stop in front of the large iron gates of Levi's Thousand Oaks mansion. Ellie peers up through the windshield, her eyes peeking through her lashes and her mouth slightly open as she takes in the view.

"This is a really… um, big house." Her voice catches in her throat.

"Levi's a pretty big deal. And money has its perks."

Once my car is parked, I round the hood to open the door for Ellie. She steps out, smoothing out the bottom half of her dress before taking my extended hand. Our hands had remained affixed through the drive here. Unable to let her go, I shamelessly hold on to her, the softness of her skin providing the solace I've just discovered.

With our hands knotted together, I lead her towards the front entrance of Levi's house. I ring the doorbell, and almost instantly, the door swings wide open to Levi's bright face.

"Rhy! You made it!" He leans in for a hug. Redness and a sheen of sweat coat his face, most likely from the drinks he must have already had before my arrival. "Better late than never."

Ellie stands to my side, hiding behind me, treating me like a makeshift shield.

"Come on in! We're still having drinks," he says. Then his eyes land on Ellie, her body peeking from my side. "You brought a date?" His smile widens, and his glazed-over eyes twinkle.

"Levi, this is Ellie."

"Ellie, nice to meet you." He extends his hand towards her, and she takes it, jiggling along as his hand aggressively shake hers. "Don't be shy! Help yourself to a drink."

"Thanks, Levi," I say, peeking down at Ellie. "Oh, did you get the gift?"

"It's already hanging in my office. Thank you, Rhylan. That was too extravagant."

"Only the best." I smile.

He turns to rejoin his party, and Ellie and I are left alone again.

"What did you get him?" Ellie's soft voice barely reaches my ear, so I stoop down closer.

"He's been obsessing about this local artist that died last year. His name is Echo Ryu. I finally got a hold of one of his pieces last month," I explain. The problem with said artist is that since his death, his work has doubled in price and been that much more difficult to acquire. But I found one out of sheer luck. I jumped on the opportunity and had it shipped all the way from Spain. I admit I had splurged a bit, but it was worth it. Levi is someone that's been there from the start of my career, and I finally feel that I'm in a place to pay him back for everything he's done for me.

"How extravagant was it?"

"I mean, since the artist died, it was a bit pricey. About forty grand," I answer her.

Her eyes go wide, her grip on me tightening. "Forty grand?!"

"Honestly, it's an investment. I know in a couple of months the value of it is going to go up even higher."

"Wow, the last birthday gift I got was a Tamagotchi pet for Claire," she says softly, her words almost coming out as a whisper with the shock still in the tone of her voice.

"I'm sorry. A what?"

"It's this little digital pet," she explains, her fingers pinching together to show how small this gift was. "You're supposed to feed it and, like, love it, or else it dies. She said she lost hers when she was a kid, and I happened to see one so…" Her voice trails off. I'm looking at her with a suppressed smile, trying to hold back my creeping laughter. "We thought it was funny!" Her shock finally falters, and a smile spreads across her face. She playfully swats my arm and pouts, coming off even cuter than before.

My laugh is genuine and boisterous. "That's actually the most adorable thing I've ever heard."

She rolls her eyes at me and gently pushes me away, pressing her hand into my chest. Having successfully pulled a smile from her face, I brush my hand against the small of her back before we simultaneously take a step further inside with a light bounce in our steps. We veer towards the table of drinks, and I pour myself and Ellie a glass of deeply fragrant merlot. Her head tilts slowly, taking deliberate sips of her wine as we both sort of exist on the sidelines of chatty conversations and casual atmosphere.

With my head bent down to get closer to Ellie's ear, I whisper quietly, "How you holding up, champ?"

She swerves her head towards me, an obvious aversion to my question. "Champ?"

"It's a term of endearment. My dad usually saved it for

when we needed a little cheering up. Like when we lost a softball game or got into a fist fight at school."

"And you couldn't think of a better one than champ?"

I shrug. "I guess I could have gone with 'tiger' or 'cupcake.'"

She cringes, her nose crinkling, with the cutest wrinkles forming in the bridge between her eyes. "Let's just stick with the basics then. I'll take champ."

"Yes, ma'am," I respond curtly with a small salute to my forehead.

She laughs as I watch some of the unease melt off of her. "But to answer your question, I think I may be able to let you know after another glass of wine or two. Once I'm more relaxed."

I hum, silently laughing at her confession. I open my mouth to tell her that I'll give her the whole bottle if it means she'll relax when we're interrupted by a high-pitched squeal.

"Rhylan!" Ellie and I both turn to see a woman dressed in a floor-length gown, sparkling in every inch of the fabric, scuttle towards me in her excessively high heels, Richard March following close behind her.

"Oh! I'm so happy to see you!" The woman is Constance, also known as Richard's wife. I've only met her a handful of times, mostly during my random visits to the studio, and she is highly overbearing. Just like she is right now, clinging to me and planting kisses on my cheek. She looks out of place in this informal dinner, as if she were attending a gala.

I reach behind her to extend my hand towards Richard, shaking his hand firmly. "Hi, Richard. I didn't know you were coming." The last time I saw Richard was at my premiere almost a month ago. I haven't spoken to him since but was aware of a conversation that he and Levi had in regards to the movie he wanted to cast me in. As soon as the script was couriered over to his office, Levi sat me down and shook his head in disapproval. He said that it wasn't the direction he wanted to take after *Unrestrained* was such a huge success.

"It's good to see you." He shakes my hand and smiles at me, not at all bothered by Constance's hands moving across my chest. I see Ellie from the corner of my eye backing away and giving space for Constance to move in closer. That's when I reach for her, taking hold of her hand and bringing her closer to me. Constance notices my movement as her eyes wander down the length of my arm to see my hand in Ellie's.

"Oh, you brought a little friend." Her eyes narrow, lips forming a straight line as she looks Ellie up and down.

I clear my throat. "Constance, this is Ellie."

"You look familiar," Richard says to Ellie, a fact rather than a question, his finger pointed in her direction as he tries to place her.

"We met at Rhylan's premiere last month. I believe my friend, Claire, is working at Paramount. She's an intern there," Ellie explains.

"Oh yes! I remember you now," Richard exclaims. He turns to Constance. "Her friend works with Hugo."

Constance's actions are overly exaggerated from the way she waves her hand before extending it towards Ellie and leans her body back in an unnecessary flourish. "Oh, I see! Nice to meet you, honey."

"Rhylan, I'm actually glad you showed up," Richard says.

His expression is serious, insistently broaching the subject that Levi had already squashed. "I know Levi already passed on our script on your behalf, but I wanted to see if we could go over it again. And maybe you can help me convince Levi. God knows how protective he is of you."

I smirk. "You know he respects you. He just wanted to make sure we go in the right direction, and I think he felt we had to pass on this one," I try to explain.

His hands move up, palms facing in my direction. "I understand. And I respect him just the same." He taps his finger to his chin. "Maybe we can talk to him right now."

"I think he's already made up his mind," I start to protest, but Richard's head is already swerving side to side as he searches for Levi. When he finally locates him, he bellows in his direction, calling his name out over the crowd of people. "Come on, Rhy. Let's go talk to Mr. Big Shot and see why he's too good to sign up his golden boy for my movie."

I shake my head and smile before turning to Ellie, silently asking her if she'd be okay if I stepped aside for a minute. She smiles reassuringly back at me. "It's fine," she whispers.

Richard clasps his hand on my shoulder and guides me towards Levi. When I turn to look back at Ellie, I see Constance already standing over her, but Ellie still looks at me, all smiles.

R hylan walks away, his head turned towards me with a sweet, apologetic smile. I smile back at him, my nose and the corners of my eyes crinkling with gratitude for his concern. When I first walked in the door of Levi's house, I was intimidated by the sheer size of it. The entire span of my living room could fit in his foyer. And that was barely the entrance of his house. I hadn't gotten past the even larger living space and the entire second story that seemed to grow taller and taller as I looked up. It expanded into the sky, and I couldn't understand how a single family could take up this large of a space and not feel like they were lost in another dimension.

Still, even with the intimidatingly beautiful home, Levi made me feel welcome. He smiled at me sincerely and received me as an extension of Rhylan, who he's obviously fond of. While I had been worried that I would feel completely out of place, Rhylan was right. It was a dinner that was just as he had explained, casual and friendly.

That was until I met Constance. As soon as her eyes landed on me, she sized me up. She looked at me with disdain and pure condescendence. Her obvious dislike for someone like me, a nobody, was obvious in her arrogance and her phony greeting, referring to me as Rhylan's "little friend."

I try to not let it bother me. Not even as she stands over me right now, her drink lazily held in her hand, with a smile that curved only in one corner, scheming her next words to sound the perfect amount of smug to still come off as polite. From the corner of my eyes, I can feel her watching me while she sips slowly and skillfully.

"You're so much prettier than the last girl Rhylan was with."

My eyes quickly revert back to Constance's, and my smile fades. Her head, topped with a heavy pile of curls, towers over me. I see her shift from side to side while placing a hand on her jutted-out hip. Her eyes continue to scan me up and down.

"Uh, thank you?" I say it more like a question rather than words of appreciation as her observation feels like a loaded statement, a backhanded compliment with an underlying insult.

"But I have to say, I didn't think you would be his type," she adds, followed by a low, throaty chuckle. "These LA girls have a certain look. Big tits, long legs, bleach blonde hair. Why, you're just the complete opposite!"

She laughs again, full of amusement from her own joke and eyes twinkling with ridicule. I politely smile, bringing my wine to my lips and taking a small sip.

She places a cold hand on my arm, fake reassurance laced in her tone. "It takes a lot of gall to show up to a party linked to someone like Rhylan and try to fit in. But I'm sure with time, you'll learn. And if not, Rhylan has a long list of women waiting at the threshold, just ready for their moment to seduce him. Some that prefer actual heels and a cocktail dress."

Her brows arch as she takes a leisurely sip of something amber colored in her tumbler. "I didn't even know they made flats for girls past puberty," she adds as she pulls her drink away from her lips, leaving behind a deep lipstick stain on the rim of her glass.

Her smile doesn't leave her face, not once. It stays, taking up half of her face, all wide and toothy. Her eyes shine bright and amused, waiting for me to respond. Instead, I stay quiet.

I look away, her words stinging. They strike a nerve that I know has been there the whole time because she isn't wrong. Not even a little bit. She laid out every worry and doubt that I felt when Rhylan brought me there. No amount of reassurance is enough to affirm that I belong in this world that feels so foreign to me. I feel like a fish out of water, flopping lifelessly on dry earth, just gasping for water. I want to go back into the deep depths of the ocean where I feel more at home.

My polite smile turns into a small frown. I haven't had a moment to evaluate my and Rhylan's relationship, or whatever this is. This is barely the second time I met him, third if I count the coffeehouse. I'm not sure what this is, but I know it won't amount to anything. It can't. We're complete opposites. He's a Hollywood movie star, someone that everyone knows and loves. I'm an ordinary girl. What do we have to offer to each other?

But everything we said, knowing that we saw a version of ourselves in each other, damaged and broken, I can't ignore that. For some reason, we both understand. We speak like we've known each other our entire lives, learning and molding into the other's thoughts and mannerisms naturally. I can't let go of the fact that when I'm with him, I feel safe. I feel like I can say the things that I keep buried deep, thoughts that I feel shameful about with others.

"Oh, honey. I hope you don't take any offense to what I said." Constance's expression changes to forced concern, her forehead creasing and eyes softening with her still-fake smile smeared across her face. "You have to have thicker skin if you're going to survive in this town."

I suddenly feel warm, my cheeks heating up and my chest feeling tight. I can feel my heart racing and the blood rushing to my ears. I feel so out of place, more so than I did earlier when I walked through those heavy wooden doors with Rhylan's hand linked to mine.

I don't belong here.

I need air.

"Excuse me," I whisper before turning and walking towards the door, my steps quick and hurried. I realize I still have my wine glass in my hand, the deep red swishing as I pick up my pace, when a splash hits the floor with an audible slap. I quickly sidestep to avoid the wine that would have hit my foot and soaked the leather straps of my sandals.

When I turn to see if anyone has witnessed the spill, I find multiple pairs of eyes on me, including Rhylan's. He had been speaking with Richard and Levi when his eyes find mine. I look at him apologetically before setting the glass down on the marble floor and walking out the door, pushing the heavy doors with my weight.

When the cool air hits my lungs, I finally feel like I can breathe. I close my eyes, and I try to even my breaths, in and out, letting the oxygen fill me and calm the creeping nerves that cause my whole body to tremble. I need to leave. I don't even know where I am, but I need to get out of here. I reach into my purse to pull out my phone. Maybe I can call an Uber. Or maybe Claire can come get me.

I'm still trying to figure out how I'm going to get home when I felt a warm, strong hand on my shoulder. The sudden touch causes me to jump and gasp. When I turn around, Rhylan is standing over me.

"Ellie," he says softly. "Are you okay?"

"Um, yeah. I'm just trying to figure out how to get home," I explain to him.

"You need to get home? I can take you." He starts reaching into his pocket to fish out his keys when my hand moves to his arm to stop him.

"No, I'm fine. I can get home on my own," I say, unable to hide the slight tremble in my voice. "Thank you for tonight. I really had a good time. You should get back to the party." My words are rushed and panicked. I smile, a weak attempt to reassure him that I'll be fine and for him to go back inside. Before he can say anything, I turn to walk away from him. My feet move down the long gravel pathway that leads to the large iron gates we drove through. I don't even know where I'm going.

A sudden chill rolls down my back, and I cross my arms to keep myself warm. But it's pointless because the chill I'm feeling has nothing to do with the temperature of the air and more to do with the insecurities that have taken over me.

"Ellie, wait!" he calls after me. I can feel his feet hitting the ground behind me as they crunch against the gravel, but I keep walking. I don't want to face him. No, I don't know *how*. What do I say to him? How do I tell him "let's not waste any more of our time" without sounding presumptuous? Because that's all this was: a waste of both our time. There was no point in all of this, and I'm not prepared to get hurt waiting around to see what will happen between us.

And then I feel his hand wrap around my wrist warmly and protectively. Every feeling that I felt before we drove through those ominous gates returns. Like the warmth that gave comfort to every bleak thought that I had. Or the electricity that buzzed between us when his fingers grasped mine, tangling them with his strong hands as if to reassure me. Even the sound of his deep voice that somehow managed to make me feel safe thawed through my guarded heart.

I stop walking, my feet still and unable to move. When I turn back to look at him, his feet move him closer. He inches towards me and fills the space between us until there barely is any. Just a fraction of air that's full of heat. My body finally turns, gravitating towards him so that I can fully face him. To see his face and study the creases that form from worry as his hands move to cup my elbows.

"What happened?" His voice is alarming and unexpected, even though I knew he was going to speak first.

"Nothing happened!" I laugh, my smile disappearing as soon as it appears. My attempt to lighten the mood fails, his face not faltering. "I just need to get home. I'm so sorry. I didn't mean to pull you away from the party…" I trail off, biting my lip as I look away.

"Did Constance say something to you?" His voice is low, trying to coax the truth out of me.

I don't nod or shake my head. When my chin begins to tremble, I angle my head down to hide it, just as he brings his hands to my face to lift it towards him.

"What did she say?"

"You know what? It's really not important," I protest as I slowly pull away. "Please, go back inside, and I can be out of your hair."

"Ellie, I don't want you out of my anything," he says, his hold on me tightening as his eyes narrow. "What did she say?"

I sigh. "She mentioned something along the lines of you having a long line of women waiting for you. You know, since I don't fit in. And some other stuff I really don't remember."

That's a lie. Of course I remember. I'll remember every word she said to me. But I don't want to repeat them. Doing so would only openly display every flaw that I'm aware of but am too scared to face when I'm with him. In the comforts of my own life, I'm only surrounded by whatever unsettled grief I've learned to live with. I don't constantly stand up to a ruler that I'll never measure up to. It's only around Rhylan I feel this way. So why am I still here, waiting instead of walking away? Standing in front of him as I set myself up for heartbreak?

And then I feel him sigh, the warm exhale of his breath hitting my cold skin. Along with it comes the realization that maybe none of that matters. Maybe what everyone thinks, everyone's opinion of seeing me alongside Rhylan, doesn't matter. I want to believe it, to cast aside fear by replacing it with the possibility of us. But it almost feels too hopeful. Because I saw it in Constance's eyes. Her judgment and the drool practically dripping from her mouth as she preyed on my own self-esteem, ready to tear it to shreds to remind me of my place.

"I forget how fucking shitty the people in this town can be," he whispers. "I'm sorry."

Unable to speak without the wavering in my voice, I shake my head and look away. My chest clenches while a part of me folds. I reach up to gently touch his biceps while running my hands over the material of his shirt to somehow let him know it's okay. When I finally try to talk, nothing comes out. Just the scratching of the words that scrape the inside of my throat, stuck there and frozen.

I should walk away now when we have nothing to lose. Tell him goodbye as I pluck myself out of his life. It should be easy, right?

He lowers his face towards me, his eyes searching mine. When I finally look back at him, I can't hide the mistiness coating my eyes. I notice his jaw clench and his mouth come together in a firm line. The furrow in his brows deepens, causing a shadow to cast over his face. But even through his hardened features, his eyes are soft. They're asking me for forgiveness. He's apologizing for something that's every bit a part of him but that he has absolutely no control over.

"It's okay." The quiet words that are barely a whisper leave my lips before his come crashing into mine.

His hands grip my waist, clinging to me before moving up my back to press me closer to him, to fill that final gap between us. Our bodies mold into each other, each curve and crevice filling until every bit of our torsos touch. As if our bodies have become one. I feel his fingers trace into my nape, grasping it as his thumb grazes my skin, eliciting a quiet whimper from me. I feel a low groan vibrate from the base of his throat as our mouths open, welcoming the weave of our tangled tongues. The hold he has on me tightens, and my hands move to his chest, gripping his shirt right where it rests on his collarbone.

We stay tangled in this kiss, his hands roaming over my body as I lean into him. Trails of static pathways linger over my body from his firm touch grasping me as if I might slip away. When we finally pull away, our foreheads touch, our breathing unsteady but in sync.

Everything I wanted to tell him, all the goodbyes and excuses, is gone. Drifted away into nothingness and forgotten. None of that seems to make sense anymore. The only thing that does make sense is me in his arms, our bodies fitting into each other and somehow causing everything to fall into place, right where everything should be. That's what he is doing. Righting every wrong, convincing me that every doubt in my mind should be thrown away and be traded for the surest thing that ever existed. Him and me.

"Let's take you home," he whispers. I silently nod as he takes my hand.

My lips are still tingling from Rhylan's kiss. My fingers trace my lower lip, a tender throbbing taking over the absence of his lips on mine. Our feet crunch along the gravel, loud and vocal in the ever so present silence. My hand is wrapped inside his, and I don't miss the strong reassurance his hold has on me. He leads the way to his car with no words between us. Just the understanding that we shouldn't be here. Not when the atmosphere is so destructive. When I'm with Rhylan, just the two of us, we're fine. Better than fine; we're ideal.

When the light slams of the car doors enclose us in Rhylan's car, I look at him, still apologetic that the night has taken a different turn because of me. Had I not been with him tonight, he would still be inside, enjoying his time while mingling with the crowd that he's familiar with.

"I'm sorry you had to leave the party," I whisper. I'm also apologizing for disrupting a part of his life that he has grown accustomed to. For the scene that I caused, leaving a deep red stain on the impeccable marble floor while Rhylan chased after me. For not being everything that should fit perfectly into his polished, Hollywood life in thousand-dollar dresses and an established taste for fine art. For almost wishing that he isn't *Rhylan Matthews* and simply just Rhylan instead.

"Ellie…" he says, his face lowered and eyes closed. His words are so soft but filled to the brim with pain. I can feel it, from the hoarseness in his voice to the strain that sits in his throat, exposing the damage that I know is there. And that's it. He doesn't say anything else. He starts his car and drives off, one hand on the steering wheel and the other on the gear shift, moving effortlessly, all while his expression stays the same.

I'm full of unease. I don't have the right words to say. Just a foreboding in my bones that I can't ignore. My eyes keep wandering to him. His hands moving in small movements, the muscles in his forearms tensing as he drives, emanating the words that are sitting between us. When he pulls to a stop in front of my house, the engine stills and quiets.

It's then that he finally looks at me, and I melt. I thought I would see resentment, but his eyes are far from any malicious thought possible. I feel all the tension thaw through my chest, leaving behind a warm sense of hope.

His jaw ticks, his brows knitted together as he considers his next words. He swallows before he speaks. "Ellie, can I ask you something?"

I nod.

"Can you be patient with me?"

Patient? With him?

I don't understand. But what I do know is that he isn't just asking for patience. He's asking me to trust him, to reserve my faith for him. I nod again. And when he sees the affirming dip of my chin, he takes my hand in his and squeezes, smiling solemnly at our connected hands before letting go.

Once inside my dark empty house, I close the door behind me, and my knees give out as my body sinks to the floor. With my face buried in my hands, I sigh and let the sudden licks from Angus's greeting take over, momentarily distracting me from one simple fact: I kissed Rhylan Matthews.

CHAPTER 19

Rhylan

My alarm blares on my nightstand. I roll over and peep my left eye open to peek at the time.

8:00 a.m.

I was dreaming. Not a good dream or a bad dream but a dream that felt real and fake at the same time. The kind of dream where you can't differentiate what's real or not, so you kind of go along with everything that's happening. Right now, I only remember flashes of it, like Ellie's brown eyes. When I looked into them, all I saw was a never-ending warmth that drew me in and wrapped me in comfort. And I remember seeing Constance's large head bobbing from left to right like a chicken, squawking in a tongue that I couldn't understand, all high-pitched gibberish. I even remember partygoers dressed to the nines laughing and drinking while Ellie and I stood on the sidelines, watching and feeling out of place. Like I said, not a good dream but not a bad dream. Just a dream that doesn't make any sense but somehow fits into the story that is my life.

I groan, still tired from a fitful sleep. The last time I looked at the glowing lights on my clock, it showed 1:47. In between the dreams, I saw Ellie's face when I closed my eyes. How hurt she was after Constance's words cut deep into her character. How I saw the tears that pooled in the corner of her eyes as she pretended like those words didn't hurt her as much as they did. And how her eyes lit with fire when I kissed her. How her breathing labored and skin heated when I touched her.

I can't stop thinking about her.

I pull myself out of bed, peeling back the covers and sitting at the edge with my elbows resting on my knees, my phone between my hands. My thumbs hover over Ellie's number.

Me: Good morning, Ellie. This is Rhylan.

I text her, starting a brand-new text message thread on my phone.

I don't wait for a response. Instead, I trudge to the bathroom and quickly wash up before the temptation of my warm bed takes over and I forgo leaving the house altogether. Once I'm dressed, I walk back to my nightstand and see a notification on my phone, Ellie's name written in bold across my screen. *She texted me back.*

Ellie: Good morning.

So sweet and simple. It almost feels too easy, these early morning greetings to start our day. Following them with *what did you have for lunch* conversations or *I hate LA traffic* rants, occurring as if we've been doing it for years. Expecting her to remain a part of my life in a way that feels natural and routine. *Too easy.*

> **Me:** Are you free today?

I fought all night with the demons that told me to get real, snap out of it, and stop acting like a lovesick teenager. And I came to the teetering conclusion: What if? What if I decide to let my heart lead the way, and I'm actually happy? What if when I decide to let Ellie in, I find a home that I never knew could exist?

> **Ellie:** I have class until about noon. And then I'm free the rest of the day.

She adds a little smiling emoji at the end of her message.

> **Me:** Perfect. I'll have someone to pick you up at your house. Is 1 p.m. okay?

The three dots indicating that she's tapping out her message pop up and then disappear. Maybe I'm being too forward. Maybe I should have waited a couple of days to see her. We were together not even twenty-four hours ago, and I'm already texting her like an overzealous teenager with raging hormones. And then, just as I brood over my impatient and eager texting etiquette, my phone buzzes, indicating a new message.

> **Ellie:** Sure. 1 sounds good.

I sigh out a breath of relief. I was starting to actually feel like that overzealous teenager. My emotions are all over the place, and I'm feeling more anxious than usual with the anticipation of seeing Ellie again. I literally have not felt like this since high school. I usually have a more blasé approach to women, just seeing what happens and letting things take their course naturally. But this is different.

When I check the time, it's almost nine a.m. *Shit!* I was so busy texting Ellie and waiting for her to respond, I haven't even realized the time had passed.

The short drive to Levi's office has turned into a long one because of the rush hour traffic, heavy with 9 to 5'ers heading into their offices. The thick layer of white sheets bound together sits on the passenger seat. I peer down and see the bold letters in the center of the front page. *Aurielle.* When I try to decide what I want my next move to be, my mind keeps coming back to this project.

My car is greeted by the valet, and I hop in the elevator right off the main lobby, remaining silent as I wait to get off on the twenty-second floor.

My feet lightly hit the marble floor as the sound of ringing telephones greets me. It's busy and hectic, but I snake my way to Levi's office. I'm greeted by his assistant who's frantic but calm, as I'm sure Levi has stressed that she is to never look frazzled and always be in control, no matter what shit storm has hit her.

"I don't really have an appointment, but Levi knows I'm coming to see him today."

She looks up at me, cordial and professional. "Of course, Mr. Matthews." She promptly picks up her phone to dial Levi. "He'll see you right away," she informs me and gestures towards the entrance of his office.

Levi is pacing the span of his office, earpiece glued to the side of his face. He quickly whispers something to whomever is on the other side of the call, something along the lines of "got to go" before he hangs up the call.

"Rhylan! How's it going?" he exclaims. He's hectic, always shooting question after question, never waiting for an answer. He's the definition of the old saying "time is money."

I hesitate a moment, stuttering through my answer. "I–I'm good." I fidget with the script in my hand, curling the edges along my thumb. I feel nervous, but Levi doesn't seem to notice.

"Great! Hey, so I heard some buzz on *Unrestrained,* and it's sounding good and loud." He claps his hands in excitement. "This might be your year for that Oscar nom. Or at least another People's Choice."

I nod. "Richard was still sounding pretty pushy about his project yesterday. Have you reconsidered?"

He shakes his head. "I know, but, like I said before, we need to take a step back and decide what we really want. With *Unrestrained* being such a success, we need to make sure we choose your next project wisely."

"That's actually why I'm here," I respond. My voice is shaky as my hold on the script grows firm. As if by treating it carelessly, it would misinterpret my intent. He looks at me, brows raised with skepticism and curiosity. "I wanted to talk to you about this."

I place the thick script on his glass desk. The word *Aurielle* in large block letters sits dead center, facing him.

"What is this?" he asks.

"Your office sent that to me a couple of weeks ago. I want the male lead." It's been a long time since I came to Levi with any prospects for a movie that I want to actively pursue. Usually, he brings the scripts to me, and it takes more than a few minutes for him to convince me to take the role. This isn't our usual exchange.

"What about the Reese Witherspoon movie? The rom-com. They're still casting and after *Unrestrained*, I think the producers want you even more."

"Yeah, but I read this script, and I want to do this."

Levi reaches for the script and flips through the first couple of pages.

"You've never done anything like this." He looks at me, surprised. He's right. I've never had any interest in starring in a tragic romance-drama. My IMDb list is full of action and rom-coms that'll bring enough entertainment for my fans to last beyond my lifetime. But I finally want to branch out. I fell into this romance between Aurielle and Thom, her husband. It's a story of soulmates.

"Okay, I'll call the producers, see if they want to see you." He sighs. "But I still think you should consider the Reese Witherspoon movie. I think you'd be a shoo-in for the part."

"I'll think about it," I agree. There's a beat of silence between us. "I also have a little favor to ask. A personal one."

"Shoot."

"You think I could use The Ladybird today?"

"Today?" He nods. "Sure, I can make a call and have it ready in a couple of hours."

"Great, thanks."

"Big party planned?" he asks.

"No, more like a date." I smile, thinking of Ellie.

"Is it the girl from the party? Ellen, is it?"

"Ellie. Yeah, it is."

He doesn't say anything as he shrugs his shoulders.

"Is there something wrong with that?"

"No, nothing wrong." His tone is unconvincing. Like he wants to say something but he's keeping his thoughts to himself.

"What?"

"Just take things slow," he finally says after a hesitant pause. His advice is guarded, one that he wants to give but doesn't feel comfortable meddling in.

"You've never seemed too concerned about my personal life before."

He hesitates before speaking again. "Yeah, but she's not from here."

"She grew up in LA."

He lowers his chin, causing his brows to furrow as he keeps his eyes on me. "You know what I mean. She doesn't understand your life. It'll only be a matter of time until she realizes how different things are in our world." His words hit me like a rock, straight to the chest while pouring over the guilt of hoping, even for a second, that Ellie and I could have evolved into something.

I huff, which comes out as a light scoff.

"Listen," he continues. "You're an adult. I'm not here to tell you how to live your life. Just don't rush into anything."

"Yeah," I answer, my gaze aimed at the floor, away from Levi.

I can't believe what I'm hearing. It's as if the second I landed my first leading role, I made a deal with the devil, selling my soul in exchange for stardom. Any hint of a life that doesn't revolve around notoriety was left in the dust, the possibility of me and Ellie buried under it, making me realize that we don't add up.

"And be careful," Levi adds.

"Will do." I pick up the script and walk towards the glass doors, leaving behind the shrill sounds of ringing telephones that never seem to stop and the obvious doubts that surround whatever is blossoming between myself and Ellie.

"**Y**ou *what*?!"

I wince at the high-pitched sound of Claire's voice playing over the Bluetooth on my speakers as I drive into school. I quietly gasp as I locate an empty spot almost as soon as I pull into the packed parking lot, a miracle for morning class hour standards.

"I told you. Rhylan Matthews showed up at my house, and he took me out for a drive. And then we went to a party, and I saw that Richard person that you work with." I jerk the gear shift into park and sit, finishing out my conversation with Claire.

"Okay, hold up. You're going to have to rewind back to the beginning. What the hell was he doing at your house?"

I sigh deeply. "Honestly, I don't even know."

"Is the guy stalking you or something?"

"No. At least, I don't think so."

"Holy shit, Ellie. What is even happening? Rhylan Matthews shows up at your house, and you talk about it so casually. Like a relative was visiting or something."

I don't know what to tell her. Was it something? Or nothing? I have no answers for her. Just the simple fact that he appeared in front of my house, completely unannounced and out of nowhere. And we kissed. We *kissed*.

My history of romantic relationships isn't that extensive. There was a short-lived boyfriend in junior high who I would hold hands with during lunchtime and pass intricately folded notes to, followed by a handful of dates to school functions like football games, homecoming, and prom. I dated around when I first started college, enjoying the party scene and meeting new people as best as I could. Claire coaxed that side of me to the surface. Without her, I would have missed out on a lot of coed experiences. Experiences that I thoroughly enjoyed and equally regretted. And then there was Jimmy. We dated a whole seven and a half months my sophomore year of college until we parted ways right before summer break when he decided to go to Spain to study abroad for his junior year. There was no passion or heartbreak, just a mutual understanding that what we had had run its course and we would part ways as friends. Last I heard, he stayed in Spain, shacking up with a local and foregoing a college degree altogether. None of those relationships were passionate or life-altering but meaningful enough to have made a dent and left a fond mark.

But this kiss…

Fireworks was the only way to explain it. I always thought describing any kind of romantic encounter as fireworks to be cliche and cheesy. I always rolled my eyes at the notion, but this was exactly that: *fireworks*. I had never been kissed the way Rhylan had kissed me, so passionate and hungry. It was enough to erase everything working against us, just for a moment.

"Okay, don't freak out over what I'm about to tell you because I honestly don't even know what it means, but it just happened, and I'm so confused and—"

"Just tell me," Claire interrupts.

"We kissed." My words are a whisper, as if someone else but Claire might hear our conversation. Or maybe it's that I don't even believe the words myself, so if I whisper them instead, I can hold on to it being a dream a little longer. Then maybe I don't have to face the reality of what that kiss meant.

Claire screams through the phone. Actually, the sound that comes out of her is a sound wave that only canines can recognize. I reach for the knob to lower the volume, wincing once again at the sheer loudness.

Then, as if intrusively invading my thoughts, I smile. Images of our night together flicker through my mind. Good ones and bad ones, all making me feel things that I can't place. My emotions are a wreck, but I can't even protest the warmth in my heart.

When Claire's high-pitched squeals have died down to the heaviness of her breathing, I throw her another bone.

"And he texted me this morning. He's sending someone to pick me up this afternoon after I get out of class."

"Eleanor! Did you sleep with him?"

"What?! No! Claire, I told you, we just kissed."

"Oh my God, Ellie. He is *so* hot. I can't even wrap my head around what's happening. You're dating Rhylan Matthews."

"What are you talking about? I'm not *dating* him, Claire."

"You guys are hanging out and *kissing*. And you're seeing

him again! That's basically dating in my book."

"That is an exaggerated assumption. Don't go calling all the tabloids now."

"I can see it now. My exclusive interview for *E! News.* 'Why, yes, I am a very close friend of the couple, and I can confirm that the two are very much in love.'"

I burst into giggles. "I have to go, Claire. I have to get to class!"

"Okay, but Eleanor. If you fuck this man, please tell me every single detail. I mean it. You have to swear on my life that you will not spare a single detail."

"Why are you so vulgar? I am not going to 'fuck' him," I respond with an emphasis on her crudeness.

"Well, just tell me every detail of what happens between you two. As your best friend, I think you owe me that," she says.

"Fine. Now, please. I really have to go!" I smile as I plead, the giddiness showing through my voice. As serious as I try to be and fail in my attempt to hide my impatience, Claire knows the gravity of the situation.

"Okay. But Ellie, in all seriousness, whatever happens between you two, just be in the moment. Don't let your crazy head take over and ruin a good thing."

I nod as I silently agree to her request. And as I try to answer her, my throat constricts, choking back my words and thinking about how it's difficult for me to do as she's saying. Already, Constance's words have taken over any shielded optimism, turning it into a sour taste in my mouth. It's the basis of the tug of war that my heart keeps playing, toying with my emotions to the point of exhaustion. It makes me want to give up, throw in the towel, and move on as if none of this ever happened. *But what if?*

"Ellie?" she calls when I stay silent.

"I heard you. I'll try," I answer softly.

"Okay, text me later."

The line turns silent, signaling the end of our conversation. I sigh.

Just be in the moment.

"Who is that?" my mom questions, fingers pulling apart the horizontal blinds to our front room window. She shifts her weight between her feet as she peers left to right, her brows knitted together in a furrow as she examines who, or what, is outside.

I peek from behind her shoulder, ready for the barrage of questions that is to come once she realizes the guest on our street is for me. My hands work furiously to pull the zipper on my floral print dress that runs along my side. It strains against the fabric and fights every tug. I had barely made it home with enough time to change my clothes and take a few deep breaths to calm the butterflies that have taken residence in my stomach since this morning.

A black Suburban had pulled up outside my house, and a man in a black suit and sunglasses steps out of the driver's seat. He walks up to my driveway, squeezing his massive build between our cars as it's the only walkway available, and stops in front of my front door. The doorbell rings, and Angus trots towards the sound, most likely waking up from his nap from under the kitchen table. He sits in front of the door, tail wagging and ready to greet our unexpected guest.

"I got it!" I call out to my mom as I rush to the door in an attempt to answer it before she does. Without even looking at her, I know she's expecting an explanation. I open the door to find the same man waiting patiently on the other side. He's all business as I face him, and he towers over me.

"Ms. Eleanor?" he asks politely.

"Um, yes. That's me."

"My name is Hank. Mr. Matthews has asked me to pick you up and escort you to where he will be waiting," he explains formally.

"Okay. Can I have a minute, please? I'll be right out," I answer.

"Of course. Take your time."

I close the door and turn, only to crash into my mom who has a shocked look on her face.

"Who is that!" She repeats her previous question, now more of a demand rather than an inquiry.

"Mom! Please, I have to go," I plead.

"Ellie! You really aren't going to tell me what that's about? Who the hell is Mr. Matthews?" She follows me to my room, practically levitating around me as I hurriedly grab my purse and search for my keys.

"It's—What are you even doing home? Why aren't you at work?"

"Don't change the subject! I had an early day and brought the rest of my work home." Her hands move to her hips as she stands her ground. "You're not going to answer my question?"

"It's Rhylan Matthews. I met him at the premiere last month when I went with Claire."

"Rhylan Matthews?!"

I sigh. Actually, it's more of a suppressed groan. I slump before hurriedly searching for my platform sandals. I hook one of them on my heel, hopping to maintain momentum as I walk towards the door.

"So is this a date? When were you going to tell me about this?"

"No! I don't know," I say, flustered. "Mom, there's nothing to tell."

"Ellie!" she yells, dragging out the last syllable of my name.

"Mom, I have to go! We'll talk about it later," I say, walking past her. I rush to the front door and leave. I hear my mom yell something to me as the door closes, something along the lines of "be safe."

I walk to the sleek car waiting for me on the street. Hank, now waiting by the car, opens the door to the back passenger seat. I slowly climb in and whisper a "thank you" to him before he gently closes the door behind me.

After a silent and awkward drive, we pull up to the marina along the sparkling blue water with a line of lavish yachts parked up to the dock. Hank gets out, opens my door, and gestures for me to exit. As I slowly step out and smooth my hands across my dress, I look up to see Rhylan walking toward me. He looks so comfortable and relaxed. His white linen shirt, loose and casual, clings to his broad chest with every sweep of the ocean breeze while his strong arms are exposed right up to his elbows, just below the folds of his rolled-up sleeves. The unkempt mess of his hair only makes him more endearing as his face brightens with a smile that's radiant and beaming. Even with his unruly hair creating a shadow shielding his eyes, I see how blue they are, almost identical to the ocean behind him.

"Hi," he says and breathes through his smile, ducking his head. He remains coy, with his head hung low and his hands in his pockets. He looks at me with a sideways glance as his smile turns into a charming chuckle.

"Hello." I smile at him. I nervously bring my hand up close to my chest and wiggle my fingers to wave at him.

"I hope the ride in was okay. I had to take care of some things here."

I nod. "It was fine. Thank you."

"Um… I thought we could make use of some privacy, so I got us a boat for the day," he explains as he gestures towards the boat parked up to the dock.

"I–I'm sorry," I stutter. "A boat?"

He turns towards said boat behind him, but it isn't just a boat. It's a yacht. And not just any yacht. It's the kind that extremely wealthy people own and buy on a whim. The kind that I would have to do a Google search to see what they look like and never actually see in person. Rhylan must sense my surprise.

"Ellie, meet The Ladybird." When all I do is stare, open-mouthed and speechless, Rhylan's face changes. "I borrowed it for the day from a friend. It's not mine," he explains in a poor attempt to humble himself.

"Oh." What am I supposed to say to him? He has a *boat*. Or, no, it's not his, so I guess that's supposed to be okay? I feel so flustered.

I sigh and look up at him. "Uh, okay. Let's get on this little ladybird," I say, my voice all squeaky and high-pitched.

Rhylan reaches for my hand to guide me onto the yacht. His fingers interlace with mine, and his thumb grazes the back of my hand. Our eyes meet where we connect, somehow reassuring me and encouraging me to trust him at the same time. When he pulls my hand towards his mouth and gently kisses the back of it, my stomach quivers with butterflies. All the shock and surprise from a minute ago has dissipated as I look up at him and smile, letting out a small laugh as I follow his lead.

We climb the steps to enter the yacht. It's so much brighter up on deck, as if the wood plankings are made of mirrors, reflecting everything under the sun. I use my hand to shield my eyes and try to refocus my vision.

"May I take your things?"

The sudden voice catches me off guard. When I turn, I see a woman dressed in a neatly pressed uniform, all colored in deep navy, extending her hand towards me. When I stare blankly, her smile tightens, her hand nudging towards the jacket slung across my arm.

"Oh," I whisper softly. I hand her my jacket as she reaches for my purse and turns towards the lower cabin to store my belongings.

Another woman dressed in an identical uniform approaches, her hand balancing a silver tray holding a bottle of champagne wedged in an ice bucket and two tall glasses. And I suppress a sarcastic "of course" when I see a third woman follow her steps carrying a large tray of fruits and chocolates, all arranged intricately. They carefully place everything on the long table next to me, one that I haven't realized I've been backed into as I take everything in.

I take a seat on the cushioned bench outlining the table, sitting right at the edge, and wait as Rhylan speaks to a man who looks like the captain in his embellished hat and uniform. They both turn and approach me.

"Hello, my name is David Aoti. I will be your captain this afternoon. The waters are clear, as is the weather ahead of us, so I have no reason to doubt a steady and uneventful journey for us," he says, reassuring me more than Rhylan.

I nod quietly and remain in my seat as Captain Aoti walks away, and Rhylan takes a seat next to me.

I hear music start to filter through the air. As I begin to assume it's coming from some hidden sound system strategically placed throughout the deck, I notice a woman sitting in the shaded corner. Her hair is pulled into a tight bun and a large cello is straddled between her legs as the deep timbre tunes of "Can't Help Falling in Love" start to pour over us.

"Is that Elvis?"

His brows lift. "You're familiar."

"It sounds beautiful."

"Champagne?" he asks, his hand already reaching for the chilled bottle.

I smile, one that doesn't quite reach my eyes, followed by a low hum that's meant to be a yes. He makes a show of unwrapping the tightly bound foil, revealing the lodged cork. When the pop of the cork startles me, he reaches for the glasses and fills them as the foam overflows the lip.

I look up at him, my shoulders hunched forward as he hands me my glass and I silently plead for an explanation.

"What?" he questions.

"What should I expect on a second date? A trip to Italy? Perhaps on a private plane?" I smile teasingly.

"So this is a date?" he teases back.

"No, I just mean… This can't be real. People don't really live like this."

"Some do. Like Jay-Z and Beyonce." He grins at me, playfulness bouncing in his eyes.

"Are you comparing yourself to Jay-Z and Beyonce?"

"Well, no. Because I don't own this yacht. And I don't have any Grammys."

"Hmm," I respond. "Technicalities."

He finally gives. "It belongs to the agency I'm part of. I usually borrow it as a way to get away from the paps from time to time. They usually can't get past the international waters, so it's a good way for me to avoid them. At least for the day."

"Rhylan," I say softly. "This is all so beautiful. The ocean, the music, the champagne. It's so wonderful, but you don't have to do this with me." I set down my glass.

None of this feels right. I want the Rhylan that I had a glimpse of last night. The Rhylan that didn't need a hundred tricks up his sleeve to feel important, wasn't hiding behind the wealthy exterior that I thought I had finally coaxed him out of.

"I would have been fine with takeout in your car again," I

add softly. I'm more thinking out loud rather than saying it to him, but it's still there, lingering between us. The realization that complicated isn't in our nature and that simplicity is what we thrive on. And I also say it because it's true. For some reason, when we're both situated inside our own personal bubble, all sense of formalities and hesitation disappear. I can say what I want to say without explanation or regrets. I just want us to be *us*.

His brows knit together. He turns to face me, his dark eyes causing my chest to tighten.

"I'm sorry," he whispers. His jaw ticks as he pauses, as if he's carefully thinking out his next words. And then they spill, all the truths pouring out of him. "This is all I know. I put on a show and expect everyone around me to *ooh* and *ahh*. It's hard for me to turn all that off. Once you strip all of that away, I'm just some guy that people are looking to tear to shreds. Looking for flaws or finding ways to poke at my life."

I reach my hand up to his cheek, the edges of his jaw meeting my fingertips. He closes his eyes and sighs, close-mouthed, letting all the tension lift away from him.

"There's not much left of me without being Rhylan Matthews. And what if that's not enough?" he finally says. It's the question that we always have in the back of our minds. What if we decide to be who we want to be, all of our walls torn down and our insides exposed, and we're rejected? *What if we're not enough?*

I let the silence fill his question, my heart aching from absorbing the pain that Rhylan so willingly let spill from him. I don't know how to let him know that we are all enough. In some way or form, we're all perfect for the right person.

I look into the distance as the ocean seems to go on and on. The reflection of the sun flashes brightly against the blue sea. I relish in the cool breeze as the engine roars to life, announcing the start of our departure. I look back into his eyes as his face turns, and he leans into my hand.

've always wondered what contentment feels like. It feels like such a broad emotion, ranging from happiness to excitement to calm. When you feel like you're enough, it must course alongside contentment. Because to feel content, you have to feel like everything you bring to the table is worth being there.

I do what I can to feel like I'm enough. I add my own flourish to things that are mundane. I stand behind my wealth and all of its perks. The perfect curtain to pull closed in front of me, to hide behind. No one's ever told me all of that's unnecessary. Until Ellie.

I pull Ellie close to me, her hair blowing in all directions as she mirrors my movements, wrapping her arms around my waist. I turn my cheek towards hers, brushing it against her skin in soft strokes.

If I can ever feel like I matter to anyone, to feel like I mean something to them and that I'm enough, I want it to be Ellie.

When I pull away from her, I see the furrow between her brows deepen as she gnaws on her lower lip and takes a shaky breath.

"I tried to kill myself when I was thirteen." As soon as the words leave her lips, she brings her thumb between her teeth, chewing at the hardened skin lining her nail painted in lavender polish. I take her hand off her lips before pressing it against my chest, my heart thumping against our tangled hands. Her downturned eyes peer up at me through her lashes. "It was about a year after my dad died, and I felt so hopeless." Her voice catches as she turns her hand in mine, weaving our fingers together while they remain over my heart. "I told you that I would shut my eyes to shut out the world, to pretend like I didn't exist in it. But that wasn't enough. So I thought that if…"

I nod, letting her know she doesn't need to finish. I already know. Shutting out the world wasn't enough. She thought ending her life would finally end the pain.

"But I regretted it. I realized that I couldn't do that to my mom… So I've been doing what I can to let her know that everything in my life is worth living for."

Her grip on me tightens.

"You need to know that you're enough too." She lifts her face, her eyes searching mine. "It doesn't matter if you're famous or not, your life is worth living for too. Just like mine."

The twisted knot in my chest pulls taut, the threads tightening and coiling as I swallow the lump formed in my throat.

"Ellie," I whisper.

Instead of answering, she nuzzles her cheek into my chest, pulling herself closer as my arms curl her towards me, my hold on her tightening.

"Thank you for telling me," I say gently into her hair. She sighs into my chest, nodding as my face buries deeper into her silky hair. I feel so touched, so honored that she would share such a raw piece of her with me. And I can't believe how brave she is to say all those things in an effort to comfort me. All so that I can know that I matter.

We stay wrapped in each other's arms, our bodies swaying as the bow and stern teeter-totters with the waves. The occasional breeze blows past us as a flock of seagulls hovers. We settle into a comfort that we somehow create, nestling within the cocoon of our pain where the solace of letting our guard down brings with it nothing but calm.

And as deeply gratified as I am that I've discovered this level of contentment, my cynical subconscious keeps reminding me that I should know better than to get so comfortable. To stop being so careless and to navigate through what's growing between us with caution.

When we return from our voyage, the sky is transitioning from a lingering orange glow to the dark blues and purples that will eventually fade into what will be a clear night. Twinkles of light peek through the sky that can only be seen over the ocean, where the air isn't tainted by the buzz of electricity and smog from the city. The air is cool and fragrant with a mixture of saltwater and oranges.

I help Ellie down the steps that lead us off the boat, her arms extended out to her sides so she doesn't lose her balance. When she steps off the last step, she trips and tumbles toward me. Luckily, my hand is close to hers, and I'm able to wrap my arm around her waist in time before she hits the ground. Both of us are barely a foot off the pavement, her hair billowing behind her, brushing the concrete.

"Are you okay?" I ask breathlessly.

She looks into my eyes and nods. I've never had her in my arms like this, holding her up with a splinter of space between us so that I could study her features up close, trailing my eyes down to her soft lips, remembering what it felt like to kiss her. Never looked so deeply, so intimately into her eyes. Her pupils are large, and her chest heaves up and down while I press her into me, as if she could still fall while I'm holding her this tight.

Her hand clings to my arm just so that she has something to hold on to. But I, too, need to hold on to her because if I don't, I feel like we would both float away. My eyes flit to her lips again as slow, uneven breaths escape her.

"Would it be completely cliché if I kissed you right now?" I whisper.

She laughs and shakes her head, the subtle movement making our noses brush. I angle my head to the side and lean in to kiss her, closed mouthed and soft. Her breath hitches, and I feel her hand grip my arm harder, clutching me as if she's telling me not to let her go. I can't let her go, not now.

I stand her upright. The sudden movement causes her to squeak, and her eyes widen. Still holding her close, I feel her pull away, and she looks up at me as a teasing smile starts to form on both of our lips.

She shakes her head at me. "Completely cliché," she finally says.

I laugh. This cliché moment feels everything but. If I was meant to dip Ellie into a long, passionate kiss with the late sunset as our backdrop, then so be it. It all seems to flow naturally.

Even though the nagging voice in the back of my head tells me that I can still stop here, walk away, and never look back, I don't want to. Whenever that voice pops in, reminding me that I'm not meant to be this happy, *this* sated, I want to tell it to fuck off and mind its own business. But I know at some point it'll come back around and tell me, *I told you so.*

Right now, with Ellie in my arms, her sweet smile looking up at me, and her tousled hair blowing in all directions, I want to actually believe that I don't have to listen to those nagging words telling me that I should know better. Right now, I just want time to stand still.

My clashing thoughts are interrupted by a high-pitched growl that comes from the nonexistent space where our torsos are touching. Ellie's eyes turn into saucers, and she covers her mouth with her hand.

"Was that you?" I ask her, stifling a laugh.

"Mm-hmm," she answers through her hand. She squeezes her eyes shut as her hands move to her eyes.

"I guess we should get you some food," I say, still laughing.

I finally let her go but still hold on to her hand. I interlace my fingers and pull her close when she attempts to keep a distance from me, bringing her hand to my lips and kissing the back of it. It's my favorite part of her to kiss. The way I take the lead but am still able to feel her bringing herself to me makes the act feel so personal and innate, like we've done it a million times.

We walk towards my car parked deep into the parking lot that's now mostly empty. When I get close, I notice shuffling in the trees and bushes that line the parking lot, behind the metal fence that closes off the lot from the main street. It's probably that I've conditioned myself to be paranoid, always being followed and never having a full moment of privacy that I get to call my own, but right then, I feel that we're being watched.

"Is everything okay?" Ellie asks.

I continue to stare, hoping that it's just my imagination. I don't see anything else, just dark shadows that are growing darker with the sun fully setting behind us.

"Yeah," I answer. "Sorry. I thought I saw something."

She continues to stare at me, waiting for me to move. I walk a little quicker, my pace picking up, then walk her to the passenger side and wait for her to get in. Once she's settled in, I don't close the door just yet. Instead, I duck my head down and kiss her. Just a light brush of my lips against hers. Her small, delicate fingers find my cheek, and her thumb strokes my chin. I pull away and smile at her.

"So, I guess we should get you some food. Shut that stomach up," I tease.

She laughs, and I close the door. When I round the back of my car, I look once more towards the back of the lot. Nothing. There are the same dark shadows that were there a minute ago. No ruffling of bushes, no shifty figures hiding behind them.

It was just my imagination.

Once I'm settled into my seat, I buckle in and start the car.

"Where are we going?" Ellie asks.

"It's a surprise." I turn to wink at her.

"You are just full of surprises today." She sits back and folds her hands in her lap.

We drive, and I turn on the stereo, the tape deck coming to life and the orange backlight marking the buttons.

"I still can't believe you have a cassette player in your car. I swear, I thought they outlawed those years ago."

I laugh. "It came with the car and was one of the only things that still worked, so I kept it. I guess I'll replace it if it goes out, but it hasn't steered me wrong yet."

I reach into the center console and pull out a cassette tape, holding it in the air between us. My eyes flit to her as she watches me.

"But it's a pain in the ass to get a hold of one of these babies."

I point the tape in the direction of the tape player. It sucks in the cassette, making clicking noises as it reads the plastic film wrapped around the spools, whirring as it takes position in the dash. I press a few more buttons and turn the dial so the volume is higher, and slow R&B music starts to filter through the speakers.

"I haven't heard music like this since my dad was alive," she says softly. "He had a soft spot for slow jams."

"Ah, your dad and I would've had a lot in common."

She smiles sweetly, blinking as she stares down at her lap. I look back at the road, knowing that the memory of her father makes her sad, reminiscent of a past that she once loved.

"Do you miss him?"

She turns to look at me, sadness covering her eyes. "Every day."

I nod. I can't tell her I understand. I've never lost someone so close to me. My parents are still alive and healthy, but I know that if anything happened to either one of them, I would be devastated.

"I'm sorry," I say. "I didn't mean to bring him up."

She shakes her head and places her hand on my arm resting on the gear shift. "No, it's okay. I hate acting like he never existed just because talking about him hurts. He wouldn't have wanted that. He would have wanted me to talk about him every day and laugh remembering how amazing he was."

I reach for her hand and bring it to my lips again, then move the back of her hand to my cheek and caress it against the stubble that has grown in since I shaved this morning. "You can talk to me about him whenever you want."

We pull into the small parking lot of a pizzeria after a slew of left and right turns, driving to the restaurant by memory. Best New York-style pizza on the West Coast, according to the large neon sign hanging off their glass entrance. I have to say, they aren't wrong. I've tried a handful of pizzas locally, and this mom-and-pop shop is the best I've had.

I park in a spot at the end of the lot, facing the busy street. We both simultaneously exit, the doors closing in unison. With a light hop in our steps, we walk into the pizza parlor to the inviting scent of floury dough and marinara sauce. In the dark parking lot, I was able to go about unnoticed, hold Ellie's hand and laugh with her without a second thought. But now, under the bright fluorescent lights, I feel the stares.

"I'll have a large cheese pizza," I say confidently to the cashier behind the register.

"Just cheese?" Ellie asks with skepticism, standing close next to me.

"Trust me." I wink at her just as I notice the clicking of phones around me, patrons attempting to be discreet as they snap candid images of me. I duck my head down, facing the counter once again. I pay for the pizza as it's being handed to me, and we both turn towards the door when the first person approaches us.

"Can we get a picture?" Two women, eyes round and twinkling in awe, look up at me, waiting for my answer.

"Uh, yeah. Sure."

I lean down, the phone turning in one of their hands. My face shows on the screen, the smile quick and fake. As soon as I hear the click go off, I stand straight, my smile shifting into a polite nod. I can see that behind them, there are more people that have gathered, waiting for their own chance to take a picture with me.

Before another person can ask, I take Ellie's hand and run, leaving behind the bewildered stares and growing clamor. We run to my car, laughing from the rush of our escape as we weave between the lot of parked cars. I have the pizza box held in one hand while I quickly open the car door to the driver's side. I don't even try to help Ellie to the passenger seat, as she's moving quicker than I am.

Once inside, Ellie's laughs die down, and she exhales deeply. "Does that happen everywhere you go?"

"Pretty much," I answer, balancing the pizza box in the

small space between us.

I drive off and find a place to park my car: a small empty parking lot that overlooks a low hill. Enough privacy for us to be left alone with no one asking me for a picture or impolitely staring.

The steam from the fresh pizza is seeping through the small slits made throughout the lid of the box. I finally open it, and the smell permeates through the car.

"Oh, that smells amazing," she groans. Her stomach growls again, this time more angrily. She moves her hand to her stomach as if trying to quiet it from the outside.

"Okay! It's coming. Sheesh!" I answer, speaking directly to her stomach.

"It's got a mind of its own," she answers. We both laugh uncontrollably while I pull out a slice using the large napkins supplied by the restaurant. The steam starts to fog the windows, making a temporary shield for us to hide behind.

"Here," I say, handing her the large slice. "Let's shut that stomach up."

She shoves almost half of the slice into her mouth, practically inhaling it without chewing.

"Mmm…" she groans. Her eyes cross as she sinks into the slice. "This is amazing."

I can't help but laugh. Watching her eat as if she's having an out-of-body experience is so cute. She finishes her slice with a couple more bites. I hand her another before grabbing my own, shaking my head and smiling with a suppressed laugh between bites as I eat my own serving a little more reservedly than her.

"What?" she asks, her mouth full.

"Nothing." I shake my head again. "You just eat like a baby panda that hasn't been fed all day."

She covers her mouth and gasps, embarrassed by my observation.

"It's good!" She defends herself, speaking with all the food in her mouth pushed to one side.

"No, I agree," I say. "It's just fascinating. Like watching a wild animal eat pizza for the first time."

She punches my arm, and I rub the spot where her small fist hit me. "Ow!"

"You know, it's not polite to comment on someone's eating habits." She holds her greasy hand up with a threat to rub it in my face.

My pizza slice drops, hitting the cardboard with a hollow thud. My hands move up to hold her wrists, my strength outmatching hers as she continues to fight me.

"Okay! Okay, I'm sorry," I exclaim, her wrists loosely wrapped in my hands.

"For…"

"For calling you a baby panda, even though I'm right."

"That's it!" She lunges towards me, her butt lifting off the seat, and my hold on her tightens. With my hands occupied, I use the only weapon at my disposal: my own greasy mouth. I pull her arms towards me, her face crashing into mine in the most playful way possible, and rub my face into hers, the oil smearing across her chin and cheeks.

"Oh my God!" she screams between breathless laughs.

My stomach hurts, the muscles tightening between my

laughs. I let go of her and grab a napkin to wipe her face. She sits patiently, her body shaking with suppressed laughter while I clean her up. Her eyes are still bright with laughter with the twinkling of tears pooling at the corners.

And then it hits me like a wrecking ball. I'm falling for her.

W e drive in silence, the soft sounds of nineties R&B filling the car. I watch Rhylan mouth along, the occasional words slipping through his lips in whispers. Not knowing the words, I watch with my head resting against the headrest, smiling and letting the wind blow my hair back.

With our stomachs full and lids heavy from a settled food coma, he's driving in the direction of my house. As exhausted as I am from the day, I'm not really ready to end the night. His car gets closer to my house, and I start to recognize the streets and landmarks that I use to find my way home on a daily basis. And then an idea pops into my head.

"Would you be willing to take a small detour?" I ask.

He turns to me, curious, with a single brow perked up. "What did you have in mind?"

"Just turn left on the third street down. On Odyssey," I explain. "And then I'll tell you where to go from there."

He follows my directions, looking carefully at the street names and watching closely so he won't miss the turns he's supposed to take. After two more lefts and a curve into a residential area, we stop in the parking lot of the YMCA.

"This is it?" he asks.

"Mm-hmm," I answer. I move first and step out of the parked car. He, too, exits and meets me at my side.

"The YMCA?"

"Mm-hmm," I say again.

"You're going to have to give me more than those 'mm-hmm's.'"

I smile at him. "I used to come here every summer up until I started junior high."

I take his hand and lead the way towards the side entrance, just past the iron gates. I find the loose door that has a trick latch that never fully locks.

"And when my parents would pick me up," I continue, unlatching the door using the finger trick that I learned years ago, "I would use this gate instead of walking all the way around to the line-up, and I found out that it had a few kinks."

The gate finally clicks open and swings wide, creaking and hitting the wall behind it.

I tip my head towards the open gate and look at him. "Come on."

I walk in, expecting him to follow, and when he doesn't, I turn back to look at him. He hesitates, looking over his shoulder tentatively. His posture is stiff as he rocks back and forth on the balls of his feet and stuffs his hands into his pockets.

"It's okay." I try to reassure him, smiling coyly. "We're only trespassing."

He huffs awkwardly and smiles. I turn to walk back towards him and link my arm through his.

"I've done this a hundred times. We're fine."

He sighs, running his hand through his hair. "Okay," he says, finally surrendering.

We take a step towards the gate as Rhylan gently closes it behind him. He looks one last time beyond the empty lot before following me, and I lead him towards another door to a large building. The metal bar clanks as I push it down to open the heavy door. Before we even walk in, I can see the glistening lights bounce off the walls like a disco ball.

"It's a pool," Rhylan states.

"Mm-hmm," I confirm. I step closer in, and Rhylan again gently closes the door behind him instead of letting it slam. He's being cautious not to make any loud noises. I walk towards the deep end of the pool and lower myself to sit on the concrete before slipping off my sandals and dipping my feet in the cool water.

"Sit," I say, smiling and patting the seat next to me. The water feels soothing, thawing the tension as it always has in the past. I lean back on my hands and close my eyes, inhaling the lingering scent of chlorine and moisture.

Rhylan saunters over and comes to a stop next to me. He slips off his boots one by one, using the other foot to unhook the heel, and rolls up his pant legs. He sits next to me and soaks his feet in the water, mirroring my movements. As the minutes pass, he relaxes. He swings his feet in the water, splashing and causing ripples that move towards the other end of the pool.

"You said you do this often?" he asks, his eyes focused on the water in front of him.

I nod. "It's close to my house, so I used to ride my bike over here in high school before I started driving. I would sneak in here in the middle of the night. The water's calming."

"Ever jump in?"

"No!" I laugh.

"Why not?"

"I don't know. It never really crossed my mind, I guess."

"Well, it should," he says with a hint of mischief in his voice. He suddenly pulls his feet out, the pull of water causing a small tidal wave to spill from the pool. I lift my legs to avoid getting wet and yelp, bringing my hands up to shield myself. Then he starts to undress, skillfully removing his shirt, pulling it over his shoulders before letting it rustle up his hair. He shakes his head when he reappears, and his eyes meet mine, playfulness written all over them. His brows wriggle upwards, teasing and making me blush in response. After unbuttoning his pants and shimmying them down, he kicks them off and leaves them on top of the rest of his clothes.

He's now in just his boxer briefs, and my eyes wander from his hard chest to his chiseled abs and down to his long legs. His lean, muscular body is so much more detailed than when I've seen him in movies. I notice every ridge and curve that defines each muscle, like the deep *V* that forms at his hips and the striated muscles that pull along the length of his thighs. He's the perfect shade of tan and smooth, coating his entire body without a single tan line. *How?*

He steps backward, making space between himself and the water. And then he starts running before launching himself towards the center of the pool and cannonballing into the water. The loud splash echoes off the high walls, the movement of the water causing the reflection to shimmer wildly.

I yelp. The water splashes me, and the bottom hem of my dress is now soaked. He then reappears from under the water, shaking his hair out, making little ripples from the droplets that land around him.

"Are you going to join me?"

I shake my head, smiling shyly and lowering my head.

"What?!" he exclaims, arguing my refusal. "Come on! You aren't going to let me swim all by myself, are you?"

He splashes water in my direction, the water hitting my face in small specks. He smiles so brightly that I can't help but wonder what it would feel like to join him, to let all of my inhibitions go and live in the moment, just like Claire told me to.

I decide I don't need to wonder.

I stand and struggle to unzip my dress, the soft material catching on the zipper. When I finally loosen it, I tug the zipper down slowly, my hands trembling and my heart beating frantically in the walls of my chest. As I pull my arms out of the capped sleeves of my dress, I see Rhylan watch me. His movements have calmed, his arms and legs coursing through the water to help keep him afloat. His expression is serious and intensely pensive, and it makes me feel vulnerable. Our eyes stay connected, and I watch him swallow when I finally lower my dress and let it pool at my feet.

I'm left in nothing but my unmatched bra and underwear. I feel so exposed, all bare and naked. I cross my arms in front of me to cover myself, but it's no use. All it does is cover my midsection. Before I lose the courage to get in the water, I dip my toes in.

I gasp. "It's freezing!" When I was just dipping my feet, it didn't feel so cold. Now, the anticipation of my whole body being submerged seems to have brought it down twenty degrees.

Rhylan swims towards me, his long arms gliding along the water and his hair flicking with wetness. "It's not too bad once you're inside."

He moves so he's leaned against the ledge and raises his hand up to help me in. I place my hand in his, slowly dipping more of my body in the water. He moves both of his hands to my waist, and then I fully immerse myself. I draw in a sharp breath, the sudden iciness of the water hitting my core. I'm against the ledge now, my back hitting the small tiles that line the edges. His hands are on both sides of me, holding on while the rest of his body bobs up and down. He's inches away from my face, the water dripping from his hair and nose.

My heart starts humming, no longer measured beats but a buzzing that I can't seem to control. His proximity is unnerving, and I can feel the heat radiating from him. He's right. It's not that bad now that I'm inside. But I don't think it has much to do with my body adjusting to the cold and more to do with Rhylan being so close to me.

But I still shiver. Nerves take over every loose thought in my mind. The trembling starts from my knees, sneaking up towards my chest, making my breathing erratic. He sees me shaking and snakes his arm behind me to bring us closer, our faces touching in light sweeps.

"I guess it is a little cold," he says. His voice is low and hoarse. He closes his mouth and swallows, his Adam's apple moving up and down his throat. I bring my arm up and drape it on his shoulder, my hand wrapping around his neck and naturally bringing us closer.

His eyes grow dark, pupils filling the blue, and it's almost frightening. And then, before I'm able to say another word or make another sound, his lips crash into mine.

Now, when a momentous event occurs in your life, you do everything you can to savor it. You try to remember the bits and pieces so that you can relive them later. But it never works out that way. When the adrenaline starts to course through your body, you forget those details. They become a distant memory, and you can't really remember if it actually happened or if you dreamed it.

That's how this moment feels. I try to delve into each movement that Rhylan makes. The way his hands move up my back and dig into my neck. How his tongue forces its way into my mouth, gliding across and coating it. How my legs find themselves wrapped around his waist just so I have something to hold on to. How the moans that escape me only urge him on, making his kisses become hungry and urgent.

Breathless, he pulls away and leans his forehead against mine. Our breathing is in sync, deep and ragged. My hand moves to his jaw, and I feel it tick under my touch. This kiss was different from our first. This was full of passion, not sorrow. It didn't come from a place of unrelenting ache. It came from a fervor that we had been trying to suppress in an attempt to avoid the buzzing electricity between us. To lie to ourselves and tell us that this wasn't different when we stood out to each other more than anyone we've ever encountered in our disenchanted past.

"What are you doing to me?" he asks, a whisper that barely leaves his lips. He looks so pained, his brows drawn together and his hold on me tightening, gripping me. As if it aches him to wonder why I'm here, ripping apart his life when it didn't need to be ripped apart.

Instead of answering, I move my hand over his heart, the heavy pulse palpable under my fingertips. "Your heart…" I whisper.

He covers my hand with his.

"It's beating so fast," I finally finish.

"I know," he whispers back. And I don't miss the way his voice stutters or the tremble in his hand. Or the rampant beating of my own heart, matching his.

CHAPTER 23

Rhylan

The heat from my shower is deliciously inviting. Even though it's still spring and LA is notorious for its warm weather, the cold from the pool hit deep in my bones. I let the water run down my back where the chill feels the worst and lean my hands against the marble tiles in the stall. Save for the trickling of water hitting the hard shower floor, it's quiet. My breathing feels echoed, the rasping of my breaths filling my ears as air moves in and out of my lungs.

After our detour to the community pool, I drove Ellie home in silence. The quiet music coming from my stereo was the only thing filling the silence. I watched from the corner of my eyes as Ellie wrung her hands in her lap, tugging down on the still damp edges of her dress. I reached for the dials on the dashboard, turning on the heat to warm her. My hands moved between us, but I didn't look at her. I couldn't.

I wish it was as easy as saying *I can promise you the world*, like a cheesy chick-flick where the guy sweeps the girl off her feet, and they live happily ever after. But it's not that easy. My *life* isn't that simple. It's complicated. And messy, and everything in between. I don't want Ellie to be a part of that life.

But I can't end this now, not when I'm in so deep. Not when I've gotten a taste of her. When I've seen how happy we can be when it's just us two. Not when I've fallen this hard for her.

I keep picturing the two of us on a secluded island. Me chasing her on the sand, us splashing water at each other. Spending our days lazily lying on the sunny beach, our bodies always touching. I picture it without the shame of forged optimism because it's just that. An idea of us that I want to dream into reality, knowing that I'm being ignorant.

I pulled up to her house, coming to a sudden stop. I dug deep to find the will to watch her walk away and trust that she'll come back, knowing that she shouldn't.

"I had fun today," she said, her tone teasing and playful, with a soft smile. She let out a small sigh, and I could see her already reminiscing about the day we had. Memories that I wish I could imbed in our minds and live off forever. Memories that I wish could fuel what we have so that it could be something great.

"I did too," I said. I finally smiled. I couldn't help it. Looking at her, watching her face and the way it expressed every thought she was thinking, softened my resentment. I couldn't help but think that if my chance of happiness were to ever present itself, it would be through her. "I can scratch 'trespassing' off my bucket list."

"And I can scratch 'riding a yacht' off of mine," she rebutted.

I took her hand and kissed the back of it. My intention was to leave it at that, not go any further until I was able to calm the raging war that had been pulling my heart into two different directions. But when she looked at me expectantly, I didn't know if I could watch her walk away without the last touch between us being our lips. I leaned in towards her, bringing my hand to her cheek. Before she had a chance to stop me, I guided her face towards me and kissed her. Not a quick brush on the lips but a deep kiss that kept me wanting more. Her full lips parted as she welcomed my tongue gliding across the ridges of her mouth. I moved my fingers to her neck and gently gripped her nape, grazing my thumb against her chin to her jaw. She leaned into me, deepening the kiss and giving a moan so soft that I felt I had imagined it.

I couldn't let go now. It was a kiss, meant to be nothing more, but it was so much. It was everything. *Everything.*

I pulled away, rested my forehead against hers, and clenched my jaw. The tightness that had balled and knotted in my chest relented to a pain that spread to my stomach. How was I going to walk away from this? How was I supposed to move on and act as if Ellie didn't exist in the same world that I did?

I didn't know how to retract, to reel in everything between us to make it mean nothing. To act as if every moment that we shared was a moment that I shared with everyone, meaningless and generic. Because that wasn't the case. None of our time together was meaningless *or* generic. It was like those moments were custom-made for us, tailored and meant only to be lived and experienced by us two. If anyone else, it wouldn't make sense, and all the pieces that should fit would fall apart.

Everything in me was telling me to drive off. To safely leave her behind and never look back. I wanted to believe that doing so would be in our best interest. An easy way not to get hurt. While all these thoughts swirled in my mind, I watched her walk away. I watched as her small movements shifted her body to face me. She wiggled her small fingers to wave goodbye before disappearing into her house.

Now, in the reality of my own home, I come face to face with the gravity of what transpired between myself and Ellie. I try to reason with my stubborn doubt. I want to tell it to stop being so uncompromising and to give love a chance. A chance to find something that'll bring me back to life. But this conflict is one that I can't seem to settle.

With a towel wrapped around my waist, I turn to look at my phone. An alert for a message pings. It's from Ellie.

Ellie: Thank you again for today.

Along with the message is an image of us on the boat with the wind blowing wildly around us as the ocean water waves rapidly in the background. Our smiles are wide, and our faces are infectiously bright, sundrenched, and drunkenly sated on bliss. Ellie's arm is draped around my shoulders, and her face is pressed close to mine so that we could both fit in the picture. Even through the blurriness of the image, she's beautiful. I don't mean an obvious beauty that women generally carry with them, although her attractiveness has always been obvious to me. Her beauty illuminates from her soul, shining through the tightly bound layers she uses to protect herself.

I can't help the smile that creeps across my face.

Me: You're welcome.

My fingers continue to hover over the keyboard as I think about what else I want to say to her. So many words that I'm keeping bottled up with the strongest dam that I can muster. And then it hits me. I'm becoming addicted. Addicted to this feeling of no longer being shrouded by a dark cloud that seemed to follow me everywhere. That cloud had now separated, and I only see sunshine. She is my sunshine, and I want to incessantly drench myself in the warmth of the sun forever.

Me: Ellie.

I carefully consider my next words.

Ellie: Yes?

Me: Please be patient with me.

I'm repeating my words, but they're my plea. My way of bargaining into her heart so that I have a reason to be there other than my own selfish reasons. Because I don't want to let her go. That's why I had initially said those words to her, to buy time. To stall so I could decide what we meant to each other. Now that I'm starting to figure it out, I need the time to prove to her that whatever trials we face, having each other is enough. We are enough for each other. To the bitter end.

My phone buzzes in my hand.

Ellie: I'm not going anywhere.

It's enough to quiet the battle in my already fragile heart, even if it's only temporary, while giving me the conviction and courage to not push Ellie away. Until the roaring of my own qualms, fighting this constant conflict, takes over.

"Ellie!"

My mom is calling me from the kitchen as if I'm still a teenager. Annoyed but curious, I get up from my bedroom floor where I had sprawled out and gotten comfortable with Angus. I walk into the kitchen and see my mom standing in front of the stove, quite literally cooking up a storm.

"So, I wanted to talk to you about meeting Mark." Her voice is cautious as her gaze is focused on the stove in front of her.

Mark?

"He's the man I told you about last month? The one I've been seeing?"

I nod. I had pushed the thought of my mom's new boyfriend (such a weird thing to say) and forgotten about meeting him. I guess I've been avoiding it altogether. Once I meet him, I won't be able to deny that he's real.

"We were talking about it and how does a quick dinner this weekend sound? Saturday? After you get off work?"

When I hesitate, she drops the wooden spoon that's in her hand and turns to face me.

"Ellie," she says. "I know this is a lot to take in, but I was hoping you could keep an open mind about it."

"Yeah, sorry." I sigh, my shoulders sagging in surrender. I force a small smile. "Saturday sounds good."

"Thank you," she says. "I really appreciate you meeting him, Ellie."

I smile deeper, the guilt of my reluctance actually convincing me to keep an open mind.

"So, this Rhylan Matthews guy," she starts, her voice carrying the implied tones of curiosity. Her hand reaches for more cooking utensils, her focus back on the stove.

I groan. "Mom, please. I don't really want to talk about it."

"I saw you two kiss in front of the house."

I look at her, surprised. Of course, she did. It wasn't as if we had kissed in some secret hideaway spot. It was right in front of our house.

"And I saw the way he looks at you," she adds.

"Are you spying on me?" I ask, trying to change the subject. I roll my eyes when she doesn't look away before bringing my hands into the air in surrender. "I don't know what it is, Mom." I sigh. Not labeling what we have may be the best thing for us. It might be what makes it work, for now.

"Well, the next time he comes by, maybe he can come to the door? Like an actual gentleman?"

"Sure, Mom."

"And maybe I can meet him?" she slyly suggests.

I deadpan, giving her a sideways glance.

She chuckles. "Anyways, don't get too comfortable. Dinner's going to be ready in a bit," she calls to me as I walk towards my room. I wave my hand in her direction to let her know that I heard her.

I smile at the mention of Rhylan's name. We hadn't been able to really make any concrete plans this week with my busy school schedule and some meetings he had with Levi and his publicist, but we've been on our phones nonstop. Last night, I sat on my bed with my phone propped up against a textbook as we FaceTimed for three hours while I attempted to study. He listened to my story about an eighty-year-old man that came into the bookstore looking for a copy of *Little Women* so he could read it to his wife who had recently been diagnosed with Alzheimer's, her memory constantly wavering in and out. He listened intently while I became teary-eyed, thinking about this man who didn't know if his wife would remember him each day, preparing for the worst but always staying by her side. While I did that, Rhylan filled me in on his days crammed with endless meetings, sifting through piles of scripts, and workouts at the gym. And then we stayed silent, enjoying each other's company in the only way that we could right now.

Through my small phone screen, I watched as whatever qualms he held in his chest dissipated. He smiled, laughed, and joked. All as if he had never asked me to be patient with him, to hold on to this idea of us. I watched more layers of him peel back as we situated into a new place in each other's lives. For those fleeting moments, I imagined a future for us, musing over what it would be like to call him my boyfriend and for him to introduce me as his girlfriend.

I slump back onto the floor in my room and lay my head down on a pillow, resting my feet upwards on the edge of my bed. My phone is held between my hands, and I scroll through the past messages between Rhylan and myself before my thumbs tap along the screen to punch out a new message.

> **Me:** My mom thinks you're not a gentleman.

I smile, knowing he's going to have something to say. He responds almost instantly.

> **Rhylan:** Apologies to milady. It was not my intention to have dishonored you. Please inform me how I may repent for my horrific actions.

I roll onto my stomach, laughing while staring at the screen. I respond back with a laughing emoji.

> **Rhylan:** Whatever I did for your mom to think I'm not a gentleman, can I make it up to you?

His tone is more serious, less mocking, even through text messages.

> **Me:** Depends on how.

> **Rhylan:** How about I start with meeting her?

I pause. Meeting my mom? My mom had suggested it too. But having the two of them actually meet, watching them exchange awkward greetings and seeing her swoon over him like she does when we watch one of his movies at home, is different. I'm not sure if I'm ready for that.

> **Me:** She did say she wanted to meet you.
> She saw you drop me off the other night.

> **Rhylan:** Then it's settled. I'm meeting
> your mom. We can't have her thinking
> that I'm not a gentleman.

He ends the conversation with a winking emoji. I hold the phone to my chest and smile.

"Come on in," I answer the door.

Rhylan stands on the other side of the threshold, his hair disheveled and slightly wet as if he has just gotten out of the shower. He's in sweatpants worn casually with a plain white undershirt. He smirks as his eyes travel down to my equally comfortable pajama pants, a plaid mesh of Christmas red and green. My hair's tied up haphazardly in a messy top bun, and my hoodie hangs loosely on my small shoulders.

It's Friday evening, and after a long week of homework, essays, and study groups, I called Rhylan to see if he was free. When he said yes, informing me he was already out, having finished an intense gym session and in need of a relaxed night in, I took advantage of the small window where our schedules didn't clash. I invited him over knowing that my mom would be with Aunt Janice for the night, though I didn't tell her that we'd have company. I offered my home as a place that felt secluded from the rest of the world, as privacy felt scarce in our relationship.

With him inside the comforts of my home, I feel like the sumptuous celebrity exterior of Rhylan has melted off, whittling us both down to the most informal and unpretentious form of ourselves. Rhylan slumps onto the couch, eyeing the selection of candies and the large bowl of popcorn sitting on the coffee table. Before he's able to make his selection, Angus comes bounding in to sniff up a storm.

"That's Angus," I inform Rhylan.

He leans forward as his hand heavily pats the top of Angus's head, Angus's tongue hanging loosely from his open mouth. "You're an old soul, aren't you?" Angus slops Rhylan with a wet kiss as his smile deepens.

"So," I start. "I have *You've Got Mail, Serendipity, How To Lose A Guy In 10 Days,* and *She's All That.*"

Rhylan reaches for a bag of Twizzlers before perusing the options I've laid out for him. "Are you trying to drown me in estrogen?"

I lift a shoulder, smiling shyly. "Something like that."

"How about *She's All That,*" he decides. "I haven't seen that one."

"Excuse me?" I say with a gasp. "How have you not seen the greatest nineties movie of all time?"

He shrugs. "It's on my queue. I just never got around to it."

"Well tonight is your lucky night, sir."

An hour into the movie with Angus's head lying heavily on Rhylan's lap and Rhylan's arm draped over the back of the couch behind me, I notice how tonight is different from any other time we've spent together. The cocoon we've created that encases us in a protective shelter from everything else in the world makes the both of us feel safe and hopeful that maybe this can be our new norm.

I'm slowly learning more things about Rhylan. Like that he's a dog person, and that he prefers the tongue-shockingly sweet flavor of candies over the savory taste of salty snacks like popcorn or potato chips. Or that he prefers drama flicks over rom-coms, even though he's starred in a dozen of them. And he's finding out similar quirks about me too. Like the fact that I incessantly talk during movies, or that, even when it's hot, I wear sweaters and cozy socks to stay comfortable.

As our attention sways in and out from the movie, he asks me questions. Random topics pertaining to my day to day.

"Do you have any plans this weekend?" he asks through a mouthful of Peanut M&M's.

"I'm having dinner with my mom and her new boyfriend." I put an emphasis on the word *boyfriend*. I'm still getting used to the word when linked to my mom, and it's still a bit unsettling.

His brows furrow. "Is this the first time you're meeting him?"

I nod through pursed lips. "I haven't told her, but… I'm a little nervous."

He doesn't ask why or question my intentions. Instead, he silently listens as I slowly pour out my wavering uncertainty.

"It's nothing against him," I explain. "I just don't know if I'm ready to see my mom with someone new. I still miss my dad, and I almost feel like the memory of him has faded away. And with this new boyfriend… It'll be like he never existed."

"Maybe talking to her might help though," he offers. "If she understood what you're going through, it could be easier for the both of you."

I shake my head. "I don't know how to bring it up to her. Everything about my dad and his death… All of that is kind of off-limits here. We don't really talk about it."

The furrow in his brows deepens as the beginning tunes of "The Rockafeller Skank" play in the background off of my TV set.

"Anyways," I say, cutting into the worrying tension spilling off Rhylan. "I just need to get through dinner tomorrow." I smile at him as his face softens and a smile peeks through. "What about you? What are your plans for the weekend?"

"I have a meeting with my publicist for lunch tomorrow about some charity event next month," he answers, his thumb running over the indent between Angus's brows.

"What kind of charity?"

"For the cancer center at the children's hospital," he answers. "Apparently, they took a liking to my car and asked me to bring it in for some pictures with the kids."

The inner corners of my brows turn up as an audible *aw* sound squeaks through my lips. "That's so sweet."

He chuckles. "It'll be nice to see the kids."

"I never really tell anyone this but my cousin Walter has been in remission from melanoma for the past eight years. My aunt and uncle caught it early, and he had a good prognosis since it's a pretty mild form of cancer, but it was a pretty big scare considering he was only thirteen when they found out."

He smiles, his grip on my shoulder tightening as I lean closer into him.

"It's really nice that you're doing this," I add.

"I wish I could say that I was doing it for the charity part," he says, somewhat strained. "But Shana digs up these events, and I usually just go wherever she points to."

"Well, I still think it's nice that you're using your fame for good."

He looks at me, his eyes almost twinkling as a small smile curves at the edges of his mouth.

"What?"

He shakes his head. "Nothing."

"I feel like it's something."

After a beat of silence, he lowers his head, the tips of his hair tickling my cheek. "I was just thinking that when you say things like that, you make it seem like I'm a better person than I actually am."

I shift on the couch, turning to face him as I tuck my feet underneath my butt. "What are you talking about, Rhylan? You *are* a good person. I don't know how you can think that every bit of you isn't made up of kindness and consideration."

"You sound like a motivational poster," he jokes through a side-eyed smile.

I shove at him, my hand pushing against his chest as he moves to cover it with his. He brings my hand up to his lips, kissing the back of it as he threads his fingers through.

"I'm being serious," I say, my voice lowered. "Rhylan, you're a good person."

"Thank you," he whispers.

His hand untangles itself from mine and moves to my cheek, cupping it as his thumb runs along my lower lip. He leans in to kiss me, his movements slow and cautious, while my hand reaches for his waist, pulling him closer to me. Our lips mold together softly, as if we're taking our time and he's wanting to discover every part of me, inch by inch. While our previous kisses felt rushed or urgent, this is the complete opposite. I don't feel an ache that dissipates as our lips move together. Instead, it feels like a warmth blooming through my chest that Rhylan had planted there.

As his hands roam down my back and mine graze over his chest, he moves to hover over me, laying me down as I sink into the cushions. Our movements become heated as I hear his breathing become rapid, matching mine in equal rhythm. As my hand dips under his shirt, my fingers tracing the hard muscles of his stomach, we're interrupted by the sloppy wet kisses that Angus showers us with.

"Angus!" I shriek as Rhylan pulls away. He sighs, his head lowering onto my chest as he nuzzles into my sweater.

"I think someone's a little jealous," I whisper, my hand reaching to pat Angus as he patiently waits for Rhylan to climb off of me.

CHAPTER 25
Ellie

'm rushing to get home. I have just enough time to clock out at six o'clock on the dot, drive home, and quickly shower before our dinner reservation. As soon as I walk through my front door, my phone buzzes with a text message.

> **Mom:** I'm with Mark right now. We'll meet you at the restaurant.

I have an hour to spare before I have to meet my mom. My phone buzzes again but continuously, indicating a phone call coming through, not just a text message. It's Rhylan.

"Hi," I answer breathlessly.

"Hey," he responds. "What are you doing? Why are you so out of breath?"

"I just got home," I answer. "I'm heading out to dinner with my mom in a bit."

"Oh, right. You're meeting your mom's boyfriend."

"Yeah," I answer, my voice somber.

"Are you okay?" he asks, sensing the sullen tone in my voice.

"Um…"

My chin starts to tremble. I'm still trying to process how my mom has moved on. The woman who I tiptoe around. Never talk about my dad's death with, never able to process my grief. The woman who had forced me to grow up too quickly and be strong enough so she didn't have to see me hurt. She has now moved on and left me behind. I don't hate that she's moved on and found someone new. I just wish she could have taken me with her. I long for the closure that I never got to have. Deep inside, I'm still that twelve-year-old girl, sitting in the hard plastic chair at the hospital, listening to my mom sob. I want to grab that girl's shoulders in my hands and tell her it's okay to move on and be happy.

I let out a deep breath, cleansing my thoughts so I can have an open mind about tonight. "It's fine. I'll be fine. I just need to get through dinner."

"How about we do something after?" Rhylan suggests. "More milkshakes?"

I finally give a light giggle, mirroring his own through the phone. "That sounds like fun."

I hear him clear his throat. "Well, you said you had to get ready. I'll let you go."

"Yeah." I sigh, my chest heaving as I inhale deeply. "I'll see you later."

I hang up, staring at my phone screen, as I let the moment of relief that Rhylan knitted into my knot of nerves settle before I realize I'm actually going to be late at this point. I hop into the shower, nearly nicking my ankle while shaving my legs as I mentally decide what I'm going to wear.

Once finished, I pull the shower curtain back and step out of the tub wrapped in a towel, my hair dripping as the moisture lingers on my skin. I'm standing in front of my open closet, still not having decided on my outfit, when the doorbell rings. I quickly pad to the door and look through the peephole.

It's Rhylan.

What the hell is he doing here?

I open the door ajar, just enough to pull taut the chain lock.

"Rhylan. What are you doing here?" I ask, peeking through the small opening.

"I'm here to take you to dinner with your mom and her boyfriend." He smiles proudly. He's dressed casually but clean. His fitted cotton jacket fits snugly, resting across his broad shoulders, while his jeans fit perfectly, elongating his legs and oddly making him look taller. His hair looks freshly cut, tousled to look sophisticated but playful.

"What are you talking about?"

His brows furrow. "Can you let me in?"

I swiftly shut the door and unlatch the chain lock to open it again. Rhylan pushes the door open wider, making his way towards the couch before he settles in and makes himself at home. Angus retreats from the kitchen, hopping onto the couch and nudging his snout into Rhylan's hand as I still process that he's here. Then I suddenly realize that I'm completely naked underneath the towel.

"Wait here. Let me get dressed, and then we'll talk."

"Sure, Angus can keep me company." He casually drapes his arms across the back of the sofa and leans further back, drawing his ankle across his opposite knee. His eyes travel from the bottom hem of the towel, where it hangs across the top of my thighs, and back to my eyes. He smirks as I attempt to cover myself more with what little material I have.

I shake my head in disbelief, and I walk to my room, leaving Rhylan with Angus. I shut the door behind me, and panic sets in. He wants to meet my mom *and* go to dinner with me to meet her new boyfriend.

My movements are calculated but only out of habit. My mind is somewhere else, probably in the living room, hovering over the situation and dissecting it to pieces. And because my brain isn't stationed in my head where it should be, my hands move on their own. Pulling the deep wine-colored dress that I subconsciously decide to wear from my closet over my head. Ruffling my hair while moving the loud blow dryer through it in haste. I'm on a perfected autopilot. But I'm stalling, as much as I can, at least. I know I'm running late, but I don't know how to face Rhylan out there. If I do, then that means he's going to meet my mom tonight. It's too much to handle in one night.

I slowly walk out of my room when I'm finished, and Rhylan rises from his sunken seat on the couch to face me.

"You look beautiful," he says softly.

"Thank you," I answer back. "Rhylan, you don't have to go with me tonight. You can meet my mom another night."

He walks to me and cradles my elbows in his hands. "I'm not here to just meet your mom. I want to be here for you. I know you're nervous about meeting your mom's boyfriend, and I just want to be there if you need someone to hold your hand through it."

I nod.

"But," he adds, "if you really don't want me to be there tonight, I won't go. I'll wait for you here. Or I can drop you off at the restaurant and wait in the parking lot, like the skilled stalker that I am."

I laugh. Maybe having him hold my hand, squeezing it occasionally to let me know he's there, will help me get through this night that I've been dreading. "Okay," I finally say.

"Okay," he says softly. He holds my hand in his, bringing it to his lips and gently kissing my knuckles. "Now, come on. You said you had an hour. We mustn't be late, milady."

The drive to the restaurant is quiet. The nerves are racking up inside of me, and Rhylan drives patiently, letting me process and prepare instead of prodding me with questions. The steakhouse my mom chose is nice, overly sophisticated, and different from the casual diners that she and I frequent.

When we arrive, the valet takes the car, and Rhylan is immediately recognized. As soon as we step up to the hostess, a manager greets us.

"Hello, Mr. Matthews. It's an honor to have you dine with us tonight. May I show you to your table?" The man is nervous, speaking quickly to get his words out without stumbling on them.

"We're actually meeting someone tonight," he answers. He then looks down at me, encouraging me to speak.

"There's a reservation for Mary Salerno," I say softly. The commotion in the restaurant has grown around us. People strain their necks to glance in Rhylan's direction.

The man looks down at the papers in front of him, his finger gliding down the list that's illegible from my angle. "Ah, yes. We've already seated your party, but we would like to move you to a more private area of the restaurant if that would be more to your liking, miss."

I look up at Rhylan, surprised. "Yes, please. Thank you."

"Right this way," he says with a smile and gestures grandly in the direction he's headed.

We quietly follow. Rhylan's hand grazes my shoulder and lowers down my back as he gently guides me to our seats.

"The rest of your party will join you shortly."

Rhylan pulls out my chair for me to sit. As he's crouching over his chair, my mom rounds the corner to our table, and he stands upright.

"Ellie! What is this? They said they moved our table over—" She cuts her sentence short when she notices Rhylan to my right.

"Hello, Mrs. Salerno. It's a pleasure to meet you," he says politely. He smiles as he extends his hand toward her.

"Oh, Rhylan Matthews. I–it's nice to meet you too," she stutters. She hurriedly shakes his hand.

Her eyes go from Rhylan to me and back to Rhylan and then me again. The silence is awkward, settling into a bubble that wraps around our table while the clinks of silverware and sharp chatter pass by us in the distance.

She's staring at Rhylan, and he continues to smile politely at her.

"Mom?"

"Huh?" She finally turns to look at me. I gave her a look, raising my eyebrows, silently asking her *What are you doing?*

"I'm so sorry. Ellie, this is Mark."

A man with dark hair and full beard steps to the side to get around my mom. He extends his hand towards me the same way Rhylan did to my mom, timorous but sincere.

"Hi, nice to meet you. This is Rhylan." My tight-lipped smile doesn't budge. But it almost falters when Mark's hand moves to grip my mom's shoulder.

"Yes, I know," he says, turning to Rhylan. "Huge fan."

Rhylan shakes his hand, and all three take their seats around me.

"I'm assuming we have Rhylan Matthews to thank for this table? It's very nice," my mom says, taking in her surroundings.

"It's just Rhylan. You don't have to say my full name," Rhylan answers with a polite smile.

"Of course. That would be weird."

I suppress the need to cover my face with my hands, cursorily rolling my eyes instead. *This is so embarrassing.*

"Mark picked this restaurant. He says they have the best steak in town." My mom beams proudly at Mark. The two look at each other with adoration. He places his hand on hers, and they look back at us.

"Are you familiar with this restaurant, Rhylan?" Mark asks.

"No, first time here. But I'm sure the food will be great," he answers. "I hope I'm not intruding on your dinner."

"Oh no! Not at all!" my mom quickly answers. "Any friend of Ellie's is always welcome to join us."

"Thank you. That's very kind of you."

Silence fills the table, the four of us sitting quietly after our short greetings. We move in synchrony as we unfold our napkins and place them on our laps before idly tracing the silverware with our fingers.

"Ellie, how did you and Rhylan meet?" my mom asks as she brings her elbows to the table, clasping her fingers in front of her.

"We met at a premiere for his new movie," I say, peering at Rhylan as he gives me an encouraging smile.

"Are you talking about *Unrestrained*? That movie was amazing!" Mark exclaims.

"Mark *loves* action movies," my mom proudly states. Her hand reaches for Mark, running it along his arm with fondness.

I angle my face towards Rhylan to look away, suddenly rushed with brief snapshotted memories, over a decade old, but sharp enough to remind me that I still haven't moved on. Like when my dad used to hold my mom against his chest, rocking side to side as her cheek lay lazily against him. Or how he would make her laugh by bringing home ice cream on Friday nights, only to create mile high sundaes as she squirted whipped cream into his mouth. All of these memories seem to grow increasingly fuzzy, and I can't remember the details that I had held on to. I can't remember what flavor ice cream was my dad's favorite or what songs he used to play for my mom when they swayed slowly in the low light of our living room. I'm not ready to let him go. Even after all these years, I want to hold on to him even if it means shutting out the rest of the world, just to live in his memory forever.

My mom continues to talk, but it's inaudible. Muted as if someone has their hands covering my ears. The feeling is all too familiar. Rhylan scoots closer to me, his arm draped along the back of my chair and his fingers lightly grazing my back. A reminder that he's here, close by.

I squeeze my eyes shut, gripping the seat as my mom's voice echoes around me. I will myself to keep them closed. To fade everything away so I never have to open them again. To shut everything out.

"Watch your step, Ellie," my mom warns as I step out of the car.

I don't respond. Instead, I silently pull myself out from the seat, using the edge of the car door for leverage. My dad's shirt is clinging to my stomach, balled up into a wrinkled mess of soft flannel. We slowly make our way to the house, the front door opening before we fully approach it. It's my aunt Janice opening the door for us, her smile forced, carrying the underlying tones of worry in her eyes.

"Hi, Ellie. Welcome home," she greets me, a little too cheerfully. "Come on in. I've got some pizza ordered for you."

I walk past her, my mom stopping behind me to give her sister a hug. I'm greeted by a hyperactive Angus jumping up and nearly knocking me off my feet. I scratch his ear, and he moves on to greet my mom, shoving his paws against her thighs and running off before he leaves to find a toy.

"Are you hungry, Ellie?" my mom asks from behind me. She closes the door softly and places my belongings bag from the hospital on the floor next to the door.

I shake my head. My hand smooths across the edge of the couch, stopping to pull on a thread that won't come off as my fingers rub into the fabric. It's almost as if I'm checking to see that this is all real, that I'm really back home where I had said my last goodbyes because for some reason, I'm back. I shouldn't be here.

I look around. I see Angus's toys strewn around the small area rug in front of the couch, my mom's half-drunk coffee sitting in a ceramic mug on the kitchen counter, the TV silently playing a commercial for breakfast cereal. Nothing's changed, but it all feels unfamiliar, as if I don't belong.

I turn towards my room, not a single word coming from my mouth, just the dragging of my feet along the carpet, my slippers making a thump, thump noise with each step. I close the door behind me once I'm in my room and sit on the bed, looking down at my feet. The flat, cold slippers are now worn and covered in dirt from the walk to and from the car. I lie down and squeeze my eyes shut.

When I finally open my eyes, I realize I had fallen asleep. The room is still, so cold and dark. A shiver runs through me as I focus my eyes to adjust to the slit of light coming in through my doorway. I walk to my door but stop when I hear muffled voices outside. And the sound of my mom crying.

"The doctors said she wouldn't talk. She just sat there, listening to them. She wouldn't open her eyes or look at anyone." She sobs, her cries muffled by the sound of her face hitting Aunt Janice's shoulder. I can see Aunt Janice holding my mom against her, caressing her back.

"Mary, she's going to get through this. She's a strong girl," Aunt Janice reassures her.

"It's my fault. If I had just gotten my shit together after Dan died, she wouldn't be in this mess."

They continue to sit in silence, holding each other. Two mugs sit on the table, steam rising as the heat drifts up between them.

"The doctors think that she has some unprocessed grief. Recommended she go to therapy," she continues. She looks up, eyes brimming with fresh tears. "I lost Dan. I can't lose Ellie too."

I slump to the floor. My eyes shut, welding tight to try to blur out the images of my mom crying into her hands and muffle the sounds of her sobs. Maybe if I didn't exist, it would all be easier. Maybe I can finally shut it all out if I stay like this.

Don't wake up. Shut it all out.

"Ellie."

I keep my head lowered, feeling Rhylan's whisper brush against my skin. His hand moves across my back, the pads of his fingers pressing into my skin as he repeats my name.

When I finally look up, I'm met with my mom's confused and concerned eyes. "Is everything okay?" she asks.

"I'm so sorry. I need to excuse myself." The legs of my chair scrape against the floor. Rhylan starts to stand before I rush out and walk to the bathroom.

I almost crash into a woman walking out of the ladies' room before I lock myself inside a stall. The latch clicks into place, the heaviness of it hitting the bolt, echoing before I lean my hands against the door. I try to breathe, focusing on the in and out of my breaths. My eyes squeeze shut again, and the sounds that echo inside the tiled bathroom ring in my ears, becoming a high-pitched thrill.

Don't open your eyes. Shut it all out.

CHAPTER 26
Rhylan

barely hear Ellie, the sound of the chair loudly scraping against the wood floor silencing her soft voice. She stood abruptly and rushed away from the table before bee-lining to the bathroom.

I thought that… I could shut out the world and pretend I didn't exist in it.

I would shut my eyes to shut out the world. But that wasn't enough.

She told me she regretted ever trying to end her life. That she couldn't put her mom through that pain again, but when I looked at her, her head hung low and her eyes squeezed shut, as if she was shutting out the world all over again, I feared that she was pushed too far to the edge for regret to even matter. And I feared death. I fear being separated from Ellie. I can't imagine a life without her in it. Without her bright smile and sweet eyes. Without her warm touch and soft lips. I want her to keep opening her eyes, over and over again, every single day for the rest of our lives.

With Ellie gone, I turn back to Mary. There's an apologetic

look in her eyes as she faces me and then Mark.

"I'm sorry. She can be a little…" She pauses. "Closed off sometimes."

Mark pats her hand that rests on the table. We sit silently, waiting for Ellie to come back.

Mark moves his hand to Mary's arm, squeezing it for reassurance. "She's a very sweet girl," he whispers to Mary.

I know I'm not meant to hear it, but I do. Ellie *is* sweet. She's kind and considerate. But she's so much more than that. Everything that she decides to hide and bury deep is what makes Ellie, Ellie. But people only see what's on the surface. They don't understand that beneath all of that, Ellie's funny and smart. She's silly and playful when you tug at the parts that cause her to loosen up. She's also someone that's suffering. She's drowning. And I'm the only one that's been able to see that.

"I'm sorry. I need to excuse myself," I finally say. I walk to the bathroom at the far end of the restaurant and wait outside for Ellie, leaning myself against the wall.

She told me there were times when she wanted to pretend like she didn't exist in this world. To close her eyes and shut out the world. I want to be there when she opens them, to show her that she has something worth opening her eyes to.

As soon as the door opens, Ellie comes crashing into me. Her pleading eyes have grown swollen and red. I look at her only to see the pain pulled to the surface. She tried to hide it. To cover it up so her mom didn't have to know how she felt. But right now, she's met her limit. It's too much, and everything she's feeling spilled over the edges. I pull her to me, her breath hitching as she leans her cheek to my chest.

"Come on," I whisper into her ear as I smooth her hair. "Let's get out of here."

"But my mom…" she starts to protest.

"Call her from the car."

I take her hand in mine, interlacing our fingers. I look down at her, letting her know that if she wants to go back to the table, she can. But she doesn't have to. She doesn't have to sit through another moment of agony watching her mom and Mark be content with the same relationship that her parents used to share. She doesn't have to idly watch something that's causing her so much pain. Because I'm here to take her away from that.

"Okay," she finally says with a sniffle.

We walk out, successfully avoiding our table and having to explain to Ellie's mom where we're going before having our orders taken. Once outside, I hand my ticket to the valet, and we wait for my car.

Ellie stands next to me, arms wrapped around herself as she shivers. I wrap my hands around her and run them along the length of her arms.

"Here," I say when my attempt to warm her is failing. I remove my jacket and rest it on her shoulders.

"Thank you," she whispers back. She looks up at me, her lips puckering together to blow out a shuddered sigh. She closes her eyes before taking a deep breath and repeats herself. "Thank you."

My hand cradles her cheek. "You're welcome."

My car finally comes around, and I open the passenger side

for her. I get in around the other side and face her.

"I don't want you to think anything funny, but can I take you back to my place?"

She nods as a hint of a smile appears on her face. I turn the ignition, and we drive in silence until Ellie pulls out her phone and dials a number.

"Mom," she says softly. I hear her mom on the other side of the phone asking what happened and where she went. "I'm fine. We just had to leave."

They continue their conversation, Ellie apologizing and letting her mom know that she'll be with me so she doesn't worry before hanging up and placing her phone back in her purse. I take her hand in mine.

"I'm so sorry. I just… I didn't know I would react this way to meeting Mark."

"You don't need to apologize," I assure.

"I was really trying to keep myself together. I think it just got too overwhelming…"

We both stay silent.

"Can you just promise me one thing?" I finally ask. I see her look at me from the corner of my eye. "Don't shut yourself out from the rest of the world."

We've come to a stop at a traffic light. I face her, giving her my full attention.

"Because I don't think I can ever wake up to a day where I don't get to hold you in my arms."

Her eyes twinkle, filling to the brim with her tears. I see her lower lip tremble before a tear trickles down her cheek.

She nods.

She reaches for my face and pulls me towards her, kissing me aggressively, the pain in her chest finally dissipating. I bring my hand up to her face, cradling her cheek then moving down to the base of her neck.

I can't promise her the world like I want to. I want to so badly because I know that's what she deserves, but the only world I can promise her is one where heartache and regret will always be a lingering presence. A constant shadow that will always remind us that happiness is just an illusion. But at this moment, when I hold her face in my hand and tears stream down her cheeks, I know that whatever I give her, it'll be my all. It will be every ounce of my being to prove to her that I never want to see her hurt like this. To show her that her life, her happiness, means more to me than my own.

The car behind us impatiently honks its horn, alerting us that the light has turned green. I pull away from Ellie and continue driving, my hand never leaving her touch.

CHAPTER 27
Ellie

t's cold and windy. I know it is because I see it. People around me shiver with the wind blowing in their faces. Laughing as they chase after their loved ones. I see a man and a woman embrace each other, leaning towards the wind so they don't blow away. I don't feel any of it. Instead, I feel nothing. But I hear it. The dark and menacing waves of the ocean crashing into each other. The mist floating along the surface of the water from the aftermath of the waves hitting the cold, fine sand swirling into the air like a tornado. My toes tickle the edges of the water. As the waves keep coming, my feet become buried under the sand. I look around, my legs feeling like they've been set in cement blocks, and all the people are gone. No sounds of echoing laughter, no more lovers holding on to each other, fighting the wind. Just me and the evading rush of water that inches itself closer.

"Ellie!"

I hear my name being called. I don't know where it's coming from, but it sounds distant and muffled. I turn to look, but I don't see anyone. I twist my waist to move my feet, but they're buried so deep, I can't pull them out. I panic. I keep trying to pull my feet out. But I *can't, so I fall, turning towards the sound of my name.*

"ELEANOR!"

I start clawing at the sand, but it's no use. My feet are stuck, embedded into the sand, with no way for me to get out. Still, I struggle, because when you think you're going to die, you do what you can to survive. You fight death.

The water keeps rising, the waves crashing into my back. I finally feel the cold, violent shivers snaking up my spine. I look back at the water. The foamy waves crashing towards me starts to roar. I hold my hands up to stop it, as if I could. As if some effort of sheer will on my end will keep me from drowning.

"Ellie?"

I open my eyes. Rhylan is crouched down next to me with the car door open. Everything around us is so quiet and still. He leans towards me, brushing my hair out of my face and tucking it gently behind my ear. My eyes are swollen, barely slit open enough for me to see his face.

"We're here." His voice is nurturing, so careful and soft, as if I could break any second. And maybe that's a truth that I keep avoiding. Maybe I'm meant to break, no longer living life as a whole but in crumbled pieces instead, being swept along and leaving behind broken parts of my heart. Either way, a whole person or pieces of one, I feel utterly exhausted.

I look past him and see a house. If that's what you would call it. It's large, expanding so far that it seems to blend into the dark sky. The modern home, made of what looks like steel and glass, reflects the moonlight against the flat surfaces.

I sigh, still waking up. "Where are we?"

"My house," he says softly.

"Right," I whisper, remembering our conversation on the road.

The tears managed to stop on the drive here, leaving me spent. But the knot in my chest is still there. That feeling of drowning is there too, reminding me that as soon as I feel the rush of air with the possibility that I can actually breathe again, it's not real. None of it's real. The only concrete thought I can hold on to is that I don't want to feel like this anymore.

I try to stand, pulling myself out of the seat. Rhylan helps me, extending his hand and carrying my weight in it. But I still feel weak. My heart feels numb, exhausted from working overtime. The exhaustion has spread into my limbs, making them feel heavy.

Without hesitating, Rhylan bends down and hooks his arm behind my knees, swooping me towards him before standing upright. I wrap my arm around his neck to give me something to hold on to.

"You don't have to carry me," I protest.

"I know," he says. He faces me, our noses almost touching. His mouth forms into a grim line, the creases in his jaw looking sharper in the shadows of the moonlight. He doesn't say anything else while his eyes remain serious. He steps slowly and carefully up the three short steps that lead up to his front door. I surrender as the exhaustion takes over me, and I bury my face into his neck. I breathe in his scent, my warm breath skirting over his skin, and I feel the goosebumps rising on his skin in the wake of my touch.

He opens his door with ease, using only one hand while the other supports my weight. Once inside, he carries me the rest of the way to his sofa where he lowers me gently and reaches for a throw blanket, laying it over me. I pull it closer to me, bunching the softness towards my face and inhaling the scent of him lingering on the fuzzy fabric.

He tries to sit on the other end, but I pull his arm towards me. I don't want him to leave my side.

"Stay with me," I whisper. I scoot over, and he fills the empty spot I made for him without a word.

Maybe it's the comfort of being wrapped up in Rhylan or the walls that have crumbled down around me, but I sink into him. I mold into the hollow between his chest and his shoulder, drinking him in. I've worked hard to keep everything in, like a dam that's ready to burst. But now that Rhylan coaxed that dam open, everything is splayed out. And it weighs a lot heavier than when I had kept it all inside.

We stay quiet, not speaking but feeling each other. He continues to stroke my arm, which is lazily draped across his stomach, and I listen to his steady breathing. It's quiet for so long that I almost think he's fallen asleep. But his movements don't stop. His hand keeps moving up and down my arm, occasionally finding itself in my hair to carefully brush it out of my face.

"Why do you think we experience heartbreak?" I ask him. My voice sounds loud and awkward after the long stretch of silence between us. Maybe it's the tightness in my chest or the tears that have finally ceased long enough for me to place some perspective on the situation, but my voice is void of emotion.

Completely raw and open to whatever hurt I need to reluctantly swallow.

I finally look up at him, waiting for his answer. "I think it just happens," he says. "People say it's a lesson that you have to learn from or some other bullshit, but in reality, shit just happens."

"I don't really know what to do to stop hurting," I say with a wavering voice. My forehead creases, and my throat feels tight again, warning me of the tears starting to prick the corners of my eyes. "I have days where I think I'm okay. I just do what I need to do to get by. But then those days don't last long. And then I…"

"Drowning will do that to you," he says. His eyes are dark and full of familiarity, letting me know that he understands. He understands what it feels like to sink with no end with nothing to pull him up, what it feels like to drown.

"Is it selfish to not want to drown anymore?" I ask him, the tears now pooling and threatening to spill. "I don't care what I have to do or who I end up hurting. I just don't want to feel like this anymore." I can't help the sob that comes from my chest, leaving my lips as a cry for help as the tears start pouring down my cheeks.

He sits up, and I sit up with him. He faces me, his hands on both sides of my face, drawing my attention to him.

"I wish it was as easy as me telling you not to feel this way anymore because if it was, I would tell myself the same thing. But it's not, and the only thing I can tell you is… I'll be here. If you ever feel like you can't go on, like you want to give up, come to me. Let me take on that suffering so you don't have to do it alone."

I've always known Rhylan Matthews to be this handsome, charming, and definitely sexy man that graced the silver screen with his presence. That isn't up for debate. It's the side of him that I've always known. But the Rhylan Matthews in front of me right now is different. He presents himself as a protector. Someone that would fend for me, body and soul. He accepts me as I am. Without condition and with full faith that there's more to me than what's on the surface.

"Just remember your promise to me," he whispers.

I nod, knowing what he's talking about. *I don't think I can ever wake up to a day where I don't get to hold you in my arms.*

I lift my face towards him. The tears that continue to flow now coat my face and moisten my lips. My eyes scan his, and the way he looks at me makes me stop for a single heartbeat. I've never had anyone look at me the way Rhylan is looking at me right now. He looks at me with a fire behind his eyes. It's fierce, and I don't know how much of it controls his actions. But I'm not scared. Instead, it fuels the erratic beating of my heart, and I can't help but wonder what would happen if he let that fire decide everything between us.

He pulls my face to him to mold my lips into his. The taste of my tears fills what creases are left in the wake of our kiss. This kiss is gentle. Every bit reserved and cautious. He's taking his time and absorbing every second we spend consumed in it. When he pulls away, his breath is still hot on my lips.

"Eleanor," he whispers, his voice caressing my skin. I can't help but feel completely and undoubtedly adored. His voice makes my heart fill to the brim with emotion that makes it clench and mourn for the moment he pulls away, whenever that inevitable moment will be.

His thumb caresses my chin, then moves to my lower lip before his lips replace it. My hands reach up to him, holding on to his shoulders then gravitating into his hair. They thread through the back of his head, and I shift my body so that I'm on top of him, my legs on either side of his lap. My face is leaned forward so it hovers over him, making my hair drape the sides of his face. With one sweep, he reaches up and gathers it all, moving it to one side. He tilts his face towards me, and our kiss becomes a cluster of mingled breaths and soft moans.

He welcomes my position as his hands graze my legs and travel slowly up my thighs. The hem of my dress slowly lifts with his fingers, leaving behind a trail of heat and static that makes it difficult for me to focus on anything else. Our kiss deepens, my tongue meeting his with equal fervor. It feels intoxicating. All of my senses are heightened, and I smell, hear, and feel everything. Like the sounds of our lips clashing and clothes rustling against each other. Or the scent of Rhylan weaving in with mine. Even the way his feather soft touch, making my core tighten and quiver at the same time, brings me to a puddled mush of languid limbs toppling over him.

My hands manage to move down his chest, searching for the buttons on his shirt. One by one, I undo them, working downwards towards where our bodies meet. The shaking in my hands is hard to hide, so I work quickly. With his chest half exposed, he lifts my dress, raising it upwards. I instinctively raise my arms, and his hands continue to graze my sides as he lifts my dress off all the way, letting my hair cascade down my bare back. He watches me in awe as his eyes skate over my body, marveling at my existence like he can't believe he's holding me in his arms. His lips part, letting out a warm, stuttered breath.

"You are so beautiful," he says breathily against my lips, making me shiver. "So. *Goddamn*. Beautiful."

He leans forward to remove his arms out of his sleeves and wraps them around my back, flicking his fingers on the hooks of my bra. Having lost all sense of control, I close my eyes and roll my head back, completely submitting. The sound that escapes me results in his hold on me tightening, my skin growing taut as his fingers pull at my waist.

I bring my face back towards him, our foreheads touching and our breaths filling the space between us.

All the heartache and pain that's been pulled to the surface effaces as I look into his eyes: cool pools of blue that darken in the smooth silk of moonlight cascading into his living room. The twinge that's taken over my heart is replaced by a thrumming beat that rattles erratically in my chest.

His eyes search mine. "Are you sure?"

I nod.

She doesn't say anything, just nods. In fact, save for our breaths, it's completely still around us. It's only us two in this world. We've transferred to that deserted island I wanted to escape to. Everything seems to have disappeared, and I feel invincible. Like we can do anything that we want.

I pick her up, her legs wrapping around my waist, and stand from the couch. We continue to kiss as I walk toward my room. Her hands skate over my shoulders before taking hold of my hair. When her hands thread through my hair, I feel heady, like she's wrapping me around her tiny finger. As if she could convince me to fight dragons or lasso the moon down to her.

Once I walk through the door to my bedroom, I lean her against the wall. My hand moves from where her knee hooks at my waist and glides up her thigh. All the while, her lips don't leave mine.

I have a moment of clarity right then. A moment where all the doubt that I carry deep in my chest pulls to the surface. It reminds me that I need to tread carefully, that I'm being reckless and throwing complete caution to the wind. It causes me to stop.

She's breaking down her barriers even though I tried to lay out the risks. I want to throw every red flag at her to remind her that I'm not good enough for her. But at the same time, I don't want to let her go. I want to hold on tight to her because right now, she feels like my only anchor.

"Rhylan?" Her sweet voice rings through my ears. Her hands move to my chin, and the way she caresses her fingers over my skin feels comforting, reassuring.

I lower my head, my hair tickling her chin. My breathing grows deep. The pain etches into my heart, which works overtime to find the right words. "I don't want you to get hurt," I say, my voice low and strained. "I–I don't know how to not hurt the people that I love."

Her eyes search mine, and I can't look at her. "Rhylan," she says, relief plied into her sigh. She hasn't said anything but my name, but I want to believe her. I want to believe her unspoken words telling me, *It's okay, you can trust me.*

She doesn't say anything else. Instead, she lowers her face to meet mine and kisses me, extinguishing all the self-doubt that always manages to rear its ugly head when I feel like I'm on top of the world. She pulls my face up towards her, urging me to keep going and never stop. So I keep going, with no plans to ever stop.

I move to sit her on my bed. We hurriedly finish undressing each other, taking off the remaining pieces of clothing that come between us, before I pull away to look at her. I look at the way her body dips and arches in the right places and how her smooth skin looks so pure against the moonlight skating over her. She's luminous, not just her skin or her hair, *her*. I bend down to loop my arm around her waist and hover over her to resume my kisses, all while laying her down as we both sink into the mattress. Her teeth lightly graze against my lower lip, sucking and teasing, eliciting a randy groan to ripple through my chest.

She reaches up to me to place my face between her hands, lifting her head and letting her hair billow softly under her. I thread my hands through her hair, scooping the back of her head and pressing her into our kiss, leaving both of us breathless.

"Eleanor," I whisper as I trail my lips towards the dip of her neck. I call her by her name. Not the moniker that she forces everyone to call her but her beautiful name that feels natural coming off my lips.

I unravel as her hands move up my stomach and across my chest, pulling me closer to her. Her body arches against mine, her head rolling back, leaving her neck exposed. I try to move gently, to not rush things, and take things slow, inch by inch. But when her fingers cling to me, I lose all sense of control. And when a needy mewl leaves her lips, I can't even remember why I was taking my time in the first place.

"Rhylan," she moans, her hands pulling at my waist with her hips pressed into me as if to relieve the built-up pressure inside of her. Her grip roams down to my ass, her nails digging into my skin, desperately pushing deeper.

"Goddamn, Ellie. You're driving me so *fucking* crazy." The whisper of my voice veils over her skin, just where her collarbone meets the hollow of her neck.

I create a pathway of kisses down her bare chest, traveling along her smooth, silky skin. I could live forever buried against her, inhaling her intoxicating scent that reminds me of citrus and vanilla. Her fingers grip my shoulders when my lips travel to parts of her that make her body tremble. The curve of her breast, the dip in her navel, the creases in her hips.

When my tongue meets the heat between her legs, finally tasting and savoring her, her back arches off the bed at the same time a sharp cry squeezes through her throat. Her fingers find their way through my hair again, gripping the roots as she tugs roughly, urging me to continue. My hands move in deep, languid strokes over her skin, squeezing and kneading while my tongue swirls in tandem.

As she writhes, her body begins to tense under me, her thighs shaking in quivering waves. She breathes out sharply, like her breath was stolen off her lips. My stomach clenches as her desperate cries shoot a zinging shock down to my core, everything in me growing fuller, pushed to the edge, waiting to spill.

Fuck, I don't think I can hold off any longer.

I move up her body, feathering her skin with light kisses before kissing her lips. I savor her lips, molding them to mine as our teeth graze and tongues flick against one another. When her hand reaches down between us to wrap her delicate fingers around me, moving in purposeful strokes, I shudder before letting out a suppressed groan.

"I could spend the rest of my life just kissing you," I murmur into her skin. "Tasting you over and over again. I would never tire of this."

She lets out a contented hum, as if plucking the decadence out of my words, all full of continued declarations for her. Her taste, her smell, her beauty, her heart.

She pulls me into a deep, hollowing kiss before looking back at me, her hand still moving over and around me, her free arm wrapped around my neck.

"I need to…" My voice scrapes against my throat. "I want to feel you. So badly."

"Rhylan," she whimpers, the inner corners of her brows turned up in plea. "Please. I need…" Her voice trails off.

Our hands and lips continue to move hungrily, all while her whimpers and cries grow more desperate and louder.

When I pull away to reach for a condom from my nightstand, she watches me, her body squirming against the white sheets. Her hand touches my back, caressing it lightly and letting me know that she's here. She's not going anywhere.

The rip of foil mingles with our heavy breaths. And when I finally position myself and move into her, we don't look away from each other. My entire body seizes, trembling and stiffening as I work through the immense feeling of being spilled over the edge. I bury my face into her neck, focusing on evening my breaths—in and out—before I look at her again. The sounds that come off our lips harmonize between us as I rock into her, vocalizing our pleasure and bringing me so much closer to the edge. It's almost painful as I fight every muscle in my body, struggling to not lose it right then and there.

Our eyes stay connected, holding on to each other as a way to convince ourselves that this is real. I know this is real because of the way Ellie molds to my body, the way she sinks into my arms and stays there, never wanting to leave. But it still feels like a dream. A dream that I never want to wake from but know that I eventually have to.

I reach for her hand, peeling it off the grip she has on my arm, and place it over my heart. To let her know that I would never feel this with anyone else. That the place she has taken in my life will be one that is embedded there by everything about her. Her sweet smile, her warm eyes, her broken heart. No matter what.

I keep moving, picking up the pace as her body meets mine, the perfect rhythm building between us. A sharp intake of breath draws into her when my hips tilt in a way that causes her knees to draw up to the sides of my waist, squeezing me, holding me against her.

Her legs wrap around me, pulling me closer as her fingers claw at my back. As if there's an endless amount of space between us that she wants to erase but can't because we will never be close enough. Our bodies will always crave more. More of each other, more of *this*. Always *more*.

Our bodies tilt and peak at the same time, a ripple of flesh coursing through us together.

She cries out, and I groan into her soft skin, saying every unspoken word between us.

I need you. I need *you. I* need *you.*

I slump, and she tightens her hold on me, our touch always a millimeter away from being satisfying because we will never have our fill of each other.

We will always crave *more*.

Every nerve ending sparks and pulls to the surface between

our bodies before the static energy slowly dissipates and we sink into each other.

I watched her succumb, completely fall apart, and it's the most salacious shift I've ever seen. She's finally let go, and so did I. We lie cradling each other, her perfect face resting on my chest with our fingers interlaced.

"Eleanor," I repeatedly whisper into her hair, surrounded by our contented silence and sated smiles. The sound of her name coming off my lips feels like music, a tune that I can never get tired of.

S orrow, regret, *heartbreak.*

Affections that I wouldn't wish on anyone, not when they said the word *love* so ardently. He didn't say he loved me. That wouldn't make sense. Not when everything between us is this new and unexpected. But he used the word to describe the people that he cared about. The ones that he inevitably hurt and let go of.

But that wasn't what this was. Nothing in this world could tear this apart and result in heartbreak. Nothing.

"Why do you call me Eleanor?" I whisper. Our breathing has leveled into a steady pace as we lie in each other's arms at the center of his bed, tangled in the sheets with the moonlight coming in from his windows, creating a veil over us. His hands continue to run across my body, sweeping over my skin in light brushes. A smile stays on my face that seems to have taken residence and replaced the tears.

"Because it sounds beautiful," he answers.

When he said my name, Eleanor, I couldn't deny the zeal that burned through his eyes. While it felt so formal coming off other people's mouths, it was different with Rhylan. When Rhylan whispered my name, I felt beautiful, cherished. As if he'd just discovered that by saying my name out loud, whispering it through his lips, he could summon everything exquisite and alluring about me, front and center. As if I had magically brought all of that to him by merely existing in his presence.

"Rhylan?" I call after a long stretch of silence.

"Hmm?" he answers.

"Who got hurt?"

His hands still, and I can feel his body tense. "What do you mean?"

"You said… You don't know how to not hurt the people you love. What happened?"

I face him, resting my chin on his chest. I want to know what hurt him. I want to know what pain keeps him from opening up and breaking his walls down. Walls that he doesn't need to have up around me.

He sighs. "I have the tendency to… shut down."

I continue to look at him, urging him to continue.

"This life isn't all that it's cracked up to be. At first, I loved it, like a fucking fool. The attention, the drama. It all felt so glamorous. And then they started talking about things that they really shouldn't have an opinion about."

"Who?" I ask, bringing my hand to his, lacing our fingers together.

"Those rag mags, the paps," he says, bunching the group of people that have peeled back the layers of glamor only to expose the ugly side of being Rhylan Matthews. "Even the fans. I make one wrong move and it's 'cancel this, cancel that.' I feel like I can never be who I want to be or even be with who I want to be with because they'll rip them apart too."

I try to remain objective. Impartial so he understands that he can tell me all of these things without feeling like he's too susceptible, too vulnerable to the life that he created for himself. But I can't help the furrow in my brows as I realize how difficult this life is for him. How I assumed he had it easy, everything coming to him on a silver platter when in reality, it's everything but.

I stay quiet, letting him talk. Letting him lay everything out on the table so I can say, *I'll take it, pain and all,* even through the ordeal I've been through tonight. Because the last thing he needs is my pity. He doesn't need someone to tell him that they care for him, love him just for the sake of commiseration. He needs someone to pummel through his walls and let him know that they would stick around, no matter what.

"So, I basically shut down," he continues. "I felt so trapped, and in the end… I pushed everyone away. My family, my friends back home. It's easy to keep my walls up so I don't have to reel everyone into my life when all I seem to do is disappoint them, but it gets kind of lonely, me alone with my thoughts. It gets pretty morbid in here," he finishes, pointing towards his head.

"I guess they glamorize it so much that people don't realize that celebrities are people too," I say softly, more to myself than to him.

"It feels like that's the whole point, to glamorize celebrities like they're gods. But I just want to be normal sometimes. You know, not worry about anyone watching me. Trespass onto private property without worrying that if I get arrested, my mug shot would be plastered on every TV and magazine cover."

I smirk at his reference to the night we spent at the YMCA pool.

"Sometimes I just want to run off to a private island and escape all this," he says wistfully.

"You think Jay-Z and Beyonce have a private island?" I ask. A smile quirks at the edges of Rhylan's mouth.

"Maybe," he says. "I wouldn't be surprised if little Blue Ivy has her own mini-island next to theirs."

We dissolve into giggles before he covers my mouth with a kiss. He pulls away and looks at me, his eyes full of what looks akin to love.

"I'm beginning to feel like this can be my own private island. Just me and you," he whispers.

I nod. "It can be."

He runs his lower lip through his teeth.

"If that's what you want, it can be," I add, pulling him to me for another kiss.

We fall asleep in each other's arms. I wake up in the early morning to a half-empty bed, right as the sun rises. The light pours through the floor-to-ceiling windows, and the view of the backyard is stunning. The pool, surrounded by a large grassy area, looks massive. As if I were at a resort, not someone's home. I didn't see any of this last night in the dark. I stand and wrap my naked body with a thin sheet and walk to the window to take in the view.

Everything from last night feels like a distant memory, fading away, making me question whether or not it actually happened. The memories of my dad, meeting Mark. It all seems to blanch into a fresh new slate now that I'm with Rhylan where we've cast away onto our own secluded island. I can't even bring myself to feel guilty for leaving my mom when our dinner was entirely for her, so that she could bridge the gap between her new life and her old one. For once, I swept myself up into what made me happy. Right now, Rhylan is what makes me happy.

"You're up," Rhylan says as he enters the room, interrupting my thoughts. I turn to look at him. He's dressed in low-hung sweatpants, his abs and chest perfectly on display as he's drying his wet hair with a towel. He saunters towards me with one corner of his mouth curled up.

God, this man is sexy.

"I was just enjoying the view," I say softly.

He comes up behind me and leans down to kiss the hollow of my neck. He wraps his arms around me, his hands meeting at my front, and I lean into his kiss as his proximity makes my entire body tingle.

I turn to face him and raise my arms to reach his neck. As I do that, the sheet pools at our feet, and he hoists me up, my legs wrapping around his waist. His hands cup my butt as he turns towards his bed. I support myself against him with my arms wrapped around his neck, and I lean closer to him, my hands moving through his hair as I kiss him. With one of his hands supporting my weight, the other moves up my back and gently grasps my nape as he deepens the kiss.

"I don't think I could ever get enough of this, Ellie," he murmurs into my ear, trailing kisses along my jawline. He lays me down on the bed and hovers over me.

I smile lazily, thinking the same thought.

His hands move to grip my hips with a playful pinch which sends me into giggles, his own laugh reverberating through me.

"You're ticklish," he states, confirming a fact that I already know. "Is it just here?" He moves higher, his fingers digging into the sensitive spot up my side. "Or here too?"

My face heats, too aware that I'm naked underneath him as his hands continue to roam. "Rhylan! Stop!" I scream, squirming.

My giggle turns into a yelp as he wrestles me against the bed, his eyes full of a torrid hunger that makes me blush. His eyes stay on mine as my laugh dissipates into a stuttered breath. He guides my hands above my head, and he pins them, holding them in place as he moves his other hand down my body. It finds itself between my thighs, causing a low and needy sound to squeak from the back of my throat. I can feel his smile against my lips as I softly moan into our slow, fervid kiss.

When he releases my hands and they dip into the waistband of his sweatpants, he sighs into my mouth. We move hurriedly as my hands pull at his sweatpants, and he pulls away to remove another condom from his nightstand.

As he moves into me, I gasp, my urgent breaths silently giving way to my desperation. He hovers over me, his trail of kisses moving down my neck. I shift, rolling over him and straddling him before he sits up, wrapping his arms around my waist as I pull his face towards me. We kiss, our hungry mouths devouring each other as I move over him.

He growls into my mouth. "I love the way you feel," he whispers over my skin as his hand threads through my hair, my head falling back.

His feverish words ignite a spark in the pit of my stomach, and I match it in equal strides with my whimpered moans and gasps.

I buck against him, moving urgently. He lifts his hips to meet mine, our bodies chasing the waves of utter bliss together.

Everything in this moment is about heat, passion, and fervor. About kindling a fiery blaze between us that seems to ignite with every touch. About learning how our bodies move together, like two partners twisted in a tango, dancing in and around a growing flame, all fueled by ecstasy.

CHAPTER 30
Rhylan

We spend the morning limbs overlapping limbs, in and out of sleep as we create an isolated island, us two the only inhabitants. As the late morning light starts to invade my bedroom, I look over at Ellie asleep again, naked and tangled in my sheets. Her dark hair, now a deep caramel color against the light, covers her face to create a soft curtain while her rosy cheeks and swollen lips peek through the wavy slits. I brush the hair from her angelic face and watch as her chest rises with every breath she takes.

My Eleanor.

I get up and mosey into my kitchen to cook breakfast. When I open my fridge and find my food supply to be sparse, I settle for eggs and bacon, knowing that Ellie won't be able to refuse the savory strips of greasy breakfast meat. The melodious humming coming from my closed mouth happens without me noticing. My head bobs up and down as I happily find the upbeat tune of "Crazy in Love" from somewhere deep within the recesses of my brain. Just as I start reciting, or rather, mumbling my personal version of Jay-Z's rap lyrics, Ellie walks into the kitchen.

The acute focus that I have on my sunny-side-up eggs shifts into an overly goofy grin once I see her. She's wearing my button-down shirt, and it reaches just up to her thigh, exposing her smooth legs and bare feet while the folded collar wraps around her slender neck. She rubs her face as a smile peeks through her fingers. Her hair is an adorable mess that she gathers with her fingers and ties into a messy pile on the top of her head using a hair tie that was secured to her wrist. The spatula slackens in my hand as I drink in the sight of her, from her shrinking in my oversized shirt to the way only her toes touch the cold tile, the rest of the soles of her feet tilted up into the air. She looks so comfortable, as if in her own home, as she tiptoes toward me.

"Good morning." She smiles, her face relaxed and blissful.

"Good morning."

She stops in front of me, and I lean down for a kiss. My spatula clumsily finds its way on the counter, and now my hands are free to give her my full attention. With a quick sweep, I lift her and settle her on top of the kitchen counter. Her hands naturally link together behind my neck, just as my mind wanders to what I would do to her right here on the kitchen counter. With those thoughts swimming through my mind, my hands gravitate to her lower back. She looks at me, one brow quirked up and a smile that's being held back.

"You know, if we don't stop, I don't think we'll ever step out of your house," she teasingly scolds.

"That's the plan." I smile back at her, biting my lower lip and flicking my brows up.

She pulls me towards her, hooking her leg around the back of my thigh and arching her body towards me, causing me to crash into her. She breathes out a soft moan when I press my body into hers. I wrap my arms around her, gripping the back of her neck as she angles her lips against mine, and I completely forget what I was doing that led up to this moment. Shivers trail down my back when her hand dips into the waistband of my sweatpants. *Fuck*, I don't want this to ever end.

"Ellie," I manage to murmur. I can feel her smile through our kiss.

We're interrupted by the spitting of oil coming out of the frying pan, hitting my bare back, causing me to flinch. "Ow!"

"Oh!" Ellie gasps, laughing as she swats my bicep. "That's what you get for getting distracted."

I help her down, and she lands with a bounce, adjusting the shirt to make sure it covers just enough of her to be discreet.

"As if that's my fault," I bite back. I playfully lift the bottom of my shirt that she's wearing, exposing the bottom curve of her ass, just enough for me to draw in a breath. She slaps my hand away.

"Easy, handsy," she says, her smile giving her away. "You better watch it, or those eggs are going to have something to say."

My kitchen fills with the scent of grease that can only come from bacon and eggs. Ellie sits patiently on a barstool while I finish cooking and eagerly brings her hands together when I start arranging frying pans and plates on the kitchen island.

Save for the clinking of plates, it's quiet between us. Ellie's stomach growls, demanding food on her behalf, and my brows shoot up at the familiar sound.

"You know, I think you need to teach that stomach some manners," I jokingly suggest. "It doesn't hurt to say 'please' and 'thank you' every so often."

"You're lucky I don't let it speak for me," she warns. "You don't want to be there when my hunger makes me angry."

"I'll keep that in mind. Maybe keep a Snickers bar in my pocket at all times."

She giggles and reaches for a still-hot piece of bacon.

"Careful. It's hot," I warn her. She blows once before biting off half of it. "Or… not, I guess." Every time I see her eat, I'm surprised by her appetite and her candidness in not hiding it.

"Coffee?" I ask. She nods at me through chews of her bacon.

I brew two shots of espresso and place them between us. We sit in silence as our utensils continue to clink between our silent chews.

"Did you have any plans for today?" I ask, breaking the silence first.

She shakes her head. "I have some studying to do, but it can wait till tomorrow."

"You want to go somewhere?" I suggest.

"Where did you have in mind?" she asks with an adorably eager smile across her face.

"I usually have a late lunch with my friends on Sundays. The farmer's market has a pretty nice selection of food trucks and baked goods. And it's pretty low-key. The crowd pretty much dies down after one."

"Your friends?" she asks as she stops the forkful of eggs

that's making its way to her mouth.

"Yeah, why? Do you not want to meet them?"

"No. I mean, yes. I just… What if they don't like me?"

I understand her apprehension. The last time I brought her around a crowd of people that I claimed to be friendly acquaintances, she ended up in tears. But my friends aren't the same LA crowd that I had subjected her to. I pull her free hand to my lips and kiss the inside of her palm. She uses her fingers to graze the underside of my jaw. "They'll love you."

Our morning continues as we eat hungrily and recharge our depleted batteries before readying ourselves for the farmer's market. Being in my home with Ellie, moving about with ease as if us eating breakfast and getting ready for the day is an everyday occurrence, feels natural. Intrinsic in a way that there's no adjustment period. We have somehow settled into this role as partners instinctively.

While I finish cleaning up in the kitchen, Ellie showers and dresses in the same clothes she wore the night before. I walk into the bathroom just as Ellie is fashioning a loose braid with her hair, a pileous tip pointing down the center of her back. We again settle into a routine that we don't realize we've established. Moving around each other as she brushes her teeth with the sealed toothbrush I left on the counter, and I reach around her for the towel to dry my hands.

When I walk out of my closet, dressed in jeans and a vintage band T-shirt, I find her waiting patiently on my bed. It's neatly made and smoothed out to conceal the wrinkles we made throughout the night. I want to mess it all up again, lay her down and kiss her, hold her close to me and run my hands along every curve and cleft of her body, but I don't. Instead, I bend down to lightly kiss her on her forehead and stand straight, angling my body towards the door.

"You have everything you need?" I ask her.

"Mm-hmm. I just had my purse," she says, patting the purse sitting on her lap.

We step into the bright afternoon light already warming with the late spring breeze. She picks up her feet, a bounce in her steps, as we walk down the stairs to my driveway. We continue our walk to the passenger side where I open the door for her, and she climbs in.

Once I'm buckled into the driver's seat, I look at her and smile. "Let's go," I say. The stupid grin plastered on my face never leaves the entire drive.

The farmer's market isn't busy, just as I had anticipated. Charles, Chuck, Jackson, and I usually like to meet a little after the lunch rush so that it's not too crowded but we still have options for food.

Still, the day is beautifully bright. The sun is shining with not a single cloud in the sky. And even though the sun is beaming down on us, the air is brisk. The breeze is cool enough that we can spend our day outdoors without an ounce of overbearing heat intertwined with it.

Families with little children are enjoying their relaxing weekend while browsing the arrangement of local cheeses, fruits, and vegetables. We walk hand in hand and stop in our tracks as a small boy and girl chase each other in front of us, each with a ripe apricot dripping from their hands.

We finally make our way to the array of picnic tables that are lined around various food trucks. Charles, already there with Amelia, is claiming a long table for us to sit at. They watch as Oliver, the older of their two boys, chases after Andy, the two giggling as they run circles around their doting parents. Chuck and Jackson haven't arrived yet.

"Come on, boys. It's time to eat!" Amelia calls to them. She sees us approach the table, and she smiles in our direction. "Rhylan! Hi." I lean down and hug her. Even before she had kids, she always carried a natural maternal kindness. She always makes me feel like family and considers me an actual uncle to her kids instead of just an honorary one.

"This is Ellie," I say as I pull Ellie to me. She stands close, both of her hands wrapped around mine.

"Hi, Ellie. I'm Amelia," Amelia answers with a smile. "It's nice to meet you."

Charles appears at her side and shakes Ellie's hand as soon as it leaves Amelia's. "Hi, Ellie! I'm Charles," he says a little too loudly. He makes no attempt to hide his eagerness. It's almost embarrassing. He looks at me with raised brows, as if silently asking me for details on this impromptu date I brought to lunch. I quickly shake my head, signaling to him not to make it weird.

"Hi. Yes, I–I know," she stammers. "I mean, hi," she says bashfully.

The boys then come crashing into me. Their giggles travel up my leg while they hang on to me and smile infectiously towards the sky.

"Hey, boys!" I greet them. I pick up Andy, who's barely over one and still learning to use his legs properly. His chubby arms wrap around my neck as he brings himself closer to embrace me. His hands feel warm and sticky, and he smells like caramel. "This is my friend Ellie."

Ellie smiles, the corners of her eyes crinkling and her nose scrunching as she waves her fingers at Andy. He reaches his arms out towards her, opening and closing his fists, signaling for her to come closer to him.

"I think he wants to go to you," I say suggestively.

Ellie looks at me, cautiously moving her eyes between myself and Andy.

"It's okay. He doesn't bite," I assure her. She rolls her eyes and smiles as she reaches her arms up toward Andy. He embraces her, wrapping his arms around her neck and resting his head on her shoulder. He starts lightly tapping her back and slumps into a contentment that is completely endearing.

Ellie accepts Andy's embrace and leans her head into his. She sighs, drinking in his warm affection.

"Aw, he really likes you," Amelia says fondly from the other side of the table, watching Ellie hold Andy. "He usually takes some time to warm up to people."

Ellie smiles proudly at me.

"I'm going to grab us some food. Anything in particular you like? They have grilled cheese. And they make really good tomato soup. Or I saw tacos too."

"Surprise me," she answers softly, speaking into Andy's hair. Their breathing synchronizes, and Ellie starts to rock him side to side, a small smile curving up on her lips.

I bend down to meet Andy's eyes. "Don't you go stealing my girl," I playfully warn him. He responds by covering his eyes and turning away from me, burying his face into Ellie's neck.

Ellie laughs. "Can you leave us alone now?" she says with a hint of feigned annoyance. She waves a free hand towards me, shooing me away.

I raise my brows at her. "You're leaving me for this guy?" I point a thumb at Andy, a playful smile creeping its way onto my face.

"He's better company."

I lower my lips to her ear and speak low so only she can hear me. "Are you sure about that? Cause it didn't seem like that last night," I rasp.

She gasps, and her eyes widen. Covering Andy's ears, she whispers back, "Excuse me, there are children here!"

She looks at me one more time before I pull away. She's teasing me, but I can see the fire in her eyes, images of last night and this morning replaying in her head. I smile, knowing what she's thinking, and wink at her.

Before I walk away, I lightly tap Ellie's ass, and Charles catches the entire exchange. Our eyes meet for a moment, and I know he's going to barrage me with questions later. For now, he leans down towards Amelia to whisper into her ear, no doubt telling her what he just witnessed. But I don't even care who sees me this happy.

I walk away and stand in line to order a mouth-watering grilled cheese sandwich with a side of tomato soup. The fresh cheese they use, the kind that strings when you separate the halves, is a taste that I look forward to every week. From where I'm standing, I see Ellie still holding Andy while talking to Amelia. The two are in an animated conversation, smiling and friendly. Andy waves at me as if he's keeping his side of the agreement not to steal Ellie away, but I think it might be a little too late. Seeing his little hand move side to side towards me makes me smile, and I wave back.

Just then, my phone rings. When I turn it over in my hand, I see that it's Shana. I step out of the line and let the person behind me go ahead as I take the call.

"Hey, Shana. What's up?"

"Rhylan. Have you looked at Just Jared recently?" she asks calmly.

My brows draw together in confusion. "No, why?"

"There are pictures of you all over their Instagram with some girl. It looks like you guys were at the marina and out to dinner in Mid City?"

My heart drops. I had the eerie feeling that paparazzi were in the distance when we were leaving the marina last week. I hadn't even noticed them last night at dinner. I thought I was being overly paranoid and brushed it off, but my suspicions were right.

I should have been more careful. Been more discerning about where we went and who saw us, but I wasn't. Instead, I became reckless as I plummeted into what it meant to fall head over heels for someone. For Ellie.

I'm not ready to share Ellie with the world. For them to tear her apart and poke at every imperfection or shortcoming as if their opinions were valid. I'm not ready to lose her.

My mouth dries, and any words I try to get out stop short of my throat. I cough into my fist before speaking again. "What are they saying?" I ask Shana, trying hard to stay calm.

"They're speculating a new romance with a mystery woman. It's hard to deny it. You two were pictured kissing. Who is she?"

"No one, Shana. Look, I've got to call you back." I look over at Ellie still talking to Amelia. We meet eyes for a second, and her smile falls when she sees the look on my face.

"Rhy, you need to let me know these things so I can speak to them. Just Jared already reached out to me, but I didn't confirm anything. Just give it some time and let me know what you want me to tell them. In the meantime, if you don't want this blowing up, lie low."

"Okay, I will. Thanks, Shana," I respond before hanging up. I quickly walk to Ellie, my hands empty, no fresh grilled cheese sandwich or tomato soup, just a mask of unease over my face.

"Is everything okay?" Ellie looks up at me with concerned eyes. Both she and Amelia look at me, my sudden presence interrupting their conversation. I know she can sense the tension set in my shoulders. I try my best to keep a straight face so she doesn't worry, but I'm doing a poor job of it. I can't see this ending any other way than badly.

"Yeah. But we should go."

"What are you talking about? I thought we were having lunch," she says. Her hold on Andy tightens as she shifts her weight.

"Something urgent came up. We need to leave," I try to

explain. I turn to Amelia. "I'm so sorry. We'll have to have lunch another time."

"No worries," she answers, taking a protesting Andy from Ellie.

I scan the area to look for Charles, but he and Oliver have disappeared. "Can you let Charles know we had to go?"

"Of course," she says. She's just as worried as Ellie is, both unsure of what's happening but worried nonetheless. She looks at Ellie and smiles. "It was nice meeting you. I hope we see you again soon."

"You too," Ellie answers, a small smile on her face that quickly fades. She embraces Amelia, and we part ways.

I grab her hand, and we both walk swiftly back to my car. She does her best to keep up with me, her feet hitting the pavement in quick steps in contrast to my long strides. I'm silent, my face hard and stone-like. I place my hand on the small of her back to guide her to the car and open the door for her, waiting on her to get in.

And then it happens out of nowhere. It usually does. They hound you down. They hunt, watching their prey until the right moment presents itself. They catch you off guard, usually at moments when your weaknesses are so openly exposed. And then they pounce. Their movements are calculated to capture just that: the money shot.

I hear the clashing of clicks before I see them. Then they're all over, surrounding us. The space around us is closing in, making it hard to breathe. I turn my body instinctively to cover Ellie, but it's no use. They're everywhere. They angle their cameras around and over me so they can take as many pictures of Ellie as they can.

Ellie's face pales in sheer horror, etched with fear. I've explained this feeling to her. The constant scrutiny, the barrage of people that invade your personal space as if you're on display, and the fact that common decency doesn't exist. I laid it out for her the best I could, but I never thought that she would have to experience this firsthand. Never did I think that I would see the look on her face that I see right now.

"Rhylan! Who's your new girlfriend?"

"Are you cheating on Bella?"

"Give us a kiss!"

"What's your name?"

"Did you break up Rhylan and Bella?"

I've always been told to ignore the paparazzi. That's what Shana always tells me. Their intention is always to get a reaction. A wild, out-of-control star is always much more exciting than a calm and boring one. But once the questions start being directed to Ellie, I lose it.

I turn on my heels and take one long step in the direction of the cameras. I don't see faces, just the intrusive lenses that poke at me like I'm a circus animal. Like they're attempting to wake the crazed lion inside me, setting my rage broken and free.

"Come on, Rhylan! Let us get a picture of you two kissing!" they continue to taunt. They start to laugh, encouraging this demand in hopes they can get what they came for.

My hands move on their own, like I don't even control them anymore. My anger is in control now. I reach behind the wall of outstretched lenses and grab the first thing my hand touches, the collar of a man half my size. When I pull him to me, nose to nose, the panic in his eyes wipes off the smug smile on his face. From the corner of my eyes, I can see that the other photographers have the same look on their faces, shocked and dazed. But then the clicking becomes louder. In the absence of the clamoring of voices, the clicking sounds violent. And everything slows. My breathing and pulse start to echo in my ears.

I stop myself, realizing how this must look. I'm not a violent person. My intention was for them to leave Ellie alone. I never intended to hurt anyone. I let go of the man. He runs his hands down his shirt, smoothing the fresh wrinkles I just made. He steps out of the crowd, stumbling over his feet, clearly traumatized by the encounter.

"Please, just leave us alone," I say in a calm voice. My eyes stay on the ground as I close the passenger door and round the hood of the car to the driver's seat. I don't look at Ellie. I can't. I can't even begin to reason with what happened. I did this to her. It's all my fault. This was the *I told you so* moment that I've been waiting for. The moment that keeps creeping in through the shadows, waving the words in front of me like a piece of meat. I feel so fucking stupid. Why did I think that even for a second, I deserve to be happy when all I do is hurt people?

Without saying a word, I peel out of the parking lot, my tires screeching behind us.

We drive in silence. I don't know how to tell Ellie that I just ruined her life. How I tainted the image of her by keeping her by my side, and now the world thinks she's some homewrecker that broke Bella and me apart. None of it is true.

There was nothing ever going on between Bella and me. Ellie is the furthest thing from a homewrecker.

But I know I can't keep doing this to her. I can't keep her by my side, exposing her to a world that's so unforgiving and works unrelentingly hard to break you down. I don't want her to end up like me, broken and detached.

"Rhylan, are you okay?" she asks softly. I glance over at her and see her pained expression full of concern that I don't deserve. Her eyes are wide, twinkling as the tears begin to pool and threaten to pour. I can't believe that I'm the one that made her feel this way. My heart breaks knowing that even if I told her she shouldn't worry about me, that I don't deserve it, her kind heart wouldn't be able to help it.

"I need to take you home. Is that okay?"

"That's fine. But are you going to be okay?" She lowers her face towards her lap. Her hands are clenched together in front of her, and I see a lone tear drop onto the back of her hand.

I turn my attention back to the road in front of me. I don't know what to tell her, so I nod. If I speak, my voice might give me away.

I told myself that I wouldn't hurt her, that I couldn't for fear that I may lose her. But now, I realize keeping her close means hurting her. I can't live with myself if I continue to abuse the heart that she so openly gave to me. She's broken down her barriers and let me in. And I'm already betraying my own promise to keep her heart safe.

We drive in silence. And it is deafening. Every crevice of his car is filled with the words that we aren't saying to each other but want to.

I'm sorry.

Everything will be okay.

We still have each other.

I need you.

Don't go.

Rhylan pulls up to my house and puts the car in park. He can't even look at me, no matter how much I urge him to meet my eyes. I look at his profile. Even with the blissful daylight outlining his features, he's rigid. His expression is hard and doleful. I miss the playful Rhylan that was full of humor and flirtatious innuendos. I wish I could erase the last hour of our day.

I speak first.

"Rhylan, I'm so sorry," I whisper quietly, my voice trembling. The tears continue to fall, trailing down my cheeks and dropping off at the edge of my chin. I can't rein them in at this point, but I don't care. All I care about is that he won't leave me. That this isn't the end of us.

His jaw clenches as he squeezes his eyes shut before a shuddered sigh blows through his mouth. He feels so far from me. I want him close again, holding me, affirming that we'll get through this one way or another. I reach for his face in an attempt to soothe his pain.

"Ellie," he whispers as he melts into my hand, my fingers caressing his jawline. He's relenting, but I don't know how much. And I don't know if it'll be enough.

He turns to look at me, and our eyes finally meet. The look on his face is like a dagger to my chest. I feel every bit of his pain, the aching in his heart that he placed on his chest, unable to cover or hide it.

"You don't have to apologize."

"Rhylan, if I hadn't been there, this wouldn't have happened."

"No, it's not your fault," he replies. "They were just trying to get a reaction out of me. They wanted to see me lose it, and I did."

We stare into each other's eyes, no words as the both of us contemplate our future together. There are a dozen different thoughts that pass through his face, and I can't fully place a single one. Minute flashes of regret, remorse, hurt, wistfulness, and even goodbye.

"Ellie, I'm so sorry you had to go through that. I never wanted to get you involved in this life. It was never my intention for this… any of this—"

I cut off his words with a kiss and I can feel him relax. The edge that he carries through his words dull, and for a fraction of a second, I feel a fleeting moment of hope. I want to fade away all the fears that he carries. I want to tell him it's okay as long as we have each other. But I don't know how to tell him so it doesn't sound like a broken record, repetitive and pointless. Because my words are anything but pointless. It's a conviction that I want him to believe. To understand that we're not as fragile as he thinks.

I feel a painful groan rumble through his chest. Even through the pain, his kiss is hungry, fervent and frenzied. But this isn't a kiss of passion. It's a kiss of farewell.

He pulls away and places his warm hand over my heart, his fingers brushing over the heavy thumping as if he's trying to remember the rampant beats like the tempo in a song. And just as quickly, he lowers his hand, leaving me empty in the absence of his touch. His movements are sudden and abrupt but thoroughly calculated. As if he already knows his next move and every decision is with purpose, regardless of if it's for the right reasons.

"We'll talk later." His voice is hoarse and rough, the ache seeping through his words. His hardened expression, the beat of the tick in his jaw, the shakiness of his voice—it's all almost unbearable. He's pushing me away, and I'm utterly frightened.

I want to scream his name. I want to sob, loudly and unrelentingly. I want to cling to him, to tell him no. *No, I'm not going anywhere.*

But instead, I do the complete opposite. I turn and walk away from him.

"Okay," I whisper quietly before I slowly exit the car.

I shut the door softly and watch him. He never looks in my direction, not once. Instead, he looks straight ahead and drives off without so much as a wave goodbye.

I suffocate the fresh wave of tears that's welling up inside of me. Long enough for me to get through my front door. Thankfully, the house is empty. Slowly, I walk to my room and sink into my bed, my knees drawn to my chest so I can hold on to something before I drift off into nothingness. The tears start rushing out again, uncontrollably this time. The dam is broken now, crumbled down into dust, letting everything spill. And I have no intention of stopping it any time soon.

"Ellie!"

I hear banging coming from the front door. The lingering darkness has now transitioned into pitch-black. I look around, disoriented and confused.

"Ellie! Open up!"

The pounding on my door continues. I get up to see who it is and find Claire peeking in through the window. When I open the door to let her in, she rushes past me.

"Claire, I'm really not up to talking right now." My fists rub my eyes, trying to erase the blurriness, but instead, a fresh wave of ache starts to form in my chest and begins to spread through my body. I'm all cried out. No more tears are left in me, so I shudder out a breath instead. Exhausted and completely dejected, I slump into my couch, the soft cushion sinking below me.

"Ellie." She stands over me. "I was just scrolling through

Instagram, and look at what I saw on Just Jared." Her face is serious as she thrusts her phone into my face. My curiosity piques, and I sit up to take her phone from her.

On the small, dimly lit screen, there are grainy pictures of Rhylan and me in an embrace. They're from the two of us at the marina after our voyage on his borrowed yacht. I scroll through the pictures, and there's another one from last night, at dinner with my mom. I looked visibly upset while we waited for the valet. I can even see Rhylan trying to console me. I continue to read the caption below the image.

Hollywood heartthrob and star of the recent Unrestrained, Rhylan Matthews, was seen with a mystery woman all around town. It seems the two are serious as they shared a passionate kiss after a romantic boat ride and what looks like an intense conversation after a dinner date. Does this mean the sizzling romance between Matthews and Bella Raven is over?

It's been six hours since it was posted, and it has already acquired over 100,000 likes and thousands of comments. I scroll down to read the comments.

"How could Rhylan cheat on Bella? This girl is such a homewrecker."

"She is so ugly. Rhylan could do so much better."

"What a bitch! She KNEW Rhylan was with Bella!"

"Rhylan is so disgusting! How could he cheat on Bella? She's so perfect!"

My heart sinks to my stomach, and a thousand-pound ball of dread settles there. "Oh my God," I say out loud. I hear my own voice, but it doesn't feel like my own. As if I'm watching everything unfold from the outside and everything happening in my own home is all part of some weird third dimension drama.

How did they even get this picture? And the things people are saying. Labeling me as a homewrecker and Rhylan as a cheater. Rhylan denied his relationship with Bella to me.

I don't belong to anyone.

Was he lying this whole time? My mind goes back to that evening, but everything is a blur. The room spins around me. I place the phone on the sofa cushion as I try to stop the dizziness. My hand goes to the sides of my head as if it's physically spinning and I can somehow stop it from rotating right off my shoulders.

"Are you okay?"

"I need a minute," I manage to whisper.

"Ellie, there's more."

I look at her, panic smeared across my face as my mind races. What else could there possibly be that's worse than those comments?

"What are you talking about?"

She takes her phone back and swipes through it, stopping to show me a full article covered by TMZ.

Pictures of Rhylan and me rushing to his car at the farmer's market are captured all over, with stills of my shocked and disoriented face and Rhylan's uncontrolled anger. I zoom in on the pictures of Rhylan attacking one of the paparazzi before I read the article.

Hollywood 'It' Star Rhylan Matthews was seen at The Country Way Farmer's Market this afternoon with the mystery girl he's been seen all over town with. The mystery girl, who we have identified as twenty-two year old UCLA student Eleanor Salerno, was seen wearing the same clothes from the night before when the two were seen leaving a dinner date, leaving little to the imagination. More shocking, Matthews, 26, lost his cool and attacked a paparazzi photographer after an altercation between the two.

According to the paparazzo, Rhylan's attack was "completely unprovoked" and was the "reaction of yet another star that has become unhinged."

It seems any speculation of a romance between Matthews and his Unrestrained *co-star, Bella Raven, 29, are forgotten as Rhylan appears to have a new leading lady in his life.*

I can't believe what I just read. Pictures of Rhylan and me all over the internet, along with these assumptions about our relationship. Lies that Rhylan randomly attacked someone for no reason. I don't even know how they know who I am. Their invasion of my privacy, exposing who I am to the world without a single consideration for my permission, makes me sick.

Claire's phone drops to the floor. I run to the bathroom sink and dry heave into the sink. Nothing comes out, but I can't control the unbearable lurching from my stomach.

I run to my room and frantically search through my purse for my phone to call Rhylan. I need to talk to him. I need him to tell me everything will be okay, that he can fix this. He doesn't answer his phone. It goes to voicemail barely after two rings, so I hang up and frantically punch out a text message.

Me: Please call me.

I don't know what else to say. I don't know what to do.

"Ellie…" Claire's voice trails off. She's standing behind me. As if she's there to catch me if I fall. I turn to her and cry into her shoulder as her hands envelop me, soothing me and allowing me to cry, to let it all out. My sobs grow deeper. The shock is slowly fading, and reality is finally settling in. We stay like this for what seems like forever, our bodies sunken into my bed as I lean into her.

What will happen to us, to Rhylan and me?

Just as my cries settle down, Claire stills. Her hands that were stroking my back in an attempt to soothe me come to a stop as she turns her head towards my door.

"What the hell?" She stands and I follow her, wiping away my tears with the back of my hand. I watch as she walks towards my door and peers out the window. It's when she splits an opening with her index finger and thumb through the horizontal blinds that I see the flashing of lights from outside.

"What the hell!" she screeches, repeating herself. But not as a question, more of a demand.

When she opens the front door and I peer over her shoulder, it's then I see where the lights are coming from. Lined up along the curb leading up to my house, a line of paparazzi clamors to get a picture. The roar of clicks and people calling my name muffles against my head as my body numbs. A prickle of static courses through my body, traveling through my stomach to the tips of my fingers. I'm stuck, frozen with my fingers gripping my door while my cavernous breaths can't seem to catch up with my hammering heart.

"Hey!" Claire calls. She's yelling, her arms thrown in the air as she wards off the photographers. "Get the hell out of here!"

She takes a step off my stoop before I reach for her, my hand grasping at her wrist as I yank her back into my house and slam the door shut.

"Claire," I whisper, my hands covering my mouth as tears brim the edges of my eyes. "What do I do?"

She guides me to my couch, sitting me down as she takes her phone in her hands.

I don't remember anything after that. With my eyes squeezed shut and my hands gripping the cushions until my knuckles turn white, I fade away. Until I've shut out the world around me.

"Ellie?"

I stir, the soft voice coaxing me out of my temporary state of paralysis. I feel a warm hand smoothing down the mussed tangles of my hair as my name is repeated. "Ellie."

When I open my eyes, I see my mom. She's hovering over me as I blink away my lethargy.

"Mom?"

"Hi, honey."

"Where's Claire?" I ask, my voice rough and dry. I sit up, scanning my dark living room. There's no more flicker of flashes peeking through my window. Instead, a steady stream of moonlight cascades through the blinds, leaving behind a soft glow while showcasing the aftermath of the day.

"It got late, so I told her to go home."

My hands move to my face, rubbing through my tear-stained cheeks and clearing the blurriness.

"What happened to all the people outside?"

"Claire called the police," she answers. "And I got home as they showed up."

"Oh." I nod.

"The officers told them to leave and stayed for a little bit until everyone cleared out." She pauses for a minute, her eyes searching me for any sign of life, of hope. "Claire told me what happened," she adds softly.

I nod again, remaining silent as I avert my eyes to the floor.

"Have you talked to Rhylan?"

I shake my head. "I don't think he wants to talk to me."

"Ellie, he needs to know what happened. He needs to know what's going on. If not for his own sake then for yours."

"I tried calling and he didn't answer," I say, defeated. "And he hasn't called me back."

"Then try again," she argues.

My chin trembles. I'm so scared. Scared that he won't answer. That he had already said his goodbyes with his kiss. Scratched me off of his life when he realized that I didn't fit into it and drove off without a second glance.

"Claire seems to think that he needs to know what happened. So he can do something about it. And I think I agree with her."

I finally look at her. She's right. He needs to know what happened. Not just to fix things, but for him to know how I feel. Forget the paparazzi and all the false rumors. He needs to know that we're worth fighting for. That we're just beginning, and that I'm not going anywhere.

I sigh, knowing what I need to do as I place my heart on my chest, unsure if it can come out of this unscathed. But it's worth the risk. It has to be. Otherwise, I don't know what will be left of me.

The drive home was quiet, no radio, no chatter. No sounds of Ellie's laughter echoing in the background. Just silence. The occasional honking and whirring of LA traffic whizzed by me, but that was it. Only utter silence that screamed at me, begging me to turn around and run back to Ellie.

I sit in the overpowering silence of my home where it feels like time stands still and everything that happened was just a dream. Or a nightmare. In the still darkness, the reality of never seeing Ellie again settles into my chest, and it *fucking* hurts. Like someone punched a fist-sized hole right where my heart used to be so that all I feel is pain. Sheer pain and nothing else.

It's self-destructive behavior, but I look through every article that has my name attached to it, new ones posted within the last couple of hours. Unsurprisingly, they've identified Ellie, plastering her name all over the internet. Everything personal about her is left out for everyone to pick through and have an opinion about. Save for her Social Security number and mother's maiden name, it seems every detail about her is up for grabs. The things that people are saying about her are just as obnoxious. All inimical comments about Ellie, about how I cheated on Bella with her. How she purposely came between us, only to break me and Bella apart. Shunning her as someone nugatory and noxious while labeling her the way I knew she would be once her attachment to me came to light.

There are things that I do to cope. Push people away, isolate myself, close people off to keep my distance. All so I don't hurt anyone and I don't get hurt in return. It's everything I never imagined doing to Ellie. Because why would I push away the one person that I meant to keep by my side forever? The one person I thought I couldn't live without. Turns out, it doesn't matter if I can't live without her. I'm going to have to.

Ellie called already, just as I thought she would. I knew that in a state of panic, she would reach out to me. I mean, I'm the one that's supposed to know how to handle these situations, how to ward off the public and live in solitude. And maybe I am the expert, with me pushing people away as a coping mechanism. But Ellie doesn't need to live like that. She should be free without the reins shackling her down to a life like mine.

I should talk to her. I *want* to talk to her. To hear her voice, if not for any other reason but to hear her call my name one more time. To savor it, embed it into my heart so that it can echo in the soundtrack of my life. If I can't have her in my life, then I at least want to engrave the memory of her into my mind as deeply as I can.

Instead of calling her back like I've been wanting to for the past couple of hours, I settle into the haze that comes with my fourth glass of whiskey, letting the day distort. I want to forget, to fog up all the good that I'm letting go of so that my heart can stop hurting. I linger from room to room with a glass tumbler loosely hanging from my fingertips, ending up in my bedroom, where the images of Ellie lying in my bed flood my mind. I still see the silhouette of her perfect body traced through the thin sheets. The sheets that still smell of her, intermingling with the softness of the fabric.

With the whiskey now settled into my bloodstream, I lie down on my bed and drink in her scent so I can hang on to this one keepsake of her for as long as I can. Sear Ellie's scent into my skin so I don't have to say goodbye. So I can hold on to her.

My phone rings in my hand, held there loosely with my body lying in the prone position. Shana's name lights up on the screen. I'm surprised that she's calling this late but regardless, I answer, preparing myself for her wrath.

"Rhylan! What the *fuck* happened?!" she demands through the phone. "There are pictures of you all over TMZ with that girl. And you hit someone?!"

"No, Shana. I didn't hit anyone. I just grabbed him," I say, my voice raspy and tired as I sit up.

"Well, that's not what they're saying. He's claiming you attacked him. And the things they're saying about this girl. Rhy, it doesn't look good," she says, softer and more exasperated.

I bury my face into my free hand, rubbing my temples as I listen to Shana laying everything out in front of me. How I quite possibly ruined my future, Ellie's future. "Shana, things just got out of hand."

"I mean, I don't even know how they found out who she is."

"You know how it goes." I sigh, my voice hoarse. "They bribe the right people and dig in the right places. They've done it before."

"Regardless, I think you need to make some sort of statement. And since everyone's claiming this girl came between you and Bella Raven, I need something official from you. Are you two together?"

I grimace at her words. I didn't mean to pull Ellie into this mess. Bella means nothing to me, and now people are speculating that Ellie broke us apart. If I continue to see Ellie, I'll only end up hurting her, and I don't know if I can live with that.

"No. It's nothing. Just tell people that we're friends, nothing more," I respond coolly. I take another sip, draining the final contents of the whiskey as the burn trickles down to my stomach.

"Okay. I'll write up something for you, a statement of apology for the incident. Hopefully that pap won't press charges. And then..." She pauses. "I–I think you should lie low," Shana instructs hesitantly. She sympathizes with the incident. She knows that the reports of me attacking someone, as false as they may be, and having that on record could end my career if handled badly.

I sigh, defeated and thoroughly exhausted. "Yeah, okay, Shana."

"Okay," she answers. "I'll call you tomorrow."

We hang up, and my phone rings almost instantly. It's Ellie. I answer this time, knowing what I need to do.

"Rhylan?" She speaks so softly, so gently. The sound of her

voice makes my chest tighten into a painful knot. *I have to let her go.*

"Ellie," I slur out, the resentment shifting to bitter sarcasm. No room for compassion. Only pain seeping through the pores so all she hears is harsh virulence. "Man, I thought I would never hear from you again."

I don't know when the blurred buzz turned into an intoxicated fog of poor judgment and out of place reasoning, but it's pouring into the cracks of my voice. As a result, all that comes out is an acrid bitterness that bites at my tongue while swimming in the drunken haze that makes the hate and desperation simmer.

"Rhylan? Where are you?" she speaks more firmly, her timidness gone.

I laugh. Not because anything's funny but because it's so completely unbelievable how *not* funny things are. How I will never find the will to laugh or smile again. How I will never be able to hold Ellie in my arms, never whisk her off to that secluded island I wanted to escape to. How instead, I'm preparing to say goodbye to someone that I'm realizing I can't live without.

"I'm at home! I'm sitting here, looking at my bed and thinking about how I fucked you last night." The words coming out of my mouth feel like acid eating away at my anger. I'm angry at the world. So pissed off that my one chance of happiness was stolen from me. And I'm taking it all out on Ellie, knowing full well that it isn't her fault. But the corrosiveness that's dissolving the layers of my heart is taking over, and I don't know how to rein it in.

She doesn't say anything, but I can feel her recoil at my vulgarity.

"Rhylan, we need to talk. Can I see you?" she finally responds, her tone matching mine in irritation.

I let out a shaky sigh, holding back the lump in my throat. "No, I don't think so. I don't think I have anything to say to you."

"What are you talking about?"

"I don't know how much clearer I can be. I don't want to see you anymore." I hold back the tears that are forcing their way out of me. I don't mean it. I don't mean any of it, but I know it's the only way that I can keep Ellie away from me. I couldn't protect her heart. Instead, I damaged it further. I need her to stay away from me before I do irreparable damage. I'm not meant to be happy, and I'm sure as hell not meant to make anyone else happy. I've come to terms with this, and now I'm ready to lie in the bed that I made.

She stays silent. I can hear the muffled sobs that she's trying to silence. The tears start streaming down my face as I picture the hurt that I just lashed at her. I want to run to her, to tell her it was all a lie, to beg for forgiveness. Most of all, I want to disappear with her, drag her to our secluded island away from everything.

"Look, Ellie, what we had was fun, but don't you think it's run its course?"

She stays silent for a while longer. I almost hang up, assuming she no longer wants to speak to me, but then I hear her strangled voice.

"Rhylan," she cries. "They came to my house! Claire had to

call the police. I…" A sob cuts off her words. "What do I do? I need you to tell me what to do."

"Ellie…" I whisper. My voice no longer carries the added edge from the pent-up anger. Instead, it's been replaced by every type of pain and ache that I've ever experienced, all placed there by the sounds of Ellie's cries and tears. "There's nothing I can do. I told you, I–I don't want to see you anymore." My voice is weak, lacking conviction, wavering instead.

"Rhylan!"

I don't say I'm sorry like I want to, for all the pain that I seared in her heart. I don't tell her that everything will be okay, lying through my teeth in an attempt to calm her. Instead, I let her go.

I place my phone down on my nightstand and stare at my bed. Our own secluded island we created out of love. Now, that dream feels so far from me. So distant that it leaves a spiteful chill running up my spine. I slump down onto my bed and sob into my hands. There's nothing in this world that can mend the damage that was done to Ellie. To my heart. It has broken into a million little pieces, its remains blowing away with the wind, leaving me empty.

CHAPTER 33
Ellie

"Ugh."

Why is it always so bright in the morning? My curtains feel so pointless, all pretty in lavender and lilacs, with daylight streaming through the almost sheer material. I climb towards my window to adjust my curtains to no avail before burying myself under my covers once again.

It's been just over two weeks since my late-night phone call to Rhylan. But the wounds are still fresh. The acidity in his tone that was full of emotionless resentment tore me apart. As if he didn't give his hateful words a second thought and they came out naturally, with him pointedly meaning every bit of it. The paparazzi that have been following me from my home to school have died down since they haven't seen me with Rhylan. But the fear of them popping out from the bushes, digging into what little amount of privacy I have left, lingers like a predator ready to pounce on their kill. I feel watched. Like every move that I make is open for anyone to pick and prod.

In the meantime, my recovery has been time-consuming

and painful. Each day is still passing by, going back to long stretches of dark haze. The hours blend into each other, disorienting me into oblivion.

My phone buzzes. I already know it's Claire. She's been checking in on me every morning since. Her outrage towards Rhylan was evident as she had repeatedly called him a "selfish bastard" over and over as I poured my heart out to her.

"Hey, El. You up?"

"Yeah, I just got up."

"You want to grab some coffee before class?"

"No, I'm good. I don't think I have time anyways."

"Okay. Just call me later."

"Okay. Bye." I hang up my phone and pull myself out of bed.

Claire's daily calls have actually helped. Just as soon as I feel like climbing under my covers and staying there forever, her call pulls me out of my slump and forces me to start my day. Quite honestly, I don't really have a choice. She would probably barge into my room and drag me out if she had to.

I pull myself up out of bed and trudge to the bathroom. It's déjà vu all over again as my day starts in a blur and continues in a thick fog. As if everything that happened between me and Rhylan was just a dream. And maybe it was, and now I've woken up, feeling the hollow hole in my chest a little too intensely.

Once I'm ready for school, I walk into the kitchen to grab a thermos for my coffee. There's a note on the counter from my mom.

Morning Ellie, I'm going out to dinner after work with Mark. Don't wait up for me.

We never talked about our dinner, the one where we were supposed to wipe away our past and lay over a new future in its place, pretending like all the pain from the last decade didn't exist. Instead, I've noticed more nights that my mom comes home a little late, having a quick dinner with Mark after work or leaving the house earlier than usual to have a cup of coffee with him, leaving our pot at home untouched. I can't help but notice how relaxed and happy she is when she's at home. As if *not* talking about everything is exactly what she wants, while I'm exploding from the inside out, everything I want to say seeping through my pores in an attempt to keep it all below the surface.

My finger taps on her scribbled message written hastily in blue ink on the back of an unopened utility bill before I fill my thermos and walk out the door.

"You know, you're better off without him, Ellie," Wes says through a mouth full of chips.

Claire swats his arm in response, signaling him to stay away from the topic of my most recent heartbreak.

"What?" he exclaims with his hands extended out. "He sounds like a total douche. Even if he's a movie star," he justifies.

"We're not talking about that asshole Rhylan Matthews," Claire says, shutting down any further conversation about Rhylan.

"It's okay," I assure them. "I don't mind, Claire. Acting like it didn't happen isn't going to make it any better."

"See! It's cathartic," Wes explains, defending himself.

Claire rolls her eyes at him and leans her head against his broad shoulder. Wes smiles down at her, flashing his small dimple, and kisses the top of her head. I smile at both of them, appreciating the time they're spending with me so I don't have to be alone.

Even Wes, who usually lets us girls have our girl time, has frequently been joining us to support Claire's undertaking of my emotional well-being until I'm no longer grief-stricken.

Today after class, Claire called to suggest another happy hour date. We're already on our third basket of chips and Claire and Wes's second round of margaritas. I'm still nursing my first.

"You know, before it all went to hell, I really thought I meant something to him. I believed it so much that *I* called *him* to tell him that. I was so confident that..." I trail off. My voice starts to crack, and I can't continue. If I do, I might break down right into the miniature bowl of salsa.

"Ellie..." Claire reaches for my hand and looks at me with a pained expression of sympathy. I hadn't realized that, while in the middle of my grieving, some of it had been transferred onto her.

A wave of guilt passes over me, and I look at her apologetically. "Claire, I'm sorry. You really don't have to worry about me. I'll be fine."

"I know. I just want to be there for you. That's all," she replies with a sincere smile.

I retreat my hand and reach for my keys sitting at the edge of the table next to my phone. I've intruded enough on Claire and Wes's time, and I know they want to be alone.

"Hey, I'm going to get out of here. I have some studying to do, and I really can't put it off till the weekend." I smile at both of them as I quickly say my goodbyes.

"El, I'll come with you," Claire starts to say as she gathers her belongings.

"No, stay. You two enjoy your night. I'll call you later."

I leave the restaurant before Claire can catch up to me, hurriedly walking to my car to drive home. When I turn on the radio, Beyonce's "Irreplaceable" starts to play on the radio before I flick the stereo off altogether, the music reminding me too much of Rhylan. After I pull into my driveway, I slowly gather my things before trudging through the front door.

"Hi, honey," my mom calls from the couch.

"Hey, Mom," I answer, surprised to see her home. "I thought you weren't going to be home till later."

"Yeah, but Mark had to work later than he thought. We just grabbed a quick bite before I left."

I nod and watch her. Her gaze reverts back towards the television while patting Angus's head lying heavily on her lap.

A bubble of frustration starts to build inside me. So many things in my life have turned upside down in the past couple of weeks, and I feel so out of control. For a sliver of a moment, when I was with Rhylan, I felt hopeful. A sense of optimism that felt so new to me presented itself, and it all dissolved so quickly. I crave that sense of control again, that sense of established resolution where I feel a part of my future is more concrete than unsure.

I change direction on the path to my room and firmly sit on the sofa facing my mom.

"Mom?" I call.

She turns to face me.

"Why don't we ever talk about Dad?"

Her eyes turn wide and her mouth slacks open. "What do you mean?"

"You know what I mean."

She sighs, her hands smoothing over her thighs. "Eleanor…"

"I'm tired of all this," I say, the frustration hiding behind my controlled voice as I attempt to remain level and calm. "Of hurting and pretending things didn't happen."

"What are we pretending didn't happen?" she asks.

"Everything!" I practically shout. "Rhylan, what happened at dinner with Mark, the fact that I tried to kill myself, *Dad*."

"Ellie, I just don't know what to say…"

"I don't either, Mom," I say, my voice softening. "But that doesn't mean I don't want to talk about it."

"I miss him," she says softly, her voice breaking. "And I'm so scared that if we start talking about him, it'll hurt even more. I'm scared that it'll hurt you. And I don't want to lose you again…"

I sigh, knowing that while I shouldn't bear the responsibility of everything, the pain that my mom feels is one that we both are living through. "But I want to talk about him," I plead. "I want him back in our lives. Even though I know he physically can't be, I want him in our home. I want everyone in our lives to know that we loved him and he loved us."

"He did love us, didn't he?" she asks, a weak smile poking through her face.

A watered-down laugh slips through my lips. "Remember the day he brought home Angus? And you got so mad because you already told him we couldn't have a dog for months?"

She laughs. "And I told him he had to sleep on the couch because Angus wouldn't stop crying at night?"

Angus lifts his head at the mention of his name, and we both smile fondly at him.

"He would have been so upset if he knew I did that to myself," I whisper. "When I…"

My mom grips my hand. "Ellie… There were a lot of things that happened after he died. I'm just thankful that I didn't lose you too."

"I'm sorry, Mom," I say. "I'm sorry that I… I only hurt you in the end and it made things so much worse for us."

"Don't apologize," she says, squeezing my hand. "All that matters is that we have each other."

I nod and curl into her, Angus inching closer as he fights for his place on my mom's lap as the unofficial younger child.

"Is this because of Rhylan?" she finally asks. "That you're saying all of this?"

I sigh, pulling away from her and slumping against the couch. "I don't know."

"Listen, you don't have to tell me what happened between you two. We don't have to tell each other *everything*. You're an adult. I don't need to know why you didn't come home after we had dinner with Mark."

"Mom," I protest.

"But," she continues, her hand coming up between us, "just know that sometimes, you have to learn to move on. Even though it's the last thing you want to do. Even if it might not feel right to you."

"Is that what made you finally start dating Mark?"

"Something like that," she says through a loving smile.

My brows turn up as my lips press into a firm line, suffocating the fresh wave of tears tightening my throat. "I'm trying."

She nods. "I… I promise I won't hide behind all the things that we—*I*—don't want to talk about. If you want to talk, we'll talk." Her apologetic face pleads for forgiveness.

"Yeah," I answer, patting her thigh. "Thanks, Mom."

"And I'm so happy that you have Claire," she adds. "Hold on to that one."

I chuckle. "I will. But I'm not going to tell her you said that because her head will just…" I mime the image of Claire's head exploding, bringing my hands to the side of my head while mimicking the sound of an explosion with my mouth, the pressure of it getting too big, causing it to finally combust.

"She might even claim she's your favorite daughter," I add. My mom laughs, shaking her head.

Once I'm in my room, lying in bed with the lights turned off and the TV volume low enough to provide the most minimal background noise, I reason with the small space between reality and possibility. Maybe what Rhylan and I had was infatuation, something that grew out of hand. And maybe it's best that this fatuous relationship ended before it turned into something that wasn't meant to be.

But the more I think about it, to call it infatuation doesn't make sense. It's not right because this was deeper than that. As much as it didn't make sense, it stemmed from a place of love. I can't deny it. No matter how much I wanted to or tried.

It doesn't matter though. Whether I love Rhylan or he loves me. None of that matters anymore. The inevitable truth is that I'm meant to live my life without him in it. Without our laughs, without our moments, without the words that were shared between only us two, completely secretive and intimate. I have to slowly learn to let all of that go, just like my mom said, and that's what is killing me. The painful goodbye that I'm putting off. I don't know how to say goodbye to a part of me that I have just learned I can't live without. But I have to, one way or another.

Even though it doesn't feel right, I have to move on. I don't have a choice.

The room is spinning. Not just metaphorically but literally. It's spinning on some rapidly rotating axis. The light is excruciatingly bright, causing me to wince and recoil. I bring my hand to my face to shield it, the stinging light still bursting through my fingers in bright rays.

A light knock hits my door, but in my current state, it sounds like a large gong booming against the walls.

"Good morning, sunshine." Charles's voice rings too loudly even though he's speaking at a regular volume. "Actually, good afternoon."

I grimace and rub my hands into my face. "What time is it?" My voice is scratchy, like it's filled with sand.

"Just after one. A little later than the normal wake-up time for a well-established adult, but who am I to judge?"

I groan an unintelligible sound. I peek through my fingers to see Charles with two mugs of steaming coffee, the aroma filling the room and slapping away my hangover almost instantly.

"At least you look better than Quasimodo outside. You

know he's not wearing any pants?" Charles is referring to Chuck. We both stumbled into my living room at three a.m., with me not knowing my hand from my ass, and I somehow managed to land in a spot comfortable enough to fall asleep. I'm surprised I made it into bed at all.

"I guess we uh… We went a little crazy last night," I say through a dry, hoarse voice. I reach for the mug and nod thanks to him.

"Yeah, you could say that." Charles brings his mug to his mouth and sips loudly. My head pounds, the sounds of Charles's slurping echoing off the walls, causing my temples to throb. "So, what's going on?"

I look at him through the steam coming off my mug. "What do you mean?"

"You've been doing a lot more drinking than usual lately. I don't think I've seen you this wasted since our early party days. It's a lot even for him." He points a thumb towards the door.

I look up and stretch out my neck, trying to loosen up the tension that has built up between my shoulders. "I've just been… distracted, I guess."

We quietly sip. I can feel Charles's eyes watching, waiting for a real answer.

"Are you going to tell me the truth, or am I going to have to drag it out of you?" He sits on the side of the bed that's empty, smoothing out the rumpled sheets before he sinks into the mattress.

I sigh. I take my time answering, sipping my coffee before speaking. "I told Ellie I didn't want to see her anymore."

"And why did you do that?"

"You saw what happened with the paps. It was a fucking shit show. She's not cut out for this fucked up life. I'm not even cut out for it, but I have no choice." I wince. The images of Ellie standing on her stoop, her blanched face horrified and zoomed in through the grainy images, flash through shooting shocks of pain to my chest. And the sound of her cries, ringing through my ears as her sobs echo against my heart, reminds me why I had to let her go.

He nods. "Okay," he finally says, unconvinced with my reasoning.

"What?" I say, my voice annoyed.

"Nothing," he answers, his mouth downturned in an impassive shake of his head. "I was just thinking that if Ellie… When she gets tired of seeing your annoyingly pretty face, and I'm sure that day will come eventually, she should be the one to tell you."

A shaky sigh blows through my lips. The thought of taking a chance and letting Ellie be a part of my life feels freeing. As if everything that I could think of that could make me happy, could make me smile, was just a phone call away. Like I could simply tell Ellie that I was wrong and that everything I did was to protect her. But it isn't that simple. Ellie's heart isn't simple. It's distinctive, carrying characteristics that could only be present in someone like her. I was meant to handle her heart with care, but I became reckless. I fell into a drunken stupor of happiness that filled me when I was around her, and I became irresponsible. And now I'm living the consequences of it all.

Charles would never understand this. "It's complicated."

"Okay. I get it," he says. "I'm not going to pretend I

understand your relationship. That's between you two. I'm just calling it as it is. You look like shit."

"Thanks," I mutter with a smirk. "And thanks for checking in on me."

He pats my bare shoulder, making me wince from the sharp slap. "Anytime."

"Hello?" A low, sultry voice rings from the other end.

"Hi, Bella. It's Rhylan. How are you?"

Bella's deep laughter rings through the phone. "How am I? After all this time, have you finally come to your senses, Rhylan Matthews?"

I ignore the loose resentment in her tone. "Uh, yeah. Sorry about that," I say, already wanting this conversation to be over.

"So, to what do I owe the pleasure of this phone call?"

"A couple of my friends are heading out to The Velvet Room in Hollywood tonight. I was wondering if you would like to join us," I say through gritted teeth. After I spoke with Charles, it was clear, more than ever, that I needed to distance myself from Ellie. Charles didn't necessarily agree, but I knew what had to be done so that I could finally sever ties with Ellie.

My late nights partying and being seen with random women since the paparazzi incident weren't cutting it. So I called the one person that could clear the air between Ellie and me. Whatever I had to do so that her name would no longer be attached to mine, so that the images of us would stop floating around the internet, taunting and reminding the both of us of what could have been. I called Bella.

"Oh, I'll have to think about it. I'm such a busy woman," she says teasingly.

"Okay. Just text me later. We're going to head out just after midnight, so…"

"I'll let you know," she says. I can hear her smile through the phone.

"Who was that?" Chuck asks as I hang up the phone call. He walks into the living room with a bowl full of pretzels I didn't even know I had. He's holding three beers in his hand, and he tosses one to Charles before walking one over to me.

"Where did you get those?"

"I found them in your pantry. Why?"

"I would check the expiration date on those before you continue eating them."

He shrugs and plops himself on the couch. Charles shakes his head when Chuck points the bowl toward him.

"He was talking to Bella," Charles answers for me.

Chuck's eyebrows shoot up. "Bella Raven?"

"Yeah. I asked her if she wanted to join us tonight."

"Yeah?" he confirms excitedly. "You should ask her if she has a friend." Chuck smiles, raising his brows at the possibility of his suggestion.

I shake my head. "I'm going to shower. Can we order some food? I'm starving."

"Okay, 'starving.' I'll take care of it," Chuck answers, never short on the continuous supply of dad jokes.

The three of us spend the day watching TV and continuing our drinking until nighttime. Jackson joins us, bringing along a bottle of tequila, claiming it will pair perfectly with the greasy Mexican food delivered to my door as if he's talking about pairing a glass of merlot with a filet mignon.

"You don't have to get home to the kids?" Jackson asks Charles as the night settles outside.

"Amelia's out with her friends, so we got the nanny for the night."

"So you're partying with us tonight?" Chuck asks in excitement. He pours another round of shots as he waits for Charles to answer.

"Sure, but I'm not doing any partying. Just hanging out," he says with hesitation.

"What are you talking about? That's what we do!"

"Come on. Just a couple of drinks," I add. I feel relaxed, the beers and tequila loosening and fading all thoughts of Ellie. Only dimming to a distant memory though. She's always there, ever so present in the hidden corners of my mind, reminding me of the ache in my heart.

"Yeah. And that couple of drinks turns into a week-long hangover."

"Weak," Chuck bellows in Charles's direction.

As planned, late into the night, we pile into Jackson's Range Rover and drive towards Hollywood.

"Are you okay to drive?" I whisper to Jackson.

"I just had a couple of beers. I'm fine," he calls over his shoulder, reminding me of the tequila shots he repeatedly refused.

I nod, settling into the backseat behind him. Bella texts me in the car, saying she's on her way, a group of her friends joining as well. I read through her text messages, the last one a snapshot of herself dressed in a short skirt in front of a floor-length mirror. Chuck looks over my shoulder in the seat next to me.

"Holy shit. Bella Raven is so hot. She could break my heart, and I would beg for her forgiveness." He lets out a whistle through his teeth.

I quickly put my phone in my pocket. "Yeah. I'll put in a good word in case she's in the heartbreaking kind of mood."

The car comes to a halt as we approach the entrance to the club. There's already a long line formed outside. Jackson pulls right to where the line ends, and the doors open. The lights immediately start to flash, and paparazzi, screaming in every direction, call for Charles and me. Chuck, in the ever so present bantering mood he's always in, smiles and poses as if he's the star that everyone's been waiting all night for. I wrap my arm around his neck, smiling against his cheek, and drag him inside. Just as the doors open for us, I'm stopped by someone reaching for my arm. I turn and see Bella standing in front of me.

"Bella! Hi," I say, surprised even though I'm the one who invited her.

The flashing of lights becomes frenzied, the shouting growing even louder. I take the opportunity and bring Bella close to me so that the cameras can get the shot they didn't know they were waiting for. Bella eats it up. She poses alongside me, whipping her hair over her shoulders and waving as if we were on the red carpet. I then do something so bold, I didn't know I had it in me. I bring my fingers to her chin to turn her face towards me. And I kiss her.

The flashes around us become furious, the shouting that comes from all different directions shifting into a chaotic roar. Bella pulls away from our kiss and gazes up at me with hooded eyes and a seductive smile. I look at her, no emotion, no sign of lust or wanting, just vacant, void of fervency. But that moment passes. I turn to the cameras, a feigned smile plastered on my face. As quickly as the kiss passes between Bella and me, I turn towards the door and enter the building, Bella close at my feet.

As soon as we walk through the door, the music is loud. I can feel the vibrations from the bass strum through my chest. When I turn to Bella, I speak through the quiver in my chest.

"Did you want a drink?" I shout over the music. She flirtatiously leans herself towards me, casually placing a hand on my forearm and grazing her fingers up towards my shoulder. I inwardly flinch, her touch not welcome, but I try to remain indifferent.

"Sure! I'll have whatever you're having," she says. She looks around the room, and her eyes light up towards the dance floor. "My friends are over there. I'm going to say hi." Her voice is shrill as she tries to speak over the music. I nod, silently letting her know that I heard her, and walk towards the bar.

I lean against the bar top, waiting for a bartender to become available to take my order. It's busy and hectic, but I wait patiently. My hands find the corners of my lips, grazing them, the last thing they touched being Bella's lips. I hate knowing that the last lips mine touched weren't Ellie's anymore. If it was up to me, all of my kisses would be saved for Ellie. Every single one of them. I would kiss her every moment I could get. I would savor each one, holding her close to me and letting her lips linger longer than needed until every kiss that belonged to Ellie was mine.

"Hey, boss." I'm interrupted from my thoughts by the bartender with a full beard and tattoo sleeves running down to the tips of his fingers. "What'll it be?"

"I'll have a scotch, neat," I answer him. "Make that two," I add, two fingers held in the air, signaling that I want a second added to my order.

The drinks come quickly, and I open a tab. I down the first one and look around for Bella. I can't find her anywhere. I survey the span of the dance floor to where Bella walked, and I still don't see her. I down the second glass of scotch, and the slow burn travels down my throat. It hits my stomach, causing a blaze to ignite, a fire that spreads and spans throughout my body. My movements begin to feel numb, every shift following in slow motion.

"Hey! We lost you," Jackson screams into my ear. He slings his arm around my neck with a large bottle of something held in his hand, I don't even care what. I grab it from him and empty almost half of it. Already buzzed from our day spent lazily drinking tequila, the strong liquor hits my stomach, leaving a warmth spreading through my body.

I'm trying to loosen the noose that's suffocating me with the undying supply of alcohol that keeps coming my way. But the noise, the crowd, the stuffy air makes me feel like everything is closing in on me. I need to get away.

I hand Jackson back the half-empty bottle and reach my hand into his shirt pocket. I find what I'm looking for: the valet ticket for his car. I hold it up in front of him and point towards the exit.

"Are you okay to drive?" he yells, the same question I asked him on our way over here.

"I'm just going to sit in the car. I'm a little tired," I answer. He nods and continues to bob his head along to the music. He turns and weaves himself through the crowd of people, disappearing in the midst of the dancers.

I turn and find the door I came in from. As soon as I push past the doors, the cameras start again, flashing in my face and nearly blinding me. My sweat-filmed, haggard face searches for the valet so I can find Jackson's car. When I finally call them, they drive up quickly, and I hastily get in and drive off. I didn't intend on driving. I'm too inebriated. But when the door opened, inviting me into an escape from the stifling crowd, I accepted.

With the adrenaline coursing through me, I drive. The alcohol that I guzzled not even ten minutes ago is now hitting my bloodstream and making its way to my consciousness. My feet become heavy on the pedal, like bricks floating to the bottom of the ocean, sinking with no way up. Headlights flash by me, whizzing by my ear through the open window. The sounds of horns honking and people yelling and laughing in the streets become muffled, a distorted sound that squeezes the sides of my head.

What the hell am I doing? I could hurt someone like this. Why did I even get behind the wheel?

During that small window of clarity, I pull over, the sidewalk busy and crowded. I don't even know where I am. I took so many turns and ran past so many intersections I can't even tell what direction I came from. I walk out of the car, my gaze zeroed in on the ground as I stumble onto the sidewalk. All while crashing into people before finally finding a wall to lean against.

I turn and rest my back to the wall, my head following. The cool brick hitting the base of my skull takes away the fuzziness from the night as people continue to walk by me, busy on their own paths.

My eyes stay closed, the weight of my lids too heavy to keep them open. I pull out my phone to search for Charles's number, dialing with my head hung low and my vision blurred.

"Rhylan! Where'd you go?"

"Charles. I don't know where I am, but I need you to come and get me," I rasp out.

"What? Rhy! I can barely hear you."

I only hear the blaring music coming through the other side of the phone mingled in with the loud chatter overpowering Charles's voice. I remember sending him my location before letting my phone fall, and I go with it. I slump to the ground, no longer able to keep my legs straight, hobbling and weak.

"Hey! Look at this guy!" I hear a taunting voice. I feel my hair being pulled, my neck extending towards the sky. I wince from the pain. I want to pull away, to fight back, but I can't. I try to will every muscle in my body to bring my hands up, but my limbs feel like they've been filled with lead.

"He looks like he's got some money with that fancy jacket. Check his pockets," says another voice, more authoritative and serious.

When I hear the words, my hands start to twitch. They start to pull at my clothes, groping and prodding me. I finally start to fight back, moans escaping my mouth in a poor attempt to ward off my attackers. They see my arms raise, trying to curl myself inward, to protect myself. And then I feel the first blow. My ribs take the brunt of the hit, causing me to curl inward even further. The next blow goes to my face, grazing my lip and hitting my jaw. I groan loudly. Any protest stops at my throat, gurgling with the sounds of pain. The hits keep coming, hitting all parts of my body now in the fetal position on the cold, wet ground. I have no idea how long this goes on. Any notion of time is distorted. It could be seconds. It could be hours.

"Hey!" I hear from a distance. It's a familiar voice echoing through the streets full of people that are oblivious.

The men stop abruptly and run.

"Rhy!" I hear. "Oh my God. Are you okay?" It's Charles. He wraps his arm around my waist and sits me up. I cough, finally able to breathe.

"Holy shit. We need to get you to a hospital." I hear Jackson's voice. His face is the last one I remember seeing. With my eyes still closed, now swollen shut, Jackson puts his arm on the other side of me, helping Charles to get me to a standing position.

"The car's right here." I hear Chuck. They drag me to the car that I parked only a few steps away from where I was lying, the key still in the ignition. And then everything blurs. It darkens, and I disappear. I fade away into the night. But before everything becomes dark, I see Ellie's face. I see her smile, hear her laugh, and feel her touch. It's the last thing I hold on to that I know is real before I fade away.

CHAPTER 35
Ellie

Mozzarella, olive oil, and parsley.

I repeat the grocery list my mom gave me before I left the house. I should have written it down but instead, I'm risking myself forgetting one single item and having to return to the store as soon as I walk through my front door.

Mark is coming over tonight, and my mom is cooking "something special." The initial shock of my mom having met someone has somewhat dissipated, our talk having a lot to do with it, and I've finally been able to see my mom with Mark without instantly thinking of my dad. Mark has also finally become comfortable enough to come over to our house a couple of days during the week. His presence in our home has now become a regular thing, and I'm really not opposed to it. It's made the transition of him being in my mom's life easier, and I see how happy it's made her.

My hands are full because I unwittingly decided that I didn't need a shopping cart and opted to gather everything with my bare hands. She only needs a handful of items, but

I keep finding things that I'm having a sudden hankering for. As I find the parsley, I walk straight into the aisle carrying an assortment of chips and candy bars. It's a lost cause as I peruse, allowing my hand to lead the way and land on a Twix bar and a bag of Twizzlers. I add it to the growing stack of junk food I've gathered, ready to stash in my room for another night of binge-watching reality TV.

I struggle to balance everything as I walk to the checkout counter. There's a short line, but I stand and wait as my eyes wander. More impulse purchases line the aisles along with an array of magazines that are stacked in the wire racks. Then my eyes land on a recent article of *In Touch* magazine. I'm drawn to it because of the familiar faces zoomed in on, plastered on full display on the cover.

My stomach clenches, and my heart drops.

Rhylan, disheveled and dazed, has his arm draped over Bella Raven, the two locked in a kiss. In bold block letters underneath the picture, it reads: *Hot couple alert.*

What the hell? He's dating Bella?

I don't belong to anyone.

Those were his words. Words he said to me with a solemness that left little room for me to doubt him. But here he is, his lips on Bella's, contradicting every word he said to me. I feel lied to, completely bamboozled into something I thought was real. I feel like I never knew Rhylan at all.

Then I realize this doesn't concern me. None of it does. He can go around kissing Bella Raven if he wants. He can kiss anyone he wants to. I have no say. Except he still holds the reins to my heart, and he's pulling at them when I see his face like this. Like he's doing this to me, publishing these pictures to urt me on purpose.

"Miss?" A voice interrupts my thoughts. I look around and realize I'm holding up the line. The cashier looks at me, annoyed that I'm delaying the checkout procession. With my arms still full of groceries, I move along and place everything on the belt. The cashier asks me questions, none of which I hear. I just insert my card into the card reader and pay, my mind remaining in a fog, still unbelieving of what I just saw.

I reach for the plastic bag before the cashier is able to hand me my receipt, leaving him standing there with his hand outstretched holding the long piece of paper meant for me. My walk back to my car is hurried as I move swiftly through the weekend parking lot traffic.

I need to breathe. I need to eat ten candy bars. I need to hole up in my room for an unreasonable number of hours. I need to drive for sixteen hours towards the opposite coast and never look back. *I need to breathe.*

I get into the driver's seat and slam my door shut. My hands move to the steering wheel—ten and two position—and I try to steady my breathing. Everything I assumed I knew about Rhylan I question now. I don't know what was real, if any of it was. I feel so exposed, so betrayed. I feel so lost. I should be angry. I should be livid. I should assume that Rhylan is a sleazy person, someone that took advantage of me, but I can't bring myself to feel any of those things. I don't know why. I feel stupid that I can't bring out the anger in me that I know I should be feeling. Instead, I feel an overwhelming sadness take over me. A grief that I didn't know I would experience, realizing that I would finally have to let Rhylan go.

My phone rings in my purse, loud and shrill. I jump at the sudden noise, the stillness in my car having created a silence that muted my ears. I look at the screen and it's a number I don't recognize.

"Hello?" I answer.

"Hi. Is this Ellie?" the voice on the other end asks.

"Who is this?" I ask without answering the question from the caller. I make no attempt to hide my chagrin. Whoever it is on the other line, they're just going to have to understand that I'm not in the mood to play guessing games.

"This is Charles. Rhylan's friend? We met not too long ago," he says. Charles Bradley. As if I don't know who he is. He's just as famous as Rhylan. Of course I know who he is.

"Oh, hi," I say softly.

"I'm sorry to call you like this, out of the blue, but I wanted to talk to you about Rhylan," he explains. There's a moment of silence. As if he's contemplating how he needs to say his next words. I stay quiet.

"Rhylan's been in an accident, and he's in the hospital. He was attacked the other night. He's going to be okay, physically. He's just resting right now, but he's not doing too well otherwise."

"I don't know why you're telling me this," I answer, not bothering to hide the confusion. After my last conversation with Rhylan, I should be the last person that should be called. Whether he's lying in a hospital bed, convalescing after an attack, or sitting on a beach sipping a mai tai, I have no business in Rhylan's life. The pictures I just saw showed evidence of that.

"I know he would want you to know," he says. "And I think it would mean a lot to him if he saw you."

"I don't think so," I answer too quickly. I close my eyes and lean my head against the window, the cold glass providing comfort as my conscience battles out what to do. A part of me wants to see him. I want to make sure he's okay. I want to tell him that I miss him and get mad at him for getting himself hurt. But then there's the other part of me. The part that's arguing with my sense of reason, telling me that I'll only end up getting hurt. That my heart isn't strong enough to be torn apart once again.

"I know you two have had your differences, but Rhylan… He's got his own demons he's fighting. And they have nothing to do with you," Charles explains.

I sigh. The pent-up frustration leaves my chest. My chin quivers, and my throat tightens, keeping me mute.

"I understand if you don't want to see him. I just thought you should know," he finally says. I don't say anything. I just listen, my breathing becoming deep and harsh. "He's at Cedars-Sinai. This is my number. Just call me if you decide to visit. I'll make sure you see him."

The line goes silent.

CHAPTER 36
Rhylan

"Dr. Park to O.R., Dr. Park to O.R."

The voice echoing through the PA system jolts me awake. And then I feel pain. Searing physical pain. *What the hell happened?*

Clear tubes come out from my hand, as if they're an extension of me, leading up to a bulbous bag hanging from a metal pole. To look up, down, or even side to side is painful. Like every extremity of my body isn't meant to rotate and pivot as joints do. Everything feels so dry and calloused. Even the blankets lying on top of me feel rough and rigid.

It's so fucking bright in here. And cold. I wince, but I don't know if it's from the pain or the brightness. There's a curtain that surrounds me, partitioning me from the rest of the room.

God, that pain. It's unbearable.

A woman who doesn't look a day over twenty-four wearing a white lab coat pulls the curtain back. "Mr. Matthews. It's good to see you're awake."

"Where am I?" I ask. But it doesn't sound like my own voice. It sounds foreign. Like it hadn't been used in days. The coarseness that surrounds me is in my throat too.

"You're at Cedars-Sinai Medical Center. You were brought in very early yesterday morning by your friends," she answers.

I try to remember what even happened yesterday. *What day is it today?* I feel so disoriented. "Am I okay?"

"You have a couple of broken ribs, and we had to stitch your jaw up right here," she says, pointing to the gauze bandage taped to the left side of my jaw. "And your blood alcohol level was very high. Any higher and the alcohol poisoning could have become lethal."

I sigh. My hands rub my face, trying to wipe away the fog that has taken residence in my brain. My breath catches, wincing from the pain when my fingers touch my eye.

"We'll get you some ice for the eye. It's going to be swollen for a while, but the ice should help. In the meantime, call the nurses if you need anything."

She turns on her heels and leaves the room.

God, I feel like shit. I feel like retching, dry heaving. Something, anything so this sickening knot settled into the pit of my stomach can go away. I don't think I've ever felt this shitty in my life.

A nurse comes in following the doctor's exit, asking me if I want pain meds. I give a perfunctory nod as she pushes a syringe into a small port running alongside the tube at my side. As the medication kicks in, I'm lulled into a dreamless sleep. The only things I remember are flashes of Ellie's face. All of it fading into nothingness.

I spend the better part of the next twenty-four hours in and out of sleep, chasing the waves of pain with meds that seem to come around the clock. Just as a fresh wave of sharp, biting pain hits all the parts that are purple and blue, I hear clamoring echoing off the walls outside of my room followed by the pitter-patter of feet. It inches louder and louder with a harsh knock.

"Rhylan!" I look up and see Levi followed closely by Shana. She's at his heels, pushing past him to reach me first.

"Rhylan! Oh my God. Look at you!" Shana cries. She's not physically crying, but her voice is full of concern. She reaches her hand towards me but stops when I recoil from the pain that still keeps wavering in and out.

Levi and Shana both start to speak over each other. Jumbled words of false claims from every news syndicate about how drugs were involved, pressing charges against whoever attacked me, even the unspoken word that we've tried to avoid up until now: *rehab*. It doesn't look good. I ended up here because my drinking got out of hand. I wanted to dull the pain and used the only commodity at my disposal. I hadn't hurt anyone, thankfully, but it could have ended so much more badly than it did. What if next time I hurt someone? What if next time, I don't make it out alive?

They both stop talking, taking a moment to breathe before accidentally saying the wrong words. Shana smooths the coarse blanket at the foot of my bed and perches herself there. "Rhy, I'll take care of everything. You just need to worry about getting better."

"I can't believe this fucking happened! I mean, what the

hell were you thinking?!" Levi booms. His stress level is inching higher and higher. I'm worried he might actually have a stroke.

"Look, guys. I'm sorry this happened. Things just got out of control, and I made some really bad choices," I say. Images of that night start to come back to me in short flashes, forcing me to remember them. To recount them. I remember Bella, kissing her and then, just as quickly, losing sight of her. I remember all the alcohol I consumed as if it were going to waste. I also remember driving completely shit-faced and recklessly. And then the pain takes over the rest of my memories, making them fuzzy and unintelligible. I sit up, the pain in my side hitting me with a sharp ache that's still fresh and lingering, causing me to silently groan in an effort to hide my discomfort.

Shana watches me, her brows stitched together and lips in a firm, straight line. Usually, she's more assertive, more stern and strict. She's the voice of reason. Always telling me when things get out of hand and to watch my image. But now, all of that's gone. It's all been replaced by a face of what-ifs.

She leans forward, placing her hand on my knee and gently squeezing it. It's as if she's touching me to make sure I'm actually here, alive. The simple gesture reminds me of my mom, always nurturing and concerned, judgment the last thing on the agenda.

When I see the concern flash through her eyes, it makes my chest tighten and ache all over. In moments of absolute weakness, you tend to search for the people who you love. The ones who would soothe the gnawing pain so that it doesn't have to hurt anymore. The ones who were around when you were happiest. When you felt invincible.

Ellie.

I would move mountains for her. I would leave everything behind and sweep her off her feet to that isolated island, just to be with her. Just so that we could live in the happiness that I didn't know existed until her.

I look down at my lap. I can't look at Shana or Levi. I can't face anyone. The trembling of my chin starts on its own, uncontrollable and wavering. Mistiness clouds my vision, and I feel the first trickle of a tear running down my cheek. *How the fuck did I end up here?*

Shana turns to shush a still-speaking Levi. He's rambling on and on about how we have to file a report with the police department and I may need to hire a lawyer for I don't even know what. He stills, looking at me, and his face softens.

Levi sighs. "Rhy, just get some rest. Focus on getting better. We'll figure things out from here."

"Rhylan?" I hear the familiar voice, soft and meek, from behind the curtain. The three of us turn to look, and I see Ellie's worried face peek from behind the curtain.

"Ellie," I whisper. She's like a vision, a dream. Her physically being here can't possibly be true. My heart thrums in my chest, and my body tightens, fighting every muscle *not* to pull her to me and hold her so she can never leave. I sit up a little straighter and try to smooth out the mess that I've become, but it's no use. I look like how I feel, tired and hopeless.

"We'll give you two a minute," Levi says sternly. He turns, and Shana follows behind him. Ellie takes a step closer to me, her hands pulling the curtain back enough to make room for her to walk through. Her movements are cautious and hesitant.

The need to reach out to her causes my hands to lift on their own, and I clench my fists to stop myself. I can't do this. I can't *fucking* do this.

The urge to look into her eyes is too strong, so I give in. Those deep, honey-colored eyes that I could get lost in for days look back at me. Downturned and riddled with sadness to the point of tears.

I can't fucking do this.

"How did you know I was here?"

"Charles called. He thought that maybe you would want to see me," she explains.

I steal a moment to take in the sight of her. Her jeans hug her hips and stop high at her waist, where a plain white T-shirt meets it, discreetly exposing her midsection. Her hair, loose and wavy, rests across her chest and shoulders. I start to notice small details about her, committing it all to memory. Like the dainty gold bracelet that rests on her wrist or the shimmer of blush she applied to her cheekbones. Details that I noticed before but are now more prominent, knowing that this truly may be the last time I see her.

I nod and look away. The cut that sears through my lower lip screams as I run my teeth along the edges. But the physical pain is nothing compared to the pain that seeps through me from watching Ellie as she becomes even more distant from me. She's here, within arm's reach, but she's somehow so far away.

I imagine what it would feel like to hold her in my arms. To drink in the scent of her and whisper into her ear. To hold her face between my hands so that I could stare into her eyes without limitations. To kiss her.

"Thanks for coming to check on me, but you really didn't have to. I'm fine." My voice is cold, annoyed with forged irritation.

She averts her eyes, looking at her feet and shuffling them beneath her. She nods before looking up again. I finally see the tears forming in her eyes, pooling along the rim, urging to trickle down her beautiful face. I shake the impulse to wipe them away or cradle her face.

"I'm glad you're okay. Charles seemed concerned that you might not be."

"Yeah. Well, I guess he worried for nothing."

"Okay," she says. She shuffles her feet again, shifting her weight from one foot to the other. Her hands come together in front of her, her fingers twisting and straining against each other.

"I don't know if you know, but I'm seeing Bella now. She should be here any minute, actually." My voice is growing even colder, pushing her away as best as I can. It's all a lie. Bella probably doesn't even know that I'm lying up in a hospital. The last time I saw her, she was walking away from me in a crowded club.

"Right," she says. She ducks her head down, and I see the drop of a tear hit the denim of her jeans, leaving a darkening stain seeping into the fabric. She turns her head to the side, bringing her palm to her face and discreetly wiping her cheek. She looks back at me, a forced smile peeking through her tears. "I'm happy for you, Rhylan."

The stiffness in my face slacks, and my expression softens. I wish she would yell at me, call me names, tell me that I'm dead to her. Anything so that she can hate me, blame me for hurting her instead of taking in all the pain on her own.

"Ellie…" My voice is weak, pathetic. I hate myself. I loathe every bit of myself for doing this to her.

"Take care." She turns and leaves before I have a chance to say anything else.

And she's gone. The emptiness she leaves behind is so pronounced, so obtrusive.

I hunch over and cry. No, I bawl. I sob through the pain, my muscles and bones screaming at me to stop. I don't care anymore. Physical pain and all, I just want everything to stop hurting. I want Ellie to come back. Instead, I cling to the blankets so I have something to hold on to. I wrap my arms around myself so that I can somehow soothe the pain coursing through me. But in the end, all I feel is numbness. Complete paralysis. So I don't fight it. I just lie there, defeated.

H ope is such a fiendish emotion. Everyone needs hope, whether it's for motivation or purpose. Its intent is to keep the unknown in a state of possibility. But there's the wretched side of hope. When those moments actually make you feel optimistic, invincible. As if a differing outcome isn't possible when in reality, it's the most likely scenario. That was what caused me to call Charles back. Hope. Hope that his words were true and Rhylan actually wanted to see me. Hope that what we had was real and that there could be a future for us.

But I was wrong. The most likely scenario that I tucked away because of hope surfaced and reared its ugly side.

After I left the hospital, I came home and licked my wounds. I cleaned and dressed those fresh cuts with self-affirmations that I would somehow get through this. Without Rhylan. Everything from here on out would be without Rhylan, like I had originally planned. All of my daily routines, my future, my life. It would all have to be without the person who I wanted to share it with. And I would have to learn to do so, even if I didn't want to.

So I continued. Weeks passed and I went on with my life, burying deep the cold rejection that Rhylan threw at me and trying to live my life. Minute to minute, hour to hour, day to day. They all blurred into one.

Today, with my hours blending into days, I drive towards The Cottage Bookstore after school. I usually don't work weekdays, but Mrs. Le has plans tonight, so she asked me to close the store. I arrive to Mrs. Le frantically packing a small stack of hardcover books in her worn-out Trader Joe's canvas bag. She reaches into her purse to pull out a deep wine-colored lipstick and swiftly applies it as she uses the display counter as a makeshift mirror.

"Thank you so much for coming in today, Ellie. Paul made these dinner plans last month, and I completely forgot about them."

She fluffs her hair in an attempt to make it more presentable. Mrs. Le's style has always struggled to keep up with current fashion trends. She even thought gaucho pants were still in style until her kids told her she looked like she was bringing back a late nineties era fashion trend. She always wears the same wool cardigan underneath the red brick apron she puts on every morning before opening the store.

But tonight, she's trading it all in for a simple black dress for a night out with her tech executive husband, even swapping out her New Balance sneakers for kitten heel pumps.

"Oh, it's no problem. I'd probably be at home watching Netflix or something anyways. This is much more productive."

She smiles at me while she swings her bags over her

shoulder with heft. "Call me on my cell if you need anything. I'll see you tomorrow."

The clicking of her heels echoes against the pavement as she scurries to her car. I watch as she drives off. It's just past five o'clock. The day is starting to get cooler, and the sun is gradually setting behind the trees that line the plaza where the bookstore sits in a corner lot.

I settle myself behind the counter and flip through one of the books on display. With the store being empty and eerily quiet, I put the book down and tap my nails against the counter. I'm used to the in and out of customer traffic on the weekends, and this uncomfortable silence is making me needlessly restless.

Just then, the door jingles, announcing a customer's entrance to the store. I look up and see Austin from my statistics class looking just as surprised to see me as I am to see him.

"Ellie! I didn't know you worked here."

"Hi, Austin," I answer with a small wave along with a sheepish smile that naturally comes with running into someone in public.

"This is how you're spending your Friday night? That's no fun," he says with a small chuckle.

"I usually don't work weekdays, but my boss asked me to pick up an extra shift tonight. She has a hot date." I smile at the notion of Mr. and Mrs. Le sharing anything other than a basket of sliced bread with a side of cold butter and an overpriced bottle of wine.

"Lucky her," he answers as he looks around the store to see if there's anyone else. He leans his elbows against the counter and faces me. The sleeve of his denim jacket brushes up against my hand that's resting on the glass. "I actually came here looking for a book that my little sister needed. I guess it's for her English class. You have *The Great Gatsby?*"

"Um, yeah. I'm sure we do." My body swerves, turning to walk out of the small nook behind the counter. I keep my eyes on the shelves, tracking the alphabetic sequence to locate *F* before my eyes land on Fitzgerald. Austin stays close, his toes inches away from my heels.

"Here it is," I say in a strained voice as I stretch my arms up to reach the top shelf. I balance on my toes and let my fingers graze the edges of the shelf before I search for a step stool.

"Here, let me get that." Austin's large hands reach up behind me to grab the book instead. I can feel his body lightly press against mine. When I turn and come face to face with his broad chest, I slightly jump, realizing how close he is.

He takes a step back and turns the book in his hand, a cheesy smile on his face.

"I'll ring you up at the register," I say softly, my voice timid and faint. I lead the way back to the counter to ring him up, and he follows closely before placing it on the counter for me to scan.

"That'll be $10.94."

He pulls his wallet out of his back pocket as he shuffles through the cash that was neatly placed in the bifold. I place the book in a small paper bag as he hands me a twenty-dollar bill, to which I give him change. The silence between us is awkward, audible through the crumpling of paper and clicks of the register. Even so, he smiles through the entire exchange.

I look up to thank him for his purchase, our standard greeting after every transaction, but he cuts me off before I speak. "Hey. So, I was going to tell you the next time I saw you in class, but I guess I'll tell you now. My aunt runs this publishing company right here in LA, and she's hiring assistants. It's a bit of grunt work, but I guess you can work your way up," he explains.

"Oh," I say between his pauses.

"Anyway, she was asking if I had any friends or classmates that might be interested, and I realized that you're the only one that I know that would fall into that category. Is it something that you might be interested in?"

"Oh," I answer. "Maybe…" My voice trails off.

"Okay." He nods. "Just think about it and text me. I can help you set something up with her."

I tilt my head. "Yeah, I will. Thanks."

"I'll see you in class." He smiles, the right corner of his mouth curving up, exposing a hint of a dimple pressing into his cheek.

"Bye," I say shyly before he leaves the store.

A job opportunity. Even with my mom's continued pressure to find a job, one that had a more promising future and quite possibly health benefits and a 401(k), I haven't even begun to look. Instead, I brush her off and continue to come to the bookstore to work my shift every week. But an actual job opportunity for a publishing company. The idea stirs something in me that vaguely mirrors excitement. An expectation that this, the hours blending into days, doesn't have to be the end-all, be-all. I can have a future, one that I'll build for myself. One that I get to dictate, to make mistakes, to celebrate milestones. Pain doesn't have to be the center of my life; heartbreak doesn't have to control me.

The last hours before the store closes drag on. Once it finally hits nine p.m., I turn off the lights, empty the register, and turn the Open sign to Closed before arming the store and locking the doors.

I walk to my car located amongst the busy parking lot and watch the buzz of Friday night festivities between locals pass by me. People spill from the stores with their frivolous purchases and laugh as they pile into their cars, driving off with loud music blasting through their speakers. All while singing along off-key to their favorite pop songs.

I unlock my car and sit in the driver's seat before starting the engine, and I lazily back out of the parking spot before driving home.

When I pull into my driveway, I'm surprised to see Claire's sleek black Mercedes-Benz parked against the sidewalk. She's standing on my front step, jumping and waving at me as I put my car in park.

"Claire, what are you doing here? Did you call me?" I ask as I look at my phone, worried that I may have missed a call from her.

"No! I wanted to surprise you." Her usually bright smile is even brighter tonight. She's here to tell me something, and she's bursting at the seams with anticipation.

"Okay... What's going on?" I look at her quizzically.

"Let's go inside, El." Her hands are bunched together in front of her mouth as if she's physically trying to keep from spilling what she wants to tell me too soon.

We enter my house, which is not surprisingly empty, and settle into my room. Claire bounces on the edge of my bed, and I ask her again what is going on.

Instead of answering me, she holds out her left hand, palm side down. It's then I notice a sparkling diamond on her ring finger. Wide-eyed at the realization, I pull her hand towards me, practically yanking her off the bed to examine it more closely.

"Wes proposed." She smiles bashfully. "After our talk about moving to Australia, he realized that whatever future we had, he wanted it to be together."

I'm speechless. Her diamond ring, beautiful and brilliantly bright, sparkles like a disco ball even in my dimly lit room.

"When did this happen?" I'm still shocked, overjoyed that such a momentous event occurred for my best friend. And a little sad that I hadn't been there to witness it.

"Last night. Wes convinced me to skip my classes this morning for a little getaway. We drove to Joshua Tree and stayed in a little camping dome. Ellie, he literally proposed to me under the stars."

"Claire!" I scream. She stands, and we both jump up and down as we cling to each other.

"Ellie!" she screeches back. We laugh uncontrollably. My best friend is getting married. The joy bursting from my heart can't be contained.

"Where is he?" I ask as our jumping settles into small hops before we both sit back down on my bed.

"He's at his place. I'm going over there right now. I told

him that I needed to come and tell you in person."

I hug her again, and we tumble backward as I'm unable to contain my joy for her.

"Oh my God, El. It was so magical. He said he wanted to wait until I graduated, but once he got the ring, he said he couldn't wait any longer."

"So does this mean you're officially moving to Australia with him?" I ask, worried to hear that Claire won't be by my side for much longer.

"No." She shakes her head. "He decided that our lives are here. I mean, I would have gone with him if that's what he wanted, but he knows how much it means for my career if I stayed here. He already told his boss he's staying in LA."

I hug her again, the realization of her staying in LA bringing me a fresh wave of relief. We continue to talk for a while, discussing plans for a possible spring wedding and the finer details of Wes's well-planned proposal.

As the hour passes, I can feel Claire's impatience to get back to her new fiancé.

"You should get back to Wes. You two need to celebrate," I suggest after the third time she's checked my clock for the time.

"Yeah, he's going to be waiting for me." She stands as she turns to me for another hug. "I called my parents last night. They want to throw a big engagement thing soon. I'll let you know the details when they get back to me."

"Of course. I'll be there."

"Ellie! I'm getting married!" she exclaims one last time before pulling me in for a hug once again. I laugh at her excitement, truly happy to share this moment with her.

"Call me tomorrow. We'll have dinner over the weekend to celebrate," I suggest.

I walk her to my door, and I lock it behind her.

So many things are changing around me, and I feel like I'm staying stagnant. My mom actually met someone, and her relationship with Mark is getting more and more serious each day. Claire's getting *married*.

I've always viewed change with dread. An overwhelming awareness of consternation would flow through me, and I did whatever I could to avoid the inevitable. But evolving is a part of human nature. We live to change and learn to adapt. At least, those around me do. I do my best to stay at a standstill, hoping that if I do, the natural shift that I should welcome would fly past me.

But maybe the fact that I work so hard to avoid change is the reason I feel so lost. Rhylan had said it was drowning, that we both were drowning. When I was with Rhylan, I didn't feel like I was drowning anymore. Maybe that was because of the way he transformed my life into something worth living. And, even if all that's left between me and Rhylan is the messy heartbreak that's scattered around us, maybe I can at least hang on to the one thing that he gifted me: freedom. The knowledge that we both had a glimpse of what it feels like to not drown, to not feel suffocated but to actually *live*, freely and unapologetically.

I look for my phone and search for Austin's number. Past messages about homework and midterms pop up as I hesitantly tap out a text.

Me: Hey Austin. Sorry, it's a little late, but I think I'm going to take you up on that assistant job.

Instantaneously, my phone dings a response.

Austin: Yeah? Awesome! I'll give my aunt a call.

Change is good.

The bruises that are spread over my eyes and cheeks are transitioning into a bile-colored yellowish green, and my stitches are healing, leaving behind a scraggly scar that will serve as a constant reminder of my actions. Stories of my brush with death and my overactive partying have died down over the past few weeks, while the images of Bella and I kissing have remained. It's a constant reminder that my actions have dire consequences, most of which Ellie has to pay.

The paralysis hasn't gone anywhere, but now it's a manageable numbness that I somehow maneuver around. Today, that numbness has lingered lightly into my chest as I drive towards downtown Los Angeles where Chuck's high rise is located in the heart of it.

He started a small business specializing in men's wear about six years ago that he built from the ground up. His parents advised against it, urging him to use his finance degree more productively, but he didn't listen. Instead, he emptied more than half his trust fund into this business. Today, his company, Suits & Whistles, is going public. This is a big deal, a very big deal, and we're celebrating.

Ever since I was hospitalized, Charles, Chuck, and Jackson have been careful. Limiting their partying and drinking and making sure that none of it got out of hand, even driving me to my sessions with Dr. Greene so I didn't miss a single one. Tonight, on a night that we would normally spend celebrating into the late hours, Chuck decided to invite people over to his penthouse and have a low-key celebration. Just catered food and cocktails.

With my car parked in the parking structure, I take the elevator up to the forty-fourth floor, humming as it ascends. When the elevator doors open directly into the foyer, I walk in to find a small collection of people standing around in even smaller clumped groups. Everyone has a cocktail in their hands, most likely made by the bartender stationed in the far corner of Chuck's living room. Light music fills the air with the hushed chatter of people blending into it.

"Rhy! You made it!" Chuck comes practically sprinting towards me while balancing a glass tumbler. His wide grin spread across his face is infectious.

I smile back, pride emanating from my grin. I know he worked hard to make this company a success and, as one of his top investors, I couldn't be more honored to be a part of it.

"Nice turnout, no?" His actions are exaggerated as he gestures toward the room. All of his furniture has been moved out, and now the room is an open space with a scattering of small tables throughout.

I smirk, my head tilted proudly towards him. "Yeah."

He pulls me in for a bear hug, his embrace disarming.

With a strong pat on my back, he steps back and snags a flute of champagne from a waiter walking past us making his rounds.

He hands me the glass.

"To Suits & Whistles," he says, gleaming with joy, raising his own glass towards me.

I clink the champagne to his glass and chuckle. "To Suits & Whistles."

"Mmm. I have someone I want you to meet!" he exclaims, his mouth coming off his glass with urgency. He waves towards a tall, attractive woman not too far from us. She smiles brightly at Chuck and saunters toward us. She stops next to Chuck, a good three inches taller than him, and smiles as she drapes her slender arm along Chuck's shoulders.

"This is Sonia," he says to me. "Sonia, this is Rhylan."

"Hello, Rhylan. It's so nice to finally meet you. Chucky here has told me so much about you." Her voice is silky, just like the olive tone of her skin. She tucks her jet-black hair behind her ear and looks down at Chuck. The two look into each other's eyes, lost in them as if I'm not here.

I clear my throat. "Nice to meet you too," I say loudly to get their attention. "Although I'm sorry to say, Chucky hasn't mentioned you before."

She laughs heartily. "Chucky has been keeping me a secret."

Chuck continues to smile up at her, his gaze lingering on her eyes, then traveling down her neck. She turns to wave at a new set of guests that have walked through the door, her smile brightening in recognition.

"I'm going to say hi to some friends," she says softly into Chuck's ear before turning to face me again. "It was nice meeting you."

She extends her hand towards me with a warm smile, and I shake it before she steps away. We both watch her as she meets her friends at the door, her enthusiastic greeting able to be heard from where we're standing.

"Chucky?" I say to Chuck once we're alone again. My brows are raised in amusement as I don't even bother to hide the mocking tone in my voice.

"Shut up," he responds, embarrassed but not completely so. He's relishing in the attention that Sonia was giving him and simply being in her presence.

"So, who is she?"

"I've been seeing her for a couple of weeks. I met her at a party, out in the Valley."

"The Valley?"

"Yeah, but she doesn't live there. She's from this side of LA. Like me."

I nod. "And it's serious." It's not a question. It's more of an educated assumption based on their body language.

He sighs, his smile spreading millimeter by millimeter. "Man, I never thought this relationship bullshit was real. Who the fuck would settle down when there's this many beautiful women in LA? But Sonia…" He whistles.

"That good, huh?"

"It's like, from the beginning, she tells me, 'Cut the shit.' She told me to tell her who I really was, not the spoiled, rich-boy part of me but who I *really* was." Head shaking, he looks down at his feet as if he still can't believe Sonia walked into his life, that she's already staking a place in a way he never imagined. "I told her everything, my future, my plans for Suits & Whistles, everything. And she actually sat there and listened. She doesn't even care about the money. She has her own with her modeling agency that she started seven years ago. She's an actual responsible adult with dreams and ambitions. I didn't realize how fucking sexy that shit was."

I listen to his every word, hanging on to it as he pours his admiration for this woman that entered his life just weeks ago. That's not a long time. Not long at all. Yet, she's made an impression on him that will last a lifetime. This is a side of Chuck that I've never seen, never even thought existed.

I'm jealous. Envious but not in a malicious way. More so that I want what he has: freedom. Expectation for things that I couldn't even dream of while bringing out a part of me that I thought had died long ago.

That was exactly what Ellie had done to me. While our relationship was flawed, I can't deny that what we had was real. I never gave us the chance to fully experience the extent of what our relationship could offer, but I know that if we did, it would have been magic. Pure magic. Here's Chuck, ready to experience it all from the beginning with nothing but optimism.

I clear my throat. "I'm really happy for you, Chuck. Everything is turning out to be such a success. We're all proud of you, man."

"Thanks. I am too." He smirks, still surprised and not used to his success.

The elevator doors behind me ding open, and an older couple dressed to the nines in Chanel and a tailored suit walk in. "Oh shit. It's my parents," Chuck whispers. He hurries away and greets them, their expressions serious but intrigued. Chuck's body language changes too. He's seeking approval, praise from the people that he never cared for approval from in the past. Yet here he is, a new leaf turned and hoping that his parents would be proud that he's made a name for himself.

"You meet Sonia?" a voice behind me says in a hushed tone. I turn and find Jackson close to me, his face hovering over my shoulder. Behind him, Charles and Amelia stand close by.

"When did you guys get here?"

"I got here before the party started. I helped set up the tables and shit," Jackson answers. He points a finger toward Charles and Amelia. "These two walked in barely ten minutes ago."

"We had to drop the kids off at my parents'." Charles defends his tardiness.

I take a step toward Amelia to embrace her. "Hi, Amelia. How are you?"

"I'm good," she answers warmly.

"So did you meet the new girl?" Jackson repeats his question.

"I actually did. Just right now. She seems nice," I say matter-of-factly. "And Chuck seems to have taken a liking to her."

"Oh, that dude is head over heels! I never thought I would live to see the day," Jackson teases.

Charles interjects. "She is nice. Even Amelia likes her."

"What?! When have I never liked anyone?" Amelia exclaims.

"You didn't like Chuck," Charles points out.

"Because he was half drunk and tried to hit on my sister the first time I met him."

"He really has come a long way, hasn't he?" I say, realizing that the Chuck Amelia is referring to is in the past. It seems as though a new and improved Chuck has made his appearance with no plans on going anywhere.

"Look at our Chucky. All grown up." Jackson fakes a sniffle and pretends to wipe a tear from his cheek as Chuck joins us.

"So, what did your parents say?" I ask him. He's a ball of nerves. Whatever they said to him has him all amped up and jittery.

"They said they're impressed. They didn't realize how big Suits & Whistles had gotten until one of my dad's partners mentioned it to him." He pauses and smiles. "They said they're proud of me."

"Hey! That's great!" Charles beams.

Sonia walks over to Chuck, matching his enthusiasm. "Hey, baby," Chuck croons to her. "Come on, I want you to meet my parents."

Sonia follows him, her hand in his as he leads the way to where his parents are standing. I watch as they smile and embrace her with open arms as he introduces her to his mom and dad.

"They look happy, don't they?" Charles says to me.

"They do," I answer, unable to help a small smile.

"So have you talked to Ellie?"

My body stiffens at the sound of Ellie's name. I know that he was the one that called her when I was in the hospital. He did it because he knew seeing her would bring me some sort of comfort. But it wasn't the right thing to do. Instead, I had to push her away even further. I haven't gotten upset at him. I'm just choosing not to talk about it. Avoidance has been the most adept path for my recovery, and I have no plans to hash everything out now.

"Uh, no. I haven't. I don't think I'm going to see her again."

He doesn't say anything. Doesn't argue with me, doesn't get frustrated because he knows that I let go of the best thing that ever happened to me. He simply furrows his brows and looks at me.

"Okay," he finally says. Simple. One word to let me know that he heard me but doesn't agree with my decision.

I know what he wants to say. He wants to tell me that I'm a fucking idiot. That I should have chased after her that day in the hospital instead of letting her slip through my fingers. It was what I wanted to do. In fact, I had to fight every fiber in my body to not reach out for her and idly watch her walk away instead.

My longing for her doubles just then, causing a sharp pain to radiate from my chest to the rest of my body. It's just the sound of her name, but it brings back so many memories. I miss her. I miss her smile, the way she looked up at me with curious eyes, hanging on to every word that came out of my mouth. I miss how her hand felt against my face, soft and nurturing. I felt adored in her hands. As if her love for me was enough to erase all the hate I carried.

I had gone on for so long, drowned by the overwhelming thought of life itself. Consumed by everything around me to the point that I felt more comfortable shadowed in the darkness. I had become so comfortable there that I didn't believe I could be happy. As soon as things turned for the worse, I assumed it was because it was my lot in life to stay discontented. I thought that I could never make anyone happy. I believed it so wholly that I pushed Ellie away as soon as it got tough. I pushed away my sunshine just so I could stay in the dark.

I did all of that even though a part of me wanted to believe that we could be happy as long as we had each other. That we could make each other happy no matter what obstacle came our way. Ellie believed in me, in us, so much that she laid open her whole heart only for me to break it into so many halves that I didn't know how she would mend it back together. I wanted to have faith in us, to have faith in myself, but I was scared to disappoint her. I didn't want to break her heart into more shattered fragments than it already was, because the love that I had for her wouldn't have allowed me to live with the fact that those broken pieces would have been my doing.

I loved her—*still* love her.

I'm not just addicted to her. I love her in the most absolute and unequivocal way possible.

I love her enough to push her away from me to try to protect her heart. In my twisted mind, this made sense the last time I spoke to her. I didn't know of any other way to love. When someone I cared for got too close, I felt it was my obligation to push them away to protect them from me. That's exactly what I had done with Ellie. I pushed her away, knowing that if I kept her close, I would only hurt her.

I look up to face Charles, a grim smile matching my

downturned eyes.

He pats my shoulder, giving it a light squeeze, almost as if he knew that my thoughts were consumed in Ellie and our past. "Listen, why don't you come over for dinner sometime this week? Just you. Amelia can cook, and the boys can see you."

I empty my champagne glass, the bubbles tickling my throat as they hit my stomach. "Sure, that sounds good."

My phone is glued to my ear, my shoulder holding it up as I neatly tuck my resume into a folder that I carefully slide into my leather tote. My heels click loudly against the pavement while I move in quick strides as I hurry to meet Austin.

"Are you almost here?" Austin's voice on the other end is breaking up, coming out in cut-off sentences, but I know he's around the corner.

When I finally reach the entrance of the tall building facing a row of wide stairs with people rushing in and out, I see Austin's sunny face, one hand holding his own phone to his ear. I breathlessly approach him with a panting smile.

"You made it!" he says, his smile beaming with his greeting. He looks down at his phone. "And with ten minutes to spare."

"I told you, you didn't have to come with me. I can meet your aunt on my own."

"Eh." He nonchalantly waves me off. "It'll give me a chance to say hi. Come on. Let's head up!"

After I texted Austin, he worked quickly to set up a

meeting with his aunt. The next day he called, saying that we could meet her the following Wednesday afternoon and I could celebrate my new job afterward by treating him to a round of drinks. It's a sweet gesture, flirtatiousness written all over it, and I worry that Austin may expect more from this once it's all said and done.

I obediently follow Austin, shadowing his movements as we check in through security, obtain a guest badge, and ascend up the building through the elevator. When the doors finally open, we're welcomed to a busy but friendly office floor fully equipped with a large reception desk that showcases what looks like a Christmas tree made of books. Behind the reception desk, a logo with bright red flowers adorns the agency's logo, Poinsettia Press, written in elegant cursive.

"Hi, Austin," the young woman behind the desk greets us, making it obvious that Austin is a familiar face around the office. "Are you here to see Paula?"

"Yeah, we actually have an appointment for Ellie. Under Eleanor Salerno." He turns to look down at me, my hand clasped around the strap of my bag as I smile politely at the receptionist.

"Okay, I'll let her know that you're here."

Austin taps his hand on the counter. "Thanks."

"Do you come here often?"

Austin laughs. "Guilty," he answers, bashfully ducking his head. "She's more of a mom to me than an aunt. I grew up with her and my cousins, so we're really close."

"Oh," I say softly. I'm about to tell him how sweet it is that he has such a close relationship with his aunt and how endearing it is that as an adult, he still manages to maintain that relationship with her. But then I see a woman dressed casually in loose slacks and a cozy sweater beam at us as she walks out from the bullpen of an office.

"Austin!" she squeals with affection for her nephew.

"Hi, Aunt Paula," he says warmly. The two hug in a quick embrace before he pulls away and motions towards me. "This is Ellie. The friend that I was telling you about."

"Oh yes! Of course." She turns to me, her bright smile never changing, and greets me attentively. "Austin has told me a lot about you."

"He's told me a lot about you as well," I respond, smiling and shaking her outstretched hand. "Thank you for the taking the time to meet with me."

"Why don't we go back to my office and have a chat," she suggests. Already, I feel welcomed and valued simply based on Austin's endorsement of my literature background and our friendship. As I follow Paula to her private office, I turn to look at Austin one more time. He smiles back at me with two thumbs up and a nod of encouragement.

Once settled behind the heavy glass doors of Paula's office, the chaotic noises from outside die down. I watch Paula as she rounds her large desk cluttered with manuscripts and multiple half-drunk paper cups of tea and coffee. She sits and gestures her hand out for me to take a seat in one of the matching cushioned chairs facing her.

"So," she exclaims, loud and clear, "Austin tells me you're a literature major."

I nod.

"Why literature?"

I smile. "I–I," I stutter before finding the right words, sighing as they finally pour out of me. "I can't imagine a world without using words to describe every image and feeling. Being able to say 'I'm sad' or 'I'm happy' without actually using those words but through an expressive language instead feels like actual magic to me."

She smiles, nodding and exuding genuine cognizance. I explained reading words and understanding every thought and emotion a writer tries to convey as a specific experience, one that most may not be able to relate to. Yet, she understood every bit of it.

"I was introduced to books at a really young age. My dad… He made sure I was surrounded by books. I don't think there's ever been a time in my life where it didn't center around reading or hunting down gems in a used bookstore. Even now, I work part time at an independent bookstore," I continue. "But I've learned more than to just appreciate books. I want to read and write and introduce others to a world that I've come to love and appreciate."

I don't know where I found those words. What I do know is that I've always felt connected to my dad through books. And this interview, this step towards my future, is about weaving those bits and pieces of him into my life so that the absence of him no longer creates a lingering ache that I can never be rid of. It's about blending my past and my future in an attempt to move on. I'm suddenly rushed with the urgency that I want this job. To know that with the strength I gain from the slowly resolving grief, I could use this connection to my dad to have a future. One that *I* control, no one else.

"Well," she responds with an exhaled breath. "I don't think I've ever heard anyone speak so passionately about the written word."

I smile shyly.

"And why Poinsettia Press?"

"Well, Austin speaks so highly of you and this entire publishing agency. I know that the agency was only founded six years ago, which makes it fairly new to the industry."

She nods, encouraging me to continue.

"That makes it all the more perfect for me. I want to learn and grow with the company."

She sifts through a large stack of papers sitting in a letter tray to procure a paper and hands it to me. When I look just below the agency's letterhead, my eyes scan over the jumbled words, only catching key phrases.

Junior editor.

Seattle.

I look back at her, confused.

"So, I have a small proposition that Austin may have not mentioned to you." She clasps her hands together, leaning forward and resting her elbows on her desk. "We have a headquarters in Seattle that is in dire need of help."

My attention piques. I nod.

"I was looking for assistants here to work with our editors, but I'm extending the offer to some who may be interested in relocating to our Seattle office."

"So the position would be in Seattle?" I ask.

"Yes. It's not an assistant position like the one I have here but a junior editor position instead."

My eyes widen. *Junior editor?*

"What do you think?"

"Me?" I squeak.

She chuckles politely. "I know it's a bit intimidating, but with how highly Austin speaks of you and how passionate you sound about literature, I think you may like it. And I think it might be the right fit for you if you're willing to relocate."

I stay silent, muddling over the offer. It's huge, life-altering. To pack up my entire life, the past twenty-two years, and move to a new state. It sounds scary. It sounds exhilarating.

"Could… Can I think about it?"

"Of course. I would expect you to think it over if you were in the slightest bit serious about the offer," she responds with understanding. "It's a big change, moving to a new city and all, so of course, take your time."

"Thank you," I say softly. All of the confidence that I oozed talking about literature is gone. I'm hesitant. Even with her and Austin's vote of confidence, I don't know if I have the courage and poise to accept such an offer and know that I would be successful.

"And if you decline, we still have positions here. Ones that don't have as many responsibilities as a junior editor would of course, but still with a lot of opportunities."

Her computer dings with an alert, and she squints, moving her mouse along the surface of her desk. "Oh, shoot."

I look up, watching her brows furrow.

"I'm so sorry, Ellie. I just got called into a meeting that got moved up an hour."

"Oh, that's okay."

"I wanted to show you around the office, but we may have to do that another time."

"Of course. That's no problem at all."

We stand in unison. Paula's steps are hurried as she walks me out of her office and back to the reception desk, where I find Austin sitting on a cushioned bench casually flipping through a magazine.

I turn to face Paula. "Thank you for your time," I say, my hand extended towards her to shake.

"It was nice to meet you. And make sure you give me a call once you have an answer."

I smile. "I will. Thank you again."

Paula waves a quick greeting towards Austin before rushing back in the direction of her office. I turn to face Austin again, and he stands, waving to the receptionist one last time before we walk back to the elevators.

"So how did it go?" Multiple people have gathered around us, all waiting for the elevator to arrive. I look at Austin with nervous eyes, wanting to wait until we have more privacy to speak.

Once outside, Austin looks at me eagerly. "So?"

I laugh, bringing my hand up to his arm. "It went well."

"She offered you a position?"

"She did. In Seattle."

His smile drops, eyes wide and puzzled. "Seattle?"

"Yeah, I guess there's a need for a junior editor at the office there, and she offered the position to me."

"So, you would be moving to Seattle?"

I nod. "Yeah."

"Wow, that's huge."

"I know," I agree softly. "I… I think I'm going to take it."

"Really?"

I nod eagerly. Saying it out loud, acknowledging my decision, feels scary but exciting. Like I've been waiting for an opportunity like this to come along without realizing how badly I wanted it.

"Well, shit. If I had known setting up this interview meant you'd be moving to another state, I wouldn't have said anything."

I laugh, playfully swatting his arm. I'm smiling, but he's not. His eyes turn serious, and he looks at me with a hint of intensity that I've never seen in him.

I clear my throat. "Let's grab a cup of coffee," I suggest, pointing to a small pop-up coffee shop right next to the entrance of the building.

We order our coffees in silence, moving within the small, busy shop before stepping back outside and sitting on the steps of the entrance.

"You've pretty much made up your mind?" Austin asks again, confirming my answer from earlier. He's close to me, his arm touching mine, and I can feel his eyes on me as he waits for my answer.

"I think so. I can't really pass up an offer like this."

"I'd miss you, Ellie. A lot."

I look at him. "I'll miss you too, Austin."

And without missing a beat, he kisses me. It's quick and soft, so fleeting that I barely have a minute to process it happening.

"Austin…"

"I'm sorry." His voice is soft, yet hoarse.

I shake my head. "I know I never mentioned it to you before, but I was kind of seeing someone and…"

"You aren't over him."

I look at him apologetically and nod. And at that moment, I see what it would be like to be with someone without all the complicated mess that I had to endure with Rhylan. Without all the doubts and uncertainties. To be able to be with someone and just *be* with them. To know that what we have is a good thing and holds a future, instead of merely promising a few stolen moments sprinkled over the pain.

I want to look at Austin and welcome his kiss. I want to be able to kiss him back and tell him that I feel the same way. That I can imagine a future for us beyond graduation and claiming a stake in our careers. One that we can build a life around.

But I can't.

"Is that why you're taking this job? Because of this guy you aren't over?"

I consider his question. Am I? Am I using this change, this opportunity, to get away from Rhylan and the mess that we had somehow created? Maybe I am. And maybe it's foolish of me to think that I can run away from my problems.

"Maybe," I answer honestly. "I just think it might be a good change for me. To move on, I guess."

"Well, if that's the case, I hate this guy." A small smile has finally reappeared, and I see the playful, goofy Austin that I'm comfortable with. I smile too, leaning my head on his shoulder and feeling sincerely grateful for our friendship.

"We're still friends?" I ask.

"Ouch," he answers, bringing a hand to his chest. "I think being friend zoned hurts more than just being rejected."

I roll my eyes and laugh before standing, hovering over him. "Come on."

"Where are we going?" he asks, standing quickly and brushing off the back of his pants.

"I owe you a drink, remember?"

The sun setting over the horizon, facing west, is gorgeous. The perfect swirl of orange, yellow, and purple mingles together for what looks like the most tranquil backdrop that Los Angeles has to offer. The drive up the winding hillside is leisurely, and I use the time to clear my head.

Taking him up on his offer for dinner at home with his family, I had called Charles. His home is located on the outskirts of Calabasas, and while we live in the same town, it still takes me a good thirty minutes to arrive at his doorstep. Once I arrive at his beautifully structured, secluded home, I ring the doorbell with a bottle of wine in my hand.

I stand and wait for the door to open when I hear the pitter-patter of feet gradually getting louder before coming to a halt behind the door. The door swings open, and I find both Oliver and Andy giddy and out of breath.

"Uncle Rhy!" Oliver shrieks.

"Rah Rah!" Andy babbles.

"Hey, boys!" I kneel down to pick up a wobbly Andy as Charles rounds the corner, jogging to keep up with his rambunctious boys.

He lets out a breath, bent over with his hands to his knees. "Hey, Rhy, you're just in time."

I close the door behind me as Charles takes Andy from me with one arm while accepting my offering in the other. "Amelia's in the kitchen. Come on in."

I follow him through the foyer towards the massive kitchen to find Amelia pulling a rectangular ceramic tray out of the oven.

"Rhylan!" She's distracted as she greets me. Charles sets Andy down to help Amelia with the oven door. "Come, sit! Food's just about ready."

Oliver takes my hand and pulls me towards the dining table situated diagonally from the kitchen. "You sit next to me, Uncle Rhy."

His too-big-for-his-face blue eyes veiled by thick, blonde eyelashes look up at me, urging me to accept his request.

"Sure, buddy! I'd love to sit next to you."

We're followed by Charles balancing three wine glasses and the bottle of wine I brought squeezed under his armpit. "Sorry it's so hectic. The boys are going to have a quick bite with us, and the nanny's going to get them into bed."

"Hey, don't worry about it. I'm just hanging out with my buddy here." I squeeze Oliver's hand in mine, and he beams at me in response.

Amelia follows with a large tray of food and continues back and forth from the kitchen to the table until it's brimming with a decadent array of dishes.

We enjoy our meal, the heavy chitter-chatter of the kids

interrupting much of our conversations, and the kids are whisked away by the nanny at eight p.m. sharp. The adults are left alone to talk.

"So, this girl," Charles starts. He's rolling the stem of his wine glass between his fingers. I stiffen, the mention of Ellie making the hairs on the back of my neck stand. I need the company of someone after so many nights in my empty house, someone who I trust and who would understand. But talking about Ellie is refreshing wounds that have long since been opened. They aren't even scarred yet. Instead, they're sitting there, oozing with pain and guilt.

I nod, and then I groan into my hands, the words I should be saying caught in my throat.

When I don't say anything, Charles continues. "When I called her, I thought, 'This is perfect. This idiot can realize that he let go of a good thing and apologize.' But your dumb ass did the complete opposite. You pushed her away."

"I know." My voice is muffled, stifled by my own hands still covering my face.

"And now, you look like this sad little pit bull, all angry and scowling but sad."

I sigh. "This is so stupid. I fucked up so bad, and I don't even know how to fix it. I don't even think I should. I feel like I should just let her go, let her move on, but I can't get her out of my fucking mind. And I feel like it's too late."

Charles and Amelia listen as I pour my heart out.

"I pushed her away when she needed me. I told her that I didn't want to see her anymore. That we were over." I look up at the sparkling chandelier hanging over the table as if I'm begging for an answer as to why I said the things I said to Ellie. "And then I saw her cry, and it felt like someone punched me in the gut. I wanted so badly to tell her it was all a lie. I even told her I was seeing Bella. *Bella!* I couldn't care less about Bella. I really thought I was protecting her from me. I just got so scared that I was going to keep hurting her."

All of the pain that's built up inside of me rushes out, the words vomiting out of me until my throat tightens up again. I stop when I feel like I can't go on, the tightness balling up as the tears start to well.

Amelia and Charles glance at each other. "You know, this shit isn't easy. This love thing. Amelia and I definitely had our ups and downs," Charles explains. I look at both of them sharing a small, knowing smile.

"We laugh about it now, but it was… difficult, to say the least," Amelia adds. "Barely a year into our marriage, we didn't know if we were going to make it. So many times, we contemplated divorce. Hollywood isn't very forgiving. Rumors every time they get pictures of us right after an argument. They once got a picture of me just two weeks after I had Andy, and they picked that picture apart, nitpicking my weight and implying that Charles could do so much better. They even went as far as starting rumors of Charles having an affair. We began to resent each other so much. Things got tough, but we both wanted to work through it. We didn't want to give up on each other."

Charles leans towards me. "This relationship stuff, it's a lot of work. You just have to decide if it's worth it. And trust me, it doesn't come without the heartache. It's always there. It's still there for us, even now. But once you both decide you want it, the good *and* the bad, it's worth it. Every bit of the hurt is worth it." He takes Amelia's hand and brings it to his lips for a kiss, just the way I used to do to Ellie. Amelia responds by leaning her head onto Charles's shoulder.

I consider both of their takes on their relationship. I was never aware that they had struggled and that they still do. I've always assumed that their marriage is smooth sailing, that every marriage should be that way. It's never occurred to me that the expectation of a perfect relationship is unrealistic. It's about compromise and learning to work through our problems, not running away from them as I had with Ellie.

"I didn't know…" My voice trails off, not knowing how to respond while trying to sympathize with the struggles they've endured.

Charles waves his hand, brushing off the gritty details that line the pitfalls of their relationship. "We're working through it, going to therapy and whatnot. I'm not telling you this for you to feel sorry for us. I'm telling you this so that you understand the sacrifices you have to make. I know you don't want to hurt Ellie, but it's not your job to protect her from the challenges that come with every relationship. It's your job to love her and to let her know that you do."

I nod, truly understanding Charles's advice. I had lowered my expectations of Ellie, so much so that I didn't have faith in her to be able to work through our struggles. It wasn't fair to her. I had decided for the both of us that our relationship wasn't worth salvaging, so I bailed like a complete coward. I was so fucking scared to give us that chance, so instead, I broke her heart.

But I don't want to be scared anymore. I want to face my fears with Ellie by my side. I want to prove to myself, and to her, that I can keep us together.

We continue the night, talking about nothing and everything. No need for formal conversation, just words that lead into an organized tangent between friends. Our conversation moves in chapters. Short stories about our set days, the adorable incidents that the boys get themselves into on a daily basis, random trivia in relation to our careers. None of it necessarily vital but salutary.

"I should go check on the boys. They've been known to give the nanny a hard time." Amelia excuses herself as our conversation dwindles. She stands and leans down to kiss Charles and turns to me. "Thanks for coming over. The boys really enjoy your company. Including this one," she adds, pointing to Charles.

"Thanks, Amelia." I smile at her sincerely. Charles and I remain quiet as she walks away. "You know, I should head out." I reach for my phone and keys as I stand.

"You don't have to leave. Amelia just likes to go down early to wake up with the boys."

"Nah, it's fine. I've had a long day, and I'm getting pretty tired too."

Charles nods before standing to follow me as I lead the way back to his front door.

"Thanks again for having me over. I appreciate it," I say, turning to face him.

"Sure, the door's always open."

I take a pause, a moment to put my words of gratitude together. "And I never really thanked you. For Paris."

"You don't need to—" he starts, but I cut him off.

"Yes, I do," I answer seriously. "You covered for me then. And I was in a really dark place that I don't think I could have pulled myself out of if you weren't there."

He lets out a small chuckle as he averts his eyes to the ground before looking back at me with a sincere smile. "Anytime."

I nod.

"Take care, Rhy," he says, his hand patting my back. I turn and wave at Charles as I walk out the door.

It's dark out when I leave. The star-scattered sky reminds me of the night I spent in the Hollywood hills with Ellie. I remember how the melancholy that spread across her face had shifted into acceptance that night. Acceptance of possibility. She opened herself up to me, allowed me in even though her better judgment told her not to.

Once in my car, I look at my phone, scrolling through pictures of Ellie. Blurred snapshots of us in bed, eyes half-open and hair rumpled but our smiles bright, drunken from the blissful cocoon we enveloped ourselves in. Her smile radiated sunshine, beaming as we basked in our contentment, all lazy and relaxed. I've been doing that a lot lately, looking through the curated gallery I created on my phone. As if the mere images of her are enough for me to fill the empty hole her absence has left. But I know it isn't. Who am I kidding? How are pictures, still images of her happy, lively smile, supposed to replace the touch of her? Her warm body like sunshine, flush against me, filling all the gaps and crevices so that I feel whole. I want so badly to feel whole again.

My fingers swipe through my phone until they still underneath Ellie's contact info. The green button, signaling a call to her, glares back at me. My thumb trembles, hovering above it.

I can't call her.

I know I can't, but all I hear is the singsong ringing of her voice calling my name. Her playful laugh that starts with a low, throaty giggle and spreads to her eyes, reminding me of my sunshine. Her fingertips grazing my skin as she traces the shape of my jaw. I feel a sharp pang in my chest, and I remember the feeling of melting into her hand, feeling like I could never tire of the way my cheek felt in her palm.

Without thinking twice, I call her, my thumb grazing over the call icon. The phone rings and continues to ring, the loud echo telling me to hang up. To let her go. And then it goes to voicemail.

My instinct is to hang up. This is a sign. I'm supposed to let her move on. But I can't.

When her voicemail system beeps, signaling me to leave my message, I go silent. I'm at a loss for words. What can I say to this perfect woman that will make her see that I made a mistake?

"Ellie, I… don't know if this is okay. I don't really know what's okay anymore."

I sigh before the words start pouring out.

"I *miss* you, Ellie. I miss you so much. I know I hurt you, and I don't deserve to ever hear from you again but… God, I fucking miss you. It fucking hurts, and I don't know what to do."

The tears start rolling down my face. It's my turn to completely and absolutely bare my heart to her. To risk it all.

"What I said before, over the phone and at the hospital, I didn't mean it. I saw what they did to you, and I was scared I was going to keep hurting you. I don't want to hurt you anymore, but I don't know how to live without you."

I pause, not knowing what else I can say to let her know that I'm a man who's living with the consequences of his actions. Actions that were made based on the false assumption that my hands were plaited with harm. But I was wrong. The harm that I believed I would lash onto those I cared about was only there because I thought myself to be unworthy.

So I say the only thing that I know to be true. The one thing that I've been clinging on to, helping me realize that maybe I am worthy. That maybe I am deserving of the happiness that I dream of. With Ellie.

"I lo—"

I love you.

The phone beeps, signaling the end of my message. I look back at my phone as the automated message continues, giving me instructions on how to complete my message delivery. I hang up.

I rub the tears from my face and blink back at Charles's house. The lights are all turned off except for the one coming from his bedroom. I see Charles and Amelia embrace before turning the lights out.

They said their marriage isn't perfect, that the hurt that

comes and goes is worth the love. They each made sacrifices so that they could see their marriage through. I don't care what sacrifices I need to make so that Ellie knows that I made a mistake.

I'm willing to do what it takes to mend her heart and promise that whatever heartbreak we have to go through, we'll do it together. I'm willing to work through it all, to see it to the end.

CHAPTER 41
Ellie

"**W**hat a cheap shot! Foul!" Wes's voice echoes through the bar as he shakes a very frustrated fist towards the big screen.

"That was a bullshit call," Austin shouts, agreeing with Wes.

I raise my eyebrows at Claire and smile. We share a judgmental glance as the boys continue their irate yelling. She rolls her eyes at me in response.

On our search for whatever local bar was serving happy hour, I got a call from Claire to join her and Wes at The Cave, a sports bar which was only a ten-minute drive from Poinsettia Publishing. With the NBA playoffs coming up, Claire had given up fighting for Wes's attention and decided to join him as he had screaming matches with the TV screen. Eager to celebrate with Claire and hold my promise to treat Austin to drinks, I agreed, knowing that she could use the company as well. What I didn't expect was for Austin and Wes to warm up to each other so quickly.

"I give them fifteen minutes before Wes throws something

at the TV and we get kicked out," Claire states matter-of-factly.

"I hope not. These wings are amazing."

After I broke the news that I was going to accept a job offer in Seattle, Claire pouted. She was thoroughly upset that I would be moving away from LA and leaving our cozy little lives behind, even though those changes after graduation would be inevitable. Everything is changing a mile a minute, and with this new job offer, I finally feel optimistic instead of scared.

Still, with the forged optimism that I "hadn't accepted the job yet" and hoping that I may change my mind, Claire quickly moved on to happier topics. We glazed over our graduation outfits, wedding plans, and just how many wings we could eat before we actually exploded.

With our fingers and mouths covered in sauce, we're interrupted by the waitress bringing us more drinks. A frosty whipped-cream-topped strawberry milkshake lands right in front of me.

"I ordered that for you," Austin says over my shoulder with a wink.

"Oh, thank you," I say quietly.

The last time I had a milkshake was with Rhylan. I've been staying away from them since then. Memories of the quaintly lit dance floor mingling with fifties era music flood my mind. My fingertips graze my lips, thinking of the strawberry and vanilla flavored kisses Rhylan and I shared. No matter how hard I try to forget him, I can't.

The TV screen goes to a commercial break, and the boys turn their attention back to us.

"This game's going to go into overtime," Wes comments.

"Yeah, unless the Lakers get their shit together." Austin looks over at me, smiling with BBQ sauce smeared across the corner of his mouth.

"You have a little something…" I point to his mouth and smile.

"Oh, thanks." He wipes the opposite corner. "Did I get it?"

I cover my mouth and laugh, trying my best not to embarrass him. "No, the other side. Here, let me."

I wipe the sauce with a napkin, and his smile never leaves his face, only growing wider as I affectionately clean him up.

"Thanks!" He continues on with his wings, getting even more sauce on the edges of his mouth and all over his fingers, causing me to roll my eyes.

We all look at the TV screen when a trailer for *Unrestrained* comes on and images of Rhylan flash through the thirty-second commercial.

"I've been wanting to see that. I heard Rhylan Matthews is amazing in it," Austin claims.

Our table falls silent as Claire, Wes, and I share a set of stiff glances.

"What?" Austin asks nervously, sensing the awkward shift.

"We don't talk about Rhylan Matthews," Claire answers for all of us.

"What?" Austin asks again with a laugh, which quickly fades when he realizes it's not a joke. "I'm sorry. Did I miss something?"

We all continue to remain quiet until I finally speak, breaking the awkward tension that has settled right over our wings and beers.

"Remember I told you that I was seeing someone recently?"

Austin nods.

"I was seeing Rhylan Matthews."

His eyes go wide. "What!"

I quickly cut him off, bringing my hands up between us. "It was nothing. Like I said, it ended really fast. But we just don't really talk about him."

"Ellie, I don't know why you downplay it," Claire says to me. She turns to Austin. "He broke her heart."

I flinch at her words, even though she's right.

Austin takes a moment to absorb this new detail of information. He raises his hands, palms facing me in surrender. "Okay, we don't talk about Rhylan Matthews."

I give him an appreciative squeeze on his forearm and continue to drink my milkshake. Just on cue, the game starts up again, and the attention is shifted back to the TV.

The game continues into overtime, just like Wes predicted. I spend the rest of the evening bent over in my seat, trying to distract myself from the fresh memories of Rhylan that have resurfaced. He's everywhere. If not swirling in the mixture of ice cream and strawberries sitting right in front of me, then plastered over a big screen, his serious eyes singling me out.

Claire and I become weary. Our seats, after we've sat for so long, have become uncomfortable, and we've eaten all the food we could possibly consume in one sitting. Nonetheless, we wait for the game to finish as we patiently sit with our chins resting in our hands and elbows digging into the tabletop.

I mindlessly reach for my phone in my purse, something to keep my hands busy as Claire is already doing the same. When

I turn my phone in my hand, I notice a missed call.

It's from Rhylan.

I freeze. He called me. I expected to never hear from him again.

I don't want to see you anymore.

His words echo through my head, and a fresh wave of heartache hits my chest. I physically cower.

"Ellie? Is everything okay?" Claire asks. She sees my phone lit up in my hand, the alert for a missed call glaring in the low light of the bar. "Did someone call you?"

I retract my hand and shove my phone into my pocket.

"It's no one." But I can't look at her. I know if I meet her eyes, I'll start crying. I'll sob Rhylan's name to her, begging for her to tell me what to do.

I want to hear his voice, to call him back just to hear him say my name or even a quick, breathy "hello." I crave his soft whispers muffled against my hair, calling my name as if he'd just discovered a sacred meaning to it. *My Eleanor.*

The game finishes with a devastating loss for the Lakers. Both boys, frustrated and disappointed, finally suggest we leave. We exit the bar, welcoming the fresh spring air. Everyone is content, stomachs full and spirits light.

Everyone except for me. My mind is a million miles away, right next to that call from Rhylan. I check my phone again and see that he left a voicemail. What can he possibly have to say to me?

"Hey, babe. I'm going to ride with Ellie. Just to make sure she gets home safe," Claire calls out to Wes on our way out, even though she was the one that consumed three plus beers in comparison to my sodas and milkshake.

Austin and Wes are in deep conversation about sports trivia, animated as they gesture wildly with their hands. Claire and I watch as they continue to act as if we're no longer there.

"Sure. We're going to Austin's. They're playing some highlight reels, so I'll hang out for a bit," Wes answers.

"Okay," Claire replies. She turns and laughs at the quick comradery they've developed. I respond with a smile and turn towards the parking lot.

"Bye, boys," I call out before getting into my car. Claire hurriedly gets in through the passenger side.

"You don't need to come with me. I didn't have anything to drink. Unless you count the three Cokes I had." I breathe an unconvincing laugh, but Claire is serious. My smile fades immediately. She knows something is up.

"Who called you?"

I look down, the expression on my face solemn. "It was Rhylan."

"What the hell does he want?"

"I don't know," I whisper. I look up at her, my eyes on the brink of tears. The confusion clouds my mind full of questions I know will never be answered. "But he left a message."

She turns to face the front of the car and huffs. "What an asshole. After all this time, he leaves you alone just enough for you to barely get your life back, and then he calls out of the blue."

I look down at my wrung-out hands, twisting them as I contemplate what to do. I want so desperately to hear Rhylan's voice, to hear him call for me and to tell me that everything he said to me, pushing me away and telling me that Bella was now a constant presence in his life, was all a lie. But then my mind goes back to the hurt that he caused me. The gut-wrenching pain that I had to go through in his absence. The only truth that I can cling to is that the pain I thought had subsided in increments is still fresh. I thought I was healing and moving on with my life, but I was wrong.

"I'll be fine," I finally say to Claire. I'm unconvincing with my wavering voice. She remains silent, allowing me to resolve, to finally come to a decision. I know she wants to ask me if I want to listen to his voicemail. And maybe I should, at least for a hint of closure, but I don't know if my heart can handle hearing his voice without the hope of something more.

"Ellie, it's okay to not be okay. You don't have to pretend like you aren't hurt." Claire reaches for my arm and gently caresses my shoulder. Her reassuring touch causes me to crumble inside before I quickly gather myself. I can't dwell on this, not now. If I do, I might not come back from it.

I take a deep breath before looking back at Claire. I need to move on from this. I need to live my life.

"You want to come over and watch a movie?" I ask with a defeated smile. I have nowhere else to go but home, but I don't feel like being alone.

She smiles back. "Sure."

I look over my shoulder as I back out of the parking spot. Wes and Austin are long gone.

"Austin and Wes seem to get along well," Claire comments.

"Yeah, Austin's a great guy."

"I think he likes you." Her eyes twinkle as she tells me this.

"I know. We kissed earlier, after the interview."

Claire lightly slaps my arm, and I playfully flinch in response. "I swear, you live a double life. You never tell me these things! So there's something there?"

My lips purse together in a firm line with my gaze on the road ahead. I wish to myself that I could offer Claire something other than a defeated shake of my head. "I told him I wasn't ready," I say. "I thought I was when I kissed him, but it only made me realize that I needed more time."

"Well, I like him. And Wes *loves* him." Claire laughs.

I smile and look over at her. She reaches for my arm to silently let me know that I should take all the time I need. That she'll be there to support me through whatever reparative journey I need to take.

I pull into my driveway and park my car, and we quickly make our way into my house. We lazily make ourselves comfortable on my bedroom floor and surround the soft carpet with blankets and pillows, letting the long day melt off of us as we decide what to watch.

The nagging reminder that Rhylan's voicemail is still unchecked, unlistened to, pokes at me. It reminds me that his presence is still around me, no matter how hard I try to forget him.

With a warm bowl of popcorn and two cans of Cherry Coca-Cola nestled between us, we finally decide on the saddest movie we could think of: *The Fault in Our Stars*. Maybe we're masochists, or maybe misery really does love company, but we watch Hazel Grace and Augustus fall in love despite everything working against them. We watch knowing that we'll end up in a heap of tears and used tissue, just like every other time we've seen this movie together.

It's well past one in the morning when Claire yawns and stretches. "Can I spend the night?"

"Yeah, of course. I didn't feel like taking you home anyways," I say through the contagious yawn she passes along to me.

Claire throws a pillow at me before she drags herself off the floor and walks to the bathroom while I set out clothes for her to sleep in.

Hours later, Claire is asleep by my side, snoring softly. But I'm still wide awake.

I put my phone in the top drawer of my dresser when we got back home. I needed to put it away, to keep it from distracting me. But out of sight definitely doesn't mean out of mind because the possibility of hearing Rhylan's voice is all I can think about.

I look over at Claire to make sure she's not awake. Her arm is draped over her forehead as her snoring grows louder, indicating that she's fallen into a deep sleep. I slowly climb out from underneath the covers and open my dresser drawer to retrieve my phone. Once in the bathroom, the only room in the house with some privacy, I flick on the lights and softly close the door behind me.

I unlock my phone and look at the missed call from Rhylan, along with the voicemail that he left me. For a long time, my finger hovers over the play button.

What do you want, Rhylan? Why are you calling me?

I'm barely existing, hanging on to whatever it is that's

keeping me on the surface. I don't know why Rhylan called. What could he possibly have to say to me? Whatever it is, good or bad, I don't know if my heart can move on from what it's already been through.

Sitting at the edge of the bathtub, I bring my knees up to my chin and continue to stare at my phone. Everything blurs in front of me. A familiar haze glazes over my eyes, and the tears start to form. They roll down my cheeks, reminding me of all the hurt that I've gone through since I met Rhylan. Love isn't supposed to hurt like this. There may be the occasional heartache with every relationship but not the kind of pain that leaves you completely and utterly hopeless. I hurriedly wipe my tears as my phone glares back at me, reminding me that a piece of Rhylan was sitting in my phone in the form of an unchecked voicemail.

And then I do it. I press the play button and brace myself for the sound of Rhylan's voice.

"Ellie..."

The sound of his voice, raw and aching, fills the room. It echoes, bouncing off the tiled walls, caging me in and surrounding myself within him once again.

"I miss you..."

My heart stops. My entire body goes numb. Of all the reasons he called, I didn't imagine it would be because he misses me.

"...I don't know what to do."

The anger begins to course through me. *You don't know what to do? How about NOT break my heart!* Fresh tears that I didn't know I still had in me begin to pour down my face. I muffle my sobs against the inside of my elbow. After all this time, my heart is still sore from the sharp ache that it suffered through. The anger quickly subsides, and I feel frustrated. Frustrated that he decides to call me to tell me he *misses* me, only leaving me confused and hoping for more.

"…I don't know how to live without you."

I don't know how to live without you either. The sadness returns as the longing ache I've had for him resurfaces. I don't *want* to live a life without him. I want to call him back and tell him everything that's running through my mind. I want to tell him that everything he's feeling, I'm feeling too.

His message cuts before he finishes. I let the tears continue to fall. My body, exhausted from the roller coaster of emotions it's been put through, slumps to the cold bathroom floor.

The mixed emotions that course through me are giving me whiplash. I miss him so much. So much so that I wish I could tell him.

But my walls are back up. I don't know how I can learn to trust him again. To let him back in. The first time, he barged in. Saw through me, right into my soul, as if he belonged there. I didn't fight it or question it because it felt so right.

I still feel the presence of him, a ghost of him wrapped around me, trying to let me know that I'm safe. I want to succumb to that. To wrap myself into him and forget everything that happened between us that brought us to this moment. But I can't.

I leave the lingering sounds of Rhylan's voice and my cries in the bathroom. I walk back into my dark room and climb into bed. A stuttered sigh escapes me, hitching at my throat as the fatigue finally settles.

"I listened to his voicemail."

Claire is waking, ahead of my alarm clock, rubbing her eyes before stretching her arms above her head. Her head jerks up and faces me sitting on my bedroom floor. My knees are drawn up to my chin. I can't look at her. I won't be able to hold back everything I'm trying to keep at bay.

"What?"

"He said he misses me."

"WHAT!" She's sitting upright. Her face goes from confused to indignant. "What does he want from you?"

I finally look up at her. As soon as my eyes meet hers, the tears start forming, and I bury my face in my hands before they start falling. Claire crawls over the blankets to join me.

"Ellie," she whispers as she holds me. I lean into her.

"I thought he was going to call to apologize so we could both move on, maybe even get some closure, but I didn't expect this. I don't know what to do." I let the tears fall, the fresh heartache settling in with the reality of Rhylan's words.

"El, he tossed you aside and didn't even look back. Whatever his reason, he still hurt you." She urges me to listen when I lower my head onto her shoulder. With a sigh, she continues. "Whatever you do, if you want to call him or forget him for the rest of your life, I'm here for you. Just… protect your heart, no matter what."

I lift my face and look up at her, considering her words. Another sob escapes me.

I miss you too, Rhylan. Please don't break my heart because I don't know if I can survive it.

CHAPTER 42
Rhylan

t's been one week since I called Ellie. Seven tortuous days sitting by my phone, waiting for her to call back. But nothing but complete radio silence. I keep thinking to myself that it was a mistake that I called her. She doesn't want anything to do with me. How could she? I broke her heart and left her to fend for herself after I promised myself I wouldn't hurt her.

Yet there's another part of me that doesn't care. I know that's extremely selfish. But all I want is to see her, to hold her and whisper into her hair, telling her how sorry I am. I want to beg for another chance, let her know that I'm willing to spend the rest of my life proving to her that I will never hurt her again.

The wait to hear back from Ellie has been excruciating. I'm getting restless. I toss and turn at night, in and out of sleep. I can't focus on anything. My days are returning to the endless blurs they used to be. The hope of seeing Ellie had brought me back to the surface, and now I'm slowly being dragged back down.

The frustration is building up inside me, bubbling until it

sits in my chest, becoming a balled-up knot in my stomach. I pound my fist onto the counter and groan loudly, lowering my head into my hands. I don't know how much more of this I can take.

My phone rings loudly from my couch. I lunge for it, tripping over my feet.

"Hello?!"

"Hey, Rhy." It's Charles. His cheerful, singsongy voice rings through the phone.

Without even thinking, I sigh, frustrated and disappointed. "Hey."

"Whoa, don't sound too excited to hear my voice."

"Sorry, I'm just a little distracted."

"Is everything okay?"

"Yeah, I guess."

He pauses a minute before speaking again. "Well, we're heading out to dinner tonight. I think Chuck made some reservations somewhere downtown for Sonia's birthday. Want to join us?"

"Um, I think I'm just going to stay in tonight. Maybe get some rest or whatever."

"Okay," he answers hesitantly. "You sure you're okay?"

"Yeah." I sigh. "I'll be fine."

"Okay," he says, clearly unconvinced. "I'll talk to you later."

"Sure." I hang up the phone and stare at it.

I breathe out a puff of air. I feel like I'm playing a waiting game and the odds are against me. I need to clear my head, get some air.

I grab my keys and walk out to my car, overcast skies

hovering above with the threat of rain. I sit for a minute with the ignition started, debating on where to go. But I have nowhere to go. My life has always been my work and this home that I made out to be a sanctuary, but the quiet and emptiness inside is stifling, making it everything but a place of refuge. So I pull out of my driveway and drive.

My mind wanders, and I drive aimlessly. For hours, I have no destination. And then, as the day begins to settle, I end up in front of Ellie's house. I have no plan, no strategy. Just the idea that if Ellie is in front of me, things will right themselves. I have to face the reality that she may not want to speak to me, not want to have anything to do with me. But none of that matters. I have to see her.

My heart beats erratically, feeling like it's jumped into my throat. As soon as I walk up to her front step, the door opens before I even have a chance to knock. But it's not Ellie. It's her friend, Claire.

"I saw you pull up," she answers my unspoken question. Her arms are crossed in front of her. She looks at me with annoyance, and it's clear that she's aware of every word Ellie and I exchanged. "She's not here."

"Do you know where I can find her?"

She scoffs at my question. "Why? So you can break her heart all over again?"

I flinch. "I just need to talk to her," I try to explain.

I cling to one thought. That I need a chance. Just a moment with her so I can explain what happened. Even if she doesn't want me anymore, I need her to know how I feel. She needs to know that I regret everything I said, and I grieve for every second I didn't get to spend with her.

"I don't think that's a good idea. Actually, I think you need to leave." She starts to close the door, taking my chance to talk to Ellie with her.

"Wait!" I put my hand up to stop the door from closing.

She turns on her feet to face me, the sudden movement causing me to take a step back. "Do you even know why I'm here? Watching her like a fucking hawk like she's some fragile porcelain doll?" she asks, her voice trembling with anger. "I'm here because I'm waiting for her to fall. She's barely holding herself together, so I'm here to catch her when she does. Do you even know what that's like? To watch her barely hold herself together? Because *you* put her there?"

I sigh deeply, my brows furrowed before I plead. "Look, I know I fucked up. I know that to my core. But… this life isn't easy. The constant criticism. Privacy isn't something that I have an abundance of. And they tore her apart. I didn't want to keep hurting her, so I pushed her away." Claire's hands drop to her sides as she continues to listen to me speak. "But that wasn't fair. I… I need her to know that I messed up. I made a mistake."

She sighs. "I've seen her in a dark place. She's been through a lot. She has these walls up that she thinks no one notices. And now, they're up so high that even *I* can't get past them. Please, don't break her heart any more than you already have," she pleads to me. Her anger towards me has dissipated. It's been replaced with earnest concern for her best friend.

"I know I don't deserve a second chance. But I will spend the rest of my life fighting for it. I need to make things right.

I love her."

She wears a stunned look on her face, although she's trying to hide it. But it's the honest truth. I fell in love with this woman that unconditionally accepted who I am. I fell completely in love with her, and I can't walk away from that.

Claire finally surrenders, her gaze settling past me as she works through her reluctance. "She's at work."

I feel victorious, hopeful that I'm getting somewhere. Maybe a bit closer to Ellie, even if it's a mere inch. I'll take what I can get. I look at her, waiting for her to continue.

She reaches her open hand out to me. "Give me your phone. I'll Google search the bookstore for you."

I comply, handing it to her and waiting patiently as she types in the address.

"She gets off in an hour. I was supposed to pick her up, but I guess you can meet her there," she says as she hands me back my phone. "But if you ever hurt her again, I will literally hunt you down and kill you."

"If I hurt her again, I'll supply you with the pitchforks and mob to come hunt me down." My eyes scan my phone, skimming through the driving instructions. "Thank you," I whisper quickly before I hurry back to my car.

I spend the drive thinking about what I'm going to say to Ellie. But nothing clear comes to mind. All the words I want to say are mixed up and jumbled in my head. How am I supposed to convince the woman I love that I messed up? That I'll do anything to prove to her that I'll protect her heart from here on out?

I pull up to a spot in the parking lot leading right to the

entrance of the bookstore. From the glass doors, I can see Ellie behind the counter. So much time has passed since I saw her when she visited me at the hospital, and the sight of her makes me float. All the memories of my time with her come rushing back like a tidal wave. Like how soft her glowing skin felt underneath my fingertips, delicate and mesmerizing. Or how when I kissed her, I felt like we were the only two people in the world, spellbound to this feeling of disappearing from everything.

Even from a distance, I can see that her brightness is gone. She smiles politely at customers, but the smile never leaves her lips. It never reaches her eyes where I know her happiness shines from. She's going through the motions of life but not living it. I want to go inside and pull her to me, to hold her and tell her that I'm sorry. I want to be able to tell her everything that I'm thinking without fear that she might reject me.

I sit in my car. I've come all this way to stall, to exist in the presence of her. But I know that I'll regret it if I don't get out and talk to her, or at least try. If I decide to leave and drive off, the idea of us will always nag at the back of my head. I will always be reminded of what could have been. I'll regret not giving my all while baring every bit of myself to her so she can know how I feel.

My hand reaches for the door handle, and I open it slowly. Every inch I make to get closer to Ellie while the inevitable fear of what may come haunts me. I stand and look around. It's a lot more crowded than I had anticipated. People walking by start looking in my direction, making second glances. Then the whispers start. People begin to circle back towards me after they've walked by.

I've been recognized.

I step onto the sidewalk and begin my walk towards the storefront, but I'm stopped as people start to approach me.

"Rhylan Matthews!" I hear it loud and distinctly though the voices are hushed. I don't make it far before people gather around, causing me to withdraw back towards my car.

"It's Rhylan Matthews!"

CHAPTER 43

Ellie

"Hey, Ellie. You got any plans after work?" Kevin, Mrs. Le's son, asks me as I finish ringing up my last customer. My shift is almost over, and Kevin came in an hour ago to take over and close out the store for the night.

"My friend is picking me up, so we'll probably just order in and watch movies or something." Claire had come over in the morning. We had an early breakfast before she dropped me off at work. After I listened to Rhylan's voicemail, Claire has been more attentive, even more so than before. She's hardly left my side, only to go home or to spend an hour or so with Wes.

"On a Saturday night? Sounds kinda boring."

"Yeah, but it's relaxing," I answer with a polite smile. "You're going to be here tomorrow morning?"

"And next week too. I told Linda to enjoy herself. She and Paul never go on vacation, so they deserve to treat themselves."

"You know, it's so weird that you call your parents by their first names."

"Only here. I feel so childish to say 'my mom' to her employees." He chuckles sheepishly.

I laugh. Mrs. Le decided to take an impromptu vacation with her husband, traveling to Arizona to visit family. She had put the vacation off for a couple years now but finally planned to go after Kevin and Mr. Le insisted.

I reach behind the counter for my purse when I hear Kevin speak again. I stand upright, turning my attention to him.

"What was that?" I ask.

"There's something going on outside." He points his finger towards the door.

I look over his shoulder from behind him to see that a small crowd has gathered around a car that I recognize. Amongst them, a tall figure is the center of attention.

It's Rhylan.

He's backed up against his car with a crowd growing around him. He's cornered, with no way out.

Customers that were shopping in the store start to exit to join the commotion outside. I follow. When I walk out of the store, Rhylan's eyes find me.

He's here for me. He has to be.

He squeezes himself out from the crowd and walks towards me. He stands inches away, quiet and serious.

"Ellie…" He says my name softly, whispering it through a clenched jaw and pinched brows.

"Rhylan, what are you doing here?"

"I came here to see you."

I look up at him with pleading eyes. I want him to stop. I'm no longer just drowning, I'm sinking down a bottomless pit, and my heart can't take it anymore. After listening to his message, I just want to move on. I want to go on with my life and forget everything that happened between us. Even if I know I'll never forget, I still have to try.

His absence allowed me to see a future where my wounds would leave deep, distinct scars. Scars that would have served as a reminder of him and what we had.

"You can't come around expecting me to drop everything for you," I answer. My shoulders slump, so utterly exhausted. "You can't do this to me, Rhylan." My entire body trembles.

"Ellie, is everything okay?" I hear Kevin's voice from behind me. He looks at Rhylan and realizes who he is. "Holy shit. You're…"

Rhylan keeps his eyes on the ground, ignoring Kevin completely. He lifts his face to speak before letting Kevin finish.

"Eleanor, can we just talk?" He looks behind me, staring blankly ahead. Then his eyes come into focus with mine. "Please."

I'm just convincing myself to walk back inside when I start to notice the swarm of people gathered around Rhylan's car getting larger. People start pulling out their phones and taking pictures, flashing away, not even realizing how much of an impact those photos would have on Rhylan's life, just like the ones of us did.

I start to panic. I understand what this means to Rhylan's career. Being pictured with the girl that everyone deemed insignificant and a stain on his otherwise strong reputation. But while the commotion grows, Rhylan keeps his eyes on me.

He doesn't care. He doesn't care about all the people around him or what will come of the dozens of pictures that are sure to surface within the next couple of days. He doesn't care what will become of his career.

He only cares about me. About us.

"Ellie," he says, barely making a sound as he whispers my name again.

I stop him, holding my hands in front of him before he says anything else. I push myself through the crowd and swiftly walk towards his car to sit in the passenger seat, no longer able to handle the pressure of the crowd closing in on us. He unflinchingly follows and closes the door behind me, walks around his hood to the driver's side, and gets in. Shifting the gears of the car, he speeds out of the parking lot and leaves the dumbfounded crowd behind us.

We sit in silence. I clutch the straps to my worn-out purse in my closed fists, the tension rising in my chest. I wish I could say all of the things I want to, but I can't.

I want to ask him why he left me, why it was so easy for him to disappear with only the words of resentment to send me off, why he had pushed me away. I want to ask him why he's come for me after all this time, expecting me to jump into his arms as if I've been waiting for him to change his mind. I want to yell at him. I want to hold him, kiss him, and tell him that I forgive him. I don't know how to tell him all this, so instead, I stay quiet.

"I'm sorry I just showed up like this."

"No, you aren't," I spit back. I don't even think. The words just come out. He looks at me, the honesty of my words slicing through him. "If you were in the least bit sorry, you wouldn't have come."

He looks straight ahead, his lips forming a grim line.

"Where are you taking me?"

He stays quiet for a long time. Too long. I cross my arms, frustrated.

"I just wanted to talk to you. Just give me five minutes. That's it. And if you never want to speak to me again, I'll leave you alone," he pleads.

My bitter silence is my answer. That thread of hope intertwined with curiosity cuts through me, forcing me to stay quiet instead of telling him to turn around or take me home like I should. I want to give up and throw in the towel, but I don't know how.

CHAPTER 44
Rhylan

The dark clouds above us look ominous and menacing, telling us that a storm is on its way. The drive to my house is completely silent but full of an air that's screaming every word between us that Ellie wants to say. And I want to listen, to hear her words so that I can finally fix this. I *need* to fix this.

Every time I steal a glance in her direction, her face changes. When we first drove off, she looked angry, frustrated, trying to tamper down every harsh word she wanted to throw at me. Now, as the car moves towards my house, her face changes to worry. Stress is written all over her body with her wrung-out hands and scrunched brows.

A thunderous clap booms above us, and somehow the clouds are even darker. But I keep driving past the looming storm.

When we finally drive through the iron gates of my house and pull to a stop on the driveway, I kill the engine. The silence is even louder without the hum of the engine.

"Why are we here, Rhylan?"

"I wanted to talk to you. Alone."

"Why?"

I sigh. I know why I came to her and brought her back here. It was to grovel my way back into her heart. Instead of telling her that, I stick to the facts. Real, feasible truths that she can't deny. "I called you."

"I know."

But she didn't call me back. "I wasn't sure if you got my message."

"I did."

She finally turns to look at me, glaring at me to show her indignation, and I flinch. She's so cold, so distant, and I made her this way. I forced her to close off her heart, to protect it because I didn't handle it with care.

When I don't say anything, she gives an exasperated sigh and opens the car door before I follow. On the pavement, she paces, running her hands through her hair in frustration. An irritated groan emits from her throat, and she looks at me with the same anger she carried in the car.

"What do you want from me, Rhylan?!" Her sentence ends with another thunderous clap from the sky. The dark clouds continue rolling in, and I see the first fat drop of rain hit the pavement before feeling another on my head.

"Ellie, I'm so sorry. I lied about Bella. There's nothing going on," I try to explain to her, but her face never falters, not even giving me an inch. "I made a mistake. I've been suffering so much without you and—"

"*You've* been suffering?!"

"Eleanor."

"Don't call me that."

I sigh, all hints of hope slipping through my fingers. "Ellie, please. You have to understand. I was pushing you away. Please, just listen—"

"Let me move on! Let me live my life and move on. I'm moving to Seattle after I graduate, and I'm finally building this life that doesn't revolve around you! So please, just let me go!" She's pleading, begging as I watch her crumble. Her heart finally gives out, exhausted and spent, as she continues her plea for me to let her wounds finally heal.

My expression turns somber. "You're moving to Seattle?"

She doesn't answer. Instead, she looks away, avoiding my eyes altogether.

"Why?"

She scoffs. "It's really none of your concern."

My breathing grows rapid, panic filling my insides. "Don't go. I know it's wrong of me to ask, but please, don't leave. I can't imagine my life without you and—"

"You broke my *heart*!" A shuddered sob leaves her mouth, somehow saying more than her actual words as her outrage spills through the cracks in her voice.

Tears roll down her cheeks, and she makes no attempt to hide them. She's openly displaying the damage I've done to her. To show me that redemption isn't going to happen. Her words hit my chest like a double-edged dagger, and I swallow the pain that forces its way into my throat. But it's not my pain, it's hers.

It starts to pour. The rain comes down, soaking the ground and our bodies. Ellie's hair and clothes cling to her, the rainwater running down her face, etching against the pain in her eyes and meeting the tears that coat her cheeks.

I move towards her as her body starts backing away. Her stance is telling me no. No to anything and everything that I'm about to do. But I can't bring myself to care. As I close in on her, she tenses. When my arms move to encase her towards me, she shows the start of a struggle. Her arms move up to come between us, and anger takes over every muscle in her body. The pounds of her small fists hit my chest, shoving me away while I refuse to back down, pulling her closer instead.

"Why?!" she screams through her tears. "Why did you push me away?!"

Her hits become weaker, her heart caving, letting me hold her in my determined arms. My hands move to cradle her head as her sobs become muffled against my chest.

"Why?" Her final question dissolves within her tears, wavering to her weakness as she finally bends. She tried to stand her ground, refusing me from getting back in after I cast her aside.

"Baby, I'm so sorry." My voice is thick. As if I've held in everything I wanted to tell her, letting those words grow calloused and brittle.

We stand there, the rain further soaking us. The coolness from the rushed storm hits deep in our bones. But we can't move, not when this moment is more than just standing in the rain. It's about canvassing what remains of our relationship so that we can fight for it.

"I'm not drowning anymore," I whisper into her hair. The rain hitting the hard cement is loud, a pitter-patter that mingles with my voice, and I'm not sure if she hears me. Until she lifts her face to look up at me. "You make me hope, even when you aren't here. Just knowing that you exist somewhere in this shitty world makes me hopeful."

The tears in her eyes continue to pour, streaming down her cheeks and spilling off the edge of her jaw.

"I belong to you."

CHAPTER 45
Ellie

He belongs to me. He's never belonged to anyone, has never been one part of two halves that made a whole. But here he is, telling me that he finally belongs to someone. And that someone is me.

When I look at him, his eyes are rimmed red and damp, and he's working hard to keep the tears in before he gives in and they fall. Once they fall, he doesn't fight them. My eyes flit to his mouth pressed in a firm line sitting just above his perfect jaw, which ticks with each passing beat.

I hate him. I hate everything that he's done. All the hurt that I had to deal with, completely and utterly alone. I was so angry at him for it. But looking into his eyes, seeing the tears flow down his cheeks, mirroring my own, I'm reminded of everything that we shared. Every laugh, every touch, every moment where we saw our own soul reflected in the other. We're the same. Cut from the same cloth while sewn together in different patterns, somehow leading to this moment. And that hate starts to dissolve, leaving behind the watered-down anger that I can't really justify anymore.

I was once told that the opposite of love isn't hate. It's indifference. While I've become angry at Rhylan for every slice of pain he cut into my heart, I can never feel indifferent about him. I can never look at him and not feel some sort of blistering, all-consuming emotion for him. I will always feel *something*.

His hands move up to my chin, cupping the wet skin and pulling me towards him. All the pent-up anger and resentment that still lingers is telling me to pull away, to stay mad. To remind him of the damage he's done. Instead, my hands move up towards him, where they always manage to gravitate to when we're this close. My fingers hesitantly trace his outline, grazing his hard chest, trailing up towards his wide shoulders, and finally stopping once they hook around his neck.

I feel the relief set in his shoulders when his lips finally meet mine. It feels like we've been apart for a hundred years. Too much time has passed since my lips touched his, and our kiss is full of hunger, an unyielding want that I melt into. His hold on me becomes tighter, and he wraps his arms around me. Without even realizing it, I'm moving. Lifted off the ground, being carried in a direction that I don't even care where. All I know is that I'm in Rhylan's arms, and I feel like I've come home. Damaged and broken, but home.

The tips of my Converse scrape against the hard cement as we both inch closer to the shelter of his house, away from the raging storm that's happening outside and inside my heart. Where I could, just for a minute, forget that my heart is at war.

I can feel his hands move to open his door, feel the sudden slam of it as he kicks it behind him, but I'm too consumed in his kiss to do anything. My back hits the cold wall with the pressure of his weight flush against me. My shoulders press backwards, my body arching into him.

Without even thinking, my hands trail down his torso to the hem of his soaked shirt, gradually lifting it and peeling it above him. He complies, letting my hands lead the way and following willingly. We break our kiss, his beautiful face disappearing behind his wet, clingy shirt. When he reappears, he doesn't continue to kiss me. Instead, he looks down at me, bare-chested and breathing heavily, the rainwater having softened his skin as he waits for my permission to continue. I don't move or say anything. I want to keep kissing him, to keep going until the only thing left is the aftermath of our passion. He leans his forehead against mine, and a shaky, uncertain sigh leaves my lips.

"We can stop," he whispers, pausing for my answer. "If you want to, we can stop. I'm here for whatever you're willing to give me. All I'm asking is that you don't give up on us."

My heart. It takes over, telling me, *I've got it from here.* I have no choice but to give in, to let it lead the way, because if I don't, there won't be anything left of me. My hands move into his hair, grasping it to pull him towards me. With his lips melding into mine, I trail my hands down to lift the hem of my own shirt, once again breaking our kiss. With my skin bare and vulnerable, there for him to take, my hands continue to move, but with caution.

He starts pulling at the metal button of my jeans, moving deftly as his hard knuckles brush against my soft stomach. When he looks at me, his eyes so painstakingly serious, I know he sees the trepidation in my face. The sight of my heart on my sleeve, openly displaying every bit of my apprehension and doubt.

"I'm so sorry I hurt you. It was the hardest thing in my life watching you walk away because I gave you no choice." His voice cracks, guilt filling those empty spaces. I can feel my chin tremble. I look away from him, the pain only allowing a shuddered sigh to blow through my lips. I could tell him to stop here, and I know he wouldn't fight it. But I can't. So instead, my hands move to his biceps, strained and bulging, and I pull them towards me.

Don't stop. Those are the words I'm telling him, my trembling hands speaking for me.

His hands move hastily, hooking at my waistband. I aide him by lowering my jeans and removing them completely before unbuttoning his. He lifts me, holding me tenderly above him and positioning himself between my legs, both of us gasping and moaning as he moves into me.

"Is this okay?" he whispers through a strained voice, pausing before he shifts his body closer. I nod, my eyes hooded and head leaned against the cold wall.

I cling to him, arms and legs wrapped around him, hanging on as if he would let me go if I didn't. His hands grasp me just as tightly, pulling at my waist as our bodies tangle within each other. We're skin to skin, no barrier between us, even though we know the consequences. But we can't stop. Nothing can stop us.

"Oh God, Ellie. I missed you so much." A low growl emits from his chest, the rumbling vibrating against my skin.

Words finally trickle out of me, cautious but real. "I missed you too, Rhylan." A whimpered cry follows, my nails digging into his skin as his hand fists into my hair.

We move quickly. As if time is working against us, threatening to interrupt this most intimate of moments. All of the missed opportunities, moments we spent without each other, pouring together as if it's a gift from the gods and only for us to share.

His lovemaking is visceral, passionate but somehow still tender. With my heart torn in two, I find it hard to not let my emotions mix in between our urgent touches. I hadn't meant for this to happen, hadn't expected it. But here I am, completely relinquishing myself to him, and I can't bring myself to regret it. All I can regret is the time that we spent apart, time I spent wallowing and being angry. Time, I now realize, that I could have spent loving him.

With his hand leaning against the wall right next to my cheek, he breathes into my ear, his breaths sharp and ragged. My face is angled towards his jaw. I don't look into his eyes. When his lips caress the side of my face, I shiver. I try to speak, try to make sense of this, *us.*

Before I can take another breath, he whispers into my damp skin still dewy from the rain, "I love you."

Our bodies slump to the ground, leaning against the wall. He holds me close against him on his lap as his arms wrap around me, and he lays my head against his shoulder.

"I was so scared," he starts, his low voice filling the room. "I saw what they did to you and what everyone was saying. About Bella and us. And I didn't want you to become…"

He gestures his free hand outwards, not necessarily pointing out one thing but everything. His life, what it's become.

"This," he finishes. "I didn't want me to be the reason that you kept drowning. I couldn't go on knowing that I was the one that kept you underwater. You deserve better."

His hand threads through mine, and our eyes gaze at the tangle of fingers in front of us. The way they knot together, it looks intricate, no exact point where he begins and I end.

"But I love you too much to stay away," he says. "Whether it's us on a secluded island or against the world, it has to be me and you. I can't live any other way." When he tells me he loves me again, it rings more veracious than it did the first time. As if he's saying it to prove a point rather than simply confessing his love.

When I stay quiet, the silence slicing through our pain, he doesn't urge me to say anything. Instead, he stands, carrying me to his room. He lays me on his bed as he wraps his arm around me, pulling my back against his front.

He loves me.

I have a hard time accepting it, having faith that he didn't say those words in the heat of the moment, even through the conviction of his words. So it lingers as a question, not a statement of fact.

When night finally falls and the rain calms to a light sprinkle, I turn to look over at Rhylan. He's fallen fast asleep, his breathing steady, a quiet rise and fall of his chest showing that he's in a deep, contented slumber.

I lift myself from his bed in the dark. The only light comes from the dim lamp sitting in one corner of his large room. I'm exhausted, utterly spent. My emotions are everywhere, far and wide, openly splayed, making it impossible for me to collect them.

I quietly dress, my clothes still damp and smelling of rainwater, and tiptoe out the front door. By the time I'm outside, the rain has stopped completely. The only thing that remains is the moist ground and the wet air, and a sense of perspective. It's not hope, because my heart doesn't feel optimistic enough. Instead, I feel an overwhelming sadness for it. For the broken pieces that remain scattered in my life, unable to come together for it to be whole. But was it ever whole to begin with?

I call an Uber to Rhylan's house. I need some distance, time to think about us. When the Uber pulls up just outside Rhylan's gate, I climb in slowly. I don't go home though. Instead, I go to Claire's apartment, and during the ride to Claire's house, I text Rhylan.

I need time.

The narrow hallway leading into Claire's apartment feels thick, my feet moving slowly and dragging on the carpeted floor. My knock on the door is heavy. I'm holding everything in, the cries, the anger, the hurt. All up until Claire opens her door and I see her face, and I can't hold it in anymore. Everything pours out of me, my body growing limp from exhaustion, from the strength that I had to exert to keep everything at bay.

"Ellie!"

I look at her, the tears welling up again and streaming

down as I slump to the ground as soon as she closes the door behind me. Claire rushes to wrap her arms around me, and I lean my head into her.

"Ellie, what happened?"

"He told me not to give up on us," I cry.

"Ellie, he came to your house looking so desperate. If I felt that he was going to hurt you, I would have told him to fuck off," Claire says. "He told me he loves you."

I face her, confused but not completely disbelieving. As if I didn't hear those same words from Rhylan himself. I don't know why they still don't ring true to me. Why I *still* question his love.

"Do you love him?"

I don't answer her, but she knows. She knows I love him even if I don't say it out loud. But it's not enough. My love for him, his love for me… It's not enough to hold us together. To look past our pain and look forward to the future.

I stay with Claire for the rest of the night, sitting on her soft couch with a blanket draped over me to keep me warm. She's a busybody, ordering takeout and keeping the conversation going to keep my mind off Rhylan. But it's useless. He's all I can think about.

"Ellie, if you want to forget Rhylan and move on, I support you one hundred percent. But if you do, you have to move on. Don't let him dictate your future." Her voice is sudden after a long stretch of silence. The lone french fry that I've been twisting between my fingers finally snaps and falls on my lap, leaving behind a fresh oil stain.

I nod. Her words of advice are sound, reasonable, and just,

but that doesn't make my heart any less heavy. She leans her head against my shoulder as I lean my head against hers.

I don't belong to anyone.

Except me. He belongs to me now.

Rhylan returning into my life has brought on a hard slab of confusion. Decisions that I didn't know I had to make are being presented, and I'm not sure if my heart has the strength to even consider them. I wish I knew what to do. I wish whatever decision I make about my future, I can also know that it's the right one. All of the what-ifs twist and turn in my mind. What if he breaks my heart again? But what if, just *what if*, he loves me, and I love him, and that's it? Just uncomplicated and unconditional love that we can live off of.

"Can I tell you something?" I ask Claire. "And maybe you don't judge me?"

"I would never judge you."

"I know, but just…" I pause. "Maybe hold off on any reactions or opinions."

She sits up and looks at me, giving me her full attention.

"I want to give us a chance," I say, with a deep exhale. "I know he hurt me, but I want to forget all that and just be with him. Even pretend that we never hurt each other and everything bad between us never happened."

"Why would I judge you for that?"

I shrug. "Because he broke my heart. And you saw firsthand how badly he hurt me. And because it sounds stupidly naive."

"Yeah, but Ellie. You love him." She sighs, taking a pause before she carefully collects her words and continues. "I saw him. I talked to him. He didn't look like someone that tossed you aside without regret. He looked like he was in as much pain as you were."

Pain. Whenever I think of myself and Rhylan, pain seems to follow. We were never full of brightness or joy or whatever optimistic thoughts most couples get to experience. We came from hardship. Our love doesn't come easily. We have to work for it. But it's an effort that's worthwhile because when it all works out and we somehow make sense, it's magic.

It's then I finally understand. Our story, mine and Rhylan's, isn't written in the stars where everything is meant to be bright and bountiful. Our story is written in the oceans, where tenderness is laced into the beautiful waves of the dark waters, making our story intricate instead of conventional. Where the ripples map out each word we share, adding to the story that's still being written. Where every pit of darkness is a place that we learn to pull each other out of so we no longer have to drown.

My weak smile causes Claire to sigh and wrap me in her arms. "Whatever you decide, I'm here to walk you through it."

I nod, smiling at her with gratitude. "Thanks, Claire."

When I wake, it feels cold. Chills cover my body, and I realize it's because I feel empty. Ellie left in the middle of the night while I had fallen asleep. My clothes are strewn on the floor, and Ellie's are gone with her. The sudden ache from her absence returns. Having her soft skin wrapped in my arms and the scent of her filling my senses, it was like we had never changed. And then, just as quickly as she was back in my arms, she was gone again.

When I look at my phone, I see a message from her.

I need time.

It isn't goodbye.

Outside, daybreak is taking over the approaching morning sky, brighter than usual as it normally is after a storm. I can't sleep, not when the absence of Ellie is so prominent. So I get up and walk outside, sliding the heavy glass doors to the poolside right outside my bedroom. Once settled into a lounge chair, I watch the morning become brighter.

It's while sitting in the quiet morning air that I realize how much Ellie has changed me. How before, I snuffed out who I really was so that I could be who everyone wanted me to be. Now, knowing what my life could be like with Ellie by my side, purpose seems to course through me. I want so many things for us, changes that I know we deserve. I belong to her, and I don't feel tethered. I feel free because she would allow me to be who I want to be. She would never hold me back. She would always accept me for who I am. When someone comes along and loves you unconditionally like that, you don't let them go. You hold them close and cherish every moment with them. You spend the rest of your life with them.

"Good morning." When I turn around, Charles is standing there, leaning against the wall leading to my backyard.

"What are you doing here so early?"

"I was heading to the gym," he explains. "I was going to see if you wanted to get an early workout with me."

I nod. He walks over and sits in the lounge chair next to mine.

"You talked to Ellie, didn't you?"

I look at him, surprised by his accuracy. "How did you know?"

"I can see it in your face. You don't look angry. But you look sad as shit." He smirks.

I sigh, rubbing my hands through my face. "I brought her back here last night, and she left in the middle of the night… while I was sleeping."

He doesn't say anything. Instead, he lets us both sit in silence, letting me know that he's here if I want to talk.

"She said she needed time," I finally say.

"Then she needs time."

My chest constricts. What if time isn't enough? What if whatever I give her, whether it's the moon or the stars, it's never going to be enough to bring her back to me?

"I love her."

"I know you do." His voice is so calm and pragmatic, not a single ounce of doubt plaited into his words.

"I'm scared that it's not enough. Loving her and proving to her that I do, I'm scared that it'll never be enough." *That I'm not enough,* I think to myself.

"Then she doesn't deserve you," he says with sureness. "But I have a feeling it's enough. You just have to give her what she wants."

Charles extends his legs and leans back into the chair, the sun finally warming the air, allowing us to bask in its glow. Stifling a yawn, he adds his two cents. "You know, sometimes, women need a big gesture. Something that tells the world that you love them. That they belong to you."

I look at him, amused and curious. "What do you mean?"

"When I was first dating Amelia, she rejected me. Over and over again. It wasn't fun but… Man, she was the most beautiful girl I'd ever seen. Always shy and humble, never fully aware of how beautiful she is. I knew I had to have her. I finally got her to go on a date with me, and I knew I couldn't mess it up. So I did the one thing I thought I knew how to do. I tried to impress her. I took my dad's BMW. I didn't even ask him cause I knew he would say no. I picked her up and took her out to this local hangout that a bunch of us jocks went to every weekend. I acted all cocky. As if she cared that I was popular. I felt like a complete phony, but I wanted to impress her."

I smirk. He sits up to tell the rest of his story.

"She saw right through me. She called me out and told me to get real. And I did. I dropped the act and apologized for acting like a complete douche. But I couldn't just let it go without a big gesture. I had to let her know that I was being real with her. So, during one of our football games, I did just that. I ran to her in the stands right before halftime and handed her a bouquet of flowers in front of the whole school. I wanted everyone to know that she was mine. That was when I finally won her over."

A smile finally creeps onto my face, resulting in a burst of light laughter. Picturing Charles in his glory days, trying to woo the pretty, timid girl in school is a sight that I wish I could've seen in person.

"So a big gesture, huh?" I ask.

"Something that tells the world you love this girl. She needs to know that you're in it for the long run."

I consider his advice. It's good advice, but I don't know if it's feasible. In this day and age, there's no big stadium to shout to the whole student body that you love someone. But there are other options.

CHAPTER 47
Rhylan

My knuckles rap lightly on Shana's office door. Through the glass, I can see her turned towards the expansive view that comes with working on the thirty-sixth floor in the middle of downtown Los Angeles. She turns her head over her shoulder and smiles too kindly at me, waving her hand to welcome me in.

"Hey, Rhy," she says softly. Ever since she visited me in the hospital, her demeanor towards me has changed. While she usually presents herself with a no-nonsense attitude, much like Levi, she's gone soft.

"Hey, Shana." I walk the three steps it takes to settle into one of the two bright purple chairs facing her glass desk. Everything in her office is glass, even the vase carrying a large arrangement of white lilies, making her workspace too fragile and clean.

I'm in her office today, one day ahead of the charity event I am to attend, to talk over logistics. So I know where I'm supposed to go, who I'm supposed to meet, etcetera. I signed up for this charity event months ago when the children's hospital reached out to Shana, knowing my appeal towards vintage cars. While Shana usually emails me the necessary details for past events that I've attended, she's been calling me to her office for such occasions. Most likely her way of doing a welfare check. To make sure I'm still in one piece after seeing me almost fall apart.

I'm glad that she wants to see me in person though, because there's something that I want to talk to her about as well.

My right foot taps against the lush carpet, making my knee bounce like there's a spring under my heel.

"So," she remarks. "The event is going to be at Irwindale Speedway." Her eyes move to scan her computer screen, the pad of her middle finger gliding across the wheel on her mouse. "I'm going to email you the address and time. You're bringing your car, right?"

I nod. "I'm getting it detailed right after this."

"Good," she almost whispers as her focus remains on her monitor. "Sorry, I can't seem to find the email Krista sent me."

I wait patiently as she continues to search.

"But it's going to be a meet and greet with some kids that are in remission and have completed one or more rounds of chemo. And then you're going to drive through the racetrack for a couple of photo ops."

I clear my throat, but Shana's focus remains on the screen in front of her, her brows now furrowed with irritation.

"Let me call Krista into my office," she explains, referring to her assistant. "I think she can help me find the email."

"Actually, Shana," I interrupt as she picks up the receiver of her phone. "I wanted to talk to you about something. Before you get too busy." *Or I chicken out.*

I'm nervous. I don't know if it's because I'm worried Shana will tell me that I've lost my mind or if it's because what I'm about to tell her feels out of character. Either way, I feel jittery. As if everything I feel about Ellie and our relationship has culminated to this exact moment and our future is at stake.

It's then that Shana finally looks at me as she gently places the receiver back in its cradle. My eyes don't meet hers right away. Instead, they scan her cluttered desktop, finally landing on a small paperweight in the shape of a glass dolphin. I'm stalling so I can gather the courage to tell her my plan.

When she notices my hesitation, she pushes herself away from the edge of her desk, the wheels of her chair swiveling to face me. "I'm listening."

"Remember that girl?" I start. "The one that the paps got a picture of me with?"

"You mean the one that got you into all that trouble?" One of her brows is raised with suspicion, already protective and skeptical.

"To be fair, it wasn't her fault," I say in Ellie's defense. Knowing that I was the one that had put Ellie in the position where she appeared to be the center of fault in the first place brings on an onslaught of guilt. None of it was her fault. It wasn't mine either. I understand that now. Believing it was my fault was what caused me to push Ellie away. I know now that what happened simply happened because of who I am, and our relationship paid the price for it.

"Okay. I'm assuming you wanted to talk to me because of something to do with this girl?"

"Ellie. Her name is Ellie."

Her hands come together on her desk, and she leans forward as her expression softens. I don't correct her to be rude. I do it to let her know that Ellie isn't just "some girl." She's someone so much more important than that.

"I know I don't really post anything on my social media accounts, and your team mainly manages it for promotional stuff, but I wanted to post something. Something to let the world know how I feel about her."

Her eyebrows shoot up. "That's a big deal."

"I know," I answer, my voice low and solemn. "She's a big deal."

"Are you sure this is what you want? I mean, the press didn't really have a positive reaction to her. And your fans might not be too happy about her coming back into the limelight."

"That's exactly why," I say. "My fans, of all people, need to know that she's someone important to me. And I think it's important that they hear it from me, not through some shady pictures on the internet."

"Okay," she answers, tapping her index finger on the glass surface. "Why don't you come up with something, and we can proofread it. Make sure it sends the right message."

"Okay. I can do that."

"But just so you know, once you post this, there's really no going back. You have to make sure that this girl is worth it. Your time, your dedication. People are going to expect this girl—Ellie, to stick around."

"That's the plan."

She smiles at me. A sweet, genuine smile. This lovestruck

movie star that sits in front of her has found someone that's worth letting the world know, and she's admittedly happy for me.

"She makes you happy?"

"She does. But I don't know if I have what it takes to make her happy." I look down, uncertainty written all over my face. Ellie means so much to me, and I'm scared to lose her completely. What if no matter what I do, it's never enough to win her back? What if she decides that giving us another chance isn't worth the heartache?

"Why are you doing this? Shouting to the world that she's yours?"

"She needs to know how I feel. She needs to know that I'm serious about us."

"Why?" Shana asks, truly curious.

"I messed up. When the paps showed up, I saw what they did to her, and I got scared. I basically told her that I had my fun with her and I was bored. And that I had moved on to dating Bella."

She grimaces at the mention of Bella. "So you made her believe that you just used her, like some typical celebrity prick adding another notch on his bedpost."

I nod.

"You know that's not who you are?" Shana asks me.

"It sure feels like I am," I huff. I feel so ambivalent. I never meant to hurt Ellie. Or anyone, for that matter. But at the same time, I *did* hurt her. I made sure she felt used even though that was the furthest thing from the truth.

"Rhylan, do what you need to do to make things right with

Ellie. Whatever amends you have to make for her to realize that you care about her, do it. I'm here to support you. I'm just here to make sure you look good doing it." She winks at me.

The gleaming sun reflects off the glossy black surface of my car. It's freshly waxed and polished, and I can see my face looking back at me along the curve of the hood. I can't help it when my hand runs along the smooth surface, knowing that I'll probably leave fingerprints, but my baby has never looked this good.

After I left Shana's office, I went home and dug deep to find the right words. The words that embodied how Ellie had become a constant in my life and how she was to remain a permanent fixture. But most importantly, I wanted to capture what it meant for me to find someone that I loved when I didn't think I deserved it. I want Ellie to know that. That I've finally come to terms with understanding my worth, and I'm finally willing to love her without condition. Everything else, I'm leaving to fate. I'm letting the world decide how to accept the proclamation that I make very public. I'm risking it all.

For now, I put all of those emotions on pause as I shift into "celebrity" Rhylan Matthews.

My drive to Irwindale Speedway was uneventful as I drove

carefully to maintain the newly speckless condition of my car. I'm standing on a rolled-out royal blue carpet on the asphalt that extends into a large oval. Hundreds of guests and attendees fill the stadium-style seats lining one side of the track as a small procession of children make their way to the cars neatly parked near the carpet where I stand.

While the show of cars is a vision that I have trouble peeling my eyes away from, the real stars of the show are the children. Rosy and optimistic, their smiles radiate as they wave at the cameras and stand to be photographed with myself and other stars that have made an appearance for the event.

"Are you really Rhylan Matthews?" A little girl peers up at me, a denim baseball cap sitting on her too-small face to shield her from the bright sun. I kneel down, getting at eye level with her, and grin.

"I sure am," I answer, my hand coming up to pat her shoulder. "And what's your name?"

"Jessica," she answers shyly.

"It's very nice to meet you, Jessica."

Another child, much older but still carrying the innocence of youth, steps closer to be next to say hi.

"Are you going to marry that girl?" she asks boldly and eagerly. "That girl that you posted on Instagram about? She's so pretty."

I lower my head, bashful. I can't help the gratification radiating from my heart. They saw and accepted Ellie and me for who we are. Two people deeply in love and ready for the world to know how we felt about each other.

"I sure hope so," I answer, chuckling with hope bubbling

inside my gut, fear the last thing I feel knowing what I said to be true.

"I hope so too," she responds. They both smile as the younger one clings to the older one before scurrying off.

With my cheeks aching from the constant smiles and my heart full from the continued words of support, I'm ready to leave. To find Ellie and let her know that I did what I did to show her that there is nothing in this world that will keep me from her. Even if it took this long to realize it, I'm going to do everything in my power to let her know this.

I'm in my car, inching towards the exit as the line of cars is directed and funneled to a narrow archway. My fingers drum against my steering wheel as I become restless, which makes the line feel longer. I fidget with my stereo, punching at the buttons and ejecting the tape in the deck when I decide slow jams aren't what I want to listen to right now.

I lift the lid to the center console, flicking through the file-like organized display of cassette tapes. My car isn't moving, and when I realize that I've been searching for the right songs to elevate my mood rather than paying attention to the cars in front of me, there's a large gap in between myself and the car in front of me.

Then I hear the screeching of tires before I see the flash of red hurtling towards me. Wheels spin as smoke kicks from behind the cherry-colored Mustang facing my driver's side. My body seizes, frozen solid in place. There's nothing I can do but brace myself.

When faced with death, you're usually told that you see your life flash before your eyes. Large eight-by-ten glossy images of your childhood playing in PowerPoint form as death stares you straight on. At that moment, I see Ellie. I see her delicate fingers trace my face, her silky hair blowing in the wind, her amber-colored eyes surrounded by dark rings that blend with her rounding pupils as she peers up at me. She is my life. And every detail about her flashes before my eyes as I prepare to say goodbye.

And everything goes black.

CHAPTER 49
Ellie

"There's too many choices," Claire huffs, blowing a loose strand of hair off her forehead. She tosses the magazine she was studying onto her coffee table, the image of the slender model wearing a beautiful cream-colored, A-line gown staring at Claire as if taunting her. "I can't decide if I want a ball gown, an A-line, or a mermaid dress… or a damn clown suit."

I reach for one of the dozen magazines that have been neatly piled on the floor next to her foot, leisurely flipping through the pages of tuxedos, table centerpieces, and veils. "This one's pretty," I offer as I show her a new dress, fluffy with tulle and lace.

She waves her hand at me, not even looking in my direction. "I'm going to tell Wes we should just drive to Vegas and elope." She grunts, her toes gently nudging away the magazines as if she could just as easily push away the daunting task of planning a wedding.

"I think your parents would literally kill you if you did that."

She scoffs, annoyed by the truth she can't deny. Her parents, especially her mom, would never let Claire stop hearing about how they didn't get to see their only daughter walk down the aisle wearing a beautiful wedding dress surrounded by two hundred plus guests in a church filled with white roses and lilies. Their vision for Claire's wedding is almost as scary as Claire's inability to decide a single concrete detail of her and Wes's big day.

When she brings her phone in front of her face, her fingers scrolling and mindlessly entertaining her while providing her a much-needed distraction, I reach for the TV remote. We spent the last hour trying to nudge Claire into finding the right dress for her while using the voice of Ina Garten cooking saffron risotto with butternut squash as background noise. I'm thoroughly hungry without an ounce of energy to cook a meal like Ina has perfected, so I opt for changing the channel while tunneling my hand into a half-empty can of Pringles.

Rhylan has been honorable in my request for time. He texts occasionally with a quick good morning or good night greeting, but other than that, I've had some time to be alone with what all of this means. I don't know what the future holds for us, whether or not I'll be able to love him without worrying about all the what-ifs, but I'm thankful that he's giving me the space that I need so that I don't feel like I'm being surrounded by his thoughts instead of my own.

Half paying attention to the news on the TV that I clicked to and half searching for a bridesmaid dress, a task that Claire has so gracefully bestowed upon me as maid of honor, I reach for a magazine we have yet to comb through.

Claire suddenly sits up from her slumped position, her hand waving at me to get my attention. "El," she mouths, a faint whisper calling out my name.

"What?"

"L–look," she stutters as she slowly hands her phone to me. I take her phone in my hand, grabbing the edges as my eyes land on the image on the screen.

It's me and Rhylan. Our picture, posted on his Instagram page, where a blue check mark sits next to his name.

Me and him. Plastered all over the internet for everyone to see. It's the same picture I sent him after he took me out into the ocean, where we spent a day escaping reality. It was such a simpler time. When we didn't know what would become of us, and the anticipation of it only left us hopeful instead of damaged. When we leapt headfirst into what we believed could be great.

I scroll down to see what he's written in the caption.

I met someone. And I fell in love. I didn't expect this to happen, but it did. I met someone who saw me for who I am. She broke down a lot of barriers that I didn't even know I had and allowed me to be me. I don't know if soulmates are real, but I feel like this is the closest thing I could imagine soulmates ever being.

But I messed up, and I quit when I thought I was going to fail. And now I lost someone who means a lot to me.

The reason I'm telling all of you this today is so that I can come clean. To squash any rumors that you might hear and for everyone to know that this is the real deal. For now, all that I ask of everyone is to have faith in me and to not listen to all of the rumors. So that

I can set the record straight. There are a lot of truths that need to be told, and I'm starting with mine.

To all of my fans, thank you for standing by me. I love you all from the bottom of my heart.

My heart stops for a second. It skips a beat as I bring my hand over my chest to clutch it, to make sure it's still there and not dropped into my stomach where I feel it has gone. The words that he said, him confessing his love for me to the entire world. This isn't some small gesture like buying me flowers or taking me on a yacht. This is out there for everyone to see.

Even with the revelation that his words are out there, there's another one that dawns on me. He loves me. He *absolutely* loves me. He loves me enough to put everything on the line, to stand up for me so that I can stake my place in his life. To prove to me that he would do anything to bring me back to him, to bring us back together.

I need to see him, to talk to him. To let him know that I love him too. That he is enough. Everything he did, all of the hurt that we both had to endure, it won't be the end of us. It'll only add to the already growing love that I know sprang to life in the midst of our turmoil.

I'm scrambling to get my belongings, trying to retrace my steps, when I realize my keys are missing. I hear the volume go up as Claire points the remote towards the TV, the news anchor speaking distinctly while enunciating words like *flames, crash,* and *accident.*

Both Claire and I stare, our hands over our mouths and eyes bulging into saucers, as our attention becomes fixated on the screen.

"Rhylan Matthews has been rushed to San Gabriel Valley Medical Center after an unfortunate accident at Irwindale Speedway during a charity event with the Children's Hospital. It appears Matthews was struck by another vehicle while at the event when it lost control. We are unsure of Matthews's condition at this time but know that he was unconscious when he was pulled from the wreckage. Reporting from San Gabriel Valley…"

Everything around me becomes muffled. Even the news anchor, with her squinted eyes and wind blowing her hair to a fluffy ball of knotted locks, sounds distant. Her lips are still moving, but I don't hear any words leave her mouth. What I see are the images the news helicopter managed to capture while hovering around the racetrack. Charcoal smoke rising from a gnarled mess of orange flames and tarmac. Emergency response teams working furiously to contain the fire and controlling the crowd.

I also see the remnants of Rhylan's car. The taillights and back bumper are the only parts untouched as the rest is mangled in a mess of metal and glass. I cling, grasping desperately to the one fact that's keeping me from falling apart and wishing that I could be engulfed in those very flames. He isn't in there. He's far away, in the hospital. The same hospital my dad died in.

"I'll drive," Claire says, her voice stern and authoritative.

I don't argue, my eyes ping-ponging from the TV screen to her phone still held in my hand. Two images that display such different plights. Life and death.

The metal from Claire's keys scrapes across the counter before she heads towards the door. "Let's go."

CHAPTER 50
Ellie

Claire pulls to a stop in front of the emergency room doors, the familiar blaring red sign welcoming me without realizing how unwelcome I felt. How much I wish I could be anywhere else but here.

Outside the hospital, lining the edge of the parking lot and filtering onto the sidewalk, news vans and cameras are set up. Pointing towards the entrance of the building as reporters speak into their microphones. What they're saying, I don't know, but I can guess it's about Rhylan. Whether or not he's okay. If he's alive.

My hurried steps stumble me to the reception area. Everyone around me looks so unconcerned and apathetic when all I want is to scream at them that the love of my life could be dead. His body lying lifelessly in a hospital bed. I don't know what I'm saying when I approach the desk, but my hands splay in front of me on the hard counter. I plead to the woman sitting behind the partition. As if she can determine whether or not Rhylan survives this.

"I'm looking for Rhylan Matthews," I say through a

strangled voice, the tears threatening as I'm hit with a fresh wave of ache thinking about how my mom said the same words, looking for my dad. Making the same plea, bargaining with an absent god. For his life. For Rhylan's life.

"I'm sorry, ma'am," she answers, unbudging and irritable. "We can't—"

"Oh my God," another voice calls from behind the receptionist. "You're that girl."

The woman who referred to me as *that girl* steps forward, standing behind the exasperated receptionist. "She's that girl that Rhylan Matthews made a big ol' announcement about."

"Please," I beg. "I need to see him."

My shoes clack against the linoleum floor, desperately clawing to get to Rhylan. While my only objective is to find him, to hold his warm hand and hear his soothing voice, I don't know if I'm ready to face what I am about to walk into.

The last time I was in this exact situation, I walked into an image deeply carved into my brain. My dad's lifeless body, gone, with only a shell left behind, holding what he used to be. What if that's what I walk into right now? What if the only thing that remains of Rhylan is the cast aside casing of what held his warmth? Now cold and vacant, like my dad.

I repeat his room number over and over in my head, using every ounce of energy to commit it to memory. As if I'm holding on to the three single digits that point to his very location so that I can grasp on to something real. I whiz past people. Nurses and doctors, all oblivious to the raging war inside my chest. All

I hear is the pounding of my heart, thrumming against my ears as I prepare myself. Somehow coming to terms that I may have lost Rhylan.

As I approach the room, I see the light streaming into the hallway. The light chatter of conversation floats out from the room that I'm too scared to enter. I strain to listen for Rhylan's voice, unsure if I can even make it out over the echoing of my own breathing pounding against my ear drums.

I chant my own prayer, whispering my own bargaining to whoever would grant it. *Please be alive. Please be okay. Please. Please. Please.*

When I come to, the overhead lights are glaring down, causing me to flinch away. The throbbing in my head pulsates when I move my head to avoid the light.

I try to move my limbs, a test to see if I'm still alive after the last thing I remember is seeing flashing images of Ellie, my subconscious telling me to say my goodbyes. But when I try to move my legs, they feel too heavy. I look down and see my left leg nestled in a boot propped on top of a small pile of pillows.

"How you feeling, kid?"

Levi's sitting in a chair at my bedside wearing typical golf attire, his elbows resting on his knees as he smirks at me. "You must have some feline blood in you because I think you've made it down to your last four lives."

I chuckle back but wince just as quickly, my hand moving to my left side. I notice the purple and red bruises forming along my forearm and bicep as I shift my position with no avail. It hurts too much to move.

"Working on your day off?"

"You keep me on my toes," he answers, joking but unable

to hide the worry set in his eyes.

"Is my car okay?" I ask, my voice hoarse but chipper considering the situation.

He grits his teeth, frowning as he shakes his head. "Sorry," he finally says. "Believe me, I'm just as upset as you are."

Before I have a chance to mourn, we're interrupted by a soft knock.

"Rhylan?"

When I look up, I see Ellie. Her hair disheveled, eyes blotched red and hands trembling.

"I'm going to get some coffee," Levi whispers as he stands, patting a hand on my shoulder.

He walks past Ellie, smiling politely at her as she points her gaze to the ground.

Once Levi's gone, she runs to me. Her chest heaving in a sobbing mess as she blubbers incoherent words into my arms. I wince again, the sharp pain radiating to my abdomen as I lift my arm to embrace her. I do my best to hide my discomfort because I can't think of a better place to be than right here, holding and consoling her.

"What happened?" she manages to say through her tears.

"I guess the other car lost control," I answer, my voice strained as I try to hold back the grimace creeping up my face. Ellie tries to move away, her face changing when she sees that I'm in pain. "Don't move," I whisper, holding on to her wrist, preventing her from moving away from me. Pain and all, I want her as close as possible. When she stills, my hand moves to her face, brushing away the tears that have spilled down her cheek with my thumb.

"Mr. Matthews," someone calls from the doorway. When Ellie and I both look up, we see a middle-aged man in a white lab coat walk briskly past the foot of the bed. He removes a large X-ray film from an even larger manila envelope. He holds it up against the light to quickly glance at it before looking down at me, taking in the sight of Ellie's tear-stained face as she clutches to my side. "We've got the results from your X-ray, and it looks like you have a hairline fracture in your tibia."

Ellie and I both stare at him, slightly confused but relieved, as he doesn't appear too concerned with the prognosis.

"What does that mean?" Ellie asks, jumping in to demand answers.

The doctor smiles before answering her question. "It means that you're going to have to wear this nice boot and stay off the foot for a while. But the good news is you don't need surgery. Or a cast."

I feel the relief pour from Ellie as her body abates, the worry finally relenting.

"Does that mean I get to go home?" I ask, eyeing Ellie by my side with a reassuring smile.

He flips through my chart that he carried into the room along with my X-ray, reviewing it before giving a definitive answer. "I'd like to keep you overnight to make sure you don't have any other significant injuries. And because of your concussion. But yes, we'll most likely discharge you within the next twenty-four hours."

I look back at Ellie as the doctor leaves, my smile proud. "See? I'm fine."

But she doesn't smile back. Instead, her chin quivers as a

fresh wave of tears threatens to spill, pooling at the corners of her eyes.

"I thought I lost you," she whispers, inching closer to me.

I extend my arm as much as I can, allowing her to nestle into me further. She moves carefully as she settles. When she does, I sink into her, relishing in the softness of her. Her warmth, her scent, her *everything*. I press a kiss into her hairline. "Hey," I whisper. "I'm right here."

She nods into my chest as if she's finally acknowledging that I really am here, breathing. Alive.

She sniffles, her hand moving to wipe her own tears. "The last time I was running through the hospital like that... It was when my dad died."

My body stiffens at the mention of her dad. Because of me, she had to relive one of the worst days of her life.

"And when I got here," she continues, another sniffle interrupting her sentence, "I expected you to be gone. I was so scared that it was too late for me."

"Ellie, I'm okay. You heard the doctor."

"Yeah, but what if you weren't?" She looks up at me, a fresh stream of hot tears running down her face. "I never got to tell you that I love you too."

Her lips continue to tremble as another sob escapes her, her pain seeping out from her cries.

"You saw it?"

"Rhylan," she whispers, voice shaky and unsure. "Everything you said..."

"I meant it. Every single word."

It's my version of shouting from a limo moonroof with

an umbrella in my hand, holding a boom box over my head on her front lawn, or showing up at her door with cue cards and Christmas carols. I have no doubts, no second thoughts because I'm that sure of us. Of me and her, forever. Ellie is it. There would be no one else.

"You love me?" she squeaks.

"I told you I do," I say. "Why is that so hard for you to believe?"

She shakes her head and lowers her face to avert her eyes away from mine. Her brows come together and her forehead creases, as if she's unsure of how to answer my question.

"Ellie, I don't feel like I'm suffocating anymore. I'm working so hard to make peace with who I am and that I can be enough for you. Because I want nothing more than to be enough. For you." I take her hand in mine, lacing our fingers together. "I can't stop thinking about you. Everywhere I look, I see you. You were the last thing I saw when that car hit me."

She slightly balks at the mention of the accident that brought me here. I feel hesitant bringing it up, but she needs to know. She *has* to understand how much she means to me. How much I love her.

"I belong to you, Ellie." I bring her hand to my lips and kiss the back of it, not realizing how much I've missed doing that simple act. "Please let me spend the rest of my life showing you how much I regret everything I did to hurt you. I love you."

Our lips meet in the middle, right in between me and her. Us meeting at the halfway point, not one pulling the other closer. Because that's what this is: two people who love each other and don't have to convince the other of it. We understand that this is our norm from now on. Loving each other and never having to reconcile for it. It feels freeing.

I can't help but feel completely content, holding her in my arms, knowing that this is my chance. My second chance that I'm not sure I really deserve but would fight tooth and nail for.

When Ellie pulls away from me, her eyes lingering on mine, she smiles. "I love you too, Rhylan."

stand as Ellie walks out from her room wearing her shiny black graduation gown with a matching square cap held in her hand, a stark white tassel dangling from the center of it. My weight shifts from my left leg to my right as I adjust my stance to relieve the dull ache shooting up from my ankle.

"How do I look?" Ellie asks, her hands spread out like she's ready to do jazz hands. The pretty floral pattern of her dusty blue dress peeks between the opening of her gown, right where her dark silky hair meets the dip in the collar.

"Oh, Eleanor," Mary calls from her spot in the living room. "You look so beautiful." Her voice croaks through tears, and Mark wraps his arms around her shoulders as she wipes the corner of her eyes with a small tissue.

Ellie smiles at Mary, the two embracing before Mary gives a light squeeze to Ellie's shoulders. I grin wide as Ellie walks towards me. She twirls in her gown once before coming to a stop at my toes.

"Hi, beautiful," I greet her.

"Hey," she whispers as she leans in towards my chest, her

hand running up the sleeve of my navy suit. "How's the leg holding up?" She eyes the boot strapped to my left leg.

"I'm fine," I assure her. "I told you not to worry about it."

She eyes me, her lips pursed in disapproval. It's the same face, an even mixture of sternness and concern, that she's worn for the past six weeks since I came home from the hospital, making sure my recovery occurred without a stitch. While I hate the burden of playing patient while I heal, having her by my side most of the days feels like my own slice of heaven, especially after having spent so much time apart from her.

"You'll tell me if you need a break?" she asks, never breaking down the role of caretaker.

My lips turn down in a small frown, reminding her that today is about her. "I can't wait until I get this thing off next week and you can stop treating me like a big baby."

"I told you to stay home and rest," she argues. "If you did, then you wouldn't have to listen to me nag."

"First of all," I say, flicking the tip of her nose, to which she adorably scrunches her face. "I wouldn't miss this for the world. And second of all, you could never nag." I bend down to kiss the corner of her mouth.

"Not even when I had to practically chain you to the couch so you would finally stay off your feet? Or when I—"

"Not even then," I assure her, cutting her off.

She smirks with a small eye roll.

"We still have about two hours before the ceremony starts, but we should leave now so we can find parking and get good seats," Mary announces, gathering a camera and her keys in her purse.

Ellie turns to face her mom, her hand lightly placed on my forearm. "Mom, I'm going to drive my car. I wanted to make a quick stop with Rhylan before we head over there."

"Okay," Mary answers. "We'll see you there then."

Ellie turns to me. She reaches for my hand as the four of us exit the house. I walk slowly, evening my steps on the slanted driveway towards the passenger side of Ellie's car before we slide into our seats and buckle in.

"So, where's this pit stop?" I ask as she turns into the main road.

"It's a surprise," she answers. "But I promise it'll be worth the detour."

After another twenty minutes of turns and curved roads, we pull up to a large plot of land covered in the greenest grass I've ever seen, all surrounded by full trees and rows of colorful flowers filling neatly trimmed bushes. Ellie parks the car and steps out. I don't ask any questions, don't prod for more information. Instead, I follow willingly, letting her lead the way as we walk through the grassy hill riddled with bouquets of fresh flowers lying on top of polished slabs of stone and marble.

We finally come to a stop in front of a gravesite with a headstone standing about two feet tall, glossy with granite. My eyes trail the words etched into the hard stone.

Daniel Francis Salerno
December 9, 1968 - February 24, 2012
Beloved father and husband

"Hi, Dad," Ellie says sweetly into the wind. "I want you to meet Rhylan." She stoops down, and her hand runs over the top of the headstone to greet her dad. When she stands upright, I pull her close to me, wrapping my arms around her as her gown swishes around us.

We hold on to each other, our faces angled downwards, saying our silent greetings and letting the air fill with the words that her father would have said to us if he were here.

Nice to meet you, Rhylan.

I'm so proud of you, Eleanor.

I miss you and your mom so much.

After a long moment, she turns to look up at me while my fingers move to instinctively brush the hair out of her face. "He would have loved you," she says through a shaky voice.

I nod, so honored that she would share this moment with me.

She looks up towards the sky, her eyes closed with a placid smile that looks so serene. She looks so beautiful, her skin glowing with pride and her heart melting with so many emotions coursing through her. I bend down to kiss her softly at the corners of her mouth, then travel up her cheeks to her eyelids.

"You make me so happy," I say softly into her skin. "I don't know what I did to deserve you, but Eleanor..." My brows furrow as I try to find the right words. Words to let her know that everything I did, all the pain I caused her, will always be a deep reminder of our journey. Our story that will only be defined as ours. I will spend the rest of my life proving to her that my place in life is right alongside her, walking her through moments like these.

"I love you," she says, placing her hand over my heart.

"I love you too." I pull her into a deep kiss, my hands

cupping her face as her arms wrap around my waist.

When I pull away, I smile down at her. "I don't know how comfortable I feel making out with you in front of your dad."

She chuckles lightly before nuzzling her cheek against my chest.

We stay like this, our bodies interlaced with our arms wrapped around each other as if holding on to this most precious of moments, before we realize that we might actually be late to her graduation.

"Come on," she says, stepping away from me while pulling at my hand. "We should get going. If I don't get there on time to meet Claire before the ceremony, she's going to kill me."

"Well then, college graduate," I respond, "we better hurry."

We both take one last look at the headstone before saying our goodbyes. Ellie slows her steps on our walk back to her car, meeting mine as I limp along in a steady, even pace.

Once inside her car, I lean back and wrap my arm behind her on the headrest. "You ready?" I ask, turning to her with an eager smile.

She answers with an excited nod before turning the ignition.

She drives off, the afternoon sunlight catching against the windows as we drink in the cool summer air. We're ready for whatever chapter we'll move on to next, whatever the future holds for us. From here on out, it will always be the two of us. Us two against the world.

The End

EPILOGUE
Ellie

"**O**h my God. I've been waiting all night to take these off."

My hands move to the soles of my feet, kneading out the knot that had settled into the arch. I audibly moan, my throat rumbling with pleasure, as my eyes roll into the back of my head at the relief.

Rhylan watches me, amused, with one brow raised and a thin slice of cheesy pizza held in his hands midair. "If you keep making noises like that, more than your shoes are going to come off in this limo."

I roll my head towards him, shaking my head, but I can't hide the smile. "You really are insatiable."

Having already inhaled my pizza, my hands move to the thirteen-inch-tall gold statue sitting between us on the long, cushioned bench, tracing the smooth surface and the words etched into the base.

Academy Award to Rhylan Matthews.
Best performance by an actor in a leading role. *Aurielle*. 2024.

I sigh. No matter how many times I read the words out loud, it still feels surreal. The whole night feels like an absolute dream.

"Be honest, were you surprised when they called your name?"

He brings a hand to his chest. "I mean, it was an honor *just* to be nominated," he says, dripping with quipped sarcasm. He's saying the words that he's said in every interview asking the same question: "Do you think you'll finally win your first Oscar?"

My laughter is loud. Full and joyous as my grip on the award slackens from its weight.

"Honest?" He side-eyes me, his smile curving even higher. "Yeah, I knew I was going to win."

"Good to know your vanity is as healthy as ever."

It's been two years. Two years since he confessed his love for me for the entire world to see. It all led us to this moment, celebrating Rhylan's first Academy Award.

I didn't go to Seattle. I didn't run away from the home that I decided to create with Rhylan, choosing our future instead of leaving it all behind. And now, two years later, I can't even bring myself to regret it.

I told Paula that I changed my mind, and she extended me her previous offer as an assistant at the LA headquarters with Poinsettia Press. So instead of leaving, I worked my way up to junior editor, the same position I would've had if I had gone to Seattle and the same position I coveted since Paula hired me. I finally feel like my success is one that I can be proud of. I'm happy, satisfied with the work that I've accomplished, and optimistic of the ladder that I continue to climb.

This past year, we celebrated a year of many firsts. I packed up my things and moved into Rhylan's home, making it ours. He encouraged me to fill every corner of it with what made me, me. So I filled it with every bit of me. Books, pictures of me and my mom and dad, potted plants, antique furniture, and too many mugs to count. Everything that I always wanted but never had the space to occupy.

We celebrated Claire and Wes as they held an intimate ceremony for their wedding with only fifty guests, much to her parents' objection. Rhylan sat dotingly in the crowded rows as I stood by Claire at the altar in an emerald-green chiffon dress. We happily accepted when Charles and Amelia proudly asked us to be their daughter's godparents, showering her with love and spoiling her with as many toys as a newborn could have. And we stood by as Chuck proposed to Sonia, surprising the couple with a lavish engagement party that included all of our friends.

And every holiday, every weekend with exceptionally good weather, every milestone that I want to celebrate, my mom packs up a large picnic blanket while I stop by the grocery store for a small arrangement of daisies before we meet at the cemetery to visit my dad. Sometimes, Mark and Rhylan join us, but for the most part, it's just me and my mom. We talk to my dad, telling him everything that's going on in our lives, and we remember what it felt like to love him and for him to love us back. We no longer suffocate the memory of him but let him live vicariously through us.

Rhylan tosses his crust back into the empty pizza box,

wiping his hands of the shiny grease with a rough napkin. He settles back and turns to look at me.

"I love you," he whispers. A lazy smile spreads across his face, and his head tilts towards me.

"I love you too."

"Tonight was perfect."

"It was, wasn't it?" I agree.

We're still coming down from the high of the night. The flashy lights, the genuine congratulations on Rhylan's success, and the adoration and respect for *us*. After all this time since Rhylan made our relationship public, we've been rained with nothing but admiration. For the trials that we had to endure to come out stronger in the end. Even on the red carpet tonight, walking hand in hand as we celebrated Rhylan, we were shown just how accepted we were as a couple.

"You ready to go home?" I ask. Home. *Our* home.

"Almost," he answers. His voice is low, nervous, as if he is still on the unsettled high from having to go up on stage and make the acceptance speech he had been mentally practicing, ending it with a special thanks to me, his Eleanor. "You know what I said up there?"

"About you wanting to spend the rest of your life with me?" I answer. My hands spread over the ruffled material of my beautiful dress, smoothing it down and admiring the shimmery fabric.

"Yes."

"What about it?" It wasn't anything new. In fact, on a daily basis, he tells me that we'll grow old together. Until we're wrinkly and tired of each other.

He leans towards me, his face inches away. "I meant it."

"I know."

"No, I really meant it."

I laugh, gently placing my hand on his chest to push him away. "I know!"

And then his hand moves to his pocket. He reveals a square velvet box that sits so small in his large palm. "I really, *really* meant it."

My eyes go wide, and I'm rendered speechless. I let out a small gasp.

"I've imagined a life with you and without you," he continues. "And with you, forever and ever, sounds so much better." His mouth curves up in a sweet, contented smile.

He opens the box, revealing the most beautiful oval diamond that sparkles so brightly in the dark. It sits on an equally stunning eternity band, carefully placed in the vertical slit nestled in the cushioned interior of the small box.

"Marry me?" he whispers.

There's no big show with a string quartet or fireworks. No yacht taking off into the starry night. None of the unnecessary extravagance, just the two of us, exactly how I've always dreamed it to be. Just us two, a thin sheen of grease coating our hands and mouths with our stomachs full of cheap pizza, and our formal attire loosened for comfort as we slowly revert back to ourselves. And it's perfect.

"Yes," I whisper back. Tears pool at the corner of my eyes, and my hands tremble as he gently removes the ring and places it on my left ring finger. He admires it, knowing that it represents forever, and brings my knuckles to his lips.

"Oh my God!" I gasp, my hands half covering my face. "What if you didn't win? This would have been so horrible!"

He laughs. "I guess we'll never know."

His hand moves towards my face, cupping my jaw as he looks into my eyes. His expression is serious, and I can almost feel the tightness in his chest from the wave of emotions that take over the both of us. He kisses me, finally, as we both realize that this is forever. Till death do us part.

"I love you," he whispers as he pulls away.

"I love you too."

Acknowledgements

Writing a book for the first time is unimaginable without the people behind you to cheer you on as your backbone and support system. Without the village that I had standing behind me, this book would have never happened. Instead, Ellie and Rhylan's story would have been stuck in a little corner in my head, begging to be told.

The first of that village includes the Bookstagram community. Home; that is the most adept way to describe this community. The support and shared love for books in this community should be showcased like a trophy for how proud I am to be a part of it. My beta-readers: Faith, Cleo, Lek, and Katherine. Your feedback and your love for Rhylan and Ellie gave me the courage to continue on in those moments when self-doubt took over my thoughts like the plague.

And Katherine Jay. I don't know what I did in a past life to have been so wonderfully blessed with your guidance and support but I must have been a damn near saint. Katherine, without you, Written in the Oceans would have been a loosely bound stack of papers sitting on my desk collecting dust, right alongside my dreams to publish my first book. Thank you, from the bottom of my heart, for walking me through all of the challenges of this self-publishing journey and giving me the feedback that I so desperately needed. I hope that one day we can meet in person and gush over our characters while we discuss the fictional worlds that we created.

My dearest friends Cheann and Amy. After twenty years of friendship, I couldn't imagine celebrating this milestone with anyone else. As scary as this journey was, I am so grateful to have had you two by my side to cheer me on and repeatedly tell me that I could do it!

The biggest thanks to my husband for taking on the burdens of our home so that I could punch out this story when my brainstorming got the best of me, for being so freaking proud of me for publishing my first book, for always being there to listen to my book ideas, and to squash any lingering doubts I had, forcing me to push through and realize my potential.

To my dedicated team that brought Written in the Oceans to what it is today. My wonderful editor, Katie Wolf, who gave the most appropriate and constructive feedback that helped shape this book. The amazing team at Books and Moods for taking in all of my ideas and dealing with my most indecisive brain while creating this beautiful masterpiece to wrap my baby in. And the entire team at Grey's Promos for handling the release and hyping my baby up to its fullest. Thank you to each and every one of you for your hard work and dedication.

To all of my readers, thank you so much for reading this story and for giving me a chance to inhabit your imaginative mind with Ellie and Rhylan. My goal with this story was for readers all over the world to understand mental health and depression. Dealing with depression is not always about being sad, it's about living with an illness that is hidden behind multiple masks. I hope, from the deepest part of my heart, that those dealing with the same heartache that Ellie and Rhylan went through, feel seen and represented.

-Jeannie Choe

For more information on Jeannie's books and upcoming releases, visit

jeanniechoeauthor.com

About the Author

Written In the Oceans, a standalone novel in the new adult/contemporary romance genre, is Jeannie's debut novel that touches subjects on mental health while including elements of angsty romance and a happily ever after. Jeannie lives in Southern California with her hubby, two kids, and fur babies.

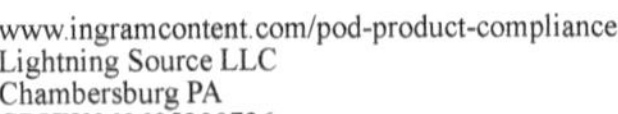

www.ingramcontent.com/pod-product-compliance
Lightning Source LLC
Chambersburg PA
CBHW060605300726
48975CB00005B/1457